# ST. MARTIN'S

# MINOTAUR
## MYSTERIES

# PRAISE FOR *O'ARTFUL DEATH*

"*[O' Artful Death]* rings subtle—and enormously satisfying—changes on the venerable tried-and-true."
—*Newsday*

"An elegantly wrought first mystery with layers within layers like carved ivory balls. . . . Rich and rewarding reading."
—*Booklist*

"A nicely puzzled plot, a closely confined rural setting, remarkable characterizations, and eminently readable prose."
—*Library Journal*

"(Taylor) has an eye for the details of rural New England. . . . Pull up an overstuffed chair and drift away."
—*The Boston Globe*

"A compelling mystery about a dark subject. One can hope she'll bring Sweeney for more sleuthing."
—*Sunday Oklahoman*

MORE . . .

# Titles by Sarah Stewart Taylor

# O' ARTFUL DEATH

Sarah Stewart Taylor

St. Martin's Paperbacks

O' ARTFUL DEATH

Copyright © 2003 by Sarah Stewart Taylor.
Excerpt from *Mansions of the Dead* © 2004 by Sarah Stewart Taylor.

Cover photography by Rachael McLean

Library of Congress Catalog Card Number: 2002191963

ISBN: 0-312-98594-0
EAN: 80312-98594-3

Printed in the United States of America

St. Martin's Press hardcover edition / June 2003
St. Martin's Paperbacks edition / July 2004

St. Martin's Paperbacks are published by St. Martin's Press, 175 Fifth Avenue, New York, NY 10010.

10  9  8  7  6  5  4  3  2  1

*For my family—Mom, Dad, and Tom*
*And, of course, for Matt*

# PROLOGUE

◆◆◆

*1890*

*"I'M IMAGINING YOU as a corpse. You'd be lovely."*

*He leaned forward to lift a strand of dark hair caught in the perspiration on her cheek and Mary burst out laughing when she saw the earnest, dreamy expression on his face.*

*"What do you mean? Corpses can't be beautiful." She rolled out from under him and propped herself up on her elbows, studying his gray eyes, the irises broken by slivers of brown and green. They reminded her of the eyes of a bird or a cat, intense and nearly unblinking.*

*It was early summer, and the Vermont hills around the colony were the bright green of the lush alfalfa in the fields, dotted here and there with sheep and stands of raucously colored wildflowers: white daisies, purple phlox, pink mallow and, farther into the woods, the tiny, hidden trilliums and jack-in-the-pulpits, shell pink and green.*

*They were lying on a blanket spread out on the thick grass of the cemetery, near where wildflowers grew along the iron fence, twining through the rails. The granite and slate stones were dull in the summer light. Outside the graveyard were the formal gardens that belonged to the big yellow house planted above them on a little rise. Up there the more pedigreed foxgloves and delphiniums and lilies filled their designated plots and below them, in the humid air, the Green River flowed placidly by, catching on a rock in the shallow bed every once in a while and swirling for a moment before moving on.*

*He was pale from working in the studio, and when he*

*leaned over to touch her again, his white hand looked like
a slap mark on her sun-pinked cheek.*

"You've always reminded me of Ophelia," he said. "I
would like to represent you lying dead in the brook, surrounded by flowers, like Mr. Millais's painting. There's
something about your black hair and your dark eyes and
your pale skin. It's as though you were made of marble, as
though you'll never change. When you haven't been out in
the sun, that is." He smiled and stroked the base of her
throat.

She frowned, then reached up to place a finger against
his lips. "Please don't," she said after a moment. "I don't
like to think about dying, I don't think it's beautiful at all."
His eyes filled with indignation, the way they did when one
of the other artists disagreed with him.

"You speak as though it were something you could choose
not to participate in," he sneered. "We all die. We all rot
away. None of us is safe from him." He gestured toward one
of the older stones, which depicted a leering, grinning skeleton holding an arrow. "And it can be beautiful. The moment
of death, when the body is frozen in still life, like a painting
or a sculpture. I've always thought about how remarkable it
would be if you could create an image of someone just as
they died, to freeze them in that instant when they are neither
dead nor alive. If an artist could represent that moment of
death, it would be a work of art like no other work of art, a
masterpiece."

"Like 'The Lady of Shalott' " Mary said carefully, reciting. He made her feel that she should be careful about details, facts and names, that they were important to him.
Besides, she felt she had said something wrong and she
wanted to make it up to him. "It's a poem I've just read in
that little book you gave me. By the Lord of Tennyson. She
looks down from her tower and sees Sir Lancelot, and leaves
her weaving. Then the curse comes over her as she dies in
the boat. 'Till her blood was frozen slowly, and her eyes
were darken'd wholly.' I imagine her lying there, and I think
she must have been the most beautiful lady, just as you say,

*in the moment that she died. Do you know that poem?"*

*"Of course. And it's by Alfred, Lord Tennyson, my dearest poet." He looked up toward the house, absentmindedly drawing circles on her neck with his fingertip.*

*She spoke thoughtfully, as though she had decided to give him a present of her words. "When I die, I want to be buried in a boat, like the Lady of Shalott," she said.*

*"In a boat?"*

*"Mmmm. A boat made of marble. And I would lie in the boat forever, singing." She stretched a bare foot out over the margin of the blanket and brushed it against the nap of grass.*

*He smiled. "What about right here? You could be buried in your boat under the willow tree, with the flowers all around, and all the colony will come visit you."*

*"The colony," she spat out. "I'm tired of the colony. I don't care if the colony comes to visit me. You think the colony is all that matters. I don't. I want to go away from here. I want to live in Europe." Her cheeks were stained with pink.*

*He stroked her hair, trying to calm her. "No you don't," he said. "This is your home. This is where you belong."*

*"I belong with you," she said, reaching up and pulling his head down to her chest. He resisted for a moment, then lay his cheek on the buttons of her dress, the bone pressing against his skin.*

# ONE

December 9

*The colony at Byzantium was a paean to the beautiful, a monument to the idea that one could live more beautifully in the country.*

*For the artists, who flocked north come summer for the heady mixture of solitude and like-minded companionship, it was a place where, above everything, aesthetic perfection reigned.*

*Beauty reigned in the rolling hillsides of the Vermont countryside, it reigned in the silhouette of the staid, silent mountain, it reigned in the graceful, lovely homes and gardens and in everything the artists did. Birth, celebration, even death—all were made beautiful in Byzantium.*

—Muse of the Hills: The Byzantium Colony,
1860–1956
by Bennett Dammers

THE GIRL'S NUDE body lay in the boat, her dead eyes staring heavenward, her long hair coiling strangely to the ground. One graceful arm was thrown across her breasts, covering them carelessly in a gesture more flirtatious than modest; the other arm trailed limply. Unmarred and impossibly smooth, the bloodless surface of her skin looked soft as soap.

Or soft as marble, thought Sweeney St. George as she flipped through the photographs she'd found lying at one end of the seminar table, for that was what the lovely, lifeless woman in the pictures was made of.

It was three weeks before Christmas, and outside the windows of the worn and very green fourth floor seminar room, Cambridge was covered in a thin layer of brand-new snow. Under the delicate coating, the buildings at this end of the Yard looked to Sweeney like gingerbread houses dusted with powdered sugar. There was something about a snowstorm that purified the city, made it cozier and even more lovely.

After removing her parka and checking the wall clock to confirm that her "Iconography of Death" students wouldn't be arriving for several minutes, Sweeney had dropped the full slide carousel into the projector, placed her notes in front of her, and settled her almost six-foot frame into one of the remarkably uncomfortable chairs around the table to look at the pictures.

The color snapshots had been taken in a New England cemetery, complete with slate and granite headstones typical of the eighteenth and nineteenth centuries and a few marble examples from the late nineteenth and twentieth. The few older Puritan stones stood at attention near the back fence, the more recent dead resting nearer to the front gate, dry autumn leaves piled around their bases. As she always did when she saw photographs of cemeteries she hadn't yet visited, Sweeney found herself wishing for a couple of hours alone with those stones and her gravestone rubbing materials. She loved the magic of making rubbings, the way long-obscured words and images revealed themselves under her hand. This one would contain a few good eighteenth-century examples, she was sure, and there would be some lovely carvings of willow trees and soul's heads. But all in all, it was a thoroughly average graveyard in every way.

In every way, that was, except for the strange, life-sized monument of the young woman. Sweeney flipped through the pile and found the best of them, a head-on shot. She studied it carefully.

The girl was limp in the bottom of the shallow, vaguely fashioned rowboat and behind her, the stern rose like a hangman's hood. Sitting jauntily upon it, and holding a scythe, was the remarkable figure of Death, his bony arms and legs intricately carved from the milky stone.

Sweeney looked again. That was strange. Images of the human face of Death were common on Puritan stones from the mid-1600s and even on stones made in the early nineteenth century, but the style of this stone was much more advanced than any Puritan stone she had ever seen. In fact, it was more like a sculpture, the dead woman's face and breasts as softly and expertly rounded as a Rodin or a Saint-Gaudens. What was the date?

She flipped through the pictures and found one that was a close-up of the tablet at the end of the stone. It was engraved with a few words and some kind of poem.

MARY ELIZABETH DENHOLM
*January 3, 1872 to August 28, 1890*

So it was late Victorian. That was puzzling. It was completely atypical for a Victorian stone. By the time this Mary Denholm had died, stonecarvers had moved on to the more familiar euphemistic images for death, such as willow trees, or romanticized cherubs and garlands. But here was this strange reaper, his figure so much more accomplished than those of his brethren on other stones. *This* Death was a man, with a man's face somehow suggested in the familiar skull. He gazed down at the girl lying beneath him, his eyes soft, a dreamy smile playing at his bony lips. There was something familiar about the way he looked down at his prey, Sweeney realized, something *loving*.

She did a quick calculation. Eighteen. The girl had been eighteen. What had she died of? Childbirth was a likely cause, but there wasn't a husband's named on the stone, as in "Mary, Beloved Wife of James," so perhaps it had been something else. She searched the marble surface, grainy in the photos. In all her years of studying gravestones and mourning jewelry, shrouds and death masks and funerary art,

Sweeney had never seen anything quite as intriguing as this lovely, eroticized sculpture of a dead girl.

The verse below the name and dates on the tablet was inscribed in small, precise letters, and Sweeney struggled to make them out. She tipped the surface of the photograph toward the fluorescent overhead light and there they were, as bizarre as the work on which they'd been etched.

> Death resides in my garden, with his hands wrapped
> 'round my throat
> He beckons me to follow and I step lightly in his boat.
> All around us summer withers, blossoms drop and rot,
> And Death bids me to follow, his arrow in my heart.

There was more, but Sweeney looked up from the photograph then, for something about the dead girl, the strange poem and the smiling figure of Death had made her think of the early New England gravestones that described Indian raids or grisly murders. She wondered how this girl had died.

Voices sounded in the hall. She tucked the photographs into her bookbag and stood up to welcome her class.

"Hey, Sweeney," said Brendan Freeman, one of her senior advisees. "How's it going?"

Still two years away from her thirtieth birthday, Sweeney knew she wasn't the model of a professorial authority figure. Her class outfits tended toward jeans or whatever she'd found that week at her favorite Cambridge vintage clothes shop, and her bright red curls, which fell halfway down her back, were often unruly, hastily pinned up with a pencil or a binder clip. But she hadn't gotten to be twenty-eight without beginning to understand how she affected people, and she knew that there was something about her open, lightly freckled face, with its large green eyes and delicate nose, its almost-but-not-quite-beautiful expression of passionate expectancy, that put her students at ease, but that also made them want to work. Her department chairman had once told her he thought she was too familiar with her students, but insisting on "Professor St. George" seemed a hollow gesture.

"Hi, Brendan. Hi, everybody. How are you all holding up?"

It was the last class before the winter vacation and they filed in lethargically, lugging backpacks and textbooks. The shabby carpet and sickly green walls of the seminar room reflected their moods. When they were seated, she could see she'd lost about half of them to early flights home or late nights in the library for other classes.

She took a deep breath. She just had to get through this lecture and one more and she'd be done until January. "All right, let's get going. Today's lecture is entitled 'The Triumph of Death.' Ring any bells? Come on, let's see what you remember from the reading." A few tentative hands waved back at her.

The strange gravestone would have to wait.

Sweeney was almost through with the class when Toby DiMarco slipped in and sat down in a chair at the back of the darkened room, grinning at her and then bowing his head of dark, Italian Renaissance curls to the table in mock concentration. Toby, who was not in the class, was Sweeney's best friend and liked to come and watch her teach. They'd met their freshman year at college and, with the exception of the three years Sweeney had been in England at Oxford, had both stayed in Boston. Since returning to America almost a year ago, Sweeney had been appointed an assistant professor in the History of Art and Architecture Department and published a book on Victorian death rituals and representations called *The Art of the Grave: Death and the Victorian World.* The book had enjoyed some modest success: an NPR interview and a quirky and complimentary review in *The New York Times Book Review.* Its success had gotten Sweeney her job and made her the most disliked member of the department. Her colleagues found her area of specialty overly broad and decidedly lowbrow, and they were envious of her mainstream success. She knew her chances of getting tenure were almost nil, but she loved her students.

Toby, for his part, had made a career of graduate school.

He was forever trying to finish his novel—a Generation X
roman à clef long ago called promising by a beloved writing
professor—as well as his seemingly interminable Ph.D. thesis on an obscure American poet named James Milliner, and
would turn from one to the other at six-month intervals, announcing each time to his exhausted friends that he had finally decided to commit to whichever project it was. The
problem, which Sweeney was always trying to identify for
him without hurting his feelings, was that he didn't know
whether he wanted to be a writer or an academic. So he
continued on being neither exactly.

"If you look here, you'll see what I mean about the skeleton," she told the class, pointing to the head of a jaunty-
looking Death who leaned against an urn on a gravestone up
on the slide screen. "Anyone want to guess when this is?
Brendan, would you like to give it a stab? No pun intended."

That got a laugh from the class.

"I'd guess eighteenth century," Brendan said. "1760s?"

"Close." Sweeney grinned at him gratefully. "1750s. A
cemetery near Concord. Remember the skeleton and now,
look at this one." She pressed the "ahead" button on the
projector controls.

Up came a medieval fresco, a resurrection scene with a
skeleton lurking in the background.

"Skeletons have been used as *memento mori* symbols in
art as far back as the Greeks and Romans, who displayed
them at feasts as a reminder that they were mortal and ought
to enjoy life while they could. Skeletons were reproduced on
drinking cups and in floor mosaics, things people saw and
used every day.

"Skeletons and skulls and crossbones were common until
the end of the eighteenth century," she went on, "when they
were replaced by the more euphemistic images—cherubs,
soul's heads, and the like. These images came to stand in for
the more macabre ones. If you think for a moment about
someone walking through a cemetery, looking at the stones,
you can see what the difference would have been between
say an eighteenth-century one and a Victorian example."

Unless, she realized, you were talking about the stone she'd just seen in those photographs.

Sweeney glanced up at the clock. It was eleven.

"Well, that's it. We'll finish up in January. Thank you, everybody. Have a great holiday and safe trip to wherever you're going. I'll see you in a month or so. Remember to keep reading in Genetti and start thinking about your final paper topics."

"Hey, prof," Toby said when everyone had filed out of the room. "Good class." He looked the way she pictured him when she hadn't seen him for a while, skinny as one of her skeletons, his cherubically curly black hair too long and completely unarranged. She felt a surge of affection as he shrugged out of his black leather jacket and moved his wire-rimmed glasses aside to rub the bridge of his nose. With his pale skin and dark Italian eyes, he'd always reminded her of a goofier, geekier version of the nubile gods in rococo paintings.

"Thanks."

"By the way, which poor member of the Smith class of 1945 gave up her clothes for the cause?" He cast a disapproving look at her outfit.

"What?" She looked down at her pleated skirt and belted jacket. "Don't you think it's cool? I think it's a Balenciaga knockoff."

Toby didn't say anything. He tended to date girls who wore fashions that could be found in current fashion magazines.

"And what's that around your neck?"

"Oh, look." She showed him the small gold and black coffin, inhabited by a skeleton and hanging on a chain around her neck. It was a museum reproduction of an Elizabethan pendant and a recent purchase.

"You're weird."

"Thanks a lot. To what do I owe the honor?" She pointed to a chair and they sat down.

"What are you doing for Christmas again? Something fun

like spending it completely alone with a bottle of scotch and some thirty-two-hour BBC costume drama?"

"Shut up." She kicked his chair. "I like having Christmas by myself. And besides, I'm on an old Italian movie kick right now." She said it lightly, but his words had bitten a little.

"Well, if you can drag yourself away from Marcello Mastroianni long enough to come to Vermont with me, I've got a proposition for you."

She raised her eyebrows. "What kind of proposition?"

"A gravestone. To be precise, the gravestone in the photographs that were here when you came into the room." Leave it to Toby, with his flair for the dramatic, to leave the unlabeled photos, knowing they would spark her interest.

"You? I couldn't figure out where they came from." She retrieved the prints from her bookbag and spread them out on the table.

"So what do you think?"

"I'm intrigued." She found the close-up of the tablet and read the bizarre epitaph in its entirety this time.

> *Death resides in my garden, with his hands wrapped
> 'round my throat
> He beckons me to follow and I step lightly in his boat.
> All around us summer withers, blossoms drop and rot,
> And Death bids me to follow, his arrow in my heart.
> We sail away on his ocean, and the garden falls away
> where life and death are neighbors, and night never
> turns to day.
> A wind comes up on the water, Death's sails are full and
> proud
> My love I will go with thee, dressed in a funeral shroud.
> Now her tomb lies quiet, the shroud is turned to stone
> And where Death had been standing, is only the grave
> of her bones.*

"Hmmm."

"I know, the poem's not very good," Toby said. "But I think you'll be interested anyway."

"All right. Tell me more."

"You knew I went to Vermont for Thanksgiving, right? To stay with Patch and Britta?"

Sweeney nodded. Patch and Britta Wentworth were Toby's aunt and uncle on what Sweeney liked to call the "grand branch" of his family. They lived with their children in the former arts colony in Byzantium, Vermont, in a house called Birch Lane that had been built by Toby's great-grandfather. The great-grandfather was Herrick Gilmartin, a famous landscape and portrait painter from the 1880s on. Gilmartin, the sculptor Bryn Davies Morgan, and a host of other well-known American artists had summered or lived off-and-on in the colony at Byzantium for most of their working lives. Sweeney didn't know much about the colony, but she'd once heard a colleague say that for a time, Byzantium and a handful of other New England artists' communities had contained the greatest concentration of artistic talent in the United States.

"Well, while I was up there, I was looking around in the little cemetery near Patch and Britta's and remembered that there's always been some question about that stone. It's pretty strange for the time period, right?"

Sweeney nodded. "Really strange. The girl would be a very typical Victorian monument, if she were standing and draped over a grave or something, but the figure of Death is incredibly weird, very un-Victorian actually. And it's clearly by a real artist, a sculptor. Any idea who it was?"

"I don't think anybody knows. The assumption is that it was by someone who was a member of the colony or someone who visited, but it isn't signed."

"Who was the girl? Mary Denholm."

"Just a local girl. The family lived down below my great-grandparents' house and one of the Denholm descendants still lives in the house. Ruth Kimball. I've known her all my life."

Sweeney studied the photographs while he talked.

"So what's the proposition?"

"Come up to Vermont with me for Christmas. I already

asked Patch and Britta and they said they'd love to have you.
You can look into this stone a little, maybe get a chapter for
your book about an anomalous, heretofore-unidentified masterpiece, have some fun for a change. Christmas is great up
there, lots of skiing and wassailing. Whatever wassailing is.
And they have this giant party every year, a couple of days
before the twenty-fifth. You'll love it."

There was a note of desperation in his voice that made
her ask, a little slyly, "Why do you want to go back up to
Vermont again so soon after Thanksgiving? You could go
spend Christmas with your mom in California."

He blushed. "Well, there's this really cool woman who's
the granddaughter of one of Patch and Britta's friends. She
just moved back to the colony and I met her at Thanksgiving."

Sweeney felt a tiny, unwelcome stab of jealousy. Why
hadn't he told her about it before? "So why do you want me
along? For female companionship if things crash and burn
with the granddaughter?"

He grinned at her. "No, it'll just be more fun."

"I don't know, Toby . . ." she said, still staring at the photographs. "I'm so exhausted from finishing up this thing for
*European Art Criticism*. And you know how I feel about
staying with people. I'm always tiptoeing around and cleaning up the bathroom as soon as I'm done. I'll probably spill
a beer on the Persian carpet or something. I'd rather just be
alone. Christmas is a weird time for me."

"Come on, Sweeney. It's been a year since you got back
from England. All you've done since then is work. You
spend too much time by yourself."

When she looked up at him, he glanced away, embarrassed. She could feel her face flush, her heart catch with
hurt. *But I've been successful*, she wanted to cry out, her
own shrill voice echoing in her head. *I've seen the dividends
of my emotional exile*.

"Look, just sleep on it, okay? I know this stone is up your
alley." He kissed her good-bye and, reluctantly, Sweeney met
his eyes. He was right, of course. The prospect of her

planned holiday stretched out in front of her now, wan and depressing.

"Okay," she said, still aware of that small, ugly pang of jealous discomfort. "I'll think about it."

Sweeney was one of those Scroogeish souls for whom bright store windows and the inevitable round of Christmas parties and gifts inspired only dread and a longing for the empty, short days of early January, when winter is finally left to get on with it in earnest.

There were good reasons for this. Like many people who dislike December, she had no warm family memories to associate with the holidays. Her father had committed suicide when she was thirteen. She had some vague memories from before the defining event; emotionally complicated, largely silent dinners at her father's parents' big house in Newport; her father's last minute presents, flashlights or batteries from gas stations, wrapped in the ancient Christmas paper her grandmother had kept in a desk drawer in the study. After, she and her mother had gotten through the holidays rather than celebrated them and her Yuletide associations ran to unclean motel rooms in second-rate resort cities or take-out turkey eaten at the table of whatever house or apartment they happened to be living in.

Another reason was her occupation. Spending her days among gravestones, skeletons, and images of the dead, Sweeney could not imagine the tiny baby Jesus, tucked into the manger and wrapped in maternal adoration, without picturing the other Jesus, bleeding, dying in agony on the cross. Christmas seemed only a precursor of worse things to come.

But while she stewed inwardly, the rest of the world seemed intent on happiness. Passing through the department's second floor warren of cubicles on the way to her own tiny closet of an office, Sweeney watched students leaving for vacation hugging each other and dropping off presents for professors and Mrs. Pitman, the motherly department secretary.

After returning a couple of phone calls and sending off a

quick e-mail to a journal editor interested in her article on a family of Massachusetts stonecarvers, Sweeney took out Toby's photographs again and laid them on her desk.

Then she took down from her bookshelf some volumes on New England stones, particularly from the late nineteenth century. Her office was so small that there was only room for her most essential texts, her desk and chair, and an extra seat for student conferences. She spread the books out on her desk and after an hour and a half of reading, she was convinced her first impression had been correct.

The stone was completely, weirdly anomalous.

But before she trekked all the way to Vermont, she wanted to make sure there wasn't some kind of obvious explanation. There were all kinds of ways she could go about finding out, but the simplest option presented itself as she thought about her conversation with Toby. Why not call the descendant? What was her name? Something Kimball . . .

Sweeney looked over the notes she'd jotted down. Ruth. That was it. Ruth Kimball. It would be much too easy if Ruth Kimball could just explain the whole thing, but years of research had taught her that sometimes the obvious route to an answer was the best one.

She got the number from information and then tried to decide what to do. She had discovered over the years that people sometimes got angry when asked about long-dead ancestors. There was often enmity and resentment buried deep among the roots of family trees. She could write a letter, but something in her wanted to know now.

The phone rang six times before a woman answered with a gruff, "Yup?"

"Oh, yes. I was looking for Ruth Kimball. Is she available?"

"Yup?"

"I'm sorry. Are you Ruth Kimball?"

"I said I was. What do you want?"

Sweeney took a deep breath, picturing an annoyed older woman, scowling down the phone. "Oh, I'm so sorry. My name is Sweeney St. George and I'm a professor down here in Boston. My area of specialty is funerary art, gravestones and things like that, and well, the gravestone of an ancestor of yours, a Mary Denholm, was recently brought to my attention." Good God, she was going on. Get to the point, Sweeney. "Anyway, I found it really intriguing and I was wondering if I could ask you a few questions about it?"

"Yup."

"Well, yes. What I was wondering was . . ." She had forgotten her questions. "I mean, I'm looking for any information about the artist who created the stone. It's very strange, for the time period and for the region."

"I don't know who did it. I don't think anybody around here does anymore. Probably one of the artists from the Byzantium colony. You know about the colony?" She pronounced the word "colony" with an air of distaste. The woman's accent was unlike any Sweeney had heard before, somewhere between Boston and London, a salty, almost colonial burr, as though her settler relatives had passed it down, barely adulterated by two hundred years in the New World. She pronounced the name of her hometown *Bisantum*, the way Toby did.

"Yes," Sweeney said. "You mean the Byzantium Arts Colony?"

"That's right. One of the artists, I think."

"Oh. Well, could I ask you how Mary Denholm died? She was very young and it might have a bearing on who created the stone and why they chose such a large monument." Sweeney was thinking about Victorian monuments made to commemorate children who had died in large scale tragedies like apartment fires or mine disasters.

Then she heard a child's voice in the background and Ruth Kimball told her to hold on for a moment, calling out a muffled warning. "Well," she said when she was back on the phone, "she was supposed to have drowned, you know. That was the story that was got about. But, my grandmother Ethel, who grew up with Mary, always said she'd been killed by one of the Byzantium artists and the whole thing was hushed up."

"Killed? You mean *murdered*?"

"Yeah, murdered. That's what my grandmother always said. No one around here thinks there's anything to it but, well, they wouldn't want it to get out, would they? The colony folks."

"No, I suppose they wouldn't. I . . ." There was a knock on her open office door and Brendan Freeman came in. Damn, she'd forgotten she had an appointment with him. "Oh, hold on, Mrs. Kimball." She held up a finger, letting Brendan know she'd be off in a second. "I'm sorry, Mrs. Kimball. I have to go. Could I call you tonight perhaps, so we could talk at more length?"

"Got bingo tonight. I'll be around tomorrow, though. My daughter Sherry's working and I'm watching Charley. That's my granddaughter."

"Okay, fine. Thank you. Tomorrow evening then."

She jotted down some notes as she gestured to Brendan to sit down.

Toby's gravestone was getting even more interesting.

# TWO

RUTH KIMBALL WAS not a beautiful woman. She had not been a beautiful girl or a beautiful young woman and at sixty-seven, she was not a beautiful older woman.

But there was something about her face that pleased her as she looked into the hall mirror to adjust her hat. Her skin was lined, but clear and pink, as though she'd just been out in the cold. And her eyes, which had always been her best feature, were still a pale, icy blue, the color of forget-me-nots. "You look at people too much," her mother had always said. "It's not ladylike. You make them think you can see right through them."

Pretending it was her mother looking back at her from the glass, she stuck out her tongue and wiggled it, watching her reflection.

She found her gloves in the hall closet and yelled out to Carl that she was going for a walk. When she went through to the living room, he was sitting in front of the television, where he'd been for the past two hours, watching talk shows and smoking cigarettes and stubbing them out in one of her favorite Depression glass bowls. It seemed like ever since Sherry had brought him home four months ago and announced that they were engaged, Carl had been sitting in her living room, making her mad. Ruth took the bowl from him and carried it to the kitchen sink, bringing him an old saucer to use instead.

"When's Sherry getting back from work?"

He looked up at her, his eyes bloodshot. "Don't know. Five or so."

"I thought you were going to talk to Hank Anson about a job at the garage." After she said it, she wished she hadn't. It never did any good.

"I am," he said, still watching the television. "Hey, what's going on with the condos? You hear anything new?"

Ruth was beginning to wish she'd never told Carl and Sherry about her plan to sell the house and land to a local developer who wanted to put up vacation condominiums on it. The developer—a guy from Stowe named Peter Richmond—had approached her back in the summer. At first she'd told him she wasn't interested. The house had been in her family for 150 years. It didn't seem right somehow for her to sell. But then he'd looked around at her living room, with its old furniture, the chairs and tables that might have looked like something in an antique shop but just looked old up against her washed-out wallpaper and faded paint. "What do you want for your family, Mrs. Kimball?" he'd asked her. "What things would you like to provide for your grand-daughter as she gets older? An education? Travel? Security? She seems like a very bright little girl." He had written the figures on a piece of paper and handed it over, the way they did when you asked for your account balance at the bank. That had been it.

She'd kept it a secret from Sherry for a long time. But Carl had figured it out almost as soon as he'd moved in. She didn't know how. He'd probably eavesdropped on one of her phone conversations, or snooped in her desk. Now, he couldn't wait to get his hands on the money, asking her about it every chance he got. Ruth felt her face flush hot with anger. Well, the money wasn't going to him and it wasn't going to Sherry while she insisted on bringing Carl into their lives. Ruth had her own plans.

"Don't know for sure. The state has to approve it before I get any money or anything. The Wentworths are still trying to stop it. We'll see."

She'd meant it to sound final, but he went on. "You can't

let 'em push you around like that. Just because they're rich and they don't want their view wrecked doesn't mean they can tell everybody in this town what to do. You tell 'em that. Tell 'em it's your land and you can do whatever you want with it."

Ruth took a deep breath. "Look after Charley, will you? She's reading upstairs. I'm just going for a walk."

"Sure." His eyes were fixed on the TV again, where a teenage girl was telling her mother that she'd been sleeping with the mother's boyfriend and was going to have his baby.

Ruth glanced at Carl, trying to decide if he was stoned or not, and determined that he was all right to watch Charley. "I'm going," she said, pulling on her gloves.

It was bitterly cold outside, the sun slanting low across the fields of frozen snow. Ruth took a deep breath of the winter air, her lungs aching as she inhaled. In an architectural style repeated over and over again around rural New England, the farmhouse was connected to the old barn by a breezeway that had been falling in for twenty years. The door that had once led from the warm house directly out into the breezeway and the barn had long since been plastered over, so she headed directly to the barn door. She climbed a few unstable stairs, opened the door and slipped inside to the plaintive mewlings of the barn cats. They gathered around her legs as she scooped dry food out of a metal garbage can and shared it out among the five grubby bowls lining a wall. Her favorite of the cats, a big marmalade-colored tom, had fresh scratches on his nose and she stooped to make sure he was okay before going through to the old milking parlor to get the pistol.

It had been her father's, from World War II, and after he got back, he'd kept it in a box in this room, the ammunition beside it in a small leather pouch. She wasn't sure why he'd kept it out there—people didn't worry about children and guns in those days—except that she'd always suspected it reminded him of the war and he'd wanted to keep it out of sight and out of mind. But Ruth and her mother had known where it was in case they needed it. It occurred to her then that the gun hadn't been cleaned in years. "You have to take care of your things," her father had liked to say. "Or they won't be there when you need them."

Standing there, she had a sudden flash of recall—winter evenings, her father and brothers bent over the Holsteins, the cows' nostrils encircled by halos of steam in the cold air. There was the scent of sweet manure and woodsmoke and the creamy, warm milk as the boys dumped full buckets into the tank. Sometimes, when she wasn't needed in the house, Ruth had come out and watched them milk, listened to their talk. She found the things the men said to each other out here much more interesting than what the women were saying inside.

Her brothers had all died young and, after her parents were gone, the house and farm had gone to Ruth and her husband, Choke. Choke wasn't from a farm family; he'd grown up in town. But he'd picked up the milking all right, as long as Ruth was on hand to tell him what order everything had to be done in those first few months. The kids had helped, too, Sherry and Dwight, before his accident. They had gotten along all right. Then in the '70s, when a lot of farms in Vermont had gone under, Choke sold the cows and Ruth got a job as a secretary in an insurance office. They'd hardly known what to do with each other after that. Ruth realized that her marriage had been based on the rhythms of farm life. They had talked easily about finances and children and world events while they worked together on cold mornings and evenings in the barn. But sitting across the dinner table from each other or watching television, they'd been strangers. Choke had been dead for twenty years now. She'd almost forgotten what he looked like.

Now, she opened the box and slipped her hand under the pile of rags that the gun had always been wrapped in. It wasn't there. Frantically, she searched the shelf, thinking it might have fallen out. She'd checked for it just a few days ago, when she'd started to feel afraid. It was an insurance policy of sorts, the idea that she had it, that if anything happened, she could go get it. There was a rifle in the house, but she had never felt like it would be much use if she needed it. Too bulky, not very quick. The one time she'd used it—to shoot a raccoon that was going after the chickens—had taught her that.

As far as she knew, nobody knew where the pistol was kept, except for Sherry and Charley. Charley had probably talked about it, told Carl. That's where it was. Carl had taken it. She'd bet her life on it. Well, she'd get it back from him. That was the only thing to do.

As she stepped out of the barn again, a single shot sounded in the frigid air. Then another came, and another. Ruth stopped and listened. The shots were coming from the woods behind the cemetery. It was the Wentworth boys. Target-shooting again. They'd been at it for a few days. Patch must have gotten them new .22s for Christmas. She stood and listened for another moment, then took off through the snow. A few minutes later, the shots ceased and silence hovered in the cold air. The boys must have gotten cold, she thought, must have gone back inside. She walked out into the frozen field.

Ten minutes later, she came into the cemetery. The snow was pristine and untouched and as she swung open the gate, she felt a pang of regret that her bootprints would mar the perfect whiteness. She strode purposefully across the yard to Mary's stone, standing in front of it and staring at the strange sculpture, the coiling hair and perfect face, the smooth marble, old secrets buried in its pale depths.

She came here whenever she was unsettled about something and for reasons she'd never quite figured out, the gravestone calmed her. Strange, that professor getting wind of it. Ruth thought of her grandmother, a small, old person in her primitive wig and characteristic shawl. "Those artists killed Mary," she'd told Ruth more than once. "They were a bad lot, free loving. I was just a girl, but I always knew there was something wrong with it. The worst of it is that her parents knew and they didn't say anything."

Well, maybe now it would all come out into the open.

Ruth stood in front of Mary's stone for a few more moments before going over to see Choke. She remembered picking out his stone, on a hot summer afternoon. Sherry had been with her. "He wouldn't want you to spend too much, Ma," she'd said. She was right and so they'd gone for the simplest one, yet Ruth felt guilty about it sometimes.

"Hello," called out a voice, breaking the silence as violently as the gunshots. Ruth started and turned to see a winter-clothed figure running through the snow toward her. She waved tentatively, waiting. The silence seemed overpowering suddenly.

"Hi," she called back. "Everything okay?" The figure came closer and Ruth felt her stomach flip-flop like a dying fish gasping for air.

This was why she'd wanted the gun, she realized suddenly. This was who she'd been afraid of. The figure came into the cemetery and Ruth stepped back against the fence, trying to appear relaxed.

"What is it?" she asked. But the figure just stood there, looking terrified, hands in pockets. Ruth thought suddenly of Dwight, of the way he'd looked when he'd done something naughty. She'd always known when he'd been up to mischief, just as her father had always known about her. You couldn't hide what was in your heart on your face.

And then Ruth Kimball looked down and saw her father's Colt pistol, just as she'd remembered it, and she thought of him, of his hands and the way he laughed, the way he'd always told her she was pretty, even though they both knew she wasn't. She heard a shot. This time it wasn't from the woods, but right in front of her. In the instant before she fell to the snow, she thought of her father's eyes, staring blankly at the ceiling at the funeral home. She had known then that he wasn't anywhere, that he was just dead, and she knew that there wasn't anything else, no light, no grace, no heaven. There was just life. And then there was nothing.

# THREE

*December 10*

IT SNOWED IN Cambridge the next day, a heavy, wet, slippery snow that made the old brick structures around the Yard—which Sweeney had liked as gingerbread castles—now resemble over-decorated wedding cakes, smothered in thick, white frosting.

Even her short commute home that day was perilous and slow, and it was nearly six by the time she got to Somerville and found a parking spot. She took a hot-as-she-could-stand-it shower and wrapped herself in her favorite silk kimono, leaving her hair turbaned in a towel to dry. While friends and lovers found her mane of bright orange curls bewitching and somehow just right for her personality, Sweeney was always fighting against its tendency to become unmanageably frizzy when left to its own devices. She rummaged through the mail, adding a new stack of unopened bills to the pile on her kitchen counter, promised herself she'd open them soon, and poured herself a scotch, straight up. She hadn't thought as far ahead as dinner. Sweeney, who loved to cook, disapproved of fast food and could usually put together something respectable from the staples she kept in her cupboards. But it had been a busy end of the semester and her cupboards were bare except for a few cans of soup. She opened an uninspiring lentil concoction and dumped it into a saucepan and turned the knob beneath the gas burner. Nothing happened—the pilot light was out—so she struck a match and held it to the burner pan.

The gas had built up and it exploded with a whoosh.

Sweeney jumped, her heart racing, and turned away from the stove. Her scotch was sitting on the counter and she gulped it, trying to clear the flames from her memory, trying to erase the awful sound of the explosion, the fire sucking at the air, the sickening rush of heat. She drained her glass and poured another drink.

When her nerves had calmed, she settled down on the couch with the telephone.

She had lived on the top floor of the rundown, pumpkin-colored Victorian triple-decker near Davis Square since returning from England almost a year ago, and even after she'd published her book and gotten the teaching job, she'd stayed at the Russell Street apartment out of laziness. Though her building was still something of a monstrosity—the paint peeled and the roofline sagged, giving it the look of a haunted house—the rest of the street was undergoing a remarkably swift gentrification and the neighborhood had gotten safer and more desirable. But her rent had stayed the same, a condition of her continued residence since her bank account ebbed and flowed depending on the time of the month. Waiting for doctors or hairdressers to see her, Sweeney picked up women's magazines with articles about retirement planning or the necessity of emergency savings and put them down again, guilty and afraid.

The apartment had a large bedroom and minuscule kitchen—ironic, she thought, considering the condition of her social life. The living room/dining room was airy and bright, the walls painted a clean ivory, the floors shiny oak. She had reproductions of Holbein's *The Dance of Death* framed and hanging on the walls and black-and-white pillows were scattered on the black slipcovered couch. The floors were covered with handwoven rugs, skeletal black death's heads woven into creamy white wool. Above her desk, which was tucked into a nook at the top of the stairs, were framed black-and-white photographs she'd taken in cemeteries around the world; a bleak New England landscape of simple stones; aboveground New Orleans monuments; a romantic line of mausoleums at Pére Lachaise in Paris.

Against one wall of the living room was propped a plaster replica of an eighteenth-century gravestone Sweeney had found in a Boston shop that also made gargoyles.

She sipped her scotch and got out a pencil and the notebook into which she'd copied Ruth Kimball's phone number. A little buzz of excitement had lodged in her stomach at the prospect of finding out more about Mary Denholm, but she'd resolved she would talk to Jamie Benedetto before she called Ruth Kimball again.

Jamie, a colleague in the Fine Arts Department, was the undisputed expert on turn-of-the-century American painting. She knew he was also interested in American arts colonies, and she'd spent a couple of hours in the library that afternoon poring over some of his articles about colonies in New England.

She reread the opening of one piece she'd photocopied.

> The American arts colony was, in many ways, the direct descendant of the French *Plein-Air* movement, the idea that colors were truer when painted in nature, that painting or sculpting away from the hustle and bustle of the city could inject new life into an artist's work. American artists like the sculptor Bryn Davies Morgan found rural paradises outside of New York, Philadelphia and Boston, bringing with them their friends, students and associates. Morgan founded the well-known colony in the aptly named Byzantium, Vermont, which, like many of the colonies, enjoyed a somewhat Roman fate. The artists brought friends so there would be things to do—the parties and gala theatrical productions at Byzantium were famous for their excess and for their debauchery. But eventually, many of the artists who had sought out colony life abandoned it, complaining that the country felt just like the city.

All very interesting, but it was on another subject that she wanted Jamie's expertise.

"So, Sweeney," he said after they'd made small talk about

holiday plans and his three-year-old son. "What can I do for you?"

"I've got kind of a strange question. At some point I'll explain the whole thing, but right now I just need to know if any of the artists associated with the Byzantium colony were ever arrested or involved in any crimes or scandals that you know of. Back around the turn of the century?"

"Hmmm. Off the top of my head I'd say no, but the person you really ought to talk to is Bennett Dammers. He was at Williams for many years and he's the point man on Byzantium. Quite elderly now, but he wrote the book, literally. He lives up there now, you know. Probably in the phone book."

"Bennett Dammers?" She wrote it down. "Thanks, Jamie. Have a great holiday if I don't see you before."

"You, too. And let me know when you're ready to talk. I'm intrigued by your project."

It *was* intriguing, Sweeney thought after she hung up the phone. And Toby was right. If there was anything in it, it could be a chapter in the book on American gravestone art she was working on. It was intoxicating stuff, a young girl killed by a famous artist and memorialized in a stone that used anachronistic gravestone iconography. Who was the anonymous artist? Why had he chosen those symbols?

But she was getting ahead of herself.

She went into the kitchen and tipped the bottle of Johnnie Walker Red above her emptied glass, enjoying the pleasing gurgle of liquid filling the tumbler, then curled up on the couch again and dialed Ruth Kimball's number.

The voice that answered this time sounded younger and when Sweeney asked if she could talk to Ruth Kimball, the woman on the other end was silent for a minute and then said, "No, I'm sorry."

In the background, Sweeney could hear a blaring television set. "My name's Sweeney St. George. We talked yesterday. She's expecting my call, actually."

Again there was a long silence and Sweeney heard, over

the background noise, a man's voice demand to know who was calling.

"No one," the woman said. "Someone for Ma." Her slightly deep voice was weak and full of emotion.

Sweeney waited, and after another few moments of silence, she said, "Hello? Are you there?"

"Yes," the woman said very softly. "Listen, I'm her daughter. Sherry. You can't . . . I mean she's . . . dead. She died yesterday."

Sweeney took a quick swig of her scotch. "I just . . . I'm so sorry. It must have been sudden."

"Yeah, it was. Were you a friend of hers?"

"No. I'm working on a project and she was going to help me with it. I'm calling from Boston."

"Oh, yeah. She said. You were going to find out what happened to Mary. She was telling everyone about it."

"Can I . . . Can I ask how she died?"

But she had gone too far. Sherry Kimball said nothing and then, as static crackled over the phone line, Sweeney heard a sob. "From the bullet in her head," she said angrily and broke down crying.

"I'm so sorry . . ." But Sherry had put the phone down, leaving Sweeney listening to the insistent dial tone. She put the receiver back in its cradle and sat there for quite a long time, shaken and replaying the conversation over and over in her head. Again she heard Ruth Kimball's voice saying, *They wouldn't want it to get out, would they? The colony folks*, and then her daughter's, *From the bullet in her head*.

Guilty and shocked, she stood up and paced around her apartment, thinking. What were the chances that this woman's death was connected to Sweeney's questions about the gravestone? Sweeney didn't even know how she had died. *From the bullet in her head*. That sounded like someone had shot her. Was it possible . . . ?

She sat down again, conscious that a small locus of excitement had begun to radiate out from her stomach. For the past year she had gone about her life within its small boundaries, following her academic pursuits, her little ambitions.

She had not felt anything like what she felt now, anything like this need to know, simply put, *what had happened*. She understood suddenly what people meant by burning curiosity. She felt warm, alive, afire. There was only one way to know.

Somewhere outside a car alarm sounded in the night. Sweeney finished her scotch, dialed Toby's number, and told him she'd love to spend Christmas in Vermont.

# FOUR

❦

*December 13*

LATER, AFTER EVERYTHING that happened, Sweeney would remember that her first impression of Byzantium was of two separate landscapes, competing with each other for her attention. The first was the idyllic New England scene of calendars and magazines: the gentle, dipping hills, the peaked evergreens against the snow, the red barns and white farmhouses like exotic holly berries, nestled among the green.

But as she and Toby followed the narrow, drift-lined dirt roads in her old Volkswagen Rabbit, she noticed another landscape. This one was made up of dilapidated ranch-style houses and trailers, paint peeling, aluminum roofing coming away at the edges. As they drove through one small town, a group of sullen teenagers, cigarette smoke curling above their heads, stood glaring at passing cars. Sweeney watched them in her rearview mirror until they disappeared.

They had left Boston a little before noon, and by two they were almost there. As they passed a huge dairy farm, the black-and-white cows turning to watch them disinterestedly, she said, "Tell me about your aunt and uncle. What are they like?"

"What are they like?" He thought for a moment. "When I was a kid, I thought they were the coolest adults I'd ever met. Patch is six years younger than my mom, so he and Britta were still in their early twenties by the time I was aware of them. Compared to all of my mom's hippie friends, they were like movie stars. He was the champion of the Middlebury ski team and had almost been in the Olympics. Britta had this long blond hair that went down to her waist and she was nice to me, always buying me presents and playing with me. There's something very fairy princess about her. I had a huge crush on her, of course. I used to have these elaborate fantasies that Patch had been in a skiing accident and that she and I lived together in Vermont."

"Dirty little boy."

"Well, yeah. Patch was great, too, though, adolescent fantasies aside. The thing I always loved about them when I was a kid was that they made a big deal out of things, you know? Everything was an event. You didn't just have a birthday, Patch would plan a treasure hunt and he and all the neighbors would put on a play for you. They didn't just get a Christmas tree, they organized an expedition into the woods to cut one down and had eggnog and cookies while they put it up."

"What do they do for work? Does Patch help run the auction house?" Toby's grandfather had founded Wentworth Auctioneers, a fine art auction house in Boston.

"Only in the sense that he goes to a few board meetings and writes off his vacations as buying trips. Britta comes from money and Patch always had some from my grandparents. He studied painting after he gave up skiing competitively and he has a studio in the house, but I'm not sure he's painting all that much these days. I asked him if he was working on anything when I saw him at Thanksgiving and he was kind of weird about it. He always used to talk about writing a novel, too."

"What about your cousins? How old are they?"

"The twins are seventeen and Gwinny's fourteen now, I think. The boys are fun, they're into outdoorsy stuff, hunting and snowmobiling and all that. Gwinny is something. She was the most solemn little child and so beautiful, like some kind of mythical heroine. She's so different from Britta. You'll see what I mean."

Listening to him, Sweeney remembered the moment they'd become friends. On her second night of college, she had been sitting with a group of other freshmen in someone's

dorm room, drinking gin and tonics and trading childhoods.
She recalled everything about the little party, the damp smell
of the dorms, the clean bite of the cocktails and the way
everyone except for her and Toby had given their résumés
in a rush of suburban town names, boarding schools, and
vacation spots.

She thought suddenly of looking through the prep school
yearbook of her roommate on one of those early days. She
had been surprised to discover that each graduate had a
whole page to himself or herself. The pages were decorated
with candid black-and-white photos of wholesome looking
teenagers, supplemented by sun-rich snapshots of blond tod-
dlers on eastern beaches, and song lyrics or cryptic messages
to friends. Sweeney's own high school yearbook, hidden beneath her warmest winter sweater in her dorm room closet,
was from a public high school in Des Moines, Iowa, where
Sweeney's mother had been appearing in a production Sweeney could not now remember the name of. She had attended
the school for only six months before her graduation, a year
early, at seventeen. She recognized almost none of the posed,
rigid portraits between those pages, the girls heavily made
up, their skin airbrushed to a sheen. Her own picture was
embarrassing; she stared out, startled and alone, her hair rising in a bright, frizzy aura around her head, her retouched
face devoid of her freckles, or of any life at all.

On that second night, one of the girls on Sweeney's hall
had asked Toby where he was from. "Everywhere and no-
where," he'd said. Everyone but Sweeney thought he was
being flip. She'd gotten drunk that night and she and Toby
exchanged the details of their two strange, itinerant childhoods.

Sweeney's parents, a well-known American painter who
had killed himself when Sweeney was thirteen, and a little-
known English actress, had never been married. Toby's, a
rebellious rich girl and an Italian poet, had stayed married
for the first year of his life, then gone their separate ways,
the poet back to Italy and the rich girl to a Berkeley com-
mune where Toby had spent parts of his childhood. Both

Sweeney and Toby were ecstatic to be at college; when their
friends moaned about being homesick or overwhelmed with
work, they sought each other out, because it seemed that only
they knew the joy of a compact dorm room, the late night
silence of the library, an early morning walk beside the river.
In the seventeen years she'd been alive to that point, she
hadn't had many best friends; her mother had moved them
too impulsively around the country for that. Toby's friendship had been a delicious novelty. She remembered the feeling of anticipation before seeing him back then, of looking
forward to their wild, free-ranging conversations. Looking
over at him, she noticed a small, missed patch of whiskers
on his right cheek. It touched her somehow and she flushed
wildly. Jesus! What was with her lately?

"Hey," she said. "They don't know about my father, do
they?"

"No. Do you want me to tell them?"

"Not unless they ask."

They were silent for a few minutes, watching the landscape widen out through the car windows. "That's the Green
River," Toby said, pointing to the swathe of frozen water
that cut the land in two along the road. On both banks, the
land was flat and bare beneath its white frosting, with stubbly
stalks of faded corn or dead grass poking up here and there.
But past the flood plain, the land rose quickly, crumpling
into gentle hills that, even under snow, reminded Sweeney
of Italian landscapes. Beyond were the steeper slopes, shaped
by time and man and striped with winding trails. They were
in ski country.

"It's beautiful. I almost recognize it from the painting."

"The painting" was a landscape by the Byzantium water-
colorist Marcus Granger that Toby had hanging above the
bed in his apartment. It was a winter scene, of a stand of
bare trees and beyond, the white hills, painted softly in pale
lavenders and blues. There was about the painting—and
about the landscape that inspired it—something that made
Sweeney feel lonely and full of awe.

"Okay, turn here," Toby said. She slowed the car and

turned right onto a dirt road. Up ahead was the mouth of a covered bridge. A green sign read "Private Road. No Trespassing," and next to it was a row of six large, metal mailboxes. The car bumped over the wooden floor of the bridge and it was dark for a moment as they crossed over a wide brook rushing swiftly beneath them, carrying broken slabs of ice as flotsam.

"We're on The Island now," Toby said when they emerged. "It isn't really an island, it's just that the brook kind of bows out from the river and then comes back in again. The only way on and off is over the bridge. When I was a kid, I loved the idea that we were cut off from everybody. Oh, that's the Kimballs'." He pointed to a white farmhouse set back from the road. Sweeney turned quickly and had an impression of a ramshackle house, a messy yard filled with old cars. A police car sat in the driveway.

Toby gestured for her to turn onto a driveway flanked by two marble posts and lined with white birch trees, bare of leaves and bending gracefully in the wind.

As they came out of the trees, a large yellow-shingled mansion came into sight in the distance. It was of typical high Victorian construction, a Queen Anne with slate roofs and a wraparound porch and turrets on the third floor, a confection of lacy trim and buttery shingles. Architecturally, it didn't fit with the colonial farmhouses and federal-style homes she'd seen, and it seemed to Sweeney somehow too fragile for the wild landscape.

They were getting out of the car when three giant Newfoundlands, shaggy and black, came bounding around the side of the house, vibrating around Sweeney and Toby's shoulders, barking and jumping and drooling.

"Their names are Sheraton, Chippendale, and Hepplewhite. I swear to God. They're dumber than chairs, too." He handed Sweeney her suitcase so he could fight off one of the dogs. "Well, let's go in and say hi to everyone."

As they climbed the porch stairs, Sweeney looked back for a minute at the dark woods and gray sky. It was still early afternoon, yet there was something about the encroaching trees that made Birch Lane seem vulnerable, as though the darkness was trying to eclipse the golden house. The dogs, lured away by a squirrel darting across the snow-covered lawn and around the back of the house, disappeared, leaving Toby and Sweeney at the front door.

"That's strange. They always used to leave the house open," Toby said, trying the doorknob. He lifted a giant brass knocker in the shape of a tragic Greek mask and let it fall with a hollow thump on the shining black wood. Iron porch furniture, missing its cushions, was scattered around on the porch and Sweeney found herself imagining what it was like to sit here in the summer, gazing across green fields. Toby knocked again.

Nobody came.

"I don't know why it's locked," he said. "But I guess we should go around to the kitchen door. The house is so big that it's hard to hear someone at the front."

She followed him around the side of the house, stepping carefully on a path of slate flagstones that had been shoveled of snow. As they climbed the back porch steps, Toby stopped and pointed over the railing, saying "There are the gardens."

Sweeney looked out on a large red barn, a cluster of smaller buildings, and a white patchwork quilt of fields, sloping to the river in the distance. Nearer to the house was a stone patio, leading down to a forlorn, empty fountain. A few tall, dead plants poked out of the snow, and a high evergreen hedge made a kind of lane leading away from the house toward the woods. "You can't see it from here, but that's where the cemetery is," Toby said, "and way beyond, into the woods and down by the river, is my great-grandfather's old studio."

He opened the back door and led the way into a room filled with boots and parkas and sporting equipment. They put the bags down and took off their boots and coats. "Let's say hi first and then we'll take the bags up," he said, opening the door to the kitchen.

Immediately upon entering the huge kitchen they were assaulted by a wave of warmth from the hotly burning woodstove against one wall and the delicious odors of bread and coffee. After the frigid outdoor air and empty, stark landscape, the house was an oasis of sensual bliss. Sweeney followed Toby through an arched doorway into a big entryway at the front of the house.

The foyer, which was bigger than Sweeney's entire one thousand-square-foot apartment, was broken in half by a wide staircase that rose majestically and spread into a railing running around the outside of a hallway on the second floor. Intricately carved dark wood paneling covered the walls of the entryway, surrounding doorways and an enormous fireplace against one wall, and the space opened into a large living room carpeted in a gaudy Victorian reproduction carpet of cream and rose. The light spots on the carpet were splashed with red, blue, purple, and green light filtering through a giant stained glass window on one wall, and the effect disturbed Sweeney. It looked like spilled wine or blood. Through another doorway, she caught sight of a heavy wooden banquet table and high-backed chairs.

There was an air of Victorian formality about the house, and everywhere she looked, Sweeney found beautiful and strange things, antiques and pottery and paintings, the old mixed with the new. An abstract wash of blues and greens hanging on one wall was mirrored on its opposite by what looked like a Bierstadt. Sweeney stepped up to it. It was a Bierstadt. She rose her eyebrows at Toby and pointed. Then she caught sight of a suit of armor standing at the foot of the staircase.

"That's Sir Brian," Toby whispered. "I forgot to tell you about the family's King Arthur thing. Started with my great-grandfather, who installed poor Brian here when he built the house, but Patch is really gung-ho, named all the kids after Arthurian characters. The twins are Tristram and Galahad, but everyone calls them Trip and Gally. Gwinny's really Guinevere."

In the living room, two more suits of armor flanked the fireplace and a set of crossed swords decorated one wall. When Sweeney stepped up to the stained glass window, she saw that it depicted the young Arthur pulling the sword from the stone. On a small table against one wall was a giant chess set, the pieces exquisitely painted medieval characters, kings and queens and silvery knights. A quarter-finished jigsaw puzzle was spread out on a low coffee table. When Sweeney leaned over it, she picked out a horse and a few spots of shining armor.

Below the Knights of the Round Table motif, there was a kind of sub-layer of lovely things everywhere Sweeney looked. Venetian glass paperweights on the coffee table, a menagerie of crystal animals on a bookshelf, antique books piled on every surface. And on the walls were wonderful pieces of art, too much to take in. The cluttered richness made her dizzy.

The scream, when it came, was such a surprise that Sweeney screamed back, then grabbed Toby's arm to keep herself from falling into a side table.

A thin blonde woman stood in the doorway, one hand to her chest, the other one clutching a long rifle. She was flushed and breathing hard. Toby took the gun from her and tried to hug her, but she remained stiff and frozen, looking from Toby to Sweeney and back again.

"It's just us, Brit," he said, reaching behind him to lay the rifle on the floor against a wall. "This is my friend Sweeney."

But Britta Wentworth did not smile and say it was nice to meet Sweeney and apologize for having been startled by their entrance. Instead, she continued to stare at them with her small, hard eyes that reminded Sweeney of sapphires, panting and looking very much like a frightened horse. Her nostrils flared.

"Oh God," she said. "I thought you were the burglar."

# FIVE

❧

"WE'VE BEEN HAVING these burglaries in the colony," Britta explained, the rifle—an early Christmas present for the boys, she'd told them—stowed safely in the hall closet. The rest of the household had returned from a skiing expedition and they were all sitting around the huge kitchen table hearing about Toby and Sweeney's arrival. "And when I heard the door open, I thought it was ... I thought someone had broken in."

Standing in front of the window, Toby's aunt now reminded Sweeney of a greyhound in her elegant beige fair isle sweater and tan wool pants. Her hair was a precisely highlighted blond bob, her figure thin and flat-chested. Her face would have been pretty but for the way her skin seemed drawn across her bones, her mouth pinched and grim, the lines like scars. Her face seemed startled, as the faces of very pretty women are, by the aging process, Sweeney thought. Her hand, when she had calmed down enough to shake Sweeney's, was like the foot of a small animal, light and fragile. It was so cool, it felt nearly dead.

"Everybody's a little on edge," said Toby's uncle nervously. "We're about the only house that hasn't been broken into." He glanced at his wife. "And then one of our neighbors died last week. Actually you know her, Toby. Ruth Kimball. It's just got everyone a little, well nervous, I guess."

Sweeney met Toby's dark eyes across the table. For reasons she hadn't quite identified, she had decided not to tell him about her conversations with Ruth and Sherry Kimball.

She tried to affect a look of shock and turned to Patch Wentworth.

Where his wife seemed frail, Patch had a youthful brawny blondness and a crooked grin that reminded Sweeney a bit of Toby's. Beneath the rolled-up cuffs of his flannel shirt, his forearms were strong and sinewy. His strawberry blond hair was laced with even paler white and his close-cropped beard gave him an earnest, wholesome look. But there was a superficiality about him; he didn't look right at her, but rather over her shoulder and twice he had walked away while Sweeney was in the middle of a sentence.

"Ruth Kimball? That's strange," Toby said. "We were just talking about her. I was telling Sweeney about Mary Denholm's gravestone. What happened?"

"It seems like she probably did it herself. . . . It was uh . . . with a gun," Britta said quietly, looking over at the children. "But the police aren't entirely sure."

"That's because whenever someone dies of a gunshot wound, they have to investigate it as a possible homicide," Gwinny said authoritatively. "Everybody knows that."

Her father smiled.

Toby's youngest cousin was tall and long-limbed, with fine features and straight light brown hair, streaked with blond and hanging to her waist. She had the lithe model's frame that half of the girls in Sweeney's freshman classes seemed to have nowadays, but instead of the ubiquitous jeans and a sweater, hers was draped in a long green velvet dress, embroidered with Celtic designs. She had, Sweeney decided, ironic eyes.

Then there were the boys. As she always did when she met a pair of identical twins, Sweeney thought about how strange it must be not to own your looks. They were very blond, with blue eyes and square faces like Patch. And though they were almost as tall as Sweeney, they seemed somehow like unfinished statues, as though the artist had walked away before completing the musculature. Their faces were identical, but they were easy to tell apart. Gally had his shoulder-length hair tied back in a ponytail and was wearing a tie-dyed T-shirt and jeans. Trip was clean-cut, with short hair, and was wearing a neatly ironed button-down shirt. Gally was quiet and hesitant, and Trip struck her as charming and somewhat flirtatious. Their names suited them somehow, Sweeney thought. Or perhaps they had come to suit their names.

When Patch introduced the boys to Sweeney, he had said, "This is Trip, the actor of the family, and Gally here is going to be the archaeologist. Isn't that right, Gal?" Gally had shot his father a look that Sweeney fully expected to wither the Christmas cactus in the middle of the kitchen table.

Toby was still looking shocked. "Why would she kill herself?"

"She's been on her own since her husband died. She had money troubles, we think." Britta stood up suddenly and took her coffee cup over to the sink with an air of finality.

But her answer had gotten Sweeney's attention. "What kind of money troubles?"

Patch said, "Oh, she wanted to sell some of her land and put up condominiums. I don't remember if we told you about it at Thanksgiving, Toby. Anyway, all the neighbors on The Island were against it, of course. Can you imagine? They were going to call it Byzantium Acres or some such nonsense. The colony is the best thing this town has going for it and they wanted to blight the landscape with concrete and steel. The right of way has to be on our land, so at first we thought we were safe, but there was a mix-up with a deed and . . . anyway, obviously we were going to fight it." Patch frowned, his blue eyes crinkling at the corners, and Toby turned the conversation back to the burglaries.

"They started in the summer. Just after the Fourth of July," Patch said. "Everyone thought that it must be kids from town fooling around. But they've continued and they only seem to target the colony. The last one was just a couple of weeks ago."

"Anything valuable get taken?" Toby asked.

"Stereos, TVs, things like that, mostly. And a few pieces of art. Our friends the Rapaccis lost six or seven pieces, but nothing really valuable. They had a Léger hanging on the wall right next to this little painting by my grandfather—a not-very-good portrait, worth next to nothing—and the burglars took my grandfather's. He would have been pleased, anyway. He didn't like the French." The joke fell flat.

"Is there any idea about who it is?" Sweeney asked.

"Oh, I think the police know who it is. Sherry, Ruth Kimball's daughter, has this boyfriend. He's got some fairly unsavory characters who are always over at the house."

"Carl," Gwinny said matter-of-factly. "He's a dirtbag."

"Yes. Carl." Her father pronounced the name with the same air of distaste. "Anyway, it would be one thing if it were just an epidemic of burglaries but, as I said, it seems like someone's only targeting the houses in the colony. I've lived here off and on since I was a child and so have most of our friends. Now we feel as though someone's trying to run us out of town. There have been some other things that have contributed to it, of course, but it's the burglaries that have everyone up in arms."

Sweeney looked up at her and saw an expression of raw fear pass quickly across Britta's face.

"It's very strange," Britta said. "The burglar doesn't seem to know what he's doing or what he wants. It's as though he's just collecting glittery things, like one of those birds. What are they called?" She searched nervously for the word.

"Magpies," said a very crisp, very English voice from the doorway. Sweeney looked up to find a man standing there, listening to them. "It's magpies that like to pick up glittery things."

Patch got up to make the introductions. "Sweeney, Toby, this is our good friend Ian Ball. Ian's visiting from London for the holidays. He just arrived in the States today."

"Hello," Ian said, sitting down at the table and accepting Britta's offer of a cup of coffee.

Sweeney was good at placing regional British accents, but couldn't quite get his, a sort of generic Queen's English that she hadn't thought existed outside the BBC. It bothered her and she inspected him for a moment, his deep blue-green eyes, which were inscrutable behind horn-rimmed glasses, and his slightly floppy, waving dark hair. He looked about thirty-five and he had the kind of beaky, intellectual English charm that she had always found attractive. But there was something about the way he watched them, his eyes darting here and there like a bird's, that put her on guard. He sat down at the table, fiddling with the handle of his coffee cup until he noticed that Sweeney was watching him.

"How has the burglar been getting into the houses?" Toby asked.

"That's the thing," Patch answered sheepishly. "None of us ever locked up around here until recently."

Sweeney asked, "But who would know that? Was it common knowledge in town?"

Britta got up from the kitchen table and went over to the window, where she gazed out at the frozen landscape as though she were looking for someone. "Let's stop talking about the burglaries," she said after a moment. "I don't want to think about them anymore."

Patch cleared his throat. "Ian runs an auction house in London," he told Sweeney and Toby, glancing at his wife. "He was coming over the pond for a business trip anyway, so we convinced him to spend the holiday with us. We've known each other for years, but he's never been to Vermont." Patch turned to Ian. "Sweeney's an art historian. She studies gravestones."

"Yes, of course. I enjoyed your book. I'm actually a bit interested in all this stuff myself. I've done some cataloging of mourning items and one of my favorite pieces in my own collection is an eighteenth-century broadsheet advertising the funeral of a Londoner named Charles Henley. It's wonderful stuff, menacing skulls and crossbones, lots of hellfire and brimstone." He gestured excitedly with his coffee cup as he talked. "Are you working on anything new?"

"Yeah, a book on eighteenth- and nineteenth-century stones and monuments. I'm focusing on New England, but I think I'll have a few chapters on southern stones as well. I'm interested in the iconography and the quality of the carving and the art. Things change a lot during the period and I want to connect it to what was going on socially, culturally. There are certain images that appear on gravestones, like hour-glasses and willow trees and death's heads—or skulls. They also show up on other items, mourning jewelry and even pottery. I'm tracing the way the images develop and were brought to America from Europe."

"That's why I thought she'd be interested in Mary Denholm's gravestone," Toby told his aunt and uncle. "Apparently it's completely wrong for the period, very anomalous." He grinned around at them. "Don't I sound like I know what I'm talking about? Anyway, she's probably going to discover that some famous American sculptor actually did it. Isn't that right, Sweeney?"

She nodded and turned to Patch. "Is it true that no one knows who made the gravestone?"

There was a pause. "Yes, it's strange actually. For a community as concerned with art and artists as we are. But no one's ever known."

"Well, someone must have known at one time because it must have been commissioned at the time of her death. Would you have any records, diaries, things that belonged to your grandfather or other members of the colony that I could look at?"

"We've got a very messy attic-full. You can look if you really want to." Patch got up and took his coffee cup to the sink.

"Anyway, I thought I'd take Sweeney down this afternoon," Toby said. "So she can see it in the flesh, so to speak."

"Well, I don't know if you'll be able to get in, I mean . . ." Britta seemed flustered.

"We don't mind blazing a path through the snow," Toby said cheerily.

"No, what she means . . ." Patch said, with difficulty, looking from his children to Toby and back again. "What she means is that the cemetery may still be roped off. You see, that's where Ruth Kimball died."

# SIX

PATCH WENTWORTH FELT relief slow his blood as he watched Toby and Sweeney disappear across the back field, down toward the cemetery. He stood for a moment, looked across the field in the other direction, toward the other houses, toward one house in particular, and felt a sudden gaping loneliness. He didn't want to go back inside. He breathed in the cold air for a few moments, like a smoker taking a last drag on the porch, then lifted a load of firewood into his arms and went into the kitchen. The outdoors clung on him like cigarette smoke, a cold, gray smell, of frozen water, deadened nature.

"Brit?"

She was standing at the window, looking out over the white fields rolling down to the river and she started at the sound of his voice. She said nothing, still looking out the window, then carefully tucked a few pieces of her fine blond and gray hair behind her ear. The action was as precise as everything she did, Patch thought, an ordering of the elements that made up her world. He had once found it endearing.

"What do you think of Sweeney?" Patch deposited the wood into the box and then pushed a log into the large woodstove against one wall. It was burning just right, emanating a cozy cloud of heat and warming the huge kitchen. As a child he had liked the kitchen best of all the rooms at Birch Lane. His grandparents had been strict about children running through the house, but in the kitchen he had been allowed to spill out toys on the floor or draw at the big table while the cook and housekeeper worked away at the cookstove they'd had in those days. It was still his favorite room, where the family ate and where the children did their homework when they were all home from school. It was Britta's room, he realized. It was here that she seemed happiest and where he had glimpses of what their marriage had once been, what he had thought it might be the first time he brought her to Byzantium.

He watched her for a moment, shocked by how thin she'd become in the last few months. Then he took off his parka and boots, poured himself a cup of coffee and sat down at the kitchen table with the paper. Droplets of melted snow glistened on his blond hair until he ran a hand through it. His face was ruddy from the cold.

"She seems nice," Britta said finally, turning away from the window and going back to stirring something in a pot on the stove.

"Her father was Paul St. George. You know, the big orange paintings of Arizona or Mexico or somewhere. I asked Toby about it just now, before she came down, and he said not to say anything because she doesn't like people to know."

Britta finally turned around and looked at him. "The one who . . . ?"

"Yeah. Isn't that sad. She was pretty young, I guess." He took a deep breath. "I wish she didn't have this idea about looking into Mary Denholm's gravestone. This is hardly the time to be bothering Sherry. Don't you think it's kind of inappropriate?"

"I don't know. It was Toby's idea." She gestured at the window. "The police are back. I just saw the car."

He went to stand behind her, conscious of her thin shoulders, the rigidity of her back. He looked out the window, and saw a state trooper car parked on the road leading to the Kimballs' driveway.

"Patch, why would they bring the state police in? Wouldn't Cooper be able to handle it?"

"I'm sure the state cops get involved whenever there's a death involving a gun," he said breezily.

Britta took a pan over to the sink and stood there, her back to him, for a few minutes before the metal clattered against the porcelain.

He felt a flash of annoyance. If there was anything that defined his marriage it was that communicative clatter. It was how Britta told him what she wanted these days. "What's wrong?" he asked finally.

She hesitated, then turned to him. "Patch, they—the police—asked me what everyone was doing during that afternoon. Where we all were."

"Yes?"

"Well, I said that you were outside stacking wood, but . . ."

He waited and Britta went back to the window. She hesitated again for a long moment before saying quietly, "There's something . . . See, with everything that was going on. When you . . . well, I was in here and I was listening to the boys shooting and suddenly I felt scared, I don't know why, and I went to find you and I couldn't."

"I went around the corner. I was cutting some brush and I wanted to make sure there wasn't anything up against the house, what with all the burglaries. I didn't want anyone to be able to get in through a window."

Britta, relieved, turned and smiled at him. "That's where you were. Of course. I didn't go around the front. I just looked by the woodpile and . . . that's where you were, of course."

"Sweetheart, don't worry about this. Let's try and enjoy Christmas."

"Yes," she said, going back to the window and looking out as though she expected to see someone there. "Yes. Christmas."

# SEVEN

❦

THE BRIGHT MORNING had turned into a frigid afternoon, the late light thin and sickly on the snow. As they walked down to the cemetery, tiny puffs of mist hovered before them and Sweeney's lungs ached with the cold.

"So what did you think of *la familia*?" Toby asked.

"They're nice. And you seem really happy with them." She didn't say anything more. She wasn't sure what she thought of them yet and people were always sensitive about their own families.

They walked in silence for a few minutes, then Sweeney asked, "How did your great-grandparents end up here anyway? I thought they were from New York."

"Well, the sculptor Bryn Davies Morgan was the first artist to come to Byzantium," Toby said. "He built a house up the river a bit called Upper Pastures—I'll take you up and show you sometime—and then he convinced my great-grandfather, who was quite a bit younger, to buy some land. The story goes that Morgan was an ugly drunk and he and my great-grandfather used to get into these knock-down, drag-out fights, so my great-grandmother said she'd only move to Byzantium if they lived on The Island, so that Morgan wouldn't be around too much. They built Birch Lane and my grandfather built his studio down near the river."

He slowed down and Sweeney spotted the river, silvery and wide, snaking away from them beyond the house. "Morgan's son built over here, too," Toby went on, "because his father could be such a son-of-a-bitch when he was drinking.

And much later, in the '20s, I think, Marcus Granger, another painter, built his house at the other end of The Island. His widow, Electra, still lives here; she's a great friend of Patch and Britta's. Her granddaughter is Rosemary. She's the woman I was hanging out with at Thanksgiving." He blushed.

"Who are the rest of the neighbors? Are they all colony families?"

"Pretty much. There's Willow and Anders Fontana. Willow is Morgan's granddaughter, and she and Anders live in the house her father built. He works in Boston during the week and comes up weekends. You'll meet Sabina Dodge, too. She used to live with one of the artists. As I said, they're a pretty tight bunch."

They walked in silence for a few minutes before Toby said, "Hey. Speak of the devils." Sweeney looked up to see a small group of walkers approaching them on the path, carrying armfuls of evergreen boughs. With the deep green woods and the white-shrouded Vermont hills all around them, the effect was lovely, as though they'd stepped out of a Christmas card.

"Hello, Toby," called an elderly woman in a velvet turban, long mink coat, and rubber boots. She was a formidable physical presence, nearly three hundred pounds, Sweeney guessed, deciding she'd never seen so much mink in one place in her life.

The large woman wrapped Toby in a furry hug with her free arm when the little group had reached them on the path. "Patch said you were coming for Christmas. How delightful." She turned to Sweeney. "And you're the art historian. Patch has told us all about you. Gravestones, he said. How macabre!"

A pretty blond woman behind her gave Toby a hug, too, and Sweeney watched him hang on for a second longer than necessary. Aha. The beloved Rosemary. She flushed slightly when Sweeney met her eyes and Sweeney felt a little flash of humiliation, realizing that Toby had told this woman about her. Stop it, Sweeney, she told herself. Just stop it.

The woman in the mink waved her arm at the little group. "We," she announced, "are the neighbors."

More specific introductions ensued. The fur coat-wearing walker was Sabina Dodge. The small, old lady turned out to be Electra Granger. She was a serene-looking person, dressed in a camel hair polo coat, and she had a cloud of fine, white hair half-covered by a pink scarf. Her cataract-clouded blue eyes gazed sightlessly as she shook Sweeney's hand.

Willow and Anders Fontana and Toby's Rosemary made up the rest of the walking party.

Willow was attractive and athletic, with short brown hair highlighted with streaks of gold, and a husky voice. Her tall, shapely figure was perfectly covered by a pair of skintight black leggings and a purple ski parka. She was wearing a black headband instead of a hat and she made Sweeney feel overbundled and un-chic. She had the timeless, expensively-cared-for look of a woman who could have been anywhere between thirty-five and fifty.

Willow's husband, Anders Fontana, was a jovial, slickly handsome man with a loud laugh and a competitive hand-shake. Even on the windy winter day, his black hair shone like molded plastic. He slapped Toby on the back and looked Sweeney up and down as Sabina introduced them.

Rosemary Burgess, Electra's granddaughter, was a petite blond woman around Sweeney's age, with a glossy cap of pale hair, dark blue eyes, and a delicate, butterfly-shaped birthmark on her right cheek. As she spoke in a soft accent that Sweeney guessed was South African, she kept a gentle hand on her grandmother's elbow and kept smiling at Toby. She was, Sweeney realized, exactly his type, small and cool and quiet, and she made Sweeney feel gawky and over-tall.

"We're on our way down to the cemetery," Toby explained, when Sabina asked him where they were walking. "Sweeney's doing some research on Mary Denholm's stone."

"Oh, do you think you'll be able to . . . ? Patch did tell you about the . . ." Willow looked subdued for a second.

"Yeah, it's awful." They chatted in hushed, awkward

tones for a few minutes about Ruth Kimball's death. Sweeney just listened.

"Anyway," Toby told them, "we're going to go down and see. Maybe they'll just let us look at the stone."

"Perhaps. Make sure you watch out for her ghost. She wasn't a very nice person when she was alive. I doubt she's improved much in death." Sabina Dodge winked mischievously.

"Sabina, stop it." Willow turned to Sweeney. "Don't let her scare you. We're all sorry about Ruth Kimball's death, even if we weren't exactly on friendly terms."

"Not on friendly terms?" Sweeney asked innocently. She wasn't sure, but she thought she caught, out of the corner of her eye, Toby shooting her a suspicious glance.

"It's just that, shall we say, her loyalty to the colony was in doubt. She didn't quite appreciate what it means to everybody and how important it is to keep it exactly the way it is." Sabina nodded, pleased with her choice of words. "Now, we'd better let you go if you're going to make it before dark. We'll all be over for dinner on Monday, so we'll see you then and talk some more." She wiggled her fingers at them. "Remember what I said about ghosts."

When they were out of earshot, Sweeney turned to Toby and, trying to keep her voice even and cheery, said, "So, she's pretty, Toby."

"Yeah. I don't know. We'll see what happens." He didn't want to go into it anymore, but Sweeney couldn't stop herself.

"Her accent sounds South African. Did you tell me she only moved here recently?"

"Yeah, it's kind of an amazing story, actually. Her parents had this big falling out with Electra and Marcus and took her to England when she was pretty young. Then they moved to South Africa and she never saw her grandparents again. She said she always knew they existed, but was afraid of asking her parents about them. Then she was working in London and her parents died in a car accident. She got in touch with Electra last summer, and suggested that she come to visit. It turned out that Electra was getting older and needed someone to live with her and look after things. I think it's worked out well for both of them."

"Well, she seems nice. I look forward to getting to know her." The words sounded false, even to Sweeney's ears, and Toby gave her an odd look.

The cemetery, when they reached it, was roped off, the orange police tape girding the iron fence like a Christmas package. But there weren't any policemen around, so they slid under the tape, standing against the fence for a moment. It was very quiet—the wind had died down—and Sweeney felt suddenly, deeply alone.

As she'd deduced from the photographs, it was a typical New England burial ground, with most of the thirty or so stones dating to the late 1700s and early-to-mid-1800s. The earlier stones were typical for the period, slate carved with willow boughs or hourglasses at the top, and the name of the deceased and dates of birth and death. The later ones had more Victorian flourishes: garlands of flowers or fruit; cherubic, flying figures. There seemed to be a number of stones with the names Denholm and Perkins on them.

Sweeney, who had spent an inordinate percentage of her twenty-eight years in cemeteries, wasn't much affected by their atmosphere. But there was a feeling in this one that made the hairs on the back of her neck stand up. Perhaps it was the low light and the way the mist rose above the snow. Maybe it was her knowledge of what had happened among these stones. But Sweeney found herself looking over her shoulder as she wandered around the burial ground.

"Hey, look at this one," Toby said, calling her over to a small, slate stone. "She was only a year old. *Come little children see the place/Where infant dust must lie/There is no age that's free from this/Both young and old must die.*'"

"That's a classic epitaph. More for the living than the dead."

Sweeney wandered around and found some other stones with the name Denholm on them. Elizabeth Denholm, who she assumed was Mary's mother from the dates on the stone, was buried beneath a simple marble headstone inscribed with the words *"O' Artful Death."* There was something sad about the stone, Sweeney thought, feeling suddenly sorry for this woman who had lost her daughter so young.

Next to it was a stone marking the grave of Louis Denholm, who was the right age to be Mary's father. It was also a simple headstone, though five times the size of his wife's. The epitaph read,

> *Think my friends when this you see*
> *How Death's dark deed hath slayed me*
> *He is a thief and taketh flight*
> *Beneath the cover of the night*

She stared at the stone for a few minutes and then said, "Come on. Let's go look at Mary's before it gets too dark."

In the low afternoon light, the lines of the life-sized monument stood out in stark relief. The marble was darkened with age, a thin layer of moss covering the surface so that the woman's eyes looked real, flecked with brown and green. The coiling strands of her hair looked almost like seaweed.

What hadn't come across in the photographs, Sweeney decided, was how deeply troubling the stone was. The woman was both more beautiful and more disturbing than she'd been in the pictures. It was very clear she was meant to be dead, and with the strange, stylized skeleton peeking over her shoulder like a lecherous imp, there was a palpable sense of violence about the work. After a few minutes of clearing snow from the base of the monument with a mittened hand, she had convinced herself that there was no signature of any kind.

"This is so weird," she said to Toby. "It didn't strike me when I saw the photographs, but it's very Pre-Raphaelite."

"Rossetti and Ruskin?"

"Right, though it's not by any of the major Pre-Raphaelites. I'd be willing to put a lot of money on that. And I don't think any of them ever came to Byzantium." She walked around the monument again, mesmerized by its strangeness.

"Were there any American Pre-Raphaelites? I don't think I've ever heard that there were."

"There were a couple of painters and journalists who knew the Pre-Raphaelites in England. Thomas Buchanan Read and a guy named Stillman. It's interesting to trace the ideas, you know, how they bounced back and forth across the Atlantic. Rossetti loved Poe, was completely obsessed with him and Poe's writing absolutely influenced his work."

She thought for a moment.

"And I think there was even a group of them who called themselves the American Pre-Raphaelites or something. Thomas Farrar comes to mind. They liked to make fun of Copley and Bierstadt. But I don't think they were ever as famous as the real ones.

"There were well-known American artists like John La Farge and even Morgan who were influenced by them. And the arts and crafts movement in America came out of some of those Pre-Raphaelite sentiments, you know."

Toby said, "You'll have to ask Patch, but I think Morgan and my grandfather knew La Farge and some of the others you mentioned, in New York. I remember reading something once. That might be the connection."

"Yeah, although, I don't know of any American sculptors who were this directly influenced by them. And the subject isn't right, you know. I don't actually think the Pre-Raphaelites would have approved. The girl is typical, but the figure of Death behind her? Very strange."

She leaned over and examined the girl's face, her cheek brushing against the cold stone. "There's been a lot written about the Pre-Raphaelites and their depictions of women. The women were either saintly goddesses of domestic tranquillity or prostitutes being lured away by evil men in the streets of London. But she looks so . . . in control. Even though she's dead. Do you know what I mean? God, it's so interesting, Toby. There's got to be a great story behind this."

She paused to catch her breath. "What do you think about the poem?"

He read it again. "It's funny. I'd say the author wasn't a very accomplished poet, yet he demonstrates a knowledge of Victorian poetry in his use of symbolism. Of course, as poetry it's not very good. The language is kind of clichéd and the shift in point of view is jarring. I'm not surprised we haven't heard of the poet."

"It's weird to have a poem like that on a stone anyway. It's not exactly an epitaph. And it's not a religious verse." She thought for a moment. "You know what the main poem sort of reminds me of? Swinburne. *The Garden of Proserpine.*"

"Yeah, I know what you mean. '*Here life has death for a neighbor, And far from eye or ear/Wan waves and wet winds labor, Weak ships and spirits steer.*' "

"I don't know much about Swinburne. What's his story?"

"Well, he was one of the better-known Victorian poets. Wrote in the 1850s and '60s. *Proserpine* was part of a larger work called *Poems and Ballads* and he defended it against charges that it was a low work of sensuality or something like that. The whole point of the thing was that he wanted to show how oppressive Victorian morality had stamped out natural sexuality. But *Proserpine* is kind of weird. It's about the saturation of love, I think, and the senses being over-loaded by sensuality and lust—the fetid garden—and the narrator just wants to sleep. There's some line like '*I am weary of days and hours and buds of flowers,*' or something like that, and then he says he's tired of desire and '*everything but sleep.*' That's my take on it."

He looked around the cemetery. It was almost dark now, though the expanse of snow-covered fields gave off a moony glow in the twilight.

"Where do you think she died?"

Sweeney had spotted a phalanx of spikes decorated with orange flags against the railing on one side of the cemetery and she pointed it out to him. Above the suggested shape of a body was a bush with waxy green leaves and from a distance, there appeared to be splashes of red blood on the snow. But as she wandered closer, she saw it was an illusion. The color came from scattered holly berries.

"I've had enough for now," she said, turning away. "Let's get out of here."

# EIGHT

*The lubricants on the wheel that was Byzantium's social life were the guests. In singles, doubles or triples, they came from the cities, breathlessly happy they'd been asked to stay, determined to respect the artists' space and not to ask too many questions. Most stayed with whomever had invited them, though on the occasion someone had filled their house up, the guests were boarded at Upper Pastures or Birch Lane, where there was always extra room.*

*Many of the artists who eventually came to live at Byzantium started out as weekend guests. One of those was Myra Benton, who went on to spend five summers as Morgan's studio assistant and to become a talented and well-known sculptor in her own right.*

*Years after her fateful first visit, Benton wrote in her journal about how she came to see the guests after she was an "official Byzantine":*

*"At some point, I began to have the feeling that the guests were a kind of mirror for the colonists, that life in Byzantium was somehow produced for them. 'Look at how we live,' we all seemed to say. 'Look at how gay we are, how much fun we have.' But when the visitors were gone, we sometimes forgot who we were, and the fun just ran out of everything as though you'd punctured an auto tire."*

—*Muse of the Hills: The Byzantium Colony,
1860–1956*
by Bennett Dammers

SWEENEY WASN'T SURE whether it was the sense of death being uncomfortably near, their pleasure in being indoors on a cold and wintry evening, or the Wentworths' gratefulness in having new guests to relieve their own family dynamics, but they entered the warm dining room that night a strangely jovial and cheerful group, the children charming and helpful, the adults pleasantly tipsy from their cocktails before dinner.

"What shall we drink to?" Patch asked as they sat down at the big dining room table, lifting his wine glass and dipping it in Sweeney's direction. "To new friends?"

"To new friends," everyone intoned, lifting their glasses. As they drank, Britta and Gwinny brought in bowls of steaming linguine drenched with tomato vodka sauce and tender veal, and sprinkled with herbs. Sweeney realized that she hadn't had anything to eat all day and she was ravenous. The smell of food was as intoxicating as the wine.

"And to old ones," Patch added as they dug into the pasta. "We should also drink to old ones."

"To old friends," they said, and Patch winked at Ian.

Toby lifted his own glass. "And while we're at it, here's to acquaintances of a medium length of time who one says hello to on the street but would never invite over for dinner."

"We haven't drunk to people we don't really like at all but have to be nice to because they're family," said Patch. "And boring distant relatives who you only see at weddings and funerals."

"Yes," said Ian Ball. "And please let's drink to work chums who you see once a year at the Christmas party and whose wives you secretly fancy!"

They all laughed and Sweeney turned to look at Toby. He was grinning, his glass raised, his hair flopping over his forehead. Earlier, they had come back from their walk and stretched out on the sofa in the living room, warming their feet by the fire. He had rubbed her back and let her think out loud about Mary's gravestone and she had felt peace overtake her. He had felt it, too, she knew he had, a simple, happy peace. Now, looking at him, she flushed deeply. Could it be that she and Toby . . . ? That after all this time, she was finally ready for Toby, to find out what there might be between them besides the friendship? She looked away quickly, embarrassed.

"We saw everyone on our walk down to the cemetery," Toby was telling them. "Sabina made them all go down and collect tree limbs to decorate her house with."

"What did you think of them, Sweeney?" Britta asked her. "They can be overwhelming. The first time Patch brought me here, I felt like I'd been bowled over by a pack of dogs."

"I liked them," Sweeney said simply.

Patch said, "We're lucky to have such good friends here," and got up to pour the wine.

"Toby says you're a painter," Sweeney said to Patch. "I've always wished I could paint. Those who can't do, teach, and all that."

"I don't paint much anymore," Patch said. "But that's one of my efforts up there." He pointed to a landscape hanging on a wall of the dining room. "I realized early on that my talent didn't hold a candle to my grandfather's, but I did inherit his love for it."

Sweeney studied the painting and saw that he was right. The landscape was technically correct, everything in proportion, the rolling hills and small farm almost photographically perfect. But there was something missing. It wasn't the oft-mentioned passion—for Sweeney loved some paintings that she considered coolly dispassionate—but rather a sense of imaginative flight. The painting was no more than what it was, an exact likeness of a scene. It didn't strive to make the viewer feel or imagine anything beyond it. It didn't go for peace or loneliness or joy. It was uninformed by emotion and in that sense, it was an utter failure.

She wondered what to say that wouldn't let on that she agreed with him, and settled on "I like the way you've done the farmer," because she did.

Ian had been quiet during most of the evening, but now he said, "I've grown fascinated by the history of the colony since I've been here, Patch. Tell me about your grandfather. What was he like as a person?"

Patch didn't say much about his grandfather, but for the next hour, he told stories—oft-told stories, Sweeney suspected—about the artists, about the parties and the famous visitors who had come, about local scandals—a visitor who fell in love with someone's gardener and an adulterous painter who was blackmailed for thirty dollars a week by the local minister—about picnics and outdoor teas and grand Christmas parties, and the colony began to take shape before Sweeney's eyes. It took on life and glittering reality and she started to see what it was that they were all so passionately connected to, what it was that had drawn them here and kept them here.

She said so, when he was finished.

"That's why we felt it was so important not to have these condos," he said, still excited from his monologue. "I sympathized with Ruth, I really did, but it isn't worth any amount of money to ruin this. That's why we felt we had to fight it."

She was curious about something. "What do you mean by fighting it? Was there some kind of review process for the neighbors."

"Not exactly," Patch said. "Vermont has a law called Act 250. It's an environmentally focused law and the idea is that any major development has to be vetted. There's a board that looks at how the development would affect a whole bunch of things, traffic, the water supply, the aesthetics of the area. Neighbors and people in the community can weigh in when the board is considering a possible development. We were fighting it on the basis that this area has historical value and that they couldn't compromise it by changing the landscape. Then, as the process went on, it became clear that the only place to put the right of way was partly over the line onto our property. We refused to give permission, and it looked like it might end there, but then the Kimballs claimed that in fact the land was theirs. When our lawyers started looking into it, they found that a deed hadn't ever been recorded.

Something like that. My father always told me that his father told him he'd bought the land off of Louis Denholm. I still don't know how it will turn out."

"Anyway." He leaned back in his chair. "Let's not talk about all this awful stuff now. We're so pleased to have you all with us." He smiled around at them. "Things can't be easy for Sherry Kimball tonight. I feel very lucky to have my family and friends safe and sound and all around me."

When they had finished eating, Britta and the kids cleared the table and brought out dessert of stewed fruit and crème fraîche. Patch opened a bottle of champagne and raised his glass to them all, saying, "I think we should drink to our friends from generations past who provided us with so much beauty and so many good stories."

"Here, here," Toby said. Sweeney turned to smile at him and found that he was smiling at her.

"And what about flighty friends who are terribly late to dinner?" They all looked up to find Rosemary standing in the doorway. "I'm sorry I'm late. Granny wasn't feeling well and I wanted to wait until she fell asleep before I left."

"That's all right," Britta said, kissing her and going to get her some dessert. "I hope Electra's okay."

"Yes, I think so. Just a bit tired from our walk today, I think."

Rosemary sat down on Toby's other side and he leaned over to give her a chaste kiss on the cheek, leaving her looking embarrassed and delighted, and Sweeney just embarrassed.

Seeking a distraction, she looked up to find Gally staring at her. She met his eyes and he looked down, flushing wildly. She still hadn't gotten a handle on Toby's twin cousins. Before dinner, Trip, dressed in an oxford shirt and wool sweater, had leaned over and told her in a confidential voice that he liked her earrings. "They match your eyes," he'd said, winking at her and reaching out to roll a sparkling drop pendant between his thumb and forefinger. She'd blushed, surprised at his boldness.

Gally, on the other hand, seemed almost pathologically

shy. She had caught him staring at her a few times, and when she'd asked him about his interest in archaeology, he had seemed unable to come up with so much as a sentence in reply.

"So how long have you been teaching, Sweeney?" Rosemary asked her, leaning across Toby, who put an arm around her shoulder.

Sweeney took a deep breath. "Well, I was a teaching assistant when I was in graduate school. But I've been an assistant professor for just a year. I like it, though it's a bit uncertain. I think my department chairman hates me. And they'll never give tenure to anyone from the department. Did I mention my chairman hates me?"

"How could he?" Rosemary said sincerely. "He must be jealous."

"That's what I keep telling her," Toby said.

"Jealous or not, he's decided to supplement his non-existent course load with a couple of semesters of torturing me. If you know any voodoo, let me know. I'd love to make a little doll of him and stick pins in it or something."

"Actually," Rosemary said, smiling, "when we lived in South Africa, we were out in the bush for a while and there was this local tribal chief my father knew a little. He used to curse people. It was really weird. One day he'd say something about how he didn't like so and so, or that they had crossed him, and then sure enough, a couple of days later the fellow's gun would misfire or he'd fall off a horse or something. I couldn't tell you how he did it, though."

"Isn't she amazing?" Toby said to them. "Do you know anyone else who knows about voodoo and curses?"

Sweeney felt herself flush again. The conversation went on, but she hardly heard what they were saying. This time she looked up to find Ian Ball watching her across the table. She did not like what she saw in his face and as soon as she felt she could, she said she was tired and went up to bed.

Climbing the stairs to the third floor, she recalled it with anger and shame. He had looked at her with sympathy.

• • •

As a child, Sweeney had been terrified by the idea of sleep, the feeling of gradually surrendering her place in the earthly world. It felt like a kind of dying, and even as an adult, she often jerked awake three or four times as she fell asleep before finally giving in. Some nights, she could not give in at all and she had tried all the usual remedies, warm baths and milk and pills. Warm baths got her creative juices flowing, she hated milk, and pills made her jittery the next day. The only thing she'd found that worked was alcohol.

That night, helped along by the five glasses of wine she'd had at dinner, she had no trouble nodding off, but she awoke with a start early the next morning, conscious that something had startled her from sleep. She looked at the glowing clock on her bedside table. It was 4:30, and outside the window of her third floor bedroom, it was not quite dark, the waxing moon casting a washed-out light on the snow-covered fields.

She turned on her bedside light, awake as if she'd downed a cup of coffee. What had it been? She was almost certain that something specific had drawn her back from sleep, the sound of a voice, a presence in her room. Footsteps. That was it. She'd heard footsteps somewhere. Someone going to the bathroom, probably. But no, it hadn't been inside the house, she realized as the sound came back to her. The sound had been someone or something's footsteps on the roof. Strangely this made her feel better. It had probably been a rat or a squirrel.

That was it. All was well. But she knew with the certainty of a lifelong insomniac that further rest was impossible. She got out of bed and went to look for a book to read.

The bedroom to which she had been assigned was a cozy little chamber tucked under the eaves of the third floor and decorated in leafy green. A stenciled vine wound its way around the room, dipping and twining itself around the wall behind a four-poster bed and echoed in a vine-print throw rug and the canopy draped over the bed. The selection of books about the colony she'd borrowed from the Wentworths' library were piled promisingly on the mirrored dressing table.

She chose the one that appeared the most comprehensive, a hardback history by Bennett Dammers, the expert on Byzantium whom her colleague Jamie Benedetto had recommended she consult. She got back in bed, opening the book to the faded back jacket flap where she found a picture of a dapper-looking man with light hair styled in formidable '70s sideburns. The collar of his shirt reached almost to his shoulders, but still he managed to look preppy and formal. "Bennett Dammers was for many years the chairman of the Art History Department at Williams College," the jacket copy read. "He was born and raised in Byzantium, Vermont, where he continues to live in a house once owned by the painter Gerard Fierman. His other books include biographies of the Byzantium sculptor Bryn Davies Morgan and a history of American painters abroad."

She spent the next hour reading about the history of the colony, about how Morgan had come up from New York and seen the hills of Byzantium and bought a piece of land for his house, about how his friends and their friends had followed him here, for the natural beauty, for the solitude, for the companionship. In their rustic Byzantium studios, some of the best American artists of the late nineteenth and early twentieth centuries had found inspiration and fame.

Next Sweeney read about Toby's great-grandfather. "Herrick Gilmartin built his studio in the woods behind Birch Lane soon after the house was finished, complete with a small kitchen, woodburning stove, and overhead sleeping loft, so that he could sleep there when artistic inspiration struck him, as it often did, at odd hours."

There was a photograph of the artist at his easel, the cluttered interior of the little studio filled with canvases and jars of paint, books, and smocks.

It was now 5:30 and the sky seemed even darker outside her window. She wasn't going to get any more sleep so she decided she might as well get up and make some coffee.

"Shhh," she told the dogs as they clattered ahead of her down the stairs, their nails clicking on the wood floors. "You'll wake everyone up."

But someone was already up. From the foyer, she caught sight of Patch's blond head bowed over the coffee table in the living room.

He was working on his jigsaw puzzle.

The puzzle had progressed a bit toward completion. There was now a red-haired woman dressed in a flowing pink gown and seated on a black horse in the center of the puzzle.

"I do puzzles when I can't sleep, too," Sweeney said, standing over him and scanning the pieces. "Try that one." She pointed to a piece printed with grass and flowers. "I think that goes under the horse's front foot. Yes, like that."

Sure enough, it fit.

"Thanks." He stared at it for a few minutes, then picked up another green piece and fit it in next to the one Sweeney had spotted. "I don't think I slept at all. I kept imagining someone was breaking in down here, going through our stuff. You had trouble, too?"

"Yeah. I've been up getting some reading done about the history of the colony. I was looking at Bennett Dammers's book. I was hoping to talk to him about the gravestone and the colony."

"Well, he's the guy to talk to." He went back to the puzzle, picking out a small piece printed with pink and adding it to the flowing skirt of the woman's dress.

"Can I see it?" she asked. He handed her the cardboard box and she turned it over to find a print of Sir Frank Dicksee's *La Belle Dame Sans Merci*. In the print, the woman looked condescendingly down on a helmetless knight, one arm holding the harness of her horse, the other outstretched in a kind of supplication. In the background were a lake and a sunset and rolling hills, a typical Pre-Raphaelite landscape. She was trying to remember what she knew about Sir Frank Dicksee when she saw there was a small note at the bottom of the box.

"*La Belle Dame Sans Merci*. Dicksee (1853–1928) was not a true member of the Pre-Raphaelite Brotherhood, but he adopted many of their themes and techniques, as in this undated painting. The familiar Keatsian subject matter was popular with many of the Pre-Raphaelites."

Dicksee. An artist who wasn't a Pre-Raphaelite, but had adopted some of their themes and techniques. It gave her an idea.

"Would it be all right to look through some of your grandfather's papers now? I don't think I'll be going back to sleep, so I might as well get some work done."

Patch turned around and studied her for a moment. "As I said, I've been all through it." His blue eyes were hard. "But you're welcome to look again, of course. A lot of it has gone to various museums and libraries, but what's left is in storage up in the attic. Here, I'll show you." He got up and led the way up the main staircase, then up the narrower passage to the third floor. Sweeney had noticed the door at the end of the hallway, but assumed it led to another bedroom.

The attic, Sweeney saw, when she reached the top stair, was not the cramped overhead crawl space she had always associated with the word, but rather a full fourth floor with room for even her to stand up and walk around. Along the walls were stacked boxes and steamer trunks and file cabinets. One wall was almost entirely obscured by a large cabinet.

Patch lifted a small panel on the front and she saw that it had humidity and temperature controls. "That's for the good stuff. Not many papers in there, though. I think you'd be most interested in what's in here." He opened the top file drawer on a tall wooden storage tower. "We hired a librarian to come up and organize everything a couple of years ago. Here's the index. See, there's stuff related to Morgan, Marcus Granger. There's even a Picasso card. I don't know what that could possibly be, but you're welcome to look through all this stuff."

Sweeney flipped through the neatly organized cards. There were entries for almost any topic she could think of, "Byzantium," "Dogs," "Tax Problems." The hired librarian had been extremely thorough.

"Did he keep a journal?" She had discovered long ago

that a well-kept journal offered endless possibilities for authenticating works of art or confirming biographical information.

"Not that I've ever found, though he had a secretary toward the end of his life and she kept his appointments, I think. Anyway, feel free to root around as much as you like. I'll leave you to it."

He turned to go, the floorboards groaning under his feet, but when he reached the stairs, he waited there for a moment as though he was going to say something.

"Was there anything else?"

"No, sorry. Good luck." She watched him go down the stairs, but his hesitation seemed to hover there in the little hallway, thickening the chilly air.

For the next hour and a half, Sweeney looked through the file cabinet, finding lots that was of interest—including a letter to Herrick Gilmartin from Teddy Roosevelt—but absolutely nothing of any use.

Under "Denholm," Mary's family name, there was only one notation: "See 234871.x." But there wasn't any such entry in the file cabinet and she decided that it probably referred to a catalog of artwork. She had done some research in a family library once where the .x referred to paintings and drawings and the plain numbers represented letters and documents. She'd have to ask Patch about it.

The problem, she decided after a few more minutes of halfhearted searching, was that she didn't know what to look for. She didn't know anything about Mary Denholm and her family, didn't really know anything about the Byzantium sculptors or the other gravestones in the cemetery.

Its creator might be right under her nose.

# NINE

## December 14

AT BREAKFAST, SWEENEY announced that she was going to spend the morning at the historical society.

"I'll give you a lift," Ian Ball said, looking up from his coffee. "I'm talking to this chap at an antiques place called the Emporium. I think it's just near the historical society."

Sweeney thought fast. "Thanks, but I have to get back this afternoon. I wouldn't want you to have to rush. I've got an appointment with Bennett Dammers. He's going to help me with my research." She had found the Byzantium scholar's name in the phone book and called him earlier that morning. "I'm afraid you may find me very old," he'd said and then chuckled in a raspy voice. But he'd agreed to see her that afternoon at his home.

"That's all right. I've got some things I want to do here this afternoon anyway. I'll be ready to leave when you are."

Sweeney, seeing no other way, reluctantly told him she'd go get her bag and see him outside.

Five minutes later they were in his little rental car, speeding toward town.

The day was slightly overcast, giving the snow piled along the side of the road a lavender cast. Sweeney thought about the impressionists and how they had been pilloried for making snow lavender. It *was* lavender, the essence of it in this exact moment in time. She looked over at Ian's hands gripped on the steering wheel. They were the hands of a piano player, long-fingered and slender. She wondered suddenly who his favorite painter was.

The landscape opened up as they neared town. They drove on past a couple of neatly kept trailers, one with a big pond in front and an enormous sign that read "Daddy's Li'l Slice of Heaven."

Across the road was a stretch of field and a farm with a big white house and lots of red barns. "Van Dyke's Goat Farm," a sign in front read. "La Manchas, milk, cheese." Sweeney had a sudden vision of Don Quixote perched on a goat, tilting at windmills.

Ian smiled.

"What?"

"Nothing, it's just that farm. I had this image of Don Quixote riding a goat."

"I was thinking the exact same thing. With a little Van Dyke beard," Sweeney said. They both laughed.

"I forgot about how the English smirk."

"We don't smirk. We smile inside." He relaxed and released his death grip on the steering wheel. He really was handsome. It had taken her awhile to see it. But there was something stiff and on guard about him that she didn't find attractive.

She raised her eyebrows and nodded.

"So tell me about this research you're doing," he said after a few minutes. "An exploration into the past shenanigans of Byzantium's artists?"

"I'm just trying to find out some more about the gravestone, who might have done it, why it's so strange." She decided not to say anything about Ruth Kimball's death. After all, she had absolutely no proof that it had anything to do with Mary Denholm and her gravestone.

"And why is it so strange?"

"It's just unlike any other Victorian stone I've ever seen. Nobody was putting figures of Death on stones in the late 1800s. In fact, it would have been considered very odd. And also . . ." She hesitated.

"What?"

"Well, it's beautiful. I guess that's why I'm interested. I just want to know who made this beautiful sculpture."

"It *is* beautiful," he said as they drove into town.

The couple hundred yards of downtown Byzantium consisted of rows of colonial and federal houses, some empty and some well-preserved and converted into shops and restaurants for tourists. It was a pretty little strip, but there were discrepancies between the rarefied atmosphere of the colony and the village: a McDonald's on one corner, a rusting car abandoned in the driveway of an old gas station. Ian drove slowly down the main drag, then turned down a side street and pulled up in front of a small, yellow colonial with a sign out front reading "Byzantium Historical Society."

Sweeney got out and thanked him for the ride.

"So, I'll be back here at one," he said distractedly. "Good luck."

She slung her bag over her shoulder and was about to slam the door with her hip when she thought of something. How had he known where the Historical Society was?

He looked up at her questioningly and she shut the door.

Following the directions on a little calligraphy sign on the door, she lifted the brass knocker next to it and let it fall with a wooden thump.

Inside, footsteps padded toward her and when the door swung open, there was a tall, skinny young man with thinning blond hair and horn-rimmed glasses standing there.

"Can I help you?" he asked in a proper voice.

"Yes. I was interested in looking at some old family records."

"Of course. Follow me."

He led her through a narrow hallway and small room beyond, both lined with bookshelves and filing cabinets. The air smelled of stale paper and woodsmoke.

But the interior was very neat, with dust-free filing cabinets against one wall and old black-and-white pictures of town life in times past in gleaming glass frames along another. A poster above the desk showed an open book and cartoon characters of George Washington, Abe Lincoln, and Paul Revere popping out. "Pick up a book about history. You never know what you'll find," it proclaimed.

"We have genealogical and historical files compiled for prominent town citizens, families that have been in town for a long time," he said, lifting up the pen with which he'd been writing, and pointing it at a stack of photocopied request slips. "Just fill out one of those with the name of the family and I'll get it for you. Oh, and please sign our guest book. We depend upon the generosity of the town taxpayers for our funding and it's nice to be able to demonstrate how many people are using our resources."

Sweeney handed him a completed request form and signed her name in the guest book. Under "area of interest," she just wrote "Byzantium Arts Colony." While the librarian went to get the files, she flipped back through the book, wanting to see who else had been here recently. Her curiosity was rewarded when she saw that Ruth Kimball had been to the Historical Society back in July. She had signed her name, but left the "area of interest" column blank.

"Here we are," the historical society librarian was saying as he handed over a stack of manila folders and pointed toward a doorway on the far wall. "There are tables through there."

"Thanks." She took them into the next room and settled down at one of the three round reading tables. There were four Denholm files: "Elizabeth," "Ethel," "Louis," and, finally, "Mary."

Each had a neatly typed sheet of paper with the name, birth date and death date of the subject. In Ethel's folder, there was a photocopy of a short newspaper piece announcing that Miss Ethel Denholm, of Byzantium, was to be married to Mr. Asa Hurd, of Manchester. The file indicated that she had given birth to a son and a daughter; the son had been Ruth Kimball's father. A note in the file also mentioned that Ethel had actually been a cousin of Mary's rather than a sister, though she'd been brought up in the family.

Elizabeth's file was even more spare, filled by just the paper with her essentials. She died in 1902, Sweeney noticed, twelve years after her eldest daughter.

Her husband's, on the other hand, was much more interesting. Louis Denholm, Sweeney discovered from his file, had owned one of the more prosperous farms in town. He'd had sheep until the 1890s and then dairy cows.

Also in the file were thirty or so photocopied pages of a book. Someone had handwritten at the top, "Byzantium's Places and Faces." From the typeface and the writing style, Sweeney decided it was a locally produced history book and settled back in her seat to read the pages. The first part of the section detailed Louis's status as a pillar of the Byzantium Congregational Church. A deacon for twenty-eight years, he had helped build an addition to the church in 1875 and had been a devoted member of the "Men's Faith Club," whatever that was. The pages also recounted an anecdote about an argument at the General Store between Louis Denholm and Herrick Gilmartin about the goings-on at the Gilmartin house.

"Mr. Denholm was upset about the colony and women on the lawn during the parties, and told Mr. Gilmartin that he was corrupting his daughters," the author noted, "but William Hohrmann, the storekeeper, stepped in and the argument was soon resolved." Sweeney felt a sudden surge of sympathy for Mary and Ethel, growing up under the thumb of such a father. The history went on to say that Ethel's son Geoffrey had inherited the family's home by the river and that his daughter Ruth now lived in it with her husband William "Choke" Kimball. The book, Sweeney saw on the last photocopied page, had been published in 1971.

Also in Louis Denholm's file was a faded, yellow-tinted photo of the man himself, suited up in formal dress, with a large belly and a walrus mustache, and wearing a pair of thin spectacles. From the sheet, she saw that he had lived to eighty-four.

Sweeney had saved Mary's file for last and as she opened it, she prepared herself to be disappointed, because it was very thin. But as she turned the front leaf, it revealed an old photograph lying on top of the papers.

It was a traditional Victorian portrait of two girls and on

the back, written in a spidery hand, it said "E. Denholm and
M. Denholm, ages 10 and 17."

Sweeney sat up in her chair. The gravestone had without
a doubt been modeled on the real Mary Denholm. In the
photo, Mary's dark, waving hair was styled up on top of her
head, and she had on a dark, high-necked dress, but the
strong lines of her face were unmistakable.

Ethel, who was dressed in a white dress and had her fair
hair cut in a tomboyish page boy, seemed somehow contained, not a hair out of place, her dress perfectly pressed.
But Mary was different. Though her hair was put up neatly,
a few coiling tendrils had managed to escape and hung down
around her face. There was something wild about her eyes
and a feyness about the set of her mouth. She was a
strangely, hauntingly beautiful young woman.

Sweeney looked through the rest of the file. The last item
was another stapled sheaf of photocopied pages from the
local history book. This chapter was entitled "Byzantium
Tragedies—Past and Present" and included a macabre listing
of the untimely deaths of scores of Byzantium residents. On
the fourth page of the section was a highlighted paragraph
and a poorly rendered drawing of Mary Denholm's gravestone.

"Perhaps one of the most terrible tragedies of the 1890s
was the untimely death of Miss Mary Denholm, a local girl
who worked as a maid and housekeeper for many of the
Byzantium colonists. On a hot summer day in August, 1890,
Miss Denholm was swimming in the Green River below her
house on The Island when she was pulled under the water
and drowned. Her body was found later that day, and she
was returned to her home, where she was buried later that
week. An unusual gravestone, a monument to Miss Denholm's grace and beauty (artist unknown) stands in the Denholm family cemetery on The Island."

There wasn't anything else in Mary's file, just a handwritten note saying that researchers interested in more information about Mary Denholm could find references in the
journal of the Byzantium sculptor Myra Benton.

Sweeney took it up to the front desk, where the librarian was now typing circulation cards at an old electric typewriter. She handed him the files and he placed her request slip on a stack of other slips. Then she told him about the note in Mary's file. "I was interested in having a look at that journal," she said. "Is it something you've got here?"

"It should be here." He sniffed. "But it's in a collection of personal papers down in Cambridge. Benton had a son—illegitimate, all very scandalous back then, you know. Anyway, the son went to the University and when his mother died, he left them all of her papers. We've tried to get copies for our files, but they're pretty possessive down there."

"Oh." Sweeney tried to hide her disappointment. She could see it when she got home, of course, but she wanted to look at it now. It was only eleven and Ian wasn't coming back until one. Damn. But then she looked down the quiet street and saw a squat brick building with a sign over the door reading "Harpett Memorial Library." Her spirits lifted. There was nothing she liked better than a new and unknown library, the stores of old novels and art books yet to be discovered.

The little library was cluttered, but cheery. A fire burned in a high fireplace taking up a wall of the lobby and a couple of big leather armchairs were set around a circular oak table. In the middle of the table was a pile of books—*Gaudy Night*, Sweeney saw—and a placard reading "University of Vermont Community Reading Series. Dorothy L. Sayers, Theologian and Shamus."

She decided to sit down and work on the poem for a bit.

An academic problem—such as Sweeney's task of explaining the poem and relief on Mary's gravestone and figuring out who might have done them—had to be approached from a couple of different angles right at the beginning. Otherwise, you risked going off in the wrong direction and wasting a lot of time.

So she went to the stacks and took down books on a wide range of subjects related to the poem. Then she got out her copy and read it over again.

*Death resides in my garden, with his hands wrapped
'round my throat
He beckons me to follow and I step lightly in his boat.
All around us summer withers, blossoms drop and rot,
And Death bids me to follow, his arrow in my heart.
We sail away on his ocean, and the garden falls away
where life and death are neighbors, and night never
turns to day.
A wind comes up on the water, Death's sails are full and
proud
My love I will go with thee, dressed in a funeral shroud.
Now her tomb lies quiet, the shroud is turned to stone
And where Death had been standing, is only the grave
of her bones.*

The reference to Death's arrow was very strange. A number of early American stones featured Death or his imps holding darts or arrows over the prone figure of the hapless human who was buried beneath the stone. Sweeney had once written a paper about the iconography of the dart or arrow and she remembered how medieval peoples had assumed that Death plunged it into the hearts of his victims, since no matter what it was the victim had been suffering from, he always died when his heart stopped. But the image was hardly used by the early nineteenth century, much less by 1890.

Then there was the reference to Proserpine. She opened Bulfinch's *Age of Fable*. Sometimes it was good to go back to basics.

> In the vale of Enna there is a lake embowered in woods, which screen it from the fervid rays of the sun, while the moist ground is covered with flowers, and Spring reigns perpetual. Here Proserpine was playing with her companions, gathering lilies and violets, and filling her basket and her apron with them, when Pluto saw her, loved her and carried her off. She screamed for help to her mother and her companions; and when in her fright she dropped the corners of her apron and

let the flowers fall, childlike she felt the loss of them
as an addition to her grief.

She thought of Dante Gabriel Rossetti's Proserpine, her
crimped black hair like coal, the flowing peacock-colored
robe, and red lips.

It seemed likely that the stone had been made by someone
who was a later, much younger member of the Pre-
Raphaelite Brotherhood, or someone who wasn't a contemporary but was sympathetic to their philosophy and tastes.
Mary had died in 1890. The unnamed artist must have been
a young protégé who left England and settled in Byzantium,
or an American who had adopted the Brotherhood's themes.

Bryn Davies Morgan was the most famous Byzantium
sculptor. Sweeney knew that he had immigrated from Wales.
It was very possible that he had lived in London for a while
and taken up with the Pre-Raphaelites in his younger years.
She found a copy of Bennett Dammers's biography of Morgan in the library's small but well-stocked art section and
searched for references to the Pre-Raphaelites. There was
nothing. And when she looked through photographs of his
works, she knew she was wrong. It didn't take her Ph.D. in
art history to see that Morgan hadn't done Mary's stone. It
had to be someone else.

So she went and found the library's only book on the Pre-
Raphaelite movement and reviewed the history of the group
of English painters, poets, journalists, and hangers-on who,
in the mid-1800s, had reacted against what they saw as the
overly mannered approach of most artists since Raphael had
painted in the early 1500s.

She looked up the one Pre-Raphaelite sculptor she did
know about—Thomas Woolner. Woolner had emigrated to
Australia, though, and from what Sweeney could tell, the
gravestone wasn't his. But still, it seemed such a Pre-
Raphaelite subject.

Her heart beating a little faster, she got out the photographs of the stone. The boat. The boat was referenced in
the poem. She hadn't taken it any further than that. But

surely the boat was also a reference to another favorite Pre-Raphaelite subject—"The Lady of Shalott," the famous piece of verse by the English poet Alfred, Lord Tennyson that had always been one of her favorites. She went back to the bookshelves and got down a copy of Tennyson's collected works.

> *On either side the river lie*
> *Long fields of barley and of rye,*
> *That clothe the wold and meet the sky;*
> *And thro' the field the road runs by*
> *To many-tower'd Camelot;*
> *And up and down the people go,*
> *Gazing where the lilies blow*
> *Round an island there below,*
> *The island of Shalott.*

Sweeney shivered a little. It was almost as if the poet were describing The Island.

But the Lady of Shalott hadn't been murdered. She had sat in her tower, weaving as she looked at the world in her mirror and had brought death upon herself when she fell in love with Lancelot and left her tower.

Had Mary tried to leave her island?

Sweeney was sitting there wondering when she caught sight of a newspaper sitting on a table next to hers. "Local Woman Dead of Apparent Suicide," the headline read, and in smaller letters, "Police Say Investigation Continuing."

She began to read. "A local woman was found dead Tuesday, apparently killed by a self-inflicted gunshot wound to the head. Community members recalled a committed local volunteer and lifelong Byzantium resident this week as state and local police continued the investigation.

"Sources say that Ruth Kimball, 72, of Byzantium, went for a walk in the early afternoon. Kimball's daughter, Sherry Kimball, 35, also of Byzantium, discovered the body at about 5:30 PM in a cemetery near the family's home."

Sweeney scanned the rest of the article. State police weren't saying much, just that it looked like suicide, but that they always investigated carefully whenever firearms were involved, just as Gwinny had said. She was interested to read that the police had questioned Trip and Gally Wentworth at first since they had been target shooting nearby at the time of the murder. But, the reporter noted, a police source said that the boys had been shooting with brand-new .22 caliber hunting rifles, while Ruth Kimball had been killed with a World War II-era service pistol. Police refused to identify the weapon used or to say whether it had been owned by the dead woman, but they had reiterated that the Wentworth twins were not suspects, it was just that the possibility of an accident had to be eliminated. Sweeney thought of Britta Wentworth's drawn face. No wonder she'd been upset.

A number of community members were quoted as saying that Ruth Kimball had been a model citizen and that she hadn't seemed at all the type to do something like this. She was survived, Sweeney noticed, by her daughter Sherry and granddaughter Charley, both of Byzantium, and had been predeceased by her husband and son.

It hadn't helped much, but it had given her an idea.


"Do you keep old newspapers on hand?" Sweeney asked the librarian. "I was actually interested in really old papers, from the 1890s."

"We've got the *Gazette* and copies of the *Watertown Herald* for that period as well," the woman said. "They're in bound volumes downstairs. First door on the right. We're trying to get them all on microfilm, but it's expensive."

"Thanks. I hate microfilm anyway."

The bound volumes of both papers were stored chronologically and it was easy to find the ones marked 1890. Sweeney decided to start with the *Gazette*. She flipped through June and July and finally came to the August papers, which appeared to come out two or sometimes three times a week. Finally, after her eyes were nearly exhausted by the tiny type, she found the article she was looking for, on an inside page of the August thirty-first edition. "Tragic Drowning Accident" read the headline. But the piece contained exactly the same information as the Xeroxed book excerpts in Mary's file.

It wasn't until she hunted down the *Herald's* version of the same story that Sweeney hit paydirt. "Miss Denholm's body was found on the afternoon of the 28th by Mr. Herrick Gilmartin of Byzantium."

Now *that* was interesting.

Ian was waiting for her in front of the historical society.

"I'm sorry," she said breathlessly. "I ended up going across to the library and got wrapped up in my reading."

"That's just fine, I had to park down the street a bit," he said in a friendly voice. He took half of the stack of books the librarian had let her borrow on the Wentworths' card and tucked them under his arm.

Ian and Sweeney walked in silence for a few minutes before she spoke. "How was your afternoon? Did you find anything good?"

"Oh, yes. Everything went smoothly," he said stiffly, and the finality in his tone of voice stopped her from asking any more questions. When they got to his car, he opened the door for her and she felt a sudden flash of irritation. Chivalry was well and good, but on him, it seemed overly decorous, as though he felt guilty about something and was making up to her. "I'm fine," she said crossly, when he asked if she wanted to move her seat back.

This time, the silence in the car was awkward. Ian broke it by saying, " '*A few weeds and stubble showing last.*' It's from a Robert Frost poem." She looked at him in confusion, but then she saw that they were passing a broad expanse of snow-covered field where a few weeds and stalks poked through the white cover.

"I never liked Frost until I came to Vermont. Isn't that strange?"

"No. It's the same for me. I've always loved the Americans, but not Frost. Always found him too *rural*, I think. Then I came here and I thought of that poem about the stone walls, the . . ."

" 'Mending Wall,' " Sweeney said, and recited it. "Toby loves that poem. Loves Frost. Now I feel like I understand him a little better."

"Goodness. You've got it committed to memory."

"Oh, it's not as much a feat as it seems. I just have one of those memories. Photographic or whatever. If I've seen it on a page I can remember it, the image of it, you know?"

"Have you got plans this afternoon?" he asked as they pulled up in front of the house. "I was thinking about borrowing Patch's cross-country skis and going for a spin. Interested?"

She undid her seatbelt and tried not to flush. Suddenly, she could hardly look at him. "Oh, I'm sorry," she said awkwardly. "I've got that appointment. With Bennett Dammers. Apparently he's the go-to man on the Byzantium colony. I'm just going over to ask him some questions. For my research."

He got out of the car quickly and gathered up her books and notebooks and a small briefcase from the back seat. When he slammed the car door, Sweeney flinched.

"Fine, another time then," he said smoothly, looking into her eyes before going into the house.

# TEN

BENNETT DAMMERS'S HOUSE, Windy Hill, was in the section of the colony that wrapped itself along the curve of the river, stretching north toward town. Sweeney detected a slight difference in the architectural style of Windy Hill and the six or so estates around it. The houses in the "Upper Colony" had been built earlier and they were somehow grander, less eccentric than those on The Island.

Sitting in his study, Sweeney marveled at the small, strange worlds she and her fellow academics came to inhabit. A week ago, she hadn't known much about the arts colony in Byzantium, Vermont. Now, here she was sitting in front of the undisputed expert on the colony, a man who, more or less, lived back in the world the artists had lived in.

When Bennett Dammers talked about them, it was as though they were old friends. Gilmartin this, Gilmartin that. They might as well have gone to boarding school together.

He even dressed like an Edwardian bohemian, in a floppy bow tie and wrinkled white shirt, a black hat on a stand by the door. In the pictures of picnics and parties in the copy of Dammers's book in the Wentworths' library, the artists were mostly wearing the same thing. His fine white hair had thinned down to a cottony tuft over each ear and his eyes were pale robin's eggs surrounded by spidery red vessels.

She had told herself not to expect too much, that he was quite elderly and his memory may have failed. But except for searching for his glasses on his desktop for five minutes, he seemed as sharp as a man thirty years his junior. She sat back in her chair and looked around the chaotic clutter of the study. Books lined the walls and lay asymmetrically piled on every surface, the great teetering towers balanced precariously. Around his desk were stacks of newspapers a couple of feet high, yellowed with age. A fire burned in the fireplace and in the greenish light from the banker's lamp on his desk, he regarded her kindly, the rectangular-framed spectacles now on his nose.

"Now, Miss St. George," Bennett Dammers said finally, his withered hands folded on the desk in front of him, the cardigan sweater he had on over his shirt and tie opened in the heat of the room. "What can I do for you?"

He had the look of a very old human, the shape of his skull showing just beneath his skin and thin hair. When she had leaned in to shake his hand at the door, Sweeney had caught an odor she had come to associate with old age. She got out one of the photographs of Mary's gravestone and handed it over to him.

"Have you ever seen this?"

He held the photo out in front of him and studied it for a minute. "Oh, yes. Of course," he said finally. "Someone thought it might be a Morgan, once."

She pointed to the snapshot. "It's not Morgan, is it?"

"Goodness, no." Bennett Dammers continued studying it and then put it down on the desk in front of him. "None of the other Byzantium sculptors, either. I've always thought it must be one of the students."

"Students?"

"The old boy ran a kind of studio school. Promising young things from the Pennsylvania Academy or wherever would come up and help him out in the studio for a summer. Mix plaster, build armatures, and provide some young blood at cocktail parties. Many of them became colonists themselves and then went on to great things. Have you ever heard of Myra Benton? Frank Bellweather?"

Sweeney said she had. Still, for the next fifteen minutes, he gave her an account of the careers of the two great American sculptors, both trained by Morgan. She had to resist an overwhelming urge to bring him back to Mary's grave.

"You're sure you can't guess at who the artist here might be," she broke in finally.

He looked at it again. "It reminds me of something," he said. "But I'm not sure what."

A grandfather clock in the hall chimed three times.

Sweeney handed him the copy of the poem she'd written out. "I don't know if you remember the poem that's on the stone, but I'm wondering if you could help me out with it. I'm really at a loss."

It took him quite a long time to read it, his chin tucked against his collarbone, and Sweeney wondered if he had fallen asleep. But then he sat up and grinned.

"Well! I haven't seen it for years. It's quite something, isn't it?"

"It's pretty bad, I know. But if I can figure out who wrote it, it may bring me closer to knowing who the sculptor is."

"Well," Dammers said, "there weren't many poets and writers in the colony. A few journalists. It was mostly Morgan's sculpting cronies. And the painters, of course."

He stood up again and got a copy of his own book from a box on the floor.

"That's for you," he said. "The new edition. I write about Matthew Bentley. He wasn't a very good poet, but he wasn't that bad. Besides, his work is very different. That sounds like the ruminations of a romantic schoolgirl."

"Or someone over-enamored of the Victorians," Sweeney said. "It's like the author had made kind of a hodgepodge of different themes, if you know what I mean. The thing that strikes me as strange is that the monument is clearly by a Pre-Raphaelite. But why haven't we heard of him? Or her, I suppose." It hadn't struck her before that the artist could be a woman.

He smiled at her. "That's a very good question, my dear. I don't know. Perhaps he or she died young. As for the Pre-Raphaelites, it's interesting, you know. There were some connections. Morgan met the Rossetti brothers once, in London, before he emigrated."

"But I looked them up in your book."

"Yes, it's only in the new edition. I received a letter from a scholar at Cambridge after my book came out, telling me of the meeting. It was only a dinner, but I think it must have smoothed the way for him when he arrived in New York."

"Was Morgan influenced by them?"

"No, not really. But there may have been connections that we didn't know about. Perhaps a young protégé came over to study with him one summer."

His eyes were tired and Sweeney decided she only had a few minutes left. "There's something I've been wanting to ask you. You grew up here. What were things like between the artists and the people in town?"

"Good question." He grinned at her. "That's one of the things I've always thought is most interesting about Byzantium and other arts colonies in this part of the world." He settled back in his chair.

"You have to understand that most of the people who lived in Byzantium before the artists arrived were farmers, small town businessmen. My own father kept a feed and grain store. They didn't understand the artists, I think, didn't understand them spending days in the studio or writing, looked down on the parties.

"But then, many of the people in town—the natives, they were called by the artists—made extra money cleaning or cooking during the summers and, of course, it meant that there was a kind of interest in the town. You know, Byzantium would be written up as the most beautiful place in America, things like that. The gardens were famous. Many of the people in town modeled for the artists, too, the children especially."

"How did that work? Would they pay them."

"Yes. Not much, though. Sometimes they paid in work." He was looking over her shoulder, off into space.

"It was very complicated," he said finally. "As most things are. Colonial, almost. If you think about the word *colony*. Well, that's what it was. They *colonized* . . ." He trailed off and Sweeney had the feeling that he was winding down, like a music box. But then he seemed to come back from wherever he had been.

"The interesting thing is that you can still see the dynamic at work today. I've always fancied I was quite separate from it, since I wasn't exactly a native and wasn't exactly a colonist and most of the time I feel as though that's okay. But there are times when a dispute will come up about something and I can tell that they want me to choose sides. This thing about Ruth Kimball's land, for example.

"Of course I felt it was imperative that we keep The Island the way it was. But I was also sympathetic to her right to do what she wanted with her property. The Wentworths couldn't understand that someone might really need the money. They've never been in that position. Anyway, about your stone, I'm not sure what to tell you, my dear."

"Can you think of anyone else in town who might be able to help?"

He thought for a moment and then said, "I would think you might get useful information from some of the descendants. Willow Fontana has always been very helpful to me. Oh, and of course you could ask Patch about it. I ran into him at the historical society a couple of months ago and he said he was looking into the gravestone.

"Patch? You're sure about that?" Sweeney sat up.

"Oh yes. That's all I can suggest. In an appendix to my book, there's a list of most of the students who stayed with Morgan. Still . . ." He trailed off, then turned in his chair to look up at his bookcase.

"Mary Denholm strikes a chord somewhere up here." He tapped a finger on his temple. "You can't imagine how awful it is to lose your memory for things like this."

He got up and continued staring at his bookcase for a minute. Sweeney sat uncomfortably. It was like watching a person in a wheelchair try to get up over a curb.

"Ah!" he called out finally and took a book from the middle shelf.

As he pulled it down, his hands shaking, she saw a portrait of a woman and the name Herrick Gilmartin on the front.

Bennett Dammers looked in the index, then flipped the book open and held it out to her, his thumb holding it to a simple portrait of a young woman. "That's her," he said simply.

Sweeney stared at the oil painting reproduced on the page.

She was wearing a white dress and sitting in front of a fantasy landscape of a dark forest. The mass of dark, curling hair hung around her face in wild tendrils, setting off her pale, almost blue skin. Sweeney stared at the portrait, mesmerized. Her vague stare, the dead tint of her skin, and the coiling, almost obscene tendrils of hair made her seem lifeless.

" 'Mary,' 1890" the painting was titled. But at the bottom of the page, there was a caption that read, "The model for 'Mary' was Mary Denholm, a local girl and neighbor of Gilmartin's."

Sweeney stared at the girl. "It's creepy."

Bennett Dammers laughed. "Yes. Quite an interesting little piece of necrophilia. They were big on it, the Victorians.".

"Was she one of his regular models?"

"I have no idea," he said. "Something just made me remember it. I can't think why I didn't before."

"It's incredible." Sweeney studied the painting again. "Did you know that Herrick Gilmartin was the one who discovered Mary's body?"

"No," he said. "I don't know much about her. I think this is the only portrait I've ever seen."

"So you've never heard that there was anything . . . suspicious about her death? She died very young." She tried not to seem too eager for the answer.

"Suspicious?" He didn't understand.

"I'm wondering if there was ever anything untoward about Gilmartin's um . . . behavior. I mean as far as young girls go, if you know what I mean." She sounded like a prudish idiot. Untoward! For godsake.

The old man stared at her for a minute and then, as though something had bubbled up from deep within his body, exploded in laughter. Sweeney was afraid he was going to break.

"My dear," he almost shouted at her, still giggling. "They were sensualists. The lot of them. Young girls, young boys. Whatever adventure happened to present itself. Gilmartin and Morgan had parties here and at Morgan's New York *pied à terre* that were, well, definitely untoward. Does that answer your question?" He was grinning, enjoying shocking her.

Sweeney blushed and tried to join in the joke. "Oh," she said. "What about Mary Denholm? Do you think there may have been anything between her and Gilmartin?"

"There may well have been, but I don't know how you'd prove it. You'll have to read the Byers." He pointed to the book in Sweeney's hand. "You can borrow mine. But I don't think he mentions her much. Why are you so interested in Gilmartin's sex life, may I ask?"

Sweeney felt herself blush again. "I'm not really. It's just that I've gotten interested in Mary's gravestone and anything I can find out about who she was is going to help."

He smiled kindly at her, but Sweeney could see he wanted her to go.

"You've been so helpful," she said, shutting the book. "But I won't take any more of your time. Thank you. And thank you for the book."

"I'll keep the gravestone in mind," he said. "I want to look through my files again and see if anything rings a bell."

"Of course. I'd appreciate that. If anything comes up, try me at the Wentworths'."

"I hope you don't think I'm a nosy old coot," he said, studying her. "But I'm wondering how a lovely girl like you came to be interested in all this doom and gloom. You don't think I'm a chauvinist, do you?"

Sweeney laughed. "No," she said, honestly. "I remember seeing an English woodcut when I was about ten, of Death looking over the shoulder of a woman lying in a bed, surrounded by weeping relatives. I was fascinated by the idea that Death was an actual person, that people needed to think of all death as a kind of murder, that they made art in order to understand it, to come to terms with human mortality."

"Do you understand it, Miss St. George? Have you come to terms with it?"

He was thinking about how young she was and wondering how much of death she'd seen. Though she hated being condescended to, she wanted even less to embarrass him. What could she say? *Actually my father killed himself when I was thirteen and my fiancé died in a violent accident a year ago.*

"No," she said.

"Neither have I. Even at my advanced age." He looked sad all of a sudden. "I beg your pardon. Good luck with your mystery."

# ELEVEN

BYZANTIUM'S CHIEF OF police, Jonas Cooper, sat in the truck watching the mouth of The Island bridge and holding his gloved hands over the heater vents, trying to get warm. He'd been there for over an hour, supposedly doing speed checks on Route 20, but actually waiting to see who was driving on and off The Island today. In his experience, there was a lot to be learned from watching what people did in the days after a suspicious death. He had once caught a murderer that way, when he was still in Boston working homicide. The guy had sat stony-faced through an interview about his wife's death and then hopped in his truck and driven off to his girlfriend's house, where Cooper, having followed at a discreet distance, watched him burn a pair of pants in the driveway.

But so far, the traffic over the bridge had been pretty thin. A couple of the state crime guys had come out and waved cheerily at him, causing Cooper, who was trying to be inconspicuous, to curse under his breath. Other than that, nothing. He was annoyed, a mood, he realized, left over from this morning, when one of the state investigators had asked him where he was from when he'd suggested they look at the pattern of burn marks the pistol had made against the victim's skin. "We know our job," he'd replied simply when Cooper told him he was from Boston, but lived in Byzantium now.

He had come up to take the job three years ago, but Cooper still felt like a city slicker at least once a day. He remembered the former chief, a tall, blond, ex-basketball player from somewhere in the Midwest telling him, "It's funny about these people up here. You're either from here or you aren't. It really matters to them. They don't like to tell you things if you're not a native."

When Cooper had asked about the townspeople, the departing chief had said, "There seem to be three types. The ones whose families have lived here for generations, the colony people who have been here for a while but are in a slightly different category, and then the flatlanders—newcomers who have moved up from Boston or New York. You'll find you don't really fit in anywhere." Cooper had discovered the basketball player was right.

But there was something about the town and about Vermont that was starting to grow on him. Though he was constantly reminded of his outsider status, Cooper felt more and more that if it didn't accept him, the town had come to respect him. That was good enough, for now.

Just as he was starting to wonder whether he should head back to the station to see what was going on, a Volkswagen Rabbit, going just a little too fast, came down the road and turned onto the bridge. When he saw it had Massachusetts plates, he figured it was the young woman staying at the Wentworths. A professor of some kind, he'd heard. She was the one who had been asking Ruth Kimball about the gravestone. He had questioned Sherry Kimball about her mother's actions in the days before her death and she had told him all about Sweeney St. George. Now she was staying at the Wentworths'. Coincidence? Cooper didn't know what to think about that. He didn't think Sweeney St. George had anything to do with the death, but it raised some interesting questions.

He'd have to talk to her, he decided. And to the rest of the neighbors again. There had been something about Britta Wentworth's eyes when he'd asked her what Patch and the kids had been doing the afternoon of Mrs. Kimball's death that gave him the idea she knew more than she was letting on. And when it came down to it, the Fontanas hadn't been all that willing to tell him where they'd been. He'd definitely have to talk to them again. But first he'd go back to the station and see if the medical examiner's report was in. He had a bad feeling about this death. It didn't feel like any suicide he'd ever investigated.

# TWELVE

WHEN SHE GOT back to the house, Sweeney stood for a moment in the foyer, feeling shaken and sad. Her conversation with Bennett Dammers had conjured up feelings she thought she had gotten past months ago and, desperate for an emotional distraction, she searched the hallway for a picture to look at. She found one, a strange, moody beachscape in shades of red and coral. There was something about it that drew her in and she stood, mesmerized, looking into its depths.

"Sweeney? Are you okay?" Rubbing at her eyes, she turned to find Gwinny standing in the doorway of the living room watching her. She was wearing a long purple dress with an empire waistline and a black velvet headband in her hair and she was holding a book. Her eyes appeared to have been inexpertly made-up with purple eye shadow and the costume made her look like a medieval lady-in-waiting.

"Oh yeah. I was looking at this." She gestured to the painting.

"Were you just crying?"

"I just . . . Something that happened today made me think about a friend who died, that's all. Where is everybody?"

"My parents are taking naps. Ian went skiing." Here, Gwinny blushed a little. "I don't know where Toby and the twins are. Did you find out anything about the stone today?"

"A little bit. I went and saw Bennett Dammers this afternoon."

"He's nice. Is it true that someone killed her? Mary?"

Sweeney hesitated for a moment. "Where'd you hear that? She's supposed to have drowned."

"Oh, I used to babysit for Charley Kimball sometimes. Mrs. Kimball, the one who died, was always talking about how Mary got murdered and she was going to find out who did it." Gwinny's eyes were wide and dark in the late afternoon light coming in through the windows. The foyer was silent, the air cold. Sweeney shivered.

"What was she like? Mrs. Kimball?"

Gwinny frowned. "She was old. You know? She was tired all the time and she got mad a lot. But I think that had a lot to do with Carl. I mean, she didn't like Carl very much and Sherry was always going out with him and leaving Charley with her."

"Why didn't she like Carl?"

"I don't know. He's just kind of gross."

"Was he nice to Sherry?"

"Yeah. I guess. He was always buying her presents, jewelry and stuffed animals and stuff. Charley, too. Hey, you should go down and talk to Sherry. She could tell you about Mary's stone."

"That's a good idea. Maybe I'll do that."

She was about to go upstairs when Gwinny looked down at her feet and asked, in a low voice, "Was it your boyfriend? The one who died?" Embarrassed, she slid one black Chinese slipper along the gleaming floor.

"Yeah." She watched Gwinny take that in. If she'd been older, she might have said she was sorry, or said that it must have been awful for Sweeney.

But as Sweeney had a sudden, vivid flash of remembrance of what it was like to be fourteen, to wonder if any member of the opposite sex would ever find her too-tall body and too-bright hair pretty, Gwinny asked, "Was he the first person you were ever in love with?"

"I guess he was. I met him in graduate school, in England, though he was Irish. Yeah, he was the first person."

"I've never been in love with anyone at all," Gwinny said.

"You should feel lucky about that at least, that you were in love. You shouldn't be sad."

Sweeney smiled. "I think I'm just a little sad in general. My father isn't alive anymore and I've lost touch with my mother. I guess being around a family at Christmastime is a little weird is all."

One of the dogs came romping in from the kitchen and Gwinny grabbed it by the collar and made it sit. Then, in a perfectly serious tone of voice, she said, "Don't think our family's really great or anything. My parents are always fighting with each other. They had a big fight this afternoon, because Chief Cooper—he's a policeman—called to say that we all have to go down and tell him what we were doing the day Ruth Kimball died. They were screaming at each other about it. And they're always yelling at Trip and Gally. Especially Gally. Sometimes I can't wait to go away to school. I mean, you shouldn't feel sad about us. We're pretty pathetic, if you want to know the truth."

Sweeney smiled again. "Thank you," she said. "Why do you think Chief Cooper wants to know what everyone was doing?"

Gwinny held up the book she'd been reading, a battered old copy of H.R.F. Keating's *The Perfect Murder*. "You know how it is in books," she said. "When the police ask about alibis, it means they think someone is a murderer."

Since there was another hour or so of light, Sweeney decided to go back down to the graveyard to have another look at Mary's stone. Now that she had seen the strange Gilmartin portrait, she wanted to compare the two. She had an idea that there was something similar in them and she wanted to test the idea. So she tucked the book that Bennett Dammers had lent her into her parka and found a pair of cross-country ski boots in her size in the closet in the hall. Britta had found them for her, looking slightly shocked when Sweeney told her her shoe size. "Oh," she'd said. "You'll have to wear a pair of Patch's."

The skis were out in a barn next to the house and she

found the pair that had been assigned to her for her stay. The bindings were much fancier than the ones she had used the last time she'd skied and it took her a couple of minutes to get her boots clipped in and to find a pair of poles that weren't too short.

It was a nicer day than the one before, and even though the air had cooled as the sun set, the landscape, washed in the pinky, clear light of dusk was somehow cheerier today, less grim. It had been years since she had been on cross-country skis, but she remembered the rhythmic motion of it, right, then left, then right and left again. She skied down over the slope behind the house and reached the cemetery in a little over ten minutes.

The orange tape that had been around the cemetery fence the day before had been removed and she stepped out of her skis and walked in to find much the same scene. The only difference was the lovely light that slanted down across all the stones. It seemed to Sweeney to illuminate the stones from within, to make them glow, and to reveal new facets of their surfaces. It was calming, to be there alone in the strange light, and she looked around her for a moment before walking over to Mary's stone, the Gilmartin book in hand.

She was struck again by how similar the two works of art were. Both showed the same young woman, wearing the same expression of staring emptiness.

There were differences, though, that she could only see here in front of the monument. Gilmartin's portrait, with its drab, watery tones and fine, expert lines, showed a young woman devoid of life, yet beautiful. The sculpture on the other hand, showed a young woman who had *been* full of life, but was now lifeless. Or not lifeless exactly, Sweeney corrected herself, but somehow absent, or in another world.

She thought again of Proserpine. In the sculpture, she realized, Death was ferrying the young woman, Mary, to the underworld. Or heaven or hell or whatever it was that this artist had believed in. But she wasn't yet dead, rather she was undergoing a transformation, she was in the process of dying, as though he had caught her in a liminal moment.

Sweeney took out her notebook and, with frozen hands, jotted down a few notes.

She was turning to go when she saw that the spikes delineating where the body had been were gone, too. The police must have finished up the investigation or taken all the evidence away at any rate. She wandered over and stared down at where her memory told her the body had been. What had Ruth Kimball known? Sweeney felt a surge of anger at herself. Why hadn't she stayed on the phone another couple of minutes? She had so many questions she wanted to ask her. She walked back over to Mary's stone.

"I wish you could speak," she said aloud, and jumped when a voice said, "That's the thing about the dead, they can't speak," and she looked up to find Ian Ball watching her from outside the cemetery fence.

"I didn't hear you coming."

"I came through the woods," he said, gesturing to the line of trees not far from the cemetery gate that stretched back toward the river. "There's a path that the family takes to get down to the river. It's longer, but it's nicely packed down for skiing."

"Oh." She tucked the book back into her parka and her notebook back into a pocket. "I got back earlier than I expected, so I thought I'd come down and just . . . look around."

He asked, "So what would you like Mary Denholm to say?"

"To tell me who made her gravestone, first of all," Sweeney said.

"Because it's beautiful?"

"What? Oh." She was confused, then recalled their conversation from the morning. "Yes. And because I'm curious. It's what I do, research things, find out about them, find out what their stories are."

"Well, perhaps it's nothing very interesting," he said. "Maybe it was just some local carver who was having a good day."

"That's a risk, I guess." She looked up at the sky, annoyed

with him. "It's getting dark. I think I'll head back."

"I'll go with you. Would you like to head back up through the woods? See some different sights?"

She couldn't think of a way to say no, so she nodded. She got back into her skis and they took off through a little gap in the trees and along a well-worn path lined with an old stone wall. It looked as though it had once been a road since it was wide and quite smooth, but it was so much darker in the woods that she found she had to go carefully so she didn't stray into the trees. At one point the path branched off in two directions and Ian explained that one of them led to Herrick Gilmartin's studio and a swimming spot down by the river. They skied silently, except for the steady huffing of their breath as the path climbed, and by the time they reached the house it was nearly dark.

The silhouette of the house looked sinister in the wintry dusk and when she looked up at the sky, she thought she could pick out a moonstone white cloud, drifting overhead, shaped like a skull and crossbones.

Sweeney went to her room to read directly after dinner and was about to go to bed when she decided to go down to the second floor and ask Toby about Tennyson. She hadn't seen him during the day and she wanted to test her response to his presence after last night.

She knocked on his door. There wasn't any answer, just a muffled thump from inside, so she called out, "Hey Toby, I want to ask you a question about Tennyson," and went into the room.

It was dark inside and when she heard Toby's voice say "Hang on" and a muffled female squeal, she realized what she had done and stepped back out into the hallway, shutting the door. She was about to turn and go when she saw a narrow band of light appear above the threshold. "It's okay, Sweeney, come in," Toby called, a bit desperately, she thought.

"Oh!" She stepped into the room to find Toby and Rosemary Burgess sitting at opposite sides of the bed, Toby in a

bathrobe and Rosemary in jeans and one of his T-shirts. "I
didn't know you were here, Rosemary. I'm so sorry."

"That's fine, that's just fine. Don't think twice about it."
Rosemary blushed.

"I'll just uh . . . leave now. I'll talk to you tomorrow."
Sweeney said, turning toward the door.

"No. Please. If you have to talk to Toby, I can go. I should
get home anyway." Rosemary blushed again.

"No, don't go," Toby said. "I really don't want you to
go."

Sweeney turned away so as not to see the look on Toby's
face. She didn't want to know.

"Darling," Rosemary said, getting up and putting on her
coat. "I really do have to go. I have to get Granny ready for
bed. We have to talk to the police tomorrow and I want to
make sure she's rested." She tousled his hair and put an
affectionate hand on Sweeney's back. "It isn't you, Sweeney," she said kindly. "Your friend here has bewitched me
into staying much longer than I ought to have." She gave
Toby a kiss goodnight and left them alone.

"Sorry," Sweeney said quietly. He lay back on his bed, a
pillow tucked under his head.

"Spoiler." He grinned at her, but when he saw the look
on her face he said, "What? Are you okay?"

"Yeah. Fine. . . . Listen, *The Lady of Shalott*. Tell me
about it."

"It's a Victorian poem."

She raised her eyebrows.

"All right. Well, you know that Alfred, Lord Tennyson
was one of the foremost poets of the nineteenth century, and
he commonly wrote on Arthurian themes." She nodded impatiently. "Let's see. *The Lady of Shalott* was originally written in the 1830s, I think, and then he revised it later. There
was speculation that the character of the Lady of Shalott was
based on Malory's Elaine in the *Morte D'Arthur*, but I'm
pretty sure that Tennyson told someone or other that in fact
it was based on an Italian folktale. But then, of course, later
he found out about Elaine and wrote some poems about her.

It's funny how that happens, isn't it? How storylines sort of exist in the collective subconscious. Very Jungian, you know."

"No scholarly digressions. What else?"

"I don't know. What else do you want to know? The poem's about this mysterious woman who lives on an island. Because of some strange curse, she's doomed to spend her days in a tower, looking at the reflection of the world in the mirror and weaving what she sees. Then one day she sees Sir Lancelot riding by her window and she falls in love with him. But when she turns away from the mirror and looks at life as it is, the mirror cracks, 'from side to side,' remember? She leaves the tower and gets into a boat and sails toward Camelot, but before she gets there, she's killed by the curse." He watched her for a minute. "Oh, I see. The boat. It's like Mary's statue."

Sweeney nodded. "Yeah. I just can't figure out why someone used it as the basis for a gravestone."

His thoughts followed along the same lines hers had in the library. "Hey, Mary lived on an island. Maybe she felt there would be a curse on her if she left. What were her parents like?"

"Strict, from what I can tell."

"There you go."

"But she didn't make her own gravestone."

"Maybe someone who knew her thought the story resonated. You said yourself that the Pre-Raphaelites often painted literary themes. Ophelia and all that."

Somewhere, deep down in Sweeney's consciousness, Ophelia struck a chord.

"I don't know." She thought for a moment. "Did you know that Mary Denholm modeled for your great-grandfather? And he was the one to find her body."

"No. Who told you that?"

"I discovered it today. When I was doing research."

"Everybody around here modeled for everybody else."

"Okay." She thought for a moment.

"Are you sure you're really okay?" Toby looked concerned. "You seem kind of weird."

She looked up at him, but his eyes, when her own eyes met them, were distracted and tired. She forced a smile. "I'm just tired. So I'm going to bed."

She made it out into the hallway before the tears rushed to her eyes. She rubbed at them angrily with the back of her hand, furious with herself, and as she climbed the staircase to the third floor, she almost ran into Ian coming out of the bathroom, his hair still wet from the shower. He smelled of lemons and cloves. He looked up and saw the tears. "Oh, good night," he said awkwardly, casting his eyes to the floor.

Embarrassed, Sweeney crossed her arms over the front of her nightgown and nodded at him, then slipped into her room, shaking. She was angry at Toby, at Rosemary, at herself for caring. And most of all, she realized, she was angry at Ian Ball, though she couldn't pinpoint exactly why. It was something about the way he looked at her, as though he was trying to read her, to figure out what was behind the words she said.

She shivered and locked her door. Sweeney's bedroom, like all the rooms on the top floor, was chilly and she took the comforter from her bed and wrapped it around her shoulders as she went to the window. In the moonlight, the snow looked lovely, almost opalescent, and a beam of eerie, pearly light shone in, cutting a swathe across the floor of her room.

There was something about her conversation with Toby that was niggling at her. What was it?

Ophelia. That was it. But what about Ophelia? Something from a long-ago class came back to her. She dug the library books out of her bag and opened the one about the Pre-Raphaelites to the index. She knew that the Pre-Raphaelite painters John Everett Millais and Arthur Hughes had both created accomplished paintings of Shakespeare's Ophelia, and she flipped through a number of references to the men before she found the one she was looking for on page 126. "When Millais was painting Ophelia, his model, Lizzie Siddal, posed in a bathtub, warmed by small candles. But the candles were allowed to go out and she was numb with cold when she emerged. Later it was said that she almost died."

Then she opened the book on Gilmartin to the portrait of Mary and she knew what it was that had been bothering her. There was a huge discrepancy between the lush, lively Mary in the historical society photo and the dead, cold one in the painting. How had he achieved the effect?

She stared at the painting for a few minutes, feeling her heart speed up in excitement. She got up and paced around the room, thinking. What if Gilmartin had taken a cue from Millais and things had gone wrong?

Out of curiosity, Sweeney flipped through the rest of the Gilmartin book. She had looked through the paintings in the car after leaving Bennett Dammers and found a few other portraits that she really liked, but what she hadn't noticed until now was that the Mary painting was somewhat atypical for Gilmartin's work. Most of the portraits were more traditionally late-nineteenth-century, with full female figures executed in careful, jewel-colored brush strokes. It was as though Gilmartin had tried something new—or new to him— in 1890, and then quickly given it up. Had his abandonment of the new style been related to Mary's death?

She took a deep breath. What if Gilmartin had been painting Mary and something had gone wrong? In order to cover up his crime, he could have taken her body down to the river and pretended to find her drowned body there. It would have been that simple. But why the gravestone?

She sat down on the bed, overcome by how far her brain had taken this. If this was true, it had implications for the Wentworths and their neighbors that went far beyond the answer to an academic question. It had implications for Toby . . . for her relationship with him. She had to go carefully here. She would think about this when she was less tired, she would gather some more information. She would keep an open mind.

As she was putting away the books she'd gotten at the library, a slip of paper became dislodged from between them and drifted to the floor. It was a credit card receipt from a restaurant in Suffolk and, she saw, when she inspected it more closely, it was signed by Ian. It must have gotten stuck between her books when he gathered them up from the back seat of his car. She put it into the pocket on the outside of her research bag. She'd have to remember to give it back to him. He was probably putting in for his expenses on this trip.

She got ready for bed and slipped between the sheets, physically exhausted. But her brain failed to stop churning, and she slept only fitfully, dreaming of artists and models and ice cold water.

# THIRTEEN

*December 15*

THE GODDAMNED VACUUM needed a new bag.

Sherry Kimball bent and shut it off, silently cursing her back, which was about to seize up in painful spasms, and the line of cracker crumbs that still remained on the carpet. She had told Charley not to eat in the living room, had even promised her a new book if she would start helping to keep the house clean, but then Carl had gone and eaten a bag of potato chips while watching football and she hadn't felt like she could yell at Charley when she'd found her lying on her belly, reading a book about sharks or something and eating Ritz out of the box.

She knew she wouldn't say anything. That was the thing with Charley: she understood things too well, she would see that she had been treated differently and she would get mad, or worse, she would look up at Sherry with those big, dark, accusing eyes and walk out of the room. Sherry hated it when Charley looked at her like that, as though she saw right through her, saw how much she loved Carl, saw how scared she was that he would go back to his ex-wife. She switched off the vacuum and unplugged it from the wall outlet.

The extra bags, for some reason she'd never understood, were kept in her mother's room, at the bottom of the blanket chest. Sherry started up the stairs and then decided she'd take the vacuum upstairs while she was up there. She'd been avoiding it and this seemed like as good a time as any. She'd get the floors done at least. Changing the sheets would have to wait. There would be time for that later, after the funeral, after . . . after what?

It struck Sherry suddenly that she might wait for some day or moment that could never come. When Charley was born, she had held her and looked at her small hands and feet and waited for the instant in which she would feel, "I am a mother. She's my daughter." It had never come like that. Sometimes she looked at Charley and could barely believe she was related to her. And it wasn't just because of her skin, because it was so dark, because she looked more like her father than like Sherry. It was something about that way Charley looked at her, as though she doubted her ability as a mother, as though she knew that half the time Sherry could barely get herself out of bed and off to work, much less get Charley to school in clothes that had been washed and that fit, more or less.

And then when they had come back to Vermont, her mother had seemed to know exactly what she felt. She and Charley had shown up one day, exhausted from the bus trip, and Sherry had said, "Ma, I need to stay here awhile. Things didn't work out in Boston." That was all she'd said and to her mother's credit, she'd never asked any more questions. She'd just made up a bed for Charley in Dwight's old room and told Sherry that she'd heard they were looking for waitresses down at the diner. Sherry even thought she'd been happy about it, about having some company in the house after all that time.

Her mother's bedroom was at the front of the house on the second floor, a large square room with peeling floral wallpaper that must have once been a bright red and pink but was now faded by sun and marked by yellow patches from when the roof leaked. When they were growing up, she and Dwight hadn't ever been allowed in there, and the room still held a kind of power for her. She could count on the fingers of one hand the number of times she'd been in here since she'd been back. It smelled exactly the way it had always smelled, the very walls perfumed with a mix of mothballs and old lavender drawer sachets.

She changed the bag and went to work with the vacuum's floor attachment. It felt good to stretch her muscles, to breathe hard. She had done nothing but lie in bed or on the sofa for days.

She lifted the bedspread and pushed the vacuum under the bed, watching the dust kitties fly across the floor. When was the last time anyone had cleaned under here? Her mother had been an inconsistent housekeeper, fastidious about dishes and hygiene in the kitchen, unconcerned about dirt everywhere else. Sherry took the attachment off the hose and stuck the narrow end into the gap between the bed frame and the old mattress. She felt a satisfying rush of debris and dust up into the hose. Jesus, it was disgusting under here. She lifted the mattress and stuck the hose farther underneath. Almost smiling, she remembered finding a stack of girly magazines under her brother Dwight's mattress once. She couldn't remember why she'd gone under there, maybe looking for pot, or money. But she'd found a whole bunch of them and taken them. He'd never asked her about it, probably thought Ruth had found them. Poor dead Dwight. Everyone was dead now, except for her.

The vacuum suddenly gave a loud slurp and she heard the sound of it sucking against an object too big to fit up the hose. She shut it off, reached under the mattress, and came up with a little blue book with a fake leather cover. It was a bankbook, the old fashioned kind that people hardly ever had anymore because of ATMs and all.

She sat down on the bed and opened it, seeing Charley's name in her mother's handwriting on the first page and a list of deposits. Jesus, that was a lot of money. For Charley's college, it said. Think of it, the old bat saving up all that money and never letting on. Where had she gotten it from? Her social security and her pension from the insurance office didn't come to more than $800 a month.

Sherry went to put the book in the pocket of her jeans, then thought better of it. If Carl found out about it, he'd say they needed it for something. No, she decided, replacing it under the mattress. She'd leave it here. Charley probably knew where it was. Charley would know what to do with it.

# FOURTEEN

Every day had the same shape to it at Byzantium. In the summers, most of the colonists rose early to work and the day lasted until about three o'clock, when visiting hours would begin. Visits might be arranged the day before or they could be more spontaneous, but they never occurred before three. It was unthinkable to interrupt someone when they might be working and new arrivals learned quickly the ramifications of a too-early visit.

Colonists and their guests would get into the carriage—later the new fangled motor cars—and begin the tour, down what was then called the River Road, now Route 20.

Riva Delaney, the first wife of the sculptor Paul Evans, who came to Byzantium in 1887 as one of Morgan's students, said near the end of her life that she loved the afternoons of visiting: "Time stood still. All that mattered was the visit. Usually, we talked about the work. Hosts might show off what they were working on, if they were at a point where they could do that. Otherwise, they answered vaguely when you asked how it was going. That was the thing about Byzantium. No one pressed you. Everyone understood how it was to be an artist."

Visiting bled into the cocktail hour, which started at four or five. Cocktails happened in the gardens of the houses when the weather was nice and in the parlors when it wasn't.

And then there was dinner. There were dinner parties

*at Byzantium Wednesday through Saturday. Dress was
as formal as one could manage away from the city and
while they ate freshly killed meat and just-picked garden
produce, the artists complained about the quality of the
help, reminding themselves that there were some things
you just couldn't get in the country.*

—*Muse of the Hills: The Byzantium Colony,
1860–1956,*
by Bennett Dammers

"HE WAS SO suspicious," Willow Fontana said, holding her
wineglass at the level of her face so that the light cast by the
chandelier in the Wentworths' living room made it look like
a cup full of rubies. "It was like he thought I'd killed her.
He asked me if I was sure I didn't know anything about her
death while Billy Van Dorn, dressed up in his goddamn policeman's uniform, pretended he'd never met me before, and
sat there gloating and writing it all down."

"I was downtown today and I kept getting these *looks*,"
Sabina told them. "At the Food Basket, Anne Salvo came
over to tell me that she was 'sorry for our trouble.' Sorry for
our trouble! Can you imagine?"

"It's so hard to know what to *do*," Britta said quietly. "I
feel as though we shouldn't be eating, shouldn't be talking
or enjoying ourselves. Yet we hardly have a right to be playing the grief-stricken mourners. It doesn't seem healthy
somehow. Does anybody know what I mean?"

*"Moderate lamentation is the right of the dead, excessive
grief the enemy of the living,"* said Sweeney. Everyone in
the room looked up at her.

Toby grinned. "Very good. *All's Well That Ends Well*?"
It was one of their favorite games.

"I know what you mean," said Patch. "I feel guilty for
not being more broken up about it."

"She was our neighbor," Anders Fontana said, gulping his
whiskey and soda, "but we can hardly be expected to prostrate

ourselves with grief. I mean, let's be honest, she wasn't exactly a friend." He looked around at them. But there was only
an embarrassed silence. Sweeney watched their sheepish eyes
dart back to their drinks. He had gone too far.

*"Darling,"* Willow said quietly.

She was like a woman from a Hemingway novel, Sweeney thought, watching her from across the room. Her raspy
voice conjured up old black-and-white movies, and her almost boyish face, with its strong, determined jaw and high
cheekbones, made her, if not pretty, immensely sexy. Already, in the course of a ten minute conversation, she had
revealed to Sweeney that she loved "shooting animals with
horns" and that she went to Montana three times a year for
the fly fishing.

The Wentworth children had been quiet so far, sipping
sodas and listening to the adults' conversation, but Gwinny,
dressed in a pink satin floor-length skirt and vintage organza
blouse, flushed now and put her drink down on a side table.
"She was *my* friend," she said angrily, looking right at Anders. "I knew her. I used to babysit for her."

No one had anything to say to that. Anders directed his
gaze away from Gwinny's determined face.

Britta put a hand on her daughter's shoulder. "He didn't
mean anything, sweetheart. Why don't you go upstairs and
change into something more appropriate." Gwinny looked at
Anders again, then turned to go out of the room.

"I thought Chief Cooper seemed a bit out of his league,"
said Rosemary, who had come dressed in a black leather
blazer and well-fitting red velvet pants, looking more New
York than Vermont. "And I like Gwinny's outfit. She looks
like Grace Kelly."

Electra Granger, serene in a blue wool suit and silk scarf
printed with Monet's water lilies, put up a hand and said,
"We have to remember that Chief Cooper is just doing his
job. He may just be pinpointing when she killed herself, the
poor woman. He's a very *sharp* man. I'm sure he'll conclude
that it was a terribly sad case of suicide."

"You know what they say about Cooper," Sabina said

with a raise of her eyebrows. "He had some big job down in Boston—homicide or something—but he couldn't stay off the sauce. That's why he got sent up to us in the hinterlands." She looked magnificent, her large frame costumed in a voluminous peacock blue silk caftan.

"If it *wasn't* suicide," Willow said, "I bet it had something to do with these burglaries. Maybe she caught Carl at it and he had to do away with her."

Electra Granger held up her hand again. "Please," she said. "I don't like this kind of talk about our neighbors."

There was an awkward silence before conversations struck up around the room again.

"Now, I want to know all about what you think of us, Miss St. George." Sabina turned her gaze on Sweeney, who felt as though she were being devoured. "Have you ever been to an art colony before?"

"Oh, leave her alone, Sabina," Willow said. "Sweeney, it's nothing personal. You're just the feminine addition *du jour*. Now, Ian, tell me again what you do for a living. Furniture, Patch said . . ." Willow leaned toward him, dangling her wineglass flirtatiously.

"How is your gravestone project going, Sweeney?" Sabina asked.

"It's gotten off to a slow start, what with the . . . with all the excitement," Sweeney said hesitantly, looking around to see who was listening. "I'm afraid I haven't found out much about who the sculptor could be."

"Well, if you're interested, I've got all kinds of art related to the colony. Besides, I'd love for you to see my house."

"That would be great. I've gotten really interested in the colony."

"Wonderful. Why don't you come over for lunch. Shall we say tomorrow? Electra, why don't you come, too? Assuming we haven't all been sent to jail."

They decided on eleven o'clock.

Electra Granger turned her sightless eyes on Sweeney. "You must think our lives here are terribly dramatic, dear.

But you should know that it isn't every day we have suspicious suicides and burglary rings."

Sweeney murmured that of course it wasn't.

"Is it true you and Rosemary were the last ones to see her?" Sabina asked Electra. "Or is that just gossip?"

"No, it's true," Rosemary said stiffly. "We told Chief Cooper all about it. We had gone out for a walk and we were starting back because the weather had gotten so bad. We saw Mrs. Kimball as she was heading toward the cemetery."

"But did you stop to talk?"

"No," Electra said. "I keep thinking that if we had called her back, stopped to talk or something, she might not have done it. But I suppose you can't think that way."

When Britta announced that it was time for dinner and the group moved to the dining room, Sweeney felt as though she'd stepped into a production of the *Nutcracker Suite*.

Tiny white lights cascaded along the walls and the long table had been set to resemble a medieval banquet hall, with wreaths of evergreen boughs studded with pomegranates for centerpieces and goblets the size of small mixing bowls, filled with crimson wine that matched the velvet tablecloth. It was lovely, but slightly creepy, too, a little Martha-Stewart-gone-awry for Sweeney's taste.

She sat down at the place headed by a little red card with her name on it and a middle-aged woman in a black-and-white uniform who helped Britta with dinner parties came out with plates of rare rack of lamb, decorated with sprigs of mint and accompanied by pecan-studded rice pilaf and asparagus. Each place setting was topped by a small bowl of mint sauce.

The effect was lovely, but struck her as somehow obscene. Sweeney was of the decided opinion that vegetarians had been put on the earth merely to vex her. She loved rare lamb. But as she sat down before the bloody meat, she felt a wave of nausea roll in her stomach.

"In any case," Anders said after they'd all begun to eat, "it solves our little problem about the condos, doesn't it?"

"Anders!" His wife gave him a look that was part horror and part admiration.

"You know," Patch said. "I wouldn't be so sure about that. Now that Ruth's gone, Sherry can do whatever she wants. And if Carl gets his hooks into her, anything could happen."

"That's true," Patch said. "The sky's the limit. An amusement park, maybe? How about a casino?"

"It isn't something to laugh about," Britta snapped. "Someone's dead."

"But it isn't our fault, Britta. We didn't kill her." Willow's eyes were cold and full of challenge. Sweeney looked quickly from her to Britta and back again. There was something there, a barely concealed hostility she hadn't noticed before.

Anders took a long swig of his wine and looked around at them. The room was very quiet. "Maybe one of us did kill her."

"Anders!" Britta gave him a stern look.

Suddenly everyone glanced down at where the children were, Trip and Gally, quiet, Gwinny still in her flamboyant outfit, with a sweatshirt over the blouse.

"That's nonsense," Sabina said quickly. "But if she was murdered, I suspect it was something very commonplace. She caught the burglar. She slighted someone in town." She pronounced the words "in town" with a slight emphasis, as if to say that the colony and the town were two different things.

"If that's all it takes to commit murder, any one of us might have killed her, even you, Sabina," Willow said.

Sabina looked embarrassed. "But if I had killed her, I would have been smart enough to arrange an alibi. Isn't that what people do? As it is, I was all alone that afternoon. No one can vouch for me."

"Me, either," Anders said happily. "I had gone for a run. All by myself. What about you, Patch?"

Patch glanced down at his plate. "Guilty as charged," he

said. "I was stacking wood out back. Then I went for a run, too."

"You all sound as though you wouldn't think it was wrong if one of us *had* killed her," Rosemary said, looking shocked. "Surely murder's wrong whatever the reason or method."

"I don't know," Anders said. "Say one of us had killed her because of the condos. To preserve the colony. Wouldn't that be worth it?"

Toby's eyes lit up. "What's one life up against the preservation of the colony, you mean. It's a good question. Is the colony a historical and cultural resource so worth defending that even murder would be justified?" He loved these kinds of circular philosophical considerations.

"Of course not," Britta said. "Murder is never justified."

"It is in time of war," Toby said. "In order to defend a way of life or a political ideal. A number of times over the past century we've made the decision that we were justified in killing to protect some vaguely defined ideal of democracy. Why is it wrong to kill for an artistic ideal?"

"And is it any artistic ideal? Or would you think some more worthy of defense than others?" Ian asked, grinning. "For example, is impressionism justification for homicide, but not Dadaism?"

"Please," Britta said in a slightly desperate voice, as the hired waitress came in to clear the table. Patch turned the conversation to the weather and how the skiing had been and Sweeney was confused until the woman went out of the room again and Britta said, "I hope she didn't hear us. She's friends with Sherry Kimball, you know."

"I'm sure she didn't," Patch said. "She was in the kitchen. You worry too much, Brit." He looked around at his guests, grinning broadly.

"She's right, Patch," Willow said quietly. "We should be careful. You don't know what people might be saying." Britta looked away, biting her lip, and Sweeney had a sudden impulse to get up and hug her. Rosemary, who was sitting next to Britta, quickly engaged her in conversation about how good the lamb had been.

Dessert and coffee were brought in. The children were excused from the table and the adults talked happily about other things for nearly a half hour. By the time Sweeney got up to go to the bathroom, she was more than a little drunk. She stumbled as she went out of the room and looked around to find Ian watching her with a concerned look on his face. "Fine, I'm fine," she said, and escaped to the powder room next to the kitchen.

Her face was flushed in the mirror over the sink and she leaned in, looking at her eyes, which were glittering and feverish. It was all this social activity, she decided. She wasn't used to it. She freshened her lipstick, then re-fastened her hair up at the back of her head with a barrette.

Out in the hallway, she leaned over to pick a piece of lint off her skirt and looked up to find Trip standing in the doorway to the kitchen. He had changed into a red T-shirt and jeans since he'd gotten up from the table. "Hey," he said. "Is dinner over?"

"Oh, no. I got up for a minute. Everyone else is still at the table."

He stepped toward her. His eyes were bluer than she remembered. "I like your hair like that. Up. It looks cool."

Sweeney's hand sprang up to her head. "Thanks." She wasn't sure if she should laugh or blush. What was he doing? Was he flirting with her? "What are you guys up to?"

"Oh nothing, just watching movies upstairs." He stared at her for a moment, then brushed past her. When he was directly behind her, he reached up to touch her hand, which was still on her hair. He left it there for a moment, then kept walking. "Bye," he said without looking over his shoulder.

When she sat down again at the table the conversation had turned back to Toby's ethical dilemma.

"I still think it's an interesting question," he said. "Which works of art would be worth killing for? Is it the most aesthetically pleasing? Or the rarest? Or the most historically interesting? Which books, or symphonies, for that matter?"

Ian took a long sip of his wine. "Personally, I've always wished someone would knock off that chap who puts cows in fish tanks."

"Or Magritte," Toby nearly shouted, enjoying the exchange. "Why didn't anybody kill Magritte?" He and Ian laughed.

Rosemary turned to him, her eyes wide and angry. "The only thing worth a life is another life in danger. You can't say that a human life is worth the defense of an abstract concept, of something inanimate. I won't accept that."

"I don't know. Do you really think that some people's lives are more worthy of preservation than, say, *Guernica*?" Sweeney knew that deep down he agreed with Rosemary, but he couldn't stop himself when he was playing devil's advocate.

"He's right," Willow said. "I think beauty, the legacy of the colony, its history, all these things are more important than some of the things this country has gone to war for. The thing that our grandparents and great-grandparents made here is something special. It's worth preserving." She took a long swallow of her wine. "Yes, even if someone had to die. I'm not saying any of us did it, but . . ."

There was a gasp and Britta stood up quickly from the table. "She killed herself," she almost shouted at them. "She killed herself and I don't know why you're all talking about murder." She pushed back her chair, which teetered for a minute and fell over, and disappeared into the kitchen. Patch glared at Willow, then followed his wife.

"Ooops, darlin'," Anders said. "Looks like you've made a *faux pas*."

"Oh, Ian," Willow said loudly, flirting again. "What must you think of us?"

"I think," Electra Granger said quietly, sitting straight up in her chair as though she were chaperoning a roomful of rowdy children, "that it's time to go home."

# FIFTEEN

❦

THE AIR AT midnight was so cold that Sweeney felt as though she'd been slapped as she stepped out the back door, looking for Toby. The end of his cigarette was a bright ember against the sky; his dark figure like an ebony statue. She sought him out, her boots crunching on the snow.

"So that was quite a dinner party." Even in her parka and hat and gloves, she had to dance around beside him to keep warm.

"Yeah. I'm sorry about that. Everyone got a little carried away. They'll be best friends again tomorrow." He dragged on the cigarette, staring out across the dark, endless landscape.

"You okay?" she asked him. Toby only smoked when he was upset.

"Yeah, yeah. It's just that things are a little intense around here right now."

"Listen, Toby. There's something I need to talk to you about."

He turned to look at her, holding his cigarette down at his side. "Yeah?"

"I didn't say anything because, well, because I didn't know if it meant anything and well . . . the thing is that I knew Ruth Kimball was dead before we came up here. I'd called her to see if I could get any more information about the gravestone. We talked briefly and she told me that she'd always believed that one of the artists killed Mary. Anyway,

I didn't know what to make of that. I had to go and I called her back the next day."

Toby was staring at her in disbelief. "And she was dead?"

"And she was dead. I just can't help wondering if there isn't some connection."

"Are you crazy?"

"No, no. Just listen to me. What if they're right and she didn't kill herself? It might be because I was asking questions about Mary's death. If Ruth Kimball knew what she was talking about and Morgan or your great-grandfather or one of the other artists had something to do with it, maybe one of the descendants was responsible for her death."

"You can't be serious. You heard them. It was suicide. And if it was anything other than suicide it was because of the burglaries. What is this, some kind of fucked-up Nancy Drew impulse?"

"Toby, all I'm saying is that I'm getting a little nervous about this whole thing. I have to find out if there's anything to what Ruth Kimball told me. If there is, it might indicate that . . ."

But Toby didn't let her finish. "This is nuts. I don't know what you're thinking you're going to find out about my great-grandfather, but it isn't there." He dropped the cigarette onto the snow and covered it with his foot.

"Toby . . ."

"Don't you think that maybe, just maybe, this has something to do with your father?"

"My father?"

"You don't want to believe Ruth Kimball committed suicide because you don't want to believe your father committed suicide."

"That has *nothing* to do with it."

"Oh yeah?" He looked at her the way he looked at her when he was trying to figure out what she really meant or what was really going on with her. "What's wrong with you, anyway? You've been acting like someone else the whole time we've been here."

Sweeney looked into his eyes, trying to decide if she

should tell him. He was angry, but she went ahead anyway. "I'm having a hard time with you and Rosemary. I'm feeling, some things for you that I didn't think I was going to feel. I'm all . . . I don't know, I'm all mixed up, Toby." She stumbled through the words, almost crying, then looked away.

His reaction was not at all what she thought it would be. Silently he took off his gloves and took another cigarette out of his pocket, hunching over to light it, then replacing his gloves. When he spoke, it was in a tightly controlled voice, angry and grim.

"You know what? I'm really fucking tired of this. I don't know if I should even believe you. I don't think you know whether you should believe yourself. I like Rosemary a lot and that has to be okay. You can't come in here—out here—and just expect me to . . . I don't even know what you expect me to do. What do you want me to say? Jesus!" He threw the barely smoked cigarette down in the snow and stormed inside, leaving Sweeney shaking in the cold.

She looked up at the dark sky, the stars blurred by her tears. She and Toby argued often; they were both strong-willed and there were strong emotions between them. But there was something about this that felt different. She had said the one thing that she was forbidden to say and she realized suddenly how cruel it had been for her to say it. Six months ago, Toby had come to her and told her that he loved her. She had felt nothing for him, nothing for anyone. She had refused to talk to him for weeks. He had almost had to break down her apartment door to get her to talk about it. Now she saw herself plainly, needy and alone; she had come to him only when she was afraid of losing his friendship. She wiped her eyes with the back of her glove.

But she didn't want to think about that right now. And he was right of course, that she was meddling in something beyond the scope of her interest or skill.

*Curious cats often lose their whiskers.*

It was something Sweeney's mother, with her English love of quirky platitudes, had liked to say, when she caught her snooping in a party guest's purse or holding her mail up to the light to see what was inside. But she hadn't said it when she'd caught fourteen-year-old Sweeney looking through her journal, trying to find out how her father had died.

Her mother's version had been maddeningly incomplete, almost tantalizing. "There was an accident. Down in Mexico," she'd said that cold winter morning fifteen years ago. "Your father won't be coming back to Boston again."

And so she had snooped, in drawers and books and finally in her mother's journal, where she had found a short newspaper clipping, slipped between the pages. "Paul St. George, the painter who became well known in the past decade for his moody, sunburnt images of Mexico and the American Southwest, died on December 2 in Mexico City, an apparent suicide. Police say St. George checked into the Casa Mexico hotel shortly before a gunshot was heard in the early morning hours . . ."

That was all she'd read before her mother found her. "So you know," she'd said. "He was a coward. Don't you wish you'd left it alone?"

But she wanted to know the truth, she had told her mother, who replied that the truth was a messy, ugly, overrated thing. And so it was. Life and love had taught her that.

Later there had been more details. As she'd moved up in the department in college, Paul St. George's name had come up more and more frequently in lectures. A woman in Sweeney's class had done her senior thesis on his *Pueblo* series. And she'd picked up a magazine in the department office once and read a review of the Toronto retrospective.

"Curiously, this is the first posthumous retrospective for the American painter Paul St. George, who committed suicide in 1988. The result is both fascinating and dismaying. The work as a body seems somewhat incomplete, as though he had begun a transformation, but never completed it, stilling his talent by his own hand. . . . Particularly moving are the series of pieces featuring handguns and rifles, St. George's chosen method of suicide. In one a Mexican housewife brandishes a shotgun like a talisman against a chaotic, abstract background of swirling color . . ." She had felt suddenly numb reading those words. He was as much a mystery to her as he'd apparently been to Sweeney's classmate, who had titled her thesis. "The Happy Enigma: Images of Joy in Paul St. George's *Pueblo* Series."

Sweeney had read the thesis, a neat treatment that wrapped the enigmatic elements of her father's work within his background and manic depression.

That was what she liked about academic mysteries, as opposed to human ones. At the end of an academic pursuit there was a satisfying symmetry, complexity to be sure, but an answer that one could hold on to.

What about this mystery, which had started out as a neat little puzzle of a gravestone and was now something else entirely?

She shivered and turned around to go back into the house. But as she turned, she caught, out of the corner of her eye, a movement in one of the upstairs windows. Someone had been watching her. When she searched the rectangular panes of glass that seemed like rows of judging eyes, each one was empty and dark. Which window had it been?

Suddenly, she was afraid. The wind had come up and the woods surrounding the house seemed sinister, full of evil. The night was so dark she could barely see the path her boots had stamped in the snow. As she turned and started for the house it was all she could do not to break into a run, and when she was finally inside, she closed the back door and locked it before it struck her that the person who'd been watching her was *inside*, and not outside.

But she did feel better being inside the warm house. She left her parka and boots in the mud room and went quietly up to her room. As she passed Ian Ball's open door, she looked inside to find the room empty. She was alone on the third floor.

Tiny pricklings of fear started along her spine when she found the door to her bedroom very slightly open, the thin, vertical line of darkness showing against the lighted hallway. She pushed on it. It swung in and alarm rose up through her body. The door had an old-fashioned latch that had to be lifted and then dropped into place and she was sure that she had secured it when she'd come up after dinner to change her clothes.

She slipped inside her room cautiously and flipped the light switch, her heart pounding, then relaxing in gratitude when the bulbs in the antique fixture illuminated only the small room, everything just as she'd left it.

Or almost everything. For when she examined the surface of her dressing table, she discovered that her emerald earrings, which she had left there after dinner, were no longer lying there, glinting in the light.

Sweeney shivered and got into bed.

# SIXTEEN

❦

## December 16

*While the glamorous young couples of Byzantium provided a certain excitement, it was the old ladies who kept everything running. In 1895, Herrick Gilmartin brought his mother to live at Birch Lane and she immediately took over the role of mistress of ceremonies. Along with Geneva Clarendon, a singer who began spending summers at Byzantium in 1897, Mrs. Gilmartin presided over the social season, planning parties and enthusiastically matchmaking.*

*"I was at a cocktail party at Upper Pastures and Mrs. Clarendon told me that there was a man she wanted me to meet," Riva Delaney Evans remembered in her 1940 memoir. "And she took me over to this little group of men who were smoking pipes in the garden and one of them stepped out when he saw us coming and smiled at me. It was Paul. We were married a couple of months later and I always said it was because of the old ladies getting together and planning it all out."*

—*Muse of the Hills: The Byzantium Colony,*
*1860–1956,*
by Bennett Dammers

SWEENEY HAD LEARNED early in life that old ladies liked talking to her. She put this down to her somewhat anachronistic interests and to the string of elderly baby-sitters who had seemed to come out of the woodwork in whatever neighborhood she and her mother had landed in.

While other children had daytime caretakers, busy with hordes of children, she had spent evenings alone with the old ladies while her mother was on the stage or working at whatever job she had resorted to. She had loved those nights in front of ancient televisions, eating frozen dinners or grilled cheese sandwiches served on good china, with cloth napkins. They had watched Masterpiece Theatre and talked about books, dead husbands, long-ago loves, children who had moved away. She had always felt she had more in common with the elderly women than with her bewildering peers. She only felt at ease in those prim, well-heated living rooms.

So she wasn't expecting she'd have any trouble getting Sabina Dodge and Electra Granger to talk about the colony over lunch. She wasn't sure exactly what it was she was after—though a few juicy morsels of gossip about Mary Denholm or Ruth Kimball would be nice.

Afraid to see Toby, she had breakfasted early and gone to hide out with a book, but her plans for a quiet couple of hours reading in the Wentworths' library were disrupted when Britta came in to tell her that the police had called. "Chief Cooper would like you to come down to the station this morning," she said nervously, watching Sweeney with slightly mistrustful eyes. "Just for a few minutes. He didn't say what it was about."

Sweeney's mind raced through the list of possibilities. Her apartment had burned down, something awful had happened to one of her students, her hundreds of unpaid parking tickets had finally caught up with her. What could it be? "Right now?"

"That's what he said. I hope it's not about the gravestone." Britta looked genuinely concerned, twisting a dish towel over and over in her hands.

Sweeney put her book down and slipped her clogs back on. "But how would he know about that?"

"Oh, I think you'll find it's a very small town," Britta said quietly. "Everybody knows everybody's business. Half the town must know about you and the gravestone."

• • •

As it turned out, Britta was right. It was about the gravestone.
"Thank you for coming in, Miss St. George. I'm sorry to be
so late," Chief Cooper said, introducing himself as he walked
into the little room. She had spent the ten minutes she'd been
made to wait looking around and deciding it must be used
as some sort of a classroom. There was a blackboard against
one wall, and it was covered with strange notations. "Satis.
Conflict Res. Lst. force nec. and fll" read the chalky words.

Chief Cooper was a tall man, taller than Sweeney, and he
had reddish brown hair, a stiff auburn mustache, and sharp
cheekbones. The impression he gave was of a sharp intelligence and bottled-up anger. In his snug-fitting dark green
uniform, he looked rangy and western, like a cowboy or a
forest ranger.

He was holding a stack of manila folders and when he
deposited them on the table before sitting down across from
her, Sweeney saw that the top folder had a white sticker with
"Kimball, R." written on it in purple marker. When he caught
her looking, he turned it over. She decided immediately that
she disliked him, disliked his long, sad face, with its reddish
nose and cheeks, disliked his thin, strong frame.

"Now, you're probably wondering why you're here."

Sweeney said that she was, but that she assumed it had
something to do with Ruth Kimball's death.

"That's right. It's come to my attention that you were in
touch with her shortly before her death. I wondered if you
could tell me what it was about."

In the car on the way downtown, Sweeney had decided
she would tell him about her conversation with Ruth Kimball
and that she had known about her death before coming to
Vermont. It was a question of risk-assessment more than of
honesty. Ruth Kimball, after all, had told her daughter about
their exchange on the telephone. Chief Cooper probably
knew that already. But Sweeney had decided not to tell him
about the inquiries she'd made so far. She had very little to
go on, after all, just a vague discomfort about Herrick Gilmartin's necrophiliac portrait and a shadowy suspicion that

one or more of the colonists knew more about Ruth Kimball's death—and Sweeney's questions—than they were letting on.

When she was finished with her story, Cooper sat back and studied her for a moment before asking, "So she said nothing that would indicate to you that she had any idea about who might have killed her ancestor? If in fact her ancestor was killed?"

"Well, that's the thing. I was going to ask her about who she thought it was the next day, but then when I called . . ." She flushed. "I mean that I wondered if . . ."

"You wondered if perhaps she hadn't mentioned to someone that she knew who had killed Mary Denholm?"

"No, I mean . . . I did wonder, I suppose. But it's really the gravestone I'm interested in. And besides, she killed herself, right? There isn't any question that it was anything else?"

Before he could say anything, the door opened, and another policeman leaned in and said, "Hey, Chief. The A.G.'s in your office. He was in town for the Dadko hearing and he wants to ask about the search thing."

Chief Cooper nodded and got up. "Could you give me a minute, Miss St. George? I'll be right back."

It was after she'd been sitting there for a few minutes, reading over and over a menacing poster on the wall that read, "Never, Never, Never Shake a Baby," that she remembered the manila folder.

There weren't any windows in the little room, but still she looked around as though someone might be watching. Satisfied that there weren't any one-way mirrors or cameras about, she leaned across the table and slowly turned the folder over so that she could see the label with its messy purple writing. After listening to make sure that no one was coming, she swiftly lifted the cover and found a stack of handwritten notes. They were practically illegible, but she flipped through anyway, looking for recognizable names or details. Once she saw "Sherry Kimball" and in another place the name "P. Wentworth." The word "Alibis" popped out at her, scrawled in red marker on another sheet of paper. Cooper, or whoever it was, had written a list of names in a column headed by the word "Insufficient or Susp." There was Patch, Britta, Willow, Anders, Gwinny, Carl Thompson and Sabina Dodge. In another column, this one headed by the word "Firm," were the names Rosemary Burgess, Electra Granger, Gally and Trip Wentworth, Sherry and Charley Kimball. Sweeney thought back to the conversation about alibis at dinner the night before. What was it Sabina had said? Something about how if she'd actually been the murderer, she would have come up with an alibi for herself. Well, she hadn't.

Sweeney listened for a moment, then opened a manila envelope at the back of the folder. Inside was a stack of crime scene photos.

She had seen them in movies, large format, black-and-white pictures shown fleetingly over the shoulders of silver screen detectives.

But nothing had prepared her for these stark images of death. The gray-haired, slightly stocky woman was a dark stain against the snow. Dressed in what looked like a long skirt, boots, and a bulky parka, she lay on her back, legs folded beneath her body. She'd obviously fallen to her knees and then back, her arms outstretched as though she'd been making angels in the snow.

Half clasped in her right hand was a dark object that Sweeney recognized as a handgun. In a close-up, farther down in the pile, the barrel pointed toward the woman's bare head and forced Sweeney's eye to her face, or the dark mess where her face had once been.

For all the time she had spent among the dead, she had never seen an undoctored photograph of a body before, much less a real corpse. Her whole being recoiled at the sight of stilled life, and something deep within her wanted to turn away from the picture of the glistening wound. In that instant she remembered everything she'd ever read about superstitions related to corpses, Kenyan tribesmen who refused to be anywhere in the vicinity of a dead body, Egyptian beliefs about preparing corpses. But still she stared, overcome by a combination of repulsion and fascination.

When she heard Cooper at the door, she barely had time to put the photos back and close the folder. As he entered the room, she was busy rooting around in her purse for a stick of gum which, thankfully, she found, a bit mashed, at the very bottom. She slipped it from its wrapper and folded it into her mouth, trying to calm her jangled nerves.

"Sorry," he said, sitting down again. "Where were we? Oh, yes. You were asking me if there was a possibility that Ruth Kimball didn't commit suicide. I'll be frank with you, Miss St. George. It's not as clear-cut as one might think. It's a very simple matter to place a gun in a dead person's hand following a murder, hold it to the head, let the arm fall naturally. The thing that frequently gives such an act away is the absence of fingerprints or the presence of strange ones, but in this case . . ."

Sweeney saw where he was going. "She was outside. She was wearing gloves," she finished.

"Exactly. So we look at other aspects of the crime. The angle at which the bullet entered the body, the distance at which the gun was fired." It struck her that he was enjoying explaining the intricacies of police work to her. "I'll get to the point. At eight this morning I heard from the medical examiner. He's calling this shooting a homicide. So now I'm investigating this as a murder and if there's anything you know that you haven't told me, this would be a good time to speak up."

Sweeney, shocked, just looked back at him.

"I want you to understand the possible seriousness of the situation. If there is anything that comes to your attention, I would appreciate it if you came to me. We wouldn't want anyone else to get hurt."

There was something threatening in his words and Sweeney found she didn't have it in her to do anything but nod.

"Okay. I'm sorry to have kept you waiting." He got up and led her out into the lobby. "You know where we are. If you need us."

Again, his words were ominous rather than comforting.

• • •

Sabina Dodge's house, decidedly New England on the outside, had the feel of a Moroccan palace on the inside. When
she answered the door, she took Sweeney's hands in hers
and kissed her once on each cheek, then led her into a little
room off the front hallway and told her to sit down on a low
red couch. The walls of the room were covered with tapes-
tries and red and black rugs. Giant pillows were scattered
around on the couch. A few large cushions were arranged
around a low table, where a giant, obscenely pink amaryllis
bloomed in a low dish. A fire was blazing in the fireplace
and the warmth and closeness of the room made Sweeney
feel sleepy. She was still reeling from her conversation with
Cooper.

"It's so nice to see you," Sabina Dodge said. "Electra's
going to be joining us in a moment, but why don't I get you
some tea. Milk and sugar?" She was wearing another voluminous caftan, this one the pink of poached salmon, and a
black velvet turban from under which a few tufts of white
hair had escaped. Her gray eyes twinkled at Sweeney from
the big, fleshy, moon-shaped face. Her hands, when Sweeney
looked down at them, sparkled with diamond and sapphire
rings.

"Just plain, thanks." Sweeney tried to lean back on the
couch and found that she sank into it. A bell sounded and
Sabina went to get it, leaving Sweeney alone in the room.
There was a small table over against one wall and on it were
a group of sterling silver picture frames with photographs in
them. Sweeney went over to look at them.

One showed a group of people standing in front of Upper
Pastures. Since most of the women had on dropped-waist
flapper-style dresses, she assumed it had been taken sometime in the '20s. She recognized Marcus Granger from other
pictures she'd seen, but other than that, no one looked
familiar.

Another picture was of a girl—upon close examination
Sweeney saw that it was a much younger Sabina—with her
arm around a gray-haired woman. A German Shepherd sat

at their feet. There were a couple of photographs of children and one had an inscription at the bottom that read. "To Aunt Gilda, with all my love—Bitty."

"Hi, Sweeney," Rosemary said from behind her. Sweeney turned around quickly and found Rosemary standing next to her grandmother.

"Are you sure you can't stay, Rosemary?" Sabina asked, coming into the room with a tea tray.

"No. Toby and I are going skiing today. I'm sorry." She blushed a little.

"Of course we understand, dear," beamed Electra Granger. Next to Sabina, she was a tiny, elegant imp. They were, Sweeney decided, a study in opposites. Where Sabina was rotund and bright and showy, Electra Granger was a small, quiet presence, dressed in a camel-colored suit, dark pantyhose and a brown silk scarf. Her sightless eyes settled pleasantly on something over Sweeney's shoulder as Rosemary said her good-byes and told her grandmother she'd be home later in the afternoon.

"Tell us more about your work," Sabina said, once they had settled down with tea and cucumber sandwiches. "It sounds so interesting. Gravestones, Patch said."

"Yes," Electra murmured. "Gravestones. How *fascinating*."

Gravestones carried them through tea and sandwiches.

"What about you, Sabina?" Sweeney asked when they were done. "How did you come to the colony?"

"I came when I was eighteen, believe it or not, and I've never really left. That was in the '40s. Gilda asked me to stay and I came for the weekend and that was it. Gilda, of course, had been here for ages. She was twenty-five years older than me."

Sweeney looked confused until Sabina explained, "Gilda Donetti."

"Oh yes." Gilda Donetti had been one of the few successful Byzantium women and Sweeney remembered there had been a show of her work at the MFA recently—walls of her pastel interiors and landscapes, the colors washing over paper and canvas like the sea.

"I was in art school and Gilda kind of swept me up and brought me here. And I just fell completely in love with Byzantium and everything about it. It was glamorously primitive in those days. No one had indoor plumbing until you and Marcus came, Electra, but we would have these marvelous cocktail parties. Oh! It was such fun. I wish you could have been here. Herrick Gilmartin was still the life of the party, even though he was almost eighty."

A giant silver Persian cat had come into the room and was rubbing against Sweeney's legs. It mewled and crossed the floor to its mistress.

"What was Gilmartin like? It's amazing to be staying in his house. I keep imagining him sitting where I'm sitting or eating where I'm eating, and wondering what kind of a person he was."

Sabina glanced over at Electra. "Well, he wasn't a nice person, if that's what you mean. I mean, he was terrific company, but he was such a devil. Patch won't let anyone talk about it, but Gilmartin slept with nearly everyone. Liked to seduce all his models."

"Really?"

"Oh yes." Sabina leaned forward. "He lived in his studio for an entire summer. With a Parisian model someone brought from Chicago. The servants had to bring them food and water." Sabina grinned. "Don't look so shocked, dear. I don't know what your generation thinks we were all *doing,* anyway. Herrick was an old goat. Wasn't he, Electra?"

"He was. Herrick was terrible." Electra smiled mysteriously.

"Who were his models? Did you know any of them?"

"Both he and Marcus used a lot of local girls. We all kind of helped out now and then, too. That, for example," Sabina pointed to a nude on the wall over the fireplace, "is me in all my God-given glory. I was much younger then."

"What about Mary Denholm? I guess she modeled for him, too," Sweeney asked innocently.

"Before my time, of course, and Gilda's, too. But she did model for Herrick. It's funny actually, but Gilda always got the feeling there was something strange about Mary's death."

Sweeney put her teacup down on the table with a clatter. "What do you mean?"

"Oh, she told me once she wondered if Herrick or one of the other men hadn't done it in a jealous rage or something. He was terribly possessive of his conquests. It was an idea she'd gotten, from a servant, I think." Sabina thought for a moment and then said, "Ruth Kimball was always going on about it, getting up at meetings and telling people one of the artists had killed her ancestor."

Sweeney's heart was pounding, but she forced herself to stay calm. "I thought Mary drowned."

"Of course she did, but Gilda had this idea in her head. I wish I could remember exactly what it was she said. It wasn't anything definite, just a sort of feeling. I think the housekeeper or someone said there was something not right about the girl's death. Didn't change the way she felt about Herrick, though. In fact, I think the little bit of mystery about that death made him seem more interesting to her. They were fast friends, smoked pipes together. He called her his Sapphic Sister. In those days no one bothered about two women. Called us a 'Boston marriage.' Have you ever heard that term?"

Sweeney shook her head.

"People don't use it anymore," Sabina said. "What do you remember about Herrick, Electra?"

"Well, he was quite *elderly* by the time we arrived here, of course, but there was something about him that people were always drawn to. He *twinkled*, if you know what I mean. Always up to something. Patch reminds me of him. Patch was a very naughty little boy. Always getting into scrapes. And he had a real temper. Used to fly off the handle at people if they didn't do what he wanted. It's funny, he and Willow were both like that as children. Willow once punched a little boy in the face. Broke his nose."

"I'd forgotten that Willow grew up coming here, too."

"Oh yes, she and Patch were fast friends. Although, as I say, they both had tempers and they used to have terrible fights. They went together for a while when they were teenagers, and everyone thought they would get married eventually, although in those days nobody seemed to get married. It was all sleeping together and living together back then.

"But then they went to college and Patch met Britta and, of course, Willow lived in Italy for all those years," Electra Granger went on. "So that was that. We all thought Britta was so sweet. Such a nice girl. I'll never forget how pretty she was the first time she came to Byzantium, with that blond hair, wearing a blue sundress. She was so fragile, I thought I would break her hand when I shook it. We all liked her. So that was okay."

But Sweeney got the feeling that it had not been okay, and she began to understand what it must have been like for Britta, coming into this strange, close-knit community, the barely tolerated outsider.

"Now," Sabina announced. "May I show you my house?" Electra said that she would stay on the couch and listen to the radio and Sabina rose and offered Sweeney her hand. "I love to show people my house."

Besides the room they'd been in, the downstairs included a living room, dining room, library, and giant kitchen, where copper pots dangled from a rack and another amaryllis was blooming on the kitchen table. "I force them," Sabina explained to Sweeney. "If you put them in the freezer, you can have them all year 'round."

"That was the morning room you were in," she went on, leading the way into a room lined with bookshelves, "and this is the library."

The walls of the room were painted a pale salmon that matched Sabina's outfit. A giant blue and gold oriental rug covered the floor and paintings crowded on the walls, making a colorful collage. Sweeney looked through the books in the cases.

"You like Dorothy Sayers, too," she said, perusing the

titles. "Austen, Josephine Tey, Marsh, Chandler, Shakespeare. I think we have the same taste in books."

"You're welcome to borrow anything you want," Sabina said. "Now here's something you might be interested in." She pointed to an oil portrait hanging over the fireplace mantel. It was a simple portrait of a plain, fair girl in a high-necked lace blouse, her pale skin melting into the milky background. "That's a Gilmartin of Ruth Kimball's grandmother Ethel. It was Gilda's, and we've always had it hanging here. But a couple of years ago, Ruth Kimball claimed she'd found a letter from Gilmartin indicating that he'd wanted her grandmother to have it. She kept threatening she was going to get a lawyer and fight me for it. I don't like to speak ill of the dead, but she was a very combative woman. This is the place it should be. It's always been here."

Sweeney took in Sabina's words and decided that if she'd discovered a letter indicating a portrait was meant to go to her grandmother, she might want to fight for it, too. She looked around at the other art in the room.

A more contemporary oil of two teenage girls playing with a small child caught her eye. It was a lovely composition—the child faced a shelf to the left edge of the canvas, one side of her face buried in one of the older girl's blouse. Nearly identical, the girls looked out from the canvas with controlled, Mona Lisa smiles. They were wearing dark clothes that set off the blue of the child's eyes.

The signature, Sweeney saw when she leaned down to look, was Gilda Donetti and the date was 1969. It wasn't anything special, really, just a pretty little painting.

"Who's that?" she asked, pointing at it.

"Oh, those are Patch's twin aunts, Violet and Barbara. They were a good bit younger than his mother. Change of life babies. And that," she pointed to the small girl, "is Rosemary. It was the summer she and her parents came to visit Marcus and Electra and I think Violet and Barbara baby-sat for her a lot. I've just gotten this down so I haven't had a chance to show it to her yet. I like to switch them around."

Sweeney looked closer and saw that the child in the

painting was indeed Rosemary. The small, butterfly birthmark on the cheek was the same.

"I thought her parents were estranged from the Grangers."

"Oh they were, but there was a summer before they
moved to Europe that they came up. Before they had the big
falling out with Marcus."

"What happened?" Sweeney asked.

"It had to do with Rosemary's father. He was a real '60s
radical, the authentic article, and when they were in Byzantium that summer he said some things about the colony and
about the way everyone lived here that were really unforgiv-
able. And then when the war was heating up they fled to
England and then I guess later to South Africa. We didn't
learn that part of it until Rosemary arrived, though." Sabina
lowered her voice. "I think that Electra and Marcus would
have forgiven it, but Emily had this idea that they wouldn't,
that they condemned her for leaving the country. It went
from there and they never spoke again. If Electra were a
different sort of person, she might have made overtures. But
she was so proud. Still is. Shall we go?"

As Sweeney followed her out of the room, she caught a
glimpse, out of the corner of her eye, of a piece of sculpture,
a child sitting in a chair, hanging on a far wall. There was
something familiar about the snowy white relief, the careful
lines of the boy's thick locks of hair.

"Isn't that a lovely little relief? I've just brought that out
as well."

Sweeney went closer and saw, down in the right-hand
corner, a signature. "J.L.B." it said, in flowing, cursive script.

"Who's J.L.B.?" She had to stop herself from grabbing
Sabina by the shoulders and shaking the answer out of her.

"J.L.B?" She went over and peered at the signature. "Oh,
I see. I don't know. Gilda always thought a student of Morgan's. Such a pretty little thing. I think Gilda found it lying
around the studio and asked if she could have it. I've always
kept it. Why?"

Sweeney stared at the relief. The style was the same as
Mary's stone. It had to be the same artist. Bennett Dammers

had been right that it was a student. But which student had it been?

"Just wondering," Sweeney said. "It's really lovely."

Sabina showed her around the spacious upstairs rooms, including the one that had been Gilda's studio. It seemed to have been preserved exactly the way it had been left, an easel still set up in a corner, with an unfinished canvas on it. Sweeney went over to look at it. A winter landscape, much like the one just outside the window, was emerging from the white of the canvas. Bottles of turpentine and tubes of paint were scattered on a low table. A smock hung from a peg and a couple of finished Gilda Donetti canvases were piled against a wall.

Sabina pointed to a small pottery urn on the mantel. "That's her," she said. "I know I should have given her a proper gravestone, but I'm selfish. I wanted her here. You must disapprove."

"A gravestone is for the living, not the dead. I think it should be up to you," Sweeney said kindly. But she shivered. There was something creepy about the shrine.

"Are you cold? I can get you a sweater."

"No, I'm okay." Sweeney went over to the window and looked out at the white emptiness. "I loved seeing your house, but I suppose I should really get going. I think they're expecting me back at the Wentworths'. I can walk Electra back if you'd like."

"That would be wonderful." Sabina shut off the light and closed the door behind them. "It's a huge house for one person, but I can't bear to sell it. I feel somehow as though I would lose her if I did." Downstairs, she helped Sweeney and Electra into their coats.

"It's silly," she continued saying as she showed them out. "But I haven't really moved on, I guess. Sometimes you don't. Or can't. We live so much in the past here. Do you know what I mean?"

"Yes," Sweeney said. "I think I do. I liked hearing your stories."

"Well. Come again. You'll be at the party?"

"Oh yes, the party. Saturday, right?"

"Yes. We look forward to it all year around here, though it's such hard work for Patch and Britta. If I think of it, I'll look through Gilda's things for notes on the relief."

Sweeney and Electra stepped out into the cold. It felt good to be out of the close atmosphere of the house.

"There was a lovely portrait of Rosemary upstairs," Sweeney said as they walked arm in arm along the snow-covered road. "It was fun to see it. She seems so much a part of things here."

"Yes. She does seem to fit right in, doesn't she. She's like her grandfather, I think. Has a real love for Byzantium. Emily—my daughter and Rosemary's mother—always hated it, found it stifling, couldn't wait to get away."

"It must have been hard having Marcus Granger for a father." Sweeney had been reading about the career of Marcus Granger. Though he had resisted the century's move away from realism and landscape painting, he had made quite a name for himself as a stalwart realist and larger-than-life personality. Bennett Dammers's book was full of stories about his famous temper.

Electra smiled flatly. "Yes. But I think it went beyond that for Emily. I think she found all of us hard, I think it was the colony."

"What do you mean?"

"Well, I think what I mean is that almost all of the colony children have had trouble of some sort. We thought we were giving them the best possible life, culture and interesting people and art and more art, and it turned out what they wanted was some kind of midwestern suburban life they could reject in the end."

They walked in silence for a few minutes, Electra leaning against Sweeney's proffered arm.

"It seems like Ruth Kimball must have been a nice woman," Sweeney said awkwardly.

"Well, you know, Ruth Kimball also had a difficult time with all of us, I think. I feel badly about it now. We all do, despite our appalling show at dinner the other night. But she didn't like us much, had this idea that the colony had exploited her ancestors or something. I really feel so *sad* about what happened to her, that we were the last people she saw. Poor Ruth. She was so *strange* that last day that we saw her."

"What do you mean, strange? What was it about her that was strange?"

"Well, of course we didn't actually talk to her, but Rosemary spotted her across the field, walking toward the cemetery. And then we realized that she had dropped her hat. Most unlike her, really. She wasn't the sort of person who dropped things. So I thought that she must have been hurrying or quite worried about something to have dropped it. We called out after her, but she was too far away to hear. It was quite inconvenient for us. The weather had gotten bad, and Rosemary had to go leave the hat on the back porch, so it wouldn't get buried by the snow. We almost got caught out in the storm. Of course, it all made sense later when we heard what had happened."

Sweeney was pondering this as they arrived at the front door of Electra Granger's big, federal-style house. Sweeney got her safely inside and was about to go when she looked down into the older woman's empty eyes and saw an unguarded nervousness pass across the pale, lined face. She wondered suddenly if blind people, unable to see emotions flit across other faces, sometimes forget to check their own facial reactions.

"My dear. I wonder if I couldn't give you a word of advice? Before you go?"

"Of course."

"We're very proud of our past here. Too proud sometimes, I think. We're also very protective of it. Be careful as you look around for skeletons in closets."

Sweeney was trying to think what to say when Electra Granger smiled, her face placid again. Then she raised her eyebrows impishly as she said, "It was lovely to chat with you. I'll see you Saturday at the Christmas party, when the Byzantium colonists come out in all their glory."

# SEVENTEEN

❦

SABINA DODGE STOOD at the window in the study, watching Sweeney and Electra walk down the driveway. Nice girl, smart, a bit uptight, but interesting just the same. "Very *unique*," Gilda would have said, with a raise of her eyebrows. *Unique*, pronounced with a bit of a French flourish, had been Gilda's highest form of praise and indication that she wanted to bring someone into their social circle. There had been a time when Sabina had felt jealous of those new girls, inevitably younger, prettier, breezier, so in awe of Gilda. But after a time, they had ceased to affect her much. She remembered one visit in particular, when a young sculptress had come to stay with them. Gilda had staged a seduction and been rebuffed. Sabina had never felt more powerful than when she had comforted her that night, Gilda had not handled aging particularly well. Anyway, she would have gotten a kick out of Sweeney.

Sabina straightened a bowl on the bookshelf and looked up at the wall. Seeing Gilda's paintings there calmed her, as though she was right up there, looking down on Sabina, winking the way she always had when they were in public. That private wink. It had been a truth of their relationship that no matter how left behind and ignored Sabina felt at Gilda's art openings or parties, a wink always brought her back, made her feel loved. She looked up at the wall again. Funny how Sweeney had picked out the relief right away, asked about it.

Sabina pottered around the room, neatening up the surfaces of bookcases and tables. As she was about to go, she looked up at the wall again. There was something strange about it . . . She had never noticed it before, but there was something about the piece of art that made her uneasy. She stared at it for a few moments but couldn't figure out what it was that bothered her and went into the kitchen to fix herself a drink.

She had fetched the mail earlier and placed it on the kitchen table, and as she sat down to read it, she caught sight of a small, hand-addressed envelope. It was the invitation to the Wentworths' Christmas party. It went without saying that she was invited, of course, but Britta liked to design the invitations every year. This one was a small red card with raised holly berries and the wording in silver calligraphy: "Please join us for our annual Holiday Fête. Britta and Patch Wentworth."

She remembered suddenly, with all the retrospective rapture of her advanced age, the first Christmas party she had been to at Birch Lane. She had been eighteen, madly in love but as yet uncertain of what plans Gilda had for her. This would have been, what? 1948. She had worn a new dress, bought and paid for with money she had received as a present upon finishing art school. She had met Gilda that fall at a seminar and had been much too pleased to be invited up for a weekend just before Christmas. Her parents—German immigrants who had been beaten down and diminished in health and spirit by the experience of being foreigners during the war—didn't pay much attention to what she did. She didn't suppose they would have had the imagination to think that anything might be wrong with the visit anyway. So she had gone, traveling alone on the train, filled with a rising fear and excitement.

She had not known what Gilda's intentions were until that night after the party. But before that there had been their magical walk through the snow, and then the house, filled with greenery and light and music. Herrick Gilmartin had kissed her hand and winked at Gilda. She had danced with so many men that night, her eyes locked with Gilda's. Gilda did not dance.

The parties were different now that Patch and Britta gave them. If she was honest, she had to admit that they seemed less natural, somehow, more staged, more *deliberate*. But that was Britta, of course. Poor Britta.

She propped the invitation up on the windowsill and sorted through the rest of the mail, then poured herself a gin and tonic. It was the cocktail hour. Outside the kitchen window, the sun was dropping on the horizon. The light was cold. This was the time of day she missed Gilda most, she decided. It was when Gilda had liked to take a break from painting and they would sit in the kitchen, talking or reading the paper, listening to the late afternoon radio news. It was the time of day when it was hardest to be alone.

# EIGHTEEN

❦

AFTER WALKING BACK to Sabina's to get her car, Sweeney drove back to the Wentworths'. As she went to turn into the driveway, she stopped and sat there for a moment with her eyes shut tight. When she opened them she could see through the naked trees the looming yellow house, and she felt suddenly that she couldn't go back yet. She swung the car around and drove much too fast along the road and over the bridge.

Once she was off The Island, Sweeney took a deep breath. She could go to the library instead, and look up J.L.B., then get a cup of coffee to celebrate this important discovery. A lot had happened. She now knew that Ruth Kimball wasn't the only one who thought there was something strange about Mary's death. She also knew that there was a good chance that Herrick Gilmartin, perhaps with the help of the mysterious J.L.B., was involved. She had made progress and she wanted some solitude to process it all.

Byzantium's downtown was bustling in the early afternoon. Shoppers in hats and heavy winter coats ducked in and out of storefronts, laden with shopping bags and children. There were tiny white lights in all the trees along the sidewalks, and red and green banners hung from the power lines, giving the downtown a festive look.

With the Rabbit safely parked in a lot behind Main Street, Sweeney strolled up to the library and found that it was closed until three. The little sign stared at her and she felt a swelling of frustration.

But then she remembered Ruth Kimball's name in the guest book at the historical society. At the very least, she could find out what Ruth Kimball had been reading in the months before her death.

There was a different librarian behind the desk today and Sweeney gave a little inward prayer of thanks. She filled out a request form for the Denholm files again and when the librarian—a teenage girl with a nose ring and a platinum crew cut—disappeared into the back room, she grabbed the pile of old request forms and flipped through them, congratulating the historical society for its inefficiency when she found slips from the previous May in the pile. When she reached July, she found Ruth Kimball's slip and copied down the number of the book she had requested on a new request form.

"Oh, thanks," she said when the girl came back with her files. "I just realized I need this book, too."

The girl looked exasperated, but went and retrieved a coffee-table-sized book, which she placed on the counter. Sweeney wanted to grab it and look through it right away, but she forced herself to stay calm and take the book and the files into the reading room.

She set them down on the table. The book, with its brown paper cover, seemed full of promise.

But the title page was a huge disappointment. "A Celebration of The Bicentennial of Byzantium's Settlement, 1769 to 1969." The pictures were all of town residents in late '60s minidresses and sideburns, celebrating the bicentennial of the town.

She looked through it carefully, but found nothing remotely related to Mary Denholm or the colony. Finally she gathered the materials together and took them back to the counter, then went dejectedly out onto the street.

She spent an hour in and out of the small boutiques and gift shops, buying Christmas presents and browsing. In one, she bought Toby a cashmere scarf and a set of silver bangle bracelets for herself. In a kitchen store, she bought a blue ceramic pitcher for Britta and Patch and mugs for each of the children. The mugs, plain on the outside, had tiny ceramic animals squatting in the bottom and they cheered her somehow, with their grim creature faces.

She found relief in her shopping, and by the time she wandered into the Well Read Bookstore, she was feeling moderately happy and desperate for caffeine. The cafe in the bookstore obliged with a passable latte, and she sipped while she read a women's magazine, an indulgence that felt justified after what she considered a fruitful morning and an even more fruitful afternoon to come.

Finally it was three, and she went back to the library and made a beeline for the art section where she sat down on the floor and flipped madly through the indexes of all the books on Byzantium.

It was only after Sweeney had looked through the indexes of all of the books on the Byzantium Colony that she realized how much she'd been counting on discovering the identity of J.L.B. within their pages. But not a single one of them offered up an artist with those initials. When she looked in Bennett Dammers's book, under the lists of studio assistants who had served under Morgan, there were only three listed for the summer of 1890. They were Myra Benton, Andrew Lordley, and Franco Quatrelli. No matter how she rearranged their initials, not one of them could be J.L.B.

She'd come to a dead end.

# NINETEEN

❧

"DAMN IT, SWEENEY, where have you been?" Toby demanded as she came in through the kitchen to find them all sitting around the table.

"I'm sorry. I lost track of time." She looked from Patch to Britta. "I decided to go downtown after Sabina's and before I knew it, it was dark."

But Toby didn't let her finish. "How do you think it made us feel when we called Sabina's and she said you'd left hours ago. In case you haven't heard, the police are saying now that Ruth Kimball was murdered. What do you think I imagined when you didn't come back?" His black eyes were furious behind his glasses.

"Toby, Toby, calm down," Patch said soothingly. "She's okay. That's what matters."

Sweeney looked up to find Ian watching them. She flushed and felt a lump of anger rise up in her throat.

"I'm not five, Toby, and I would hope that you would have imagined me taking care of myself, because that's exactly what I do." It struck her that despite his protestations the night before, he believed there was something in all this, and that he believed she was in danger. And suddenly she felt awful and she wanted to tell him she was sorry.

Embarrassed, Patch said, "Why don't we all go into the living room and leave you two."

"No, that's all right," Sweeney said, and turned to Toby. "Can we go for a drive or something? I want to talk to you."

He nodded and they put on their coats in silence and went

out to the Rabbit. Driving gave her something to do as she decided what she wanted to say and they were almost to the Kimballs' house before she started, "I'm sorry. I should have called and told you guys I was downtown."

"Yeah, especially after all the stuff last night about someone being willing to kill Ruth Kimball to keep her quiet." That was sarcastic.

She waited a moment until he had calmed down and then, because she was embarrassed, she blurted out, all at once, the words tumbling over and over each other, "What I'm really sorry about is last night. You were right. I put you in a really bizarre position and the thing is, I like Rosemary and I like how you are with her and I want it to work out. But I can't help it if I'm jealous or whatever it is that I am. I shouldn't have said anything."

They drove over the bridge and Sweeney pulled the car over into a little turnout overlooking the brook.

"Yeah, that seems to be the way you and I do things," Toby said. They were quiet for a moment and then he went on, "When I . . . last summer, I don't think you knew how hard it was for me to see you. You made it out that you were the victim in all of it, that I was wrong to have told you. I don't know why I let you do that. I didn't say anything, but maybe I should have. And then, I just . . . it kind of gradually went away. I replaced it with something else and I was okay. I met Rosemary and it was the first time I'd even felt *anything* for anybody other than you. In a long time."

She listened to the brook rushing beneath them. The night was still. "I know that. And that's good." There was nothing else to say. She felt like laughing. Toby just looked at her.

"Do you think that maybe this whole thing means something? That it means you're ready for, I don't know, a normal relationship? With a man who doesn't already know that you eat condensed milk out of the can with a spoon?" The car's headlights bounced off an evergreen tree in front of them, shining on Toby's face. He was grinning.

"Is that what Dr. Berg would say?" Toby, whose mother

had put him in psychoanalysis when he was eleven, always had a Dr. Berg.

"No, you don't want to know what Dr. Berg has to say."

She started up the car. "What? Does Dr. Berg think I'm screwed up?"

"Very." They laughed. "Are you okay?"

"Yes." She wasn't yet, but she would be.

As they pulled into the driveway, he said, "Hey, what did you find out today? Anything interesting?"

She told him about the relief at Sabina's house and asked if he'd ever heard of anyone associated with the colony with the initials J.L.B.

"I don't think so, but you should ask Patch. He'd know."

Sweeney knew she wouldn't do that. She said, "I don't know. I'm ready for a break from Mary's gravestone."

"You should come skiing with us tomorrow then. We're taking the kids, I think. It'll be fun."

"Okay. Sounds good. I'm terrible, though. I might break my neck."

"Don't worry. I'll look after you." He smiled. "I always do."

# TWENTY

*December 17*

IT WAS BRIGHT and clear the next morning, a perfect skiing day. Outside Sweeney's bedroom window, the disembodied sky, a brilliant slippery, shiny blue, seemed to hang in suspension. She stared at it, half-conscious, until a passing cloud, as vague as a puff of breath in frozen air, broke her gaze.

Outside, after breakfast, they organized skis and cars. There wasn't room for everybody in the Rabbit, so it was decided that Toby would take Britta's Land Rover with Gwinny and the twins and all of the equipment.

"I'll go with Sweeney," Rosemary said.

Toby looked concerned for a moment, until Sweeney said, "Yes, good. It will give us time to talk about Toby," and he flashed her a grateful smile.

"Can I ask you something?" Rosemary said, as they passed a development of condominiums hugging the sides of the mountain. Sweeney slowed down behind an old station wagon, crawling improbably up the hill.

"Sure."

"What do you think about Toby and me?" Sweeney turned her head and saw that she was blushing, and Sweeney felt herself blush back.

But she could say honestly, "I think it's great. I'm really happy for you guys."

"He's lovely. I just keep wondering if it's just that we're on holiday, you know. And if I should be careful not to get too involved."

"Well, I can tell you that Toby takes things seriously. He always has. I don't think he would be involved at all if he wasn't serious about it. I don't know if that helps."

"Thank you," Rosemary said, smiling. "I'm a bit out of practice. I haven't dated in ages and I've kind of forgotten what you're supposed to do and not do. I asked him if he wanted to have lunch with Granny and me and then I panicked that he might think I was trying to rope him." She laughed. "See how muddled up about it all I am?"

"I wouldn't worry about that," Sweeney said, laughing, too. "Toby's usually the one who's inviting people to meet his mom after the first date."

They drove in silence for a while before Rosemary said, "And what about you? Is it my imagination or is there something going on between you and Ian?"

"Ian?"

"I thought I detected something. On his side anyway."

"I don't think so. Actually, he's been driving me a little crazy. Does he seem odd to you?"

"Other than the fact that he's English?"

Sweeney laughed. "You don't think there's something kind of sinister about him?"

"Sinister? I think he has a crush on you."

Sweeney blushed. "It feels more like he wants to kill me."

"What?" Rosemary looked shocked.

"No, I'm kidding. I don't know . . . it's just that you know when someone's always watching you and, I don't know, keeping track of you. That's how it feels. He's keeping track of me."

"I still think he has a crush on you."

Sweeney didn't say anything. She hadn't considered that possibility.

They skied all morning, Toby and the kids off on the expert slopes and Sweeney and Rosemary trying to stay upright on the easier runs. Sweeney hadn't skied for five or six years, but she remembered the basics and after a couple of runs felt that she was starting to improve. By the time they met Toby,

Gwinny, Trip, and Gally for lunch in the lodge, she felt pleasantly exhausted.

They all skied together in the afternoon and after a couple of runs, she found herself riding the lift up the mountain with Gally. He was a good skier—the best of the three kids, really, though Trip was more daring—and she told him so as they cleared the lodge and moved slowly up the mountain, the wind blowing tiny crystals of snow around his head, leaving it in his hair like glitter.

"Thanks," he said, and then lapsed into silence.

She had no idea what his eyes were doing behind his sunglasses, and she sensed that he didn't want to talk. But she went on anyway.

"Do you like being home for Christmas, or do you miss school?"

"It's all right, I guess. I don't really have a choice."

That was true. "This is a pretty cool place to spend Christmas. It must have been a fun place to grow up."

He said, "It was when I was little. We used to go swimming and hiking all the time and stuff. My dad used to come with us all the time. My mom even used to ski. She was really good."

"She doesn't do that stuff anymore?"

"No, because then she'd have to spend time with my dad."

"Oh."

She said impulsively, " "I remember how weird it was to be seventeen. It does feel like things kind of fall apart, doesn't it? Everything gets so much more complicated."

"No," he said cryptically. "I think things are the same. I think you just begin to see them the way they really are, to see things you couldn't see before. People can't fool you anymore."

They had reached the top of the mountain and in a quick, graceful motion he lifted the bar and dropped down on to the snow, leaving Sweeney fumbling for her poles. She jumped off, too, but promptly fell onto the snow, cursing the sport of skiing and wondering about Gally.

• • •

They got back to the house in the late afternoon and show-ered and changed to go out to dinner at Les Deux Canards, Patch and Britta's favorite restaurant in Byzantium.

As they were getting ready to go, Sweeney said, "It's really weird. I've lost my emerald earrings. You guys haven't found them, have you?"

"Those ones you were wearing at dinner?" Gwinny asked. "I liked those."

"I'll look around for them," Britta said. "Maybe you just misplaced them. They were lovely." Her voice was cheerful, but Sweeney thought she saw worry in her eyes.

Les Deux Canards, housed in a perfectly restored Georgian mansion on Byzantium's Main Street, reminded Sweeney of a combination of a Savoy Raclette restaurant she'd eaten in once and The Cock and Lamb, her favorite pub in Oxford. As a student, she'd often settled into a snug at the back to read and drink pints of Guinness, something her English friends had ribbed her for. The library was for coursework, pubs were for socializing, they'd said. On her last trip to Oxford, Sweeney had been dismayed to find that The Cock and Lamb was now a nightclub called—bizarrely but nod-ding to tradition—The Rooster.

The walls of this cozy little bar and restaurant were pa-pered in a cream and blue fleur-de-lis pattern and covered with landscape paintings and old photographs of the Byzan-tium artists. The long bar up at the front was ornate, a rich, dark mahogany, and at eight o'clock it was cluttered with skiers and end-of-the-workday revelers. The men seemed all to have beards and work boots and expensive jackets, and there were a lot of beautiful, earthy women with long hair.

In the car on the way to the restaurant Britta had told Sweeney that it was all over town now that Ruth Kimball hadn't committed suicide. "Gwinny was supposed to baby-sit for a family we know tonight. But they called this after-noon to say they wouldn't be needing her after all. I felt just sick. We haven't done anything!" She'd sounded as though she was about to cry.

As they'd come into the restaurant, there had been a strange, halting moment in which conversation had slowed and a few people had turned to watch them enter. Sweeney felt the attention of everyone in the room focus on them as they made their way to a table in the back. "Everyone's staring at us," Gwinny had whispered to them.

Once they were seated, Patch said quietly, "Let's have a good time. We haven't done anything wrong. We don't care what people think."

"Hey, look Gwinny," Trip said, looking at the menu. "Sweetbreads. That's brains. You should get some. Maybe it would make you smarter." He was sitting on Sweeney's other side and had been telling her about boarding school life and playing Nathan Detroit in the school's production of *Guys and Dolls*.

"Fuck you," Gwinny said nonchalantly. The twins laughed.

"Gwinny!" Britta gave her a stern look.

"I bet Ian will get sweetbreads," Sweeney told Gwinny in a loud stage whisper. "English people like all kinds of disgusting innards and brains and things. Tripe. Trotters."

Gwinny giggled.

"Only those brains belonging to American professors," Ian, who was sitting directly across from them, countered loudly, winking at Sweeney. He was making an effort to cheer them all up, she realized, and it made her warm to him.

"Because we have the best brains, is that it?" She nudged Gwinny, who laughed again.

"Yes, the brains of art historians are known to be particularly delicious. A bit tough sometimes from so much thinking, but nonetheless ..." The waitress appeared over his shoulder and everyone looked down at their menus again.

After they had ordered, Toby asked Ian about his job.

"Basically, I look for pieces that are very valuable whose owners don't know they're very valuable. I'm a bit of a confidence man, really. I don't ever want to be dishonest with anybody, but my profit margin depends on my being able to acquire something for less than it's worth."

"Ian makes himself sound like some kind of crook," Patch said. "The truth is that he's probably the most respected decorative arts guy in Britain. He headed up a commission last year that did a survey of decorative arts in country estates. It was a really important piece of work."

Gwinny took a sip of her father's wine and said, "No offense, Ian, but how did you get so interested in lamps and stuff? It isn't even art really, is it?"

Ian leaned back in his chair. "Think of it the way you think of Sweeney's gravestones. You have to have furniture, right? But what the really fine craftsmen and their workshops did was to turn it into an art. Creating a leg wasn't just about making something for the table to stand on, it was about making it the most functional and beautiful leg they could make it."

He looked over at Sweeney and smiled.

"I'm interested in that," Patch said, warming to the topic. "When you study a gravestone, are you studying it as a piece of art or a piece of anthropology? I mean, there are other media for artistic expression that are easier to work with than gravestones."

"It's art *and* anthropology. Many stonecarvers didn't have those media available to them," Sweeney said. "In America they were frequently European immigrants who had trained as sculptors back home. They carved some beautiful stones. For families who could afford special commissions, but also for families who couldn't. I like to think of them like Amish quilts. The women who made them weren't allowed to be artists. But when they created functional things like quilts, they really let loose and made things of beauty."

"What do you mean when you say art history?" Gwinny asked.

Gally said meanly, "It's the history of art, stupid."

Gwinny made an extremely unattractive face in his direction, but Ian turned to her and said kindly, "It's the study of how art has developed over the years. From cave paintings in France to Andy Warhol. Art historians trace the different movements, how one led to another and how artists reacted against, say, paintings they thought were too fancy and formal by making paintings that were more natural, that recreated nature without embellishment."

"Oh," Gwinny said. "But cave paintings aren't considered real art, are they? It's just drawings of buffalo and stuff."

"But they are absolutely art," Ian said, with feeling. "The people who painted animals on the insides of caves were painting what was familiar to them. Animals were their means of survival, they were sacred, and those cave painters drew them with loving detail, the same way the Renaissance painters would labor over every detail of the background in a painting of a madonna and child."

"But what is it for?" Gwinny asked. "I like looking at art and everything, but what is it for, other than being pretty?"

It struck Sweeney that Gwinny was acting out by questioning the usefulness of art. In this family, it was the equivalent of questioning capitalism in a family where the business was banking.

"It's for a lot of things," Sweeney said now. "For one thing, it tells us a lot about what was going on at a particular time. How people lived, what kind of houses they lived in, what kind of bowls they ate out of. Art as anthropology. When I study gravestones and things like Victorian mourning rings or Egyptian funeral practices, I learn a lot about how people felt about death.

"But that's only part of it, I think. Art is also about representing the sublime, or at least it should be. When you look at a beautiful painting, you feel that you know what feeling or atmosphere the artist was trying to capture. You experience something that's true."

The food came quickly and she ate silently for a few minutes before she looked up to find Ian staring at her.

"Have you heard anything about the little girl?" he asked after an awkward moment. "I wonder how she's doing?"

"The little girl? Oh, you mean Mrs. Kimball's granddaughter. You'd have to ask Patch. She can't be doing very well."

"Children that age react to things in funny ways. They're

very good at deflection. At least my daughter is."

"You have a daughter? I didn't know." She felt herself blush.

"Her mother and I are divorced and they live in Paris," Ian said quickly. "I don't see her as much as I'd like, but . . ."

"What's her name?"

"Eloise."

"That's pretty. I had a French friend named Eloise when I was at Oxford."

"Oxford," he said. "Well, I shall have to watch my back. I was at Cambridge. You Oxonians are notoriously treacherous, you know."

"I was only there for a few years," Sweeney said, grinning at him. "Doing graduate work. Maybe it doesn't count."

The waitress came over with another scotch for Ian and he took a long sip as Patch said something at the other end of the table that made everyone laugh.

"What part of England are you from? I'm good at accents and I guessed London," Sweeney asked.

"Ha! Sussex. But I did have a strange and unsettled up-bringing that included British schools in some of the most peculiar outposts of the world. When one has been taught by unhappy, exiled Londoners, one's accent tends to come to the middle after a bit."

"Why did you move around so much?" She looked up and down the table guiltily. She had felt for a second that they were alone.

"My father worked for what he called 'The Government,' but was actually British Intelligence. He was always going off on hush-hush little jaunts. Sometimes we went with him."

"Where?"

"Belgium for a year. Then Egypt. And then Lebanon. Then military school and France, when I was older. That's where I met Sylvie. Eloise's mother."

"That sounds so romantic. I had a roving, unsettled child-hood, too, but we just roamed around backwater American cities. What happened with Sylvie?" Being tipsy made her brave.

"Oh. I don't know." He was uncomfortable. "The usual. We were too young. We grew apart. She fell in love with her psychiatrist."

"Really?"

"Yes. Now let me ask you something. How did you get your name?"

"My mother was an actress. She had this thing about old Irish legends."

He grinned at her. "Mad Sweeney?"

"I know. I think she just liked the name, the way it sounded."

"It suits you, you know, in an odd sort of way." He studied her for a minute and she felt her heart speed up under his gaze. "I'm not quite sure why. Are your parents still alive?"

She looked down at her plate. "My father's dead. I don't see much of my mother anymore."

"I'm sorry, I didn't mean to pry."

"No, that's fine." But it was the end of the conversation. They finished their meals and lingered over dessert and coffee. They were waiting for Patch to finish paying the bill up at the bar when an older man, very drunk, stood up and turned his back to them.

"Some people have a lot of nerve," he said loudly to the bartender. "Coming down here when the cops are still sniffing around up on The Island. When old Cooper proves that one of them did her in, I'd just like to see if they have the guts to show their faces around her friends."

The bar got very quiet as Britta gasped and hustled the children out of the restaurant. Before she joined them out on the sidewalk, Sweeney saw Patch step toward the man as though he was going to say something, then put his wallet back in his coat as he followed them through the door.

Everyone had gone to bed. Sweeney lay on the couch in the living room with a glass of scotch, listening to the end of the "Hallelujah Chorus." Someone had put it on and she had no idea where the stereo was. The music seemed to come out of the walls and ceilings and floors.

So she just let it play. *Hallelujah! Hallelujah! Hall-ay-loooo-ya!* She had never much liked Handel. She'd take Mozart's *Requiem* any day.

"Feeling Christmasy?"

She jumped. Ian was standing behind her, still wearing the too-crisp black jeans and taupe sweater he'd had on at dinner. "You scared me," she said, sitting up.

"Sorry." He went over to the little bar and poured himself a scotch. "One thing about Patch. He knows his scotch. I try to send him a bottle of something interesting every once in awhile. The last bottle was Royal Brackla. Very nice. Want to try some?"

"Sure." She drained her glass and held it out for him. He frowned, put it face down on the bar and got her a new one. "Musn't mix our scotch up," he said. He was clearly drunk.

"It's lovely," she told him after taking a sip. "Smoky and kind of peaty."

"It's one thing I hate about traveling. I always feel like I have to sneak around and keep my own bottle in my room. So," he said, sitting down across from her. "Oxford. I should probably challenge you to a duel or something. You know, in the defense of dear old Cambridge."

"Really? Do you duel? Wonders never cease."

"Oh yes. All Englishmen learn to duel. It's very important." He got up and pretended to joust with the bookcase.

"I'm too drunk for a duel," Sweeney said.

"So am I too drunk, come to think of it." He went over to the bookcase and looked at the books, then picked up a little antique pistol that was lying on an ivory plate. "This is what I love about the Wentworths," he said. "This is just the sort of thing they would have. What is this anyway?"

"Looks like an itsy bitsy gun," Sweeney said.

He jabbed at the air with it. "On guard!" Then he saw her face and put it down. "Oh God! That's tasteless." He sat down again. "Forgive my boyish exuberance. We can't keep it down, all those years of pretend war at military school."

He raised his eyebrows at her. "So, Toby was pretty angry at you yesterday."

She sat up. "Oh, that? He's just really emotional. He likes to play Papa Bear. We've made up already."

Ian just watched her and it made her stumble ahead. "Toby and I have been friends for a long time . . . how do I explain it? You know how there are things that happen to you that are so overwhelming, so awful or beautiful or whatever, that whoever is with you when they happen is forever locked up in you?" Ian nodded. "Anyway, he's just an emotional person."

Ian smiled. "I don't know. As a fellow man, I can say that we don't take shows of emotion like that lightly."

"Well, you're an Englishman. Toby's the hot-blooded Mediterranean type. Though, I have to say, you talk a lot for an Englishman."

"Do I? I had no idea, I really didn't. Do you really think I do? Really? That's odd."

She laughed, and spotted *The Collected Robert Frost* on the bookshelf.

"Hand me that," she said, pointing to it. "I want to read that poem you were reciting. That day." He hesitated, then got it down for her. It was one called *Desert Places*, she saw when she looked up the first line in the index. She began reading aloud, finishing with the lines, *"They cannot scare me with their empty spaces/Between stars—on stars where no human race is./I have it in me so much nearer home/To scare myself with my own desert places."*

He had his back to her and his shoulders seemed suddenly fragile. She was silent for a moment.

Then she asked, "What's your daughter like? Eloise?"

He turned around. "She's very small and dark and Sylvie keeps her hair cut in a pageboy. Like this," he said, drawing a line across his forehead and down the sides of his face. "And she can be very serious and sort of melancholy. For a while I was terrified it was the divorce, but then I realized it's just the way she is. Sometimes she looks at me and I think she feels sorry for me.

"But she can be silly, too. She has a stuffed cat called Pierre and she likes to go for walks in the park and as much as I would like to think she does, I don't think she really likes museums. She doesn't find them *useful* somehow. I think she will probably grow up to be a successful business-woman. I adore her."

Sweeney smiled at him.

"Did you like England?" he asked. then, taking off his glasses and polishing them on the hem of his sweater. "A lot of Americans can't take it. Too rainy. People take so long to know you."

"I loved it. But then I'm sort of a gloomy, rainy person to begin with."

"Isn't it funny how we still talk about national character, even in our very global world?"

"Yes. I do think of the English as a type, though it isn't strictly true. You, for example, are both the quintessential Englishmen and not a very typical one at all."

He studied her again in a way that was becoming familiar, with serious eyes and a slight smile. "And you, I think, pos-sess the best of the American type without the more unat-tractive bits. You're industrious, but you aren't simple. I suppose that's not a very nice thing to say."

"No. Lots of us are simple. And smug. But isn't that the point about Americans? We aren't a type."

They went on like this for some time before he stopped and looked at her.

"Why don't you see your mother anymore?" he asked after a minute.

"My mother? Oh, that's very complicated." Sweeney felt her stomach muscles clamp together. "My mother is . . . sick," she said stiffly. "We just don't . . . We've lost touch is all."

She could tell that he wished he hadn't asked from the way he fidgeted and quickly changed the subject. "So why did you leave? If you liked England so much."

She looked down at the glass in her hands. "You really want to know?"

"Yes."

"I was dating this man. He was Irish, from the west, near Galway, though he'd been born in the north. He told me once that his father had asked his mother to marry him by saying, 'Would you like to be buried with my people?' I always loved that.

"Anyway, he was at Oxford. Reading history, and we met in the library. We wanted the same book, but he got there first and he said that I could have it if I let him take me out for a pint."

"What was the book?"

"Oh, a Yeats bio. I was writing something about epitaphs. He was writing something about the Irish Revival."

"That's right, Yeats's epitaph. *Horseman, pass by.* Isn't that right?" Sweeney nodded. "So what happened with your Irishman? Did you have a fight? Did you run away?" He made two fingers of his right hand, like little feet running. On his face was a strange mixture of concern and interest.

"No." For some reason she smiled.

"What?"

"He died," she said. "In a bombing on the London tube. His name was Colm."

"I'm sorry. I had no idea." He got up and took his shot glass over to the bar. "Of all the moronic . . . Can you forgive me?"

But she couldn't stop herself.

"This was a year ago, the one where they never figured out who it was. He had some things to do in London and I went up with him for the day. It was January and I remember it was really cold. We had this drafty little flat and I remember that when we woke up that morning, we could see our breath in the bedroom." As she talked, Sweeney realized that she hadn't told anyone the story since she'd told it to the police. No one had ever asked her. Even Toby had never asked her to tell him about that day.

"Anyway, I went to the Tate and then I had lunch in a pub while he did an interview with someone for his thesis. The cream they gave me for my coffee was sour. I remember

that. I was supposed to meet him on the platform at Picca-
dilly Circus and then we were going to have dinner with
some friends. He was late, but it didn't matter. I had a book
and I sat on the platform and read. Then the train came and
it was the strangest thing, when I think about it now, it's as
though it came rolling in, kind of in slow motion. I can
remember seeing the lights down the tunnel and feeling the
wind, you know the way you do? The train came slowly,
and I was searching the windows for Colm, to see if I could
see him, and for some reason I have this memory of seeing
him, standing at one of the windows, but I don't think I did,
because the train wasn't even all the way in before there was
this *sound*. I can't even describe it, it was just this sucking,
breathing sound and then a hollow boom, and fire burst out
of the tunnel and we all ran.

"That was the only reason that those of us on the platform
weren't killed too, that the train, the compartment where the
bomb was, wasn't all the way in before it went off. I was
burned. My . . . my arm. You can't see it anymore. I didn't
know for a while if he was even on the train, I . . . but they
found his wallet and then, well later they knew. But it's
weird, I still have that memory of seeing him in the window.
It's made me mistrust my own mind."

Ian was watching her and in the strange light from the
lamp near the couch, he looked very pale.

"We were going to get married," she continued.

"That was when Toby and I got . . . what did I say?
Locked up together? He came to Oxford. Took a semester
off school. Gave up his tuition money and everything. He
propped me up for months."

"Sweeney . . ." He was pleading with her.

Suddenly she found that she was irritated at herself, for
telling him about Colm, for letting herself relax around him,
for whatever it was he wanted from her.

"People involved with me always seem to end up dying,"
she said, putting her drink down and getting to her feet. "You
should be careful."

# TWENTY-ONE

*December 18*

"BUT IT'S SUCH A long drive to Cambridge, Sweeney. You won't get down there until almost eleven," Britta said. "And the Christmas party's on Saturday. We wanted you to be here for the party."

"Oh, I'll be back tomorrow," Sweeney said nervously. "It's just that if I don't have this meeting, I don't know when I'll be able to do it again. And there are a couple of errands I need to do while I'm down there. I suddenly realized I don't have anything to wear to the party." She gulped her coffee and tried to smile. Everyone else was still in their pajamas around the kitchen table, but thinking it would make it harder for them to argue with her announcement that she was going home for a day, she'd come down dressed and ready to go.

"If it's just the dress, you'd be welcome to borrow something," Britta said looking confused.

"Oh no, it's really this meeting. I know I'll be able to enjoy Christmas more if I can get it out of the way."

"Who is it you're meeting with?" Toby asked slyly. He knew her too well not to be suspicious.

"Oh, um, John Philips." John Philips taught Modern Art and though she couldn't think of a single good reason she'd have to meet with him seven days before Christmas, his was the first name that came to mind.

Toby looked skeptical.

"Well as long as you promise you'll be back for the

party," Patch said. "You haven't lived until you've been to a Byzantium Christmas party."

"I promise." She took her coffee cup to the sink and rinsed it out. "See you all tomorrow."

Ian nodded at her as she went out the door and she nodded back, embarrassed.

The day was a good one for driving, the sun bright and clean on the white snow and as she headed south, past rest stops and gas stations and fast food restaurants, Vermont and the events of the past few days began to recede. The colony seemed suddenly a distant, rich dream from another time, hardly relevant.

Murder! Detection! It sounded silly now that she was speeding along, Ella Fitzgerald and Louis Armstrong on the tape player doing *Can't We Be Friends*. Ruth Kimball had killed herself. In the bright light of day, the act seemed commonplace, like the ones you read about on the inside pages of the newspaper.

But yet . . . But yet, she felt she had to follow the string that had been offered to her when the librarian at the Historical Society had told her Myra Benton's journal was in Boston. Maybe it was the academic researcher inside her who was driving her on, but she felt compelled to follow the trail and it was just possible that there was something in the journal that might lead her to the truth. Something about Herrick Gilmartin, something about the unnamed J.L.B. She had called Bennett Dammers the night before, while everyone was getting ready for dinner and asked him if he had ever heard of a student with those initials.

"No, I don't think so," he had said in his quavering voice. "He's not in my book, you said? No. If you knew the name . . ."

But, of course, that was the whole problem. She didn't know the name.

She reached Medford by eleven and, after getting on 28, made it through Somerville and into Cambridge in good time, since there wasn't much traffic.

The yard and the rest of the campus were peaceful with

most of the students gone and Sweeney parked just off Quincy Street and found Marlise, her favorite Fine Arts Library librarian, sitting at the front desk looking bored.

"Hi, Marlise," she whispered. "How are you?" Marlise had dredlocks and a tiny pink gemstone in the side of her nose.

"Hey, Sweeney, I thought you were gone for Christmas."

"Yeah, I am. Sort of. It's a long story. Anyway, I'm trying to get hold of a collection of family papers donated to the library by Piers Benton. It would have been in 1960, somewhere around there. His mother was the sculptor Myra Benton. It's mostly her stuff."

"Hang on." Marlise tapped at the keys of her computer, and peered at the screen. "Oh yeah. Here it is—456778. Why don't you go sit down and I'll bring it over to you. It's a big box."

Sweeney sat down in her regular spot, a table tucked into an alcove under a big skylight, and spread out her notebook and a few new pens, ready for the ritual of research.

"Okay, this is it," Marlise said a few minutes later, leaving a large box on the table. "You've got . . ." She checked her watch. "An hour-and-a-half. Vacation hours."

"Oh, that's right. Thanks, Marlise. This shouldn't take too long."

Sweeney opened the box, conscious that she'd have to hurry. The first item was a copy of a letter from Piers Benton to the trustees of the University libraries dated April sixth, 1963. It stated that he was donating his mother's personal papers to the University and went on to say that she would have been happy to know that future students had access to them.

Next was a stack of photographs. Sweeney leafed through them quickly, noting familiar faces: Morgan, Gilmartin, and some of the others. She would get to them later. Right now, she was impatient to see what the journals offered up, so she put the pictures aside and took the first leather book from the pile of ten or twelve similar volumes.

It appeared that Myra Benton had begun keeping her

journal in 1886 as an art student in Philadelphia. Sweeney read carefully, enjoying the developing writing style of the obviously intelligent young woman, but growing impatient with her verbosity.

Finally.

> *June 10, 1888. We arrived into the Suffolk train station at about 9 o'clock, having slept well overnight despite the incessant ramblings of a fellow passenger who I suspected had been at the sherry most of the evening. I awakened at 7, when the sun shone through the sleeper car window and on to my berth and when I raised the shade, I saw outside the great form of the Green River and looking into its seafoam depths, I could see from whence the name had come. Beyond were hills as green as England and little farms where cattle dotted the fields. Mrs. Morgan rapped on my door before I was done dressing and when I told her I would be there in a moment, she snapped that she had been up for two hours already and that if I was going to learn to be useful in Byzantium, I would learn to rise earlier, the way the country people did. She is a terrible woman and no one at the Academy thinks she is the equal of her husband.*
>
> *As to her dear husband, he was there when we pulled into the station and kissed me once on each cheek in the European style when I got off the train. When he tried to kiss her, his own wife, she told him it had been a long journey and that it was his fault for insisting she travel with me.*
>
> *There is so much to tell, I hardly know where to begin! We drove in a smart carriage through Suffolk, a bustling little town where there are a great many factories and shops that turn out all manner of engines and machines. Dearest Bryn told me that I ought to come with him some day and see the women at work in the factories. He said it is quite amazing and that they work very hard and make their own money. We*

*followed the river out of Suffolk and started for By-*
*zantium. All along the way, field turned to forest and*
*then to field again, the green pastures dotted with*
*wildflowers and lilacs. A very sad-eyed creature,*
*standing in the road, forced us to stop so as not to hit*
*it and I recognized it as a milk cow, which Bryn said*
*I would see lots of in Vermont and I had an idea for*
*a piece featuring a milk maid, sitting by her cow. Bryn*
*said there were lots of local girls who were willing to*
*pose for the artists.*

*The house is heavenly, a white palace covered with*
*climbing vines and Mrs. Morgan's famous gardens all*
*around. They really are beautiful, sculpted out of the*
*land, the pink and blue and red and yellow spots of*
*color like a French painting. Bryn took me to the stu-*
*dio and showed me what I am to do. He said he was*
*glad to see me and that he thinks I will enjoy Byzan-*
*tium, then took me back to the house to meet Mr. Gil-*
*martin, the painter, who is only just out of the*
*Academy and very handsome and looks at one as*
*though he could see right through your skin and bones*
*and clothes. He and his wife have only recently built*
*a house over on The Island. I also met the Morgan*
*girls, Gwenda and Martha, who are cunning and*
*bright, with mischievous spirits. I think we will be*
*great friends.*

*My room is on the third floor, next to the servants,*
*which doesn't bother me, though Bryn said he felt aw-*
*fully about it, but the house is so full there were no*
*other rooms. It is very quiet, compared to the city, and*
*at night I lie in bed and listen to the sounds of insects*
*through the open window and smell the lilacs on the*
*air.*

Sweeney read on for a few pages, as Myra Benton described
her work in the studio—mixing clay and sweeping seemed
to be her main responsibilities—and a party at Upper

Pastures that she described with gusto. But it wasn't until
July third that something really interesting happened.

> *. . . Bryn took me into Suffolk to buy drink for the In-*
> *dependence Day party at Upper Pastures and on the*
> *way back we came upon Miss Mary Denholm walking*
> *along the Suffolk Road. She is the daughter of Louis*
> *Denholm, who lives next-door to Gilmartin's home*
> *Birch Lane, on The Island, and she is quite an*
> *interesting-looking girl, not exactly beautiful, but she*
> *contains beauty if such a thing can be said of some-*
> *one. And she chooses when to let it out, I think.*
>
> *She is quite thin and pale, though womanly, with*
> *remarkable, coiling dark hair like an Irish princess*
> *and haunted eyes the color of coal.*
>
> *She had the sleeves of her dress turned up and was*
> *perspiring and covered with dust from the road and*
> *when we stopped and offered her a ride, she smiled*
> *broadly and said she'd be glad of one since it was so*
> *hot. I judged her to be about 16 years of age and*
> *immediately thought of her for my Juliet piece, with*
> *her fine dark hair tumbling down around her face.*
> *When I mentioned it to Bryn later, he said that Gil-*
> *martin had also seen the potential in her and asked*
> *her parents if she might pose sometime.*

Throughout the rest of that summer of 1888, there were hardly any mentions of Mary, except for a reference to a picnic
upon the mountain which she came along on and which included Gilmartin, Morgan, and some of the children.

Thankfully, Sweeney was able to skim quickly over the
parts of the diary which were not about Byzantium and after
a somewhat exhaustive description of the end of the school
year and what appeared to have been a brief love affair and
a broken engagement, the account picked up again in a new
volume dated June third, 1889.

> *It is good to be back in Byzantium after a year away*
> *and all the trouble of these past months. I have vowed*

*not to think of Arthur and when Bryn saw me on the stairs this morning and said "Will Mr. Pettengill be coming for a visit this summer, Myra," in that twinkly, insinuating way of his, I looked him right in the eyes and told him that there was no possibility of it. He looked sad for me, but did not say anything.*

*I must work harder than ever before now. My work must be my life and my life my work, and I must throw myself into the discipline and application of my skill. Bryn knows this and he will understand it without my telling him.*

*Though I am not the same woman I was last summer, dear Byzantium is as ever she was. There is a new flowerbed at Upper Pastures and Mrs. Morgan has planted it with foxglove and lilies and delphiniums. We are to have dinner at Birch Lane on The Island tonight, and Bryn tells me that Gilmartin has changed the house extensively over the spring and made it quite modern. As I was unpacking my clothes, I saw a lovely portrait hanging on the wall and recognized the subject at once as Miss Mary Denholm and the painter as Mr. Gilmartin. When I asked Bryn about it later, he said that she had been doing quite a bit of modeling for them all and revealed herself as a willing and untiring subject. He said I should let her know if I required her services.*

*June 4, 1889—I am quite myself again, dear diary. The fresh country air and beauty all around me have convinced me to live again and Bryn said he can hardly tell the difference between me and the local girls who help in the kitchen.*

*June 15, 1889—It is a rainy, despairing morning and I and the girls and Mrs. Morgan have settled into the drawing room with a fire until it clears. After lunch, I will help with casting in the studio, for Bryn is*

*finishing his Proserpine and has dedicated himself to
its completion.*

*I must take this opportunity to recount our delight-
ful evening at Birch Lane. Mr. Gilmartin was in good
spirits as always and drank too much and leaned too
close when he spoke, but I forgave him it because of
his great kindness and warmth. I hadn't met Charis
Gilmartin, and found her a lovely and bright woman,
with a great interest in flowers and gardens, and a
palpable disdain for her husband. When I remarked
on it, Bryn said that it was just the way they were and
that I was too much an innocent about men and
women and how they got along.*

*But the most interesting thing that came out of our
evening was the appearance, around six, of Miss Mary
Denholm. We were sitting out on the terrace when she
came over with a basket of eggs. She was about to go
around to the back door when Gilmartin called her
over to speak to us. He introduced me to her and said
that he thought we might be good friends and that he
had heard anyway, through the grapevine, that I might
be interested in having her sit for me.*

*I told him that we had met last summer and won-
dered if she remembered.*

*Miss Denholm smiled and said she did remember
and that she would be happy to sit, and that I should
let her know when. She is truly a lovely girl—all tumbling hair and pale skin and a willowy figure and I
imagined that she seemed somehow older this summer
than last. Of course, she is now seventeen, only five
years younger than myself.*

*She has a younger sister, a plain girl who seems
much duller than Mary. I have not yet met Mrs. Denholm, but was introduced to her husband once at the
train station. He was a very large man, with little
spectacles and when I told him that I was working for
Morgan, he said, "Ah, a sculptress" and gestured at*

*my hair. I thought him odd until M. explained that he
was a great one for puns.*

*In any case, I am newly interested in my work and
will commit myself to the completion of a piece as
soon as possible.*

But Marlise, carrying a stack of books to put back on the
shelves, intruded upon Myra Benton's resolutions.

"Hey, Sweeney. I'm afraid I'm closing up in a few
minutes."

"Oh, shit. I didn't even . . ." Sweeney looked through the
pile of diaries. She still had a few to go. "Marlise . . . ?"

"You're going to ask me if you can take that box home
with you, aren't you?" Marlise adopted the famously stern
look that Sweeney knew terrified less intrepid researchers.

"Well, if I could just look at it for another hour . . ."

Marlise looked around the empty library. "Okay. Take the
box. Nobody but you and some guy from the University of
Wisconsin have ever wanted to see it anyway. But if something happens to it, I'm going to tell the powers that be that
I never saw it before and you must have stolen it. Right?"

Sweeney grinned. "Thank you so much. And you don't
have to worry. I'll have it back first thing in the morning
and I'll guard it with my life."

"You better. We open at eight. Just bring it in and put it
behind the desk. I'll make sure it goes back where it's supposed to go."

Sweeney carefully tucked the box into her bookbag and
patted it. "Thank you so much. I owe you one."

"All right. Have a good Christmas."

"You, too."

She walked down to Massachusetts Avenue and got a beer
and a Reuben sandwich at a little pub she'd never been to.
She desperately wanted to take the box out and keep reading
Myra Benton's diary, but Marlise would never forgive her if
she got Russian dressing on the old documents, so she found
a *Boston Globe* and read happily in a cozy corner booth. It
was heavenly warm inside and she ate slowly, listening to

other diners' conversations and watching shoppers passing
by on the sidewalk outside.

Then, with the box of Myra Benton's journals safely
locked in the trunk of her car, Sweeney decided to stop by
the office to check her e-mail and see if she had any interesting mail. There wasn't much of interest, but she spent a
happy hour reading the proofs of her *European Art Criticism*
piece and returning a couple of e-mails from colleagues interested in her book on gravestone iconography.

The air had warmed up a little by the time she got back
outside, and in the dusky late afternoon light, Sweeney could
smell the familiar odors of the city, cooking oil and fried
onions emanating from a Chinese restaurant, cigarette smoke
as a teenage girl walked by, scowling into the winter night.

The traffic was getting heavier as it got to be the rush
hour and it took her nearly twenty minutes to get back to
Somerville and circle her block twice, looking for parking.
She finally found a space a couple of streets away and
squeezed into it narrowly, then got all of her bags and the
precious box out of the car.

It was as she crossed Davis Square that she saw the red
car.

Sweeney jumped back and looked behind her for a place
to hide and watch. It was Ian's car. She was sure of it. It
had the same Vermont plates—her good memory called up
the sequence, BUI 178, and the shiny red finish and American make gave it away as a rental.

Luckily, there was a large oak tree along the street and
on the other side, a small bench offered a comfortable post.
She put her bags on the bench and sat down, pulling a hat
and scarf out of the bag and wrapping her face so she
wouldn't be recognized. She hugged the box to her chest and
waited.

It was ten minutes before she saw his tall, lanky figure
coming out of a small convenience store on the corner. He
looked to the right and then to the left and rooted in his
pocket for a few seconds, presumably looking for his keys.
Sweeney watched as he opened the car and dropped some-

thing that looked like a small paper bag on the front seat. Then he re-locked the car and started walking across the square, looking down frequently at what appeared to be a map.

After a couple of seconds, Sweeney got up, gathered her things, and followed at a safe distance. In movies, following someone looked so simple but, in fact, it was bloody difficult. He didn't walk quickly, looking straight ahead, the way bad guys were supposed to. Instead, he turned around frequently, looking up at street signs and checking them against his map. Each time he stopped, Sweeney jumped back against a building, turning away to pretend to fumble in her bag.

They went on like that for a couple of blocks before she realized where they were going. Ian looked up at the street sign and turned right onto Russell Street, walking slowly along until he came to the big pumpkin-colored Victorian triple-decker where she lived.

All of a sudden, she wasn't sure what to do. A cold web of fear had spread itself across her chest and she stood, rooted there on the sidewalk. She could confront him, of course, but the street was empty. No, she decided, it was better to wait and see what he was going to do. She ducked into an alleyway on the corner and kneeled down behind a pair of trash cans, still hugging the box.

From her post, she watched him stand on the sidewalk looking up at the house. His expression was inscrutable; he merely stood. And after a minute or two, he turned and passed by the alley, going back the way he had come.

She counted to one hundred and then stood up, her legs cramped from kneeling on the cold concrete. After looking up and down the street, she let herself in and climbed up the stairs to her third floor apartment, her heart beating and the back of her sweater damp with perspiration.

She stood in the hall for a moment, listening to the silence, then pressed the button that played the new messages on the answering machine. There wasn't much, a reminder from the video store about *Divorce Italian Style* and a message from a student explaining why he wouldn't be handing in his final paper for Introduction to Art History.

Then she poured herself a scotch and put on her favorite flannel pajamas. Comfortable and warm, she stood in front of the bay window in her little living room looking out over the square. She'd been living on Russell Street so long that she'd come to know the scene by heart, the neon-signed diner and the VFW hall across the way.

Down below, pedestrians crisscrossed the square. A couple looked for cars, then dashed across the street and disappeared into The Auld Sod, the best Irish bar in the neighborhood.

She looked down at the spot where Ian had been standing. What did he want? She hadn't been able to shake the feeling that he had some *business* in Byzantium, that he was somehow wrapped up in the mystery of Mary Denholm's death and Ruth Kimball's murder. And now he'd followed her to Boston.

She remembered the credit card receipt she'd picked up accidentally with her books the day he'd driven her downtown. She'd forgotten to give it back to him, so it was still in the front pocket of her research bag. She got it out and found the name of the restaurant, "Jane's Diner," in Suffolk, a large town next to Byzantium, and saw that he'd spent $11.93 on eggs, bacon, coffee, orange juice and a cranberry muffin. She was about to put it back when she saw the date printed in small faint purple type. It was three days before she and Toby had arrived in Byzantium.

Yet, when Patch had introduced Ian to them, he'd said he had just arrived from London. She remembered it distinctly now. Patch told them that Ian was exhausted because he'd just that day arrived from London. Sweeney couldn't imagine why Patch would have lied to them about it, so Ian must have lied to Patch.

But why?

Sweeney forced herself to stop thinking about Ian. She had the rest of Myra Benton's diary to read and she settled down on the couch. She worked her way through seemingly endless descriptions of Benton's work on a sculpture.

She had been reading for almost thirty minutes and she was growing bored of Myra Benton's confessional. There was a sly intimation of some kind of romantic adventure with a student of Gilmartin's, but no mention of J.L.B. She still hadn't reached the summer Mary died.

Finally, in May of 1890, Myra Benton was back at Byzantium.

And then:

> *July 6, 1890—The girls and I went for a lovely picnic today at the pond and asked the Denholm girls to come along as they do not have much fun on account of their father's strictness. We brought cold meat and drank water from the little spring on the way and Ethel said it was the first picnic she had ever gone on and that she was enjoying herself immensely.*
>
> *It is just the time of year when the wildflowers are blooming and as we walked, we saw flowers of every variety. They were so beautiful, I could hardly believe they were of nature and we plucked them up and made little crowns for ourselves. I came upon Mary picking the petals from a daisy and saying, to herself, he loves me, he loves me not, and I asked her who her sweetheart was and she said she would not tell me and then flushed so deeply I could not help but laugh and tell her that she looked exactly like a blushing bride.*

The next passage of interest was dated July twenty-sixth, 1890:

> *M. and J.L.B. had most terrible row tonight. I was coming back from the Ladies Guild meeting at the Church and when I had brought the horses into the stable and put them away I thought I would pass by the studio and have a word with M. about my "Hermione" work, since I have been so distracted and have made no headway these last three weeks. In any case, thinking M. might have some words of advice, I took*

*a lantern and started for the studio when I heard them
screaming at each other like jealous women.*

*"I won't have it," J.L.B. called out. "It's madness,
sheer madness. The deception, the lies, it's too much."*

*"My dear man, surely you see that it is . . . una-
voidable." M. was far more measured than J.L.B., but
still his voice rose from the studio and reached me
where I stood, shivering on the path. I would like to
say, dear diary, that I turned on my heel and went
straight back to the house, but instead I waited there
and eavesdropped, knowing they were too involved in
the discussion to leave the studio and find me.*

*Then, to my surprise, I heard G's voice also. He
spoke softly and I could hear only the fragment of a
sentence, something that sounded like ". . . and I wish
things could be different."*

*The three of them fought on like that for a few
minutes more and I was about to go when I heard M.
say something about "Mary." Mary Denholm it must
have been, because J.L.B. said shortly after "the poor
wretched girl, that Louis Denholm is a tyrant." They
must have moved to some other part of the studio because I could not afterward hear them so clearly.*

*I went back to the house and felt guilty all that
night for listening.*

M., as she already knew, was Morgan and G. was Gilmartin.
And here again was the mysterious J.L.B. What did it stand
for? She searched back through the entries from that summer
and found only a short entry, in early May, that she had
missed the first time, stating that "J.L.B. arrived from the
station."

The use of the initials indicated that Myra Benton knew
J.L.B. before he arrived in Byzantium, Sweeney decided.
Since he appeared to be using the studio, he must have been
a student who was working with Morgan.

The next entry was a few days later, on August first.

*There is something the matter with M. He spent the morning away from the house, when he usually works in the early hours. I heard him tell the housemaids that he was going to Mr. Denholm's to discuss the purchase of a piece of land, but for some reason I did not believe it to be the case. While he was gone, J.L.B. sat by the window and watched the long drive up to Upper Pastures, waiting for M.'s return. When M. came back, the two of them went down to the studio—I watched from my window—and did not return for nearly two hours. After lunch, I remarked to M. that he had not worked that day, but he did not offer any explanation for his strange behavior. For his part, J.L.B. seemed moody and snappish one minute and quite elated the next.*

Sweeney skimmed over the next two weeks' worth of entries, which detailed nothing much more interesting than a picnic at Winkle's Lake, a crow's nest discovered over the front door, and an angry little sentence about J.L.B. using the studio almost twenty-four hours a day and not allowing anyone else in. Then, with a sense of foreboding she read *August 28, 1890. I can hardly believe what has happened. Life, so short and impermanent, has been stilled by the hand of time.* Myra Benton had written the melodramatic words with a flourish of underlining and exclamation points. Sweeney's heart began beating faster—she held her breath.

*Mary Denholm is dead!*

*This morning, as I awoke, I heard one of the housemaids beneath my window, talking to the Denholms' house girl and she was saying that Miss Mary had disappeared the day previous. She had told her mother—the father was not to be told, because he did not approve of it—she was going to sit for Mr. Gilmartin and then to go for a bath in the river and she did not come back for dinnertime. When she had not returned by dark, one of the girls went over to Birch*

*Lane to ask if they had seen her and he said that they had worked in his studio by the river for three hours, after which he had dismissed her. The household was up most of the night waiting for her to return, but did not alert the colony because they suspected she had merely gone off, as she sometimes did.*

*Then, early this morning, Gilmartin rose to paint by the river and he saw her poor body and carried her out of the dark water and to her very own home, the last time ever she would enter those doors.*

*I wept in my room and when I went downstairs, found the household deep in the throes of mourning. Mrs. M. cried that the girl was so young and should not have been allowed out swimming at all, until one of her daughters reminded her that they themselves had been out the morning before and would they die, too? We assured them they would not and comforted each other as best we could. M., however, was not to be found and when I traveled down to the studio to console him, I found him hard at work, on the piece he had been at for some time, the large Narcissus for the Derringer Center in St. Louis. When I showed him that my eyes were red from weeping, he looked at me strangely and said, 'Dearest Myra, be a sensible woman. There are some things that are for the best. You must not be so sad.' I thought him cruel and heartless, told him so, and went back to the house.*

*August 30, 1890*

    *The events of the past 48 hours seem so strange I know not what to think of them, nor what to do. Today was the day of Mary Denholm's burial and what should we awake to but the news that J.L.B. had left before dawn for the continent!! He said good-bye to no one, according to Doris, and told her only that he had been called to Europe on business of the most serious kind. He drove himself in one of the carriages*

*and left it at the station in Suffolk for M. to pick up
later.*

   *What is there to say of the funeral? The women
wept terribly. Mrs. Denholm was inconsolable, though
she tried to remain calm. Dear Mary. She was a beautiful girl and so young.*

Nothing about the gravestone. Surely, Myra Benton, a sculptor, would have remarked on the strange stone. Her heart
pounding, Sweeney turned the page. But there wasn't anything more. The pages after that had been ripped out of the
journal. The deckled edges of the old paper lay against the
binding like a scar.

   She grabbed the box and went through it, looking for the
pages. But there wasn't anything to be found except for a
little note on the library's letterhead indicating that the journal had been missing the pages when it was donated. "Donated in damaged condition," the note read, indicating the
missing pages and convincing Sweeney that they weren't to
be found anywhere.

   It wasn't fair. Just when she'd been getting so close. She
went into the bathroom and splashed cold water on her face
to calm herself down. Why? Why did the pages have to be
missing. It wasn't fair, goddamnit. She picked up a bottle of
hand lotion that was sitting on the counter and flung it across
the bathroom. It bounced unsatisfactorily against the wall
next to the tub, opening and dribbling its contents over the
floor.

   She went back out into the living room and took a sip of
her scotch, then paced around the room. Okay, she didn't
have the last couple of pages, but she did have a lot. She
would work with what was there. Sweeney turned back to
her own notebook. Say Morgan *had* made the gravestone.
But it wasn't possible, was it? Dammers had said so. If he
had sculpted it, why would he disguise his style? The stone
was in the same style as the relief. So J.L.B., whoever he
was, must have made it.

   Wait a second. Sweeney flipped quickly through the diary

pages, until she came to one of the entries she had looked at cursorily because it didn't mention Mary.

> *July 28, 1890. I went down to the studio to clean up for M., since I had not done it in a week or more. I also hoped to get some work done on my Hermione, since she has sat alone and untended beneath the canvas cover for 10 days now. But when I arrived at the studio door, J.L.B. came out to meet me and announce that he was using the studio and I was not to come in. We had words about that, but he blockaded the door with his body and short of wrestling him to the ground, there was nothing I could do. When I returned to the house and told M. what had happened, he merely smiled and said J.L.B. was working on a project and I should let him be.*
>
> *It is unfair the way women are treated as second-class citizens in this world.*

# TWENTY–TWO

SWEENEY YAWNED AND stretched her pajama-clad legs beneath the table. She was tired and frustrated and the Tylenols she'd taken to suppress her hangover were starting to wear off. But she had to figure this out. What had J.L.B. been working on in the studio and why, after Mary was dead, had he left Byzantium so suddenly?

J.L.B. was the mystery here. Who was he? Where had he come from? That was what she needed to know. But there was no mention of anyone with those initials in any of the books about Morgan or the Byzantium colony. He had been in the colony a very short time, a summer only, and despite his obvious talent, he had never produced anything of distinction.

She went back and read the poem again. Until she found out differently, she would have to assume that he had also written the poem. If J.L.B. thought of himself as Death, then he must have killed her. But why? She got up and walked around the room, trying to figure it out. Was he a sociopath? Had they been lovers and had a fight? She found the latter description more interesting than the former. Or . . .

Sweeney turned back to the painting in the Gilmartin biography. She'd looked at it a hundred times, but she was as struck by it as she had been the first time she'd seen it. What about her original theory, which was that there had been an accident while Gilmartin was painting Mary? What if there had been an accident, not while Gilmartin was painting

Mary, but while she was modeling for J.L.B? That was an interesting possibility.

Racing back through the pages, she considered Myra Benton's account. J.L.B. had been working on a mysterious sculpture a week before Mary's death. If it was Mary's gravestone, then . . . Sweeney stared at the painting. Then he must have known in advance that she was going to die.

Wait a minute. She looked back through the diary. Myra Benton had overheard a conversation between J.L.B., Morgan and Gilmartin a couple of weeks before Mary's death. What had Morgan been saying?

*"Surely you see that it is unavoidable."* And Gilmartin had been there, too.

If Morgan, Gilmartin, and J.L.B. had all been talking about Mary's death long before she was dead, that meant that . . . The enormity of what she'd realized hit her. They had been in it together. And it hadn't been an accident while she was posing for a painting. They had *planned* to kill her and they had made the strange gravestone to mark her grave. But why?

That was the question she couldn't answer. It didn't make any sense. *Why?*

Stymied, she turned back to the box. From what she could tell, the rest of the material related to Myra Benton's life after she'd ceased coming to Byzantium as Morgan's student. There were letters to and from friends, including a telegram from Herrick Gilmartin congratulating her upon the unveiling of her Women Textile Workers Monument in New York.

Most of the black-and-white photographs in the box were from the 1920s and '30s and showed a much older Myra Benton with a child Sweeney assumed was her son Piers. In one, they sat on a bench in front of a body of water Sweeney recognized as Lake Geneva. In another, a plump Myra and a teenage Piers stood in front of a large house, a German Shepherd by Piers's side.

But at the bottom was an envelope of obviously much older photographs, on thick paper, sallow with age. One showed Gilmartin and a group of other colony artists sitting on a blanket in a field. In Myra Benton's hand on the back, it read "Colony picnic at the pond 1901."

A few other pictures showed similar scenes, the colonists standing around at Upper Pastures or Birch Lane—the women in long white linen dresses, their hair piled up on top of their heads. The men had on linen suits and looked jolly and drunk.

She flipped through them and then she came to a picture that made her heart stop.

Mary Denholm was standing with a group of men, none of whom Sweeney recognized. It was a rare candid shot and she was laughing in the picture, her head thrown back, a hand up in front of the camera. It made Sweeney feel good somehow, to see her so alive. She turned it over and read the now-familiar writing: "Paul Evans, ? ?, Geoffrey Church, Jean Luc Baladin and Miss Mary Denholm."

She turned it back over and stared at Jean Luc Baladin. He was a tall, dark-haired man, with a flowing mustache. There was something continental about him. His clothes were cut slightly differently than the other men in the picture, his hair left longer.

From the picture, his dark, heavily lashed eyes stared out at her. There was something romantic, but subtly sinister about his full lips and high cheekbones and she noted that his arm was wrapped tightly around Mary's shoulder; his knuckles clenched the fabric of her dress.

Jean Luc Baladin. She'd found J.L.B. She jumped up and grabbed the *Encyclopedia of American Artists* from the bookshelf above her desk. But when she turned to the Bs, there was no Jean Luc Baladin to be found. She went over to another shelf and pulled down the giant volume of European artists. It wasn't organized as efficiently as the American one and she had to hunt a bit for the Bs. But she scanned down the listings, and suddenly there it was:

> Jean Luc Baladin, 1860–1930. Born in London, the son of a French immigrant father and an English mother, Baladin was a young associate of some of the

later Pre-Raphaelites. He was considered to be a promising member of the Academy, but did not live out his
potential after his 30s. He died in Sussex at the age
of 70.

Well, so much for the theory she'd been formulating that he
hadn't left Byzantium at all. She found her address book and
quickly dialed Bennett Dammers's number. He would know
who Jean Luc Baladin was. But the phone rang and rang.
Finally, a mechanical voice told her that he wasn't home,
but that she could leave a message. She obliged, asking him
if he had ever heard of the artist and telling him she'd be
back in Byzantium tomorrow. After pouring herself another
scotch, she paced around the living room, trying to work it
all out.

She had the name now. And she was sure that Mary Denholm had been murdered. What she was also increasingly
sure of was that Ruth Kimball had been murdered in order
to keep her from revealing the truth about that first murder.

It took a moment for that to sink in, and another moment
for the implications of the realization to become clear.

To figure out who had killed Ruth Kimball, all she had
to do was figure out who in Byzantium needed to make sure
that the truth about Mary Denholm's death didn't come out.
Sweeney remembered a logic class she'd taken in college.
"If A, then B." In this case, it was "The descendant of whoever killed A killed B."

The information she'd gotten from the diary implicated
three people: Jean Luc Baladin, Bryn Davies Morgan, and
Herrick Gilmartin. Baladin was a puzzle, but the involvement
of Morgan and Gilmartin meant that there were two people
in Byzantium who had a clear and vested interest in keeping
the truth hidden: Patch Wentworth and Willow Fontana. But
then there were the rest of them, too, Britta and Sabina and
Anders and Electra and Rosemary. Hell, if she hadn't driven
up with Toby herself, she would have had to suspect him,
too. She found herself wondering where he had been on the
day of the murder and admonished herself.

And, she realized, there was Ian, who had lied about when he arrived in Byzantium.

*Why* would Ian want to kill Ruth Kimball? He had never even been in Byzantium before.

This was crazy. She could go around like this for days. She found herself wondering if Ruth Kimball had sat as she sat now, going over and over the facts, trying to figure it out. And she had figured it out. The murder proved that. But *what* had she figured out. That was the question she had to answer. That was everything.

Sweeney turned out the lights in the living room and took her drink to bed with her, setting her alarm for 6 A.M. the next morning. She'd spent the past few days resolving the mysteries of the past. The time had come to address those of the present.

# TWENTY-THREE

*December 19*

THE STORM THAT had been threatening for a day broke as Sweeney drove north toward Vermont the next morning. The Rabbit was creeping along in the early morning mist rising off the snow when the skies suddenly opened in a torrent of rain and sleet that narrowed her visibility down to a one-foot tunnel.

By the time she crossed the bridge to The Island, the brook was full and swollen, washing up against the banks, chunks of ice bobbing along violently on the current.

She parked the Rabbit in the Kimballs' driveway and picked her way through the broken toys and a few pieces of trash lying in the snow along the flagstones leading up to the house. The rain had washed away much of the snow and the landscape now looked washed out and dirty, the dark, flooded ground showing through here and there like old stains.

The house was a typical New England farmhouse, two-storied, white with black shutters and a porch on the front. Paint was peeling from the sides of the building and shutters were missing from a few of the upper story windows. Sweeney could see that part of the roof had been patched with a piece of metal. An old junk car sat in the driveway, and rusty appliances and bags of trash lay around the bottom of the porch. A barn to one side of the house had seen better days; the roof sagged in the middle like the back of an old horse.

The state of the property provoked a pang of sadness. Ruth Kimball had probably always meant to clean it up, but never gotten around to it. And now she never would.

Sweeney climbed the five steps up to the porch and knocked on the front door, her heart beating nervously. She'd been so intent on getting up, returning the library materials to Marlise, and getting back to Vermont that she hadn't planned out exactly how she was going to do this. You couldn't, after all, just blurt out, "Hello. I think someone killed your mother because of what she knew about Mary Denholm's death."

The door opened and Sweeney was about to launch into an explanation of who she was and how she'd gotten interested in Mary Denholm's gravestone when she looked down to find a little girl staring up at her. She looked about ten but her tiny, skinny body made her head of tight brown curls and the giant eyeglasses that sat on her nose look disproportionately big. Her skin was a soft cocoa color and she wore overalls and a bright pink T-shirt. This must be Charley.

"Who are you?" the girl asked, staring up at Sweeney through her glasses.

"Is your mother here?" Sweeney asked.

The girl just stared and asked again, "Who are you?"

"My name is Sweeney St. George and I'm a researcher, a professor. I was wondering if I could speak with your mother."

"I'm Charley."

"Hi, Charley. Could I come in? It's very cold."

Charley stepped aside and allowed Sweeney to walk past her into the house. "Sherry's still sleeping," she said. "I'm supposed to wake her up at eleven, but I can wake her up now."

Sweeney looked at her watch. It was 10:45. "No, no. I don't want you to do that. She'll be up soon. Is it okay if I wait?"

Charley nodded solemnly.

The living room was a Victorian interior left too long in the sun. Red-and-white wallpaper had faded to pink, and an old high-backed sofa was the color of tea-stained linen. The

rest of the furniture was made up of original pieces mixed
with new ones. Another sagging couch stood out from one
wall at an angle, as though someone had started to move it
and then changed her mind. A La-Z-Boy chair, upholstered
in blue velveteen, reclined between the couches, and the television was on to a cartoon show that featured a talking wolf.
On the low table, a game of Concentration was spread out,
half the cards turned over as though someone had been playing and then been interrupted.

"Do you want a drink?" Charley asked politely.

"Okay. If it's not too much trouble." The girl disappeared
silently and came back into the room a couple of minutes
later, holding a blue tinted glass filled with cherry Kool-Aid.
She handed it to Sweeney, who slipped out of her coat and
sat down on the couch.

"Thank you." After a few minutes she said, "I'm so sorry
about your grandmother."

Charley just stared at her. "Is that your real hair?"

"Yes."

"Sherry has red hair like that, only she buys it in a box
and puts it on in the bathroom like shampoo. That's called
dyeing. Not like being dead, but like making something a
different color."

"I always wished I had a more regular hair color. Blond
or a nice brown, like yours."

"Really?" Charley sat down on the couch next to Sweeney
and stared at her hair some more. Sweeney checked her
watch. It had only been five minutes.

"What grade in school are you in?" Sweeney had another
sip of the sweet Kool-Aid.

"Fourth," Charley said. "I'm younger than everybody else,
though, because my birthday's in December, but they let me
in anyway because I started reading when I was three."

"Three? Really?"

"Yeah. I don't remember, but Sherry says I started reading
newspapers."

"This is a nice house."

"Yuck." Charley wrinkled up her nose and looked at

Sweeney in disbelief. "No it's not. Not like the Wentworths' house. It's old outside, but new inside. They have a *white* couch. And they have suits of armor, like the knights of the round table. Gwinny let me touch one once. She's their daughter. She baby-sits for me sometimes, but next year she's going to boring school. She's going to be an actress. Have you ever read Morty Dee Arthur?"

"Yes," Sweeney said, trying not to smile. "Actually it's *Le Morte D'Arthur*, the death of Arthur." She pronounced it carefully and Charlie copied her, almost perfectly.

"Is that what that means? *Mort*. Death."

"Yes," Sweeney said. "In French. But it's not in French, *Le Morte D'Arthur*, I mean."

They were silent for a minute.

"Have *you* ever read *Le Morte D'Arthur*?" Sweeney asked, for something to say.

"No. The librarian at school told me about it. I wanted to read a book about King Arthur, but all they had were baby books, with pictures."

"That's too bad. I bet you could get it at the regular library, though."

"Yeah." She looked up at Sweeney, suddenly accusing. "You were supposed to find out about Mary."

"Yes. Did you know about Mary? Did your grandmother talk about her?"

Charley wandered over to the window and looked out. "I used to go down and look at her gravestone. I liked the poem. All about the man taking her on a trip."

God, Sweeney thought, children really are masters of euphemism.

"Charley?" A tall big-hipped woman with lank hair was coming down the stairs in a nightgown and thick wool socks and when she saw Sweeney she narrowed her eyes suspiciously. She couldn't have been more than thirty, but her face was pulled down in grief.

"I'm so sorry to barge in on you," Sweeney said from the bottom of the stairs. "I'm Sweeney St. George and I, I think I talked to you last week. About Mary Denholm's gravestone and then I think I talked to you the day after . . . I just wanted to say how sorry I am. I had no idea . . ." She was babbling.

"No, that's okay," Sherry said finally. She came down the stairs and curled up on one of the couches in the living room, pulling a pack of cigarettes out of the crack between a cushion and the side of the couch. On a table by the wall were casserole dishes filled with food, plates of brownies and a couple of pies wrapped in cellophane. One of the pies—cherry from the look of it—had a hole in the middle, as though someone had scooped out the center with a spoon.

"People keep bringing food," she said, shaking a cigarette out of the pack and following Sweeney's gaze. "I don't know what to do with it." She lit up and took a long grateful drag.

Sweeney studied Sherry's ravaged face, her pockmarked skin red and angry, and she thought about how grieving turned people's faces inside out, how you could see on their mouths and eyes the machinations of grief as it passed over and through their minds.

Upstairs, bedsprings creaked.

"Sherry?" called a male voice. All three of them watched as a man in boxer shorts and a white T-shirt came down the stairs. He was a good-looking guy, with dark hair cut short and muscular arms.

"That's Sweeney St. George, Carl," Sherry said. "Remember? She's the one that . . ." She looked nervously at her boyfriend.

"What does she want?" Carl asked. Sweeney watched him.

"I talked to Mrs. Kimball a few days before she died. She was going to help me with a research project."

He looked her up and down, his eyes predatory and chilly.

"You go back to bed, Carl," Sherry said, getting up and putting a hand on his arm. "I'll be right up." He gave Sweeney another hard look, then turned and disappeared up the stairs.

"We've had all kinds of people here," Sherry said apologetically, pushing her limp reddish hair away from her face. "Police and insurance people and reporters from the paper.

Asking bullshit questions. He's just tired of talking is all."
She took another drag on her cigarette and studied Sweeney.
"So you're the professor who was going to find out who
killed Mary, huh? I'm sorry I hung up on you. Just didn't
feel like talking about it."

"Of course. Did your mother tell you about our conversation?"

"Yeah, she said you might be able to figure out the truth
about Mary being murdered and that she was going to tell
you what she knew."

Charley was sitting on the floor staring up at them with
her huge brown eyes.

"Could we talk somewhere alone?" Sweeney asked
Sherry, who looked down at her daughter.

"Baby, go watch TV in the kitchen, okay? Just for a
minute."

Charley nodded and did as she was told.

"I've uncovered some stuff about Mary Denholm's death
that makes me think she probably was killed. What did your
mother say about it? I guess she told quite a few people in
town about her suspicions."

"Yeah, although I think a lot of that was to piss off the
Wentworths. She thought it was really crappy the way they
wanted to stop her making money from the condos."

"But where had she gotten the idea that Mary was killed?"

"Oh, from her grandmother. She always said there was
something weird about it."

"Do you know if she talked to anyone shortly before her
death? Did she tell anyone specific that I was going to be
looking into it and that it might come out that one of the
artists was a murderer."

"I don't know. She was kind of weird the last few
months."

"What do you mean?"

Sherry thought for a moment, a few strands of slick hair
falling haltingly over her face. "I don't know," she said after
a moment, and Sweeney had the feeling she had been about
to say something and decided against it. What she decided

to say was, "She was happy . . . it was like she was planning something, you know?"

"Was it the thing with the condominiums? Could that be what was making her happy?"

"Maybe. But that wasn't a sure thing yet. I mean, we weren't going to get any money until the state gave the okay. And the Wentworths and all them kept fighting it." She looked quickly up at Sweeney. "To be honest, I don't hold anything against them. You know, you can disagree about stuff and all, but we've been neighbors for a long time."

"She wasn't . . . having a relationship? With a man?"

Sherry opened her eyes wide. "My mother? No way. She didn't like my father much, and he was the only man she ever cared about. No, she wasn't seeing anybody. If she had been, she might have been more understanding about Carl." She cast her eyes toward the staircase, where he'd stood a few minutes ago, and lit another cigarette.

Sweeney picked up the Concentration cards on the coffee table, carefully turning over one that had cherries on the other side, then one with a turtle.

"I always liked this game," she said. "I think it's because I have a really good memory and I always win."

"My mother was like that, too. She only had to see something once and she'd remember it forever. She loved playing Concentration with Charley. Had to pretend she didn't know where they all were, though. Give the kid a chance. She was getting better though. Smart as a whip, Charley."

"I'll get going and leave you alone," Sweeney said finally, "but there's just one more thing I want to know. What do *you* think about this whole thing? Is there a possibility that someone who didn't want her to tell what she knew about Mary is responsible?"

Sherry looked up quickly and Sweeney could see tears welling up in her too-old eyes. "I don't know. I keep thinking that if I can remember what she looked like when I found her, it might tell me something. But then I think about it. . . . She went for a walk at lunchtime. She always did. We used to have a dog and she kind of just got in the habit, so even after the dog died, she always went for a walk then. And it started snowing that day and she didn't come back and she didn't come back and I got worried. So I went out and I was yelling for her. I could hear the Wentworth boys shooting in the woods." She stopped and looked at Sweeney. "I'm sorry. I don't know why I'm telling you this. I don't even know you."

"It's okay," Sweeney said. "I don't mind."

Then suddenly, as though the memory of finding her mother dead in the snow had just come back afresh to her, Sherry began to sob. "Oh God. Oh God. I just keep seeing her lying there, her hair. It's like a slide that's stuck and I can't get rid of it. The police keep coming back here, asking Carl if he did it, but they don't know what it was like, looking down at her. There's no way he could have . . ." The cigarette she had balanced in the ashtray was out and she lit another one, holding it with shaky hands up to her mouth. One of the cartoon characters on the TV laughed loudly.

"She was holding the gun. She was . . . Oh God!" Sherry started sobbing again and Sweeney leaned forward to touch her knee.

"I'm sorry. I'm so sorry."

"It's okay." Sherry quieted down, the tears falling silently now. "It's like, I just feel so . . . it's like everything's just wrong, that's all. My whole body is so fidgety. It's like I can't ever get comfortable. I can't get ever get comfortable with the idea that she's gone, you know."

Sweeney flashed back to the days after Colm's death, when every new minute that passed was like the minute in which she awakened each morning to realize that he was really gone. "I know, I know," she said. "I'm so sorry."

Sherry stared out the window. "I'll never forget the way I felt walking down there. I didn't know anything then. It was the last time I . . ."

"When did you see the hat?"

"The hat?"

"Didn't you find her hat on the porch? Before you found her?"

"No. What do you mean? Whose hat?"

"Forget it. I'm sorry."

"Oh shit. You'd better go." Sherry was crying again now, deep, raspy sobs that made Sweeney feel empty and impotent.

"Can I do anything?"

"No. I just . . . I ran out of cigarettes." Sherry laughed, then started sobbing again.

Sweeney put her coat on and got ready to go. "I'm so sorry," she said. "Listen, if there's anything that you think of, even something small, I think you should tell me or the police. I'll be staying up at the Wentworths' until after Christmas. Is it okay if I stop by tomorrow? There's something I want to get for Charley, a book that we were talking about."

But as it turned out, Sweeney didn't stop by the next day. Because the next day, after getting a firm identification on Carl Thompson as the man who had pawned a number of the electronic items stolen from colony homes, Chief Cooper got a search warrant for the Kimballs' home and found, hidden in the basement beneath a tarp, other items that were identified as having been stolen from the Byzantium houses.

Carl Thompson was arrested and ordered held without bail on suspicion of burglary, a charge the town was sure would soon be changed to murder.

# TWENTY-FOUR

SWEENEY HAD RETURNED to Birch Lane and found she could no longer look at the house with the same eyes, knowing as she now did that the man who had created it had played a role in Mary's death. She had examined a Gilmartin hanging over the reception table, a portrait in whites and grays of a young woman. It was a thing of beauty, the woman's small, delicate face turned slightly upward in flirtatious supplication, her fair hair silvery in the strange light coming in through a small window over her shoulder. A large gray cat lolled on her lap, his visage ecstatic beneath the woman's hand. How could a man capable of such monstrosity make something so beautiful? Sweeney had stared at the creation, at the swirls and daubs of oil paint that were the painter's words and that had always seemed to her like the fingerprints of divinity.

They spent the next day getting ready for the Christmas party.

Sweeney found herself in a strange position all that day. From the perspective of everyone else in the house, Ruth Kimball's murder had been solved, and everything was back to normal. When they had heard—from Willow and Rosemary who had come breathless and excited at lunchtime with the news—Britta had visibly relaxed, her whole face undergoing a transformation, softening and becoming prettier. Toby, who had shot Sweeney a satisfied look as if to say "See?" was positively cheerful, grinning and humming Christmas carols.

As they decorated the house, hanging evergreen boughs from the staircases and mantels, stringing cranberries on thread for garlands, and trimming the giant tree that Patch and the boys had brought from the woods, Sweeney agonized about what to do.

She knew that Gilmartin had had a hand in Mary's death. But there didn't seem to be an imperative anymore to reveal her knowledge. If that murder had nothing to do with this one, what good did it do anyone to make the truth known? And there was Toby to think about. Revealing the truth about his great-grandfather would hurt him as much as it would hurt the rest of them.

But she was a scholar. She had made an academic discovery as well as a human one.

She wondered, too, what to do about Ian. He had been careful with her since she'd been back, hardly looking at her, leaving the room when she entered. He was embarrassed, she decided, but there was something else there, too, something that smacked of self preservation, as though he were afraid to be alone with her.

She went up to her room right after dinner that night, pleading exhaustion, and after reading for an hour, put on her nightgown and got up to use the bathroom. But when she stepped out into the hallway, Ian was on his way in, wearing a bathrobe and carrying a leather toiletries case.

"I'm sorry. Did you want to . . ." He looked so completely un-sinister that she had trouble connecting him with the person she'd followed to her house only yesterday.

"No, that's fine. You go first." She ducked back into her room, her heart beating fast. The bathroom shared a wall with her room and she listened to the steady rush of the shower for a few minutes, then the sounds of him getting out, shutting the door of the shower stall and flushing the toilet. A few minutes later, she heard the door to the bathroom open, his footfall in the hall, and his own door shutting behind him.

She counted to one hundred, then went out into the hall

and knocked on his door. When he answered, he was still in his robe.

"Can I talk to you?"

"Yes. Certainly." He drew the robe more tightly around himself, gestured her into his room and shut the door.

"Sit down," he told her politely, clearing some papers off the chair at the little desk. She sat and looked around the bedroom, which was an almost identical, though more masculine version of her own, its walls a clean white, the trim painted a dark blue that matched the bedding and curtains. The room was neat, the bed made, not a single piece of clothing on the floor. A black suit was draped over the blue and red patchwork quilt.

"What um . . . what did you want?" he asked. He sat down on the bed, clutching his robe around him. With his wet hair slicked down close to his head, he looked very young.

Suddenly, she was so embarrassed, she could barely speak. But she'd already started it and there wasn't any turning back. "I saw you in Boston yesterday," she announced. "And I know that you lied to us about when you arrived in Vermont. What I want to know is why."

Ian stood up and went over to the window. For a couple of minutes he didn't say anything. Then he turned back to her.

"I wondered if anyone knew about that. I'm afraid my explanation won't make much sense to you, but I'll give it all the same. I had come all the way here and I wanted some time on my own before arriving at Patch and Britta's. I don't know, I think it was the idea of Christmas and the children and all the people. Christmas is a bit odd for me, because I'm not with Eloise. I just wanted a few days here to explore, by myself. It's one of my favorite things, getting to know a new place all on my own. So I stayed at a hotel in Suffolk, a few miles away. I'd heard from Patch and Britta that there were some great antiques in the area. I am, after all, here to buy antiques. So I looked around, went to an auction."

"What would you have done if you'd run into them downtown?"

"Don't know. I hadn't thought that far ahead, I guess. I would have told them the truth, I suppose, or said I'd arrived early and didn't want to trouble them."

She stood up and went over to him, her eyes almost level with his, so close that she could smell the particular scent of him, his sharp English smell, of lemons and spice. "But why did you go to my house yesterday? Why did you follow me to Boston?"

On the wall above the bed was a portrait of an eighteenth-century gentleman, dressed in military garb and staring imperiously down at them. She imagined that he disapproved. "Look at you," he seemed to say, "accusing a man when you've got no evidence to support your feeling that he's guilty." But she had evidence. He had followed her. She had seen him.

He stared at her for a minute, his face stricken, then turned away and slammed his open hand against the wall. "Damn, Sweeney." The violent movement surprised her. "Bloody hell. I can't . . . Close your eyes for a second. I can't talk to you like this." Not knowing what else to do, she turned away and shut her eyes.

The sounds of him getting dressed—the soft rustle of denim, his nervous breathing—seemed very loud to her and she held her breath until he said "all right," then opened her eyes to find him wearing jeans and a cashmere sweater, his feet still bare. They were pleasantly slender, the tops of his toes lightly furred, his arches pronounced, the skin pale, like the underbelly of a fish.

He reached past her to hang the damp robe up on a hook next to the door and when his hand brushed her shoulder, she stepped back so quickly she almost fell into the bed.

"I didn't follow you. I swear it. I had some business in Boston and I was about to tell everyone that I was going down yesterday when you came out with your own announcement. I couldn't say then that I was going as well because you would have thought I was following you. I had to go to an auction house. Skinner's. You can call them and check it out if you want."

He went on. "Bloody hell, it's so hard to explain. I don't know what it is, but I feel like you're afraid of me, like you think I'm up to no good. And then I put my foot in it the other night and I just felt like you couldn't stand to have me around. So I decided it was easier to say I had things to do in Vermont than to explain why I was gone all day."

"That's a very neat explanation, Ian. But why did you go to my house? What business could you possibly have had on my *street*, for godsakes?" She could feel perspiration running down her back despite the fact that it was cold in his room.

He turned away and went to sit down on the bed, pulling a hand roughly through his hair. For a matter of minutes, he seemed about to speak, as though he were wrestling with a pronouncement or a speech, shaping the words in his head, trying them out to see how they worked. Finally, she could see that he had given it up.

"I don't know," he said quietly, meeting her eyes. "I wanted to see where you lived. I looked you up in the phone book."

"Come on, you can't expect me to believe that crap. I saw you. You followed me to Boston."

She was furious with him, because she felt somewhere deep in her bones that he was lying, that he knew more about this whole thing than he was letting on, and because she realized in that moment that he had gotten to her, that she was very attracted to him and that if he were to stand up and walk over and kiss her, it might possibly be the most thrilling thing she could imagine. And then she did imagine it.

Suddenly, Ian was standing directly in front of her. She could feel a kind of vibrating warmth emanating from his body, a warmth that she wanted to step into, let wash over her like rainwater.

But he kept talking, smiling down at her. "You can't imagine how embarrassing this is. When I was in primary school I used to walk by the home of a little girl named Harriet. She was lovely, Harriet. One day she caught me and I made up a story about how my dog had run away and I was looking for him and she spent a half hour helping me look for my nonexistent dog. She felt so sorry for me. Do you feel sorry for me?"

She looked up into his eyes and he leaned forward and pressed his mouth lightly to hers, just for a second, testing her response, then looking more urgently for her lips. She leaned into the kiss, thrilled and terrified.

"No," Sweeney whispered into his mouth, normal breath gone to her.

"Good." He lifted her hair away from her neck and held it lovingly, weighing it in his hands like something very precious, then laying it back down on her shoulders.

And that was what broke the spell, for it was something that Colm had always done when he wanted to make love or when he was feeling sentimental, and she stumbled backward toward the door, mumbling that she was sorry but that she had to go.

# TWENTY-FIVE

❧

## December 21

Winter in the colony was a time of hunkering down, of keeping the houses warm with wood fires and hot coals at the bottom of the bed. And for the colonists who stayed year round, and those who came north for Christmas, it was a time of celebration.

There was ritual to the season, as there was to most things at the colony. A giant tree was felled in the woods and brought to Birch Lane and decorated by the servants. Shortly before the children were allowed to come in, it was lit. Then their parents summoned them and they waited in the dark for the doors to the parlor to be opened. There was eggnog and hot cocoa and all kinds of sweets. When she was older, Violet Gilmartin remembered Morgan's annual turn as St. Nick for the Gilmartin's holiday parties. "He would put on a red coat and trousers and big black boots and a fake beard of white wool. Then, while the children were being given hot cocoa and cookies after their sleigh rides, he would sneak in the back door and surprise them. Handing out presents from the giant bag over his shoulder, he would ask each child if they had been naughty or nice. Of course they all said nice and got a present.

"There was one concession to his character that Morgan was not willing to make and that was to wear a hat. He hated hats and so until I saw a picture of St. Nicholas in a book, I assumed that he had red hair, no hat, and a long white beard."

*—Muse of the Hills: The Byzantium Colony,*
*1860–1956,*
by Bennett Dammers

IT WAS THE next night, the night of the Christmas party, and
Sweeney stood against a wall of the living room, feeling
decidedly antisocial and overdressed in the vintage red cocktail dress and spike heels she'd brought from home. Someone
had told her once that redheads should never wear red. Usually it was a rule she liked to break, but tonight she was
wishing she'd stuck to something a little more modest.
"Who's the flashy broad in the red dress?" she pictured the
guests whispering to each other.

What must have been half the evergreens in Vermont had
been sacrificed to transform Birch Lane into an approxima-
tion of the outdoors in winter. Little Christmas trees decorated with red and purple velvet bows sat on every surface
and the giant tree in the foyer was hung with strings of silvery ornaments. Feathery boughs decorated mantels and
shelves and tables, sending off a pleasant piney scent.

It was mystical, a glorious antidote to the stark, chilly
world outdoors.

Sweeney asked the bartender to pour her a scotch and
tried to drink it slowly. Then she took up a post in a corner
of the living room, hoping no one was going to take her in
hand and make sure she had a good time. She tried not to
look forlorn.

It was eight now and the party was in full swing. A few
couples danced over by the four-piece jazz band playing *My
Embraceable You*, and everyone else stood around a velvet-
covered buffet table laden with wonderful things—smoked
meats, a whole poached salmon, little bowls of caviar with
toast and lemon wedges, oysters on a bed of crushed ice.

A dessert table in the hallway held six varieties of cakes,
homemade Christmas stollen studded with fruit, crystal
bowls of tiny, candied oranges, nuts and about twenty kinds

of Christmas cookies. The living room, with another huge
tree as the centerpiece, sparkled in candlelight.

Her efforts toward not looking forlorn obviously weren't
enough. Willow, dressed almost as formally as Sweeney in
a long blue velvet shift and Indian print silk shawl, glanced
over at her a couple of times before excusing herself from
the group she'd been talking to and coming over.

"Sweeney, you look fantastic," she said kindly.

"Thanks. I was feeling a bit overdressed, actually."

"Oh, don't worry about that. I'm always overdressed up
here. I refuse to let myself go just because everyone else
does. I like to think of myself as a fashion voice in the wil-
derness, actually. Here, have one of these. Patch always buys
the best."

Sweeney traded her tumbler for a flute. They sipped their
champagne and then Willow said, "Isn't it something about
Carl Thompson?"

The champagne was delicious and Sweeney drank it a
little too quickly, the dry, bubbly fumes tickling her throat.

"Yeah. Everyone seems so relieved. I almost hadn't realized how much it was weighing on all your minds."

Willow's eyes were artfully made up with pink and beige
shadow and dark mascara. They glanced up quickly at Sweeney, then darted away again, and she said falsely, "I know
it was weighing on mine. I always felt that someone was
going to just come in at any moment, you know? Anders
went back to Boston today and I can't tell you how much
better I feel being in the house alone, now that there's been
an arrest."

"Anyway," she added, as a gray-haired man approached
them, carrying a glass of champagne. "It's a huge relief. For
all of us. Hi, Frances." Around the man's neck was a
Christmas-themed ascot. His hair was in a ponytail and his
eyebrows looked like fuzzy gray caterpillars. "We were just
talking about Carl Thompson. Have you heard?"

"Yes," he said. "We're all relieved, although it's no relief
for poor Mrs. Kimball's family."

He offered Sweeney a hand. "I'm Frances Rapacci. You must be Sweeney."

"Nice to meet you. Wasn't yours one of the houses that he broke into?"

"That's right." He looked slightly surprised that she knew. "We didn't lose much, an old radio, a few paintings, some knickknacks, but it was a horrible feeling to think that someone had been in there."

"What paintings?" Sweeney asked.

"Oh, nothing particularly valuable. It took us a few days to even remember what they had been. The thieves left much more valuable works right on the walls. Actually it's interesting. One of the pieces stolen was a Granger, not a good one, but we realized when we looked through the insurance records that it was of Rosemary. Her grandfather did it when she was just a toddler. I wish I could have shown it to her. She was a lovely little thing." He took a sip from his glass and added, "Well, who knows. Maybe we'll get it back now."

"We've been trying to decide if we should take out a new policy for the art," Willow said. "With everything that's been going on, we realized we'd get hardly anything for what we have."

"You really should look into it. Thank God, we didn't lose some of our really valuable stuff. With the way sales have been going lately, you need to get your collection appraised every year so you'll get what it's worth if something happens."

Sweeney, who had been forgotten, quietly downed her champagne and excused herself to get another drink. Despite her best intentions, she was starting to feel slightly tipsy, and she watched the partygoers from behind a veil of displaced feeling. They danced and talked and swirled around the room, but she might as well have been on the other side of a river, watching them through a fog. She had seen Ian only once, when he'd come down looking crisp and movie star handsome in his tuxedo, then he'd disappeared into the other room.

When Rosemary came up behind her and put an arm around her waist, Sweeney jumped as though she's been tapped on the shoulder by a ghost.

"Is this as strange to you as it is to me?" Rosemary whispered. "My grandmother's been telling me about the parties they used to have. But it always sounded like kids playing dress-me-up."

They both watched Patch make his way across the room, chatting jovially and topping off champagne glasses from the bottle he carried. It struck Sweeney that he was in his element as host.

"I had a nice talk with your grandmother the other day," Sweeney said. "She's a great old lady."

"Isn't she?"

"I think I'm starting to understand what it is that drew them all here. There's a sense of belonging to something important, something beautiful, and whether you're an artist or not, you're part of it."

"You're right," Rosemary said, smiling. "That's exactly what I felt when I arrived here. It was like stepping back in time, into this beautiful world, where nice things and art mattered more than anything. I felt somehow that I belonged to this world more than I've ever belonged to any other."

They were silent for a moment, watching the guests.

Sweeney asked, "Did you hear a lot about the colony when you were growing up."

"God, no. My parents pretended that it didn't exist. They'd had a falling out with my grandmother and Marcus when I was about four. After we moved to England and then South Africa, I never heard about it again."

"So how did you get in touch with your grandmother again, after your parents died?"

"Well, I wrote her to tell her about the car accident. I thought that she should know. And she wrote me a letter back saying that if I needed anything, I should let her know. I had just ended a relationship and was thinking about switching jobs and I did need . . . It wasn't money so much as it was family. So I came to visit and it turned out that she needed someone to look after her. It worked out well for everyone. And I've fallen in love with Byzantium. It was absolutely instantaneous. I drove up and felt that I'd come home."

"Tell me about this thing with the condominiums. Was Ruth Kimball really going to sell her property?"

Rosemary looked at her curiously. "It all started before I got here, so I just know what I've heard from Grandmother. I think she did want to sell the house and move into something smaller that didn't need so much upkeep. So she'd been talking to a real estate developer who thought it would be a good spot for condominiums. Because of the ski area, people are always looking for second homes here. Everyone was furious, Patch and Anders especially. Of course the Wentworths would have been the ones looking right at them. For the rest of us, it was more the *idea* of it."

Rosemary thought for a moment. "When it comes right down to it, we were all ready to fight to keep things the way they are. We're very attached to our past here, in case you haven't noticed."

"Did Ruth Kimball know how everyone felt?"

"I think she must have. Patch had been going to town selectboard meetings where they were discussing it and spoken his mind."

Sweeney lowered her voice, suddenly conscious that someone might hear them. "The thing I don't understand is why Patch didn't just buy her out if he was so worried about it."

"I know. I wondered about that, too. I think Mrs. Kimball was being stubborn. She felt that it was her land and Patch was trying to prevent her from doing what she wanted with it. It was a lot of money, too. It probably wouldn't have broken Patch, but it might have been a little bit of a stretch."

Sabina came up behind them and said, "What are you two up to? You look as though you're plotting to overthrow the king."

"Yes," Rosemary said, in a loud whisper. "Do you want to join our movement?" They all laughed.

"I feel so relieved about this burglary thing," Sabina said. "I didn't realize how much it's been weighing on my mind."

"I know," Rosemary said. "I feel like I've shifted a ton of bricks from my shoulders."

Sweeney had been trying to keep her face impassive, but a small nervous twitch must have caught their attention because they both looked at her strangely.

"Don't you feel relieved, Sweeney?" Rosemary asked.

"I don't know . . . I . . . Yes, of course."

"Oh look," Sabina said. "There's Bennett Dammers. I didn't know he was coming." She waved at him across the room, and he waved back cheerfully, hoisting his champagne glass in the air.

Sweeney told them she wanted to say hello.

The elderly man was seasonally resplendent in a white shirt, red suspenders, and red silk bowtie. Sweeney kissed him on the cheek and traded his empty champagne glass for a full one from a passing tray.

"Happy holidays, Mr. Dammers," she said. "It's so good to see you here."

"It's lovely to see you, my dear. I was hoping I'd get a chance to speak with you tonight. I got your message and looked through my records for you, and I did find a reference to Jean Luc Baladin—what a wonderful name that was. It seems a small relief signed by him was given to the Historical Society in the 1930s. I found the transference agreement. But the interesting thing is that there was a little note that went along with it. It noted that the relief might be of interest since Baladin had visited the colony, though he hadn't been a member per se. It seems he met Morgan in Europe and Morgan extended an invitation. So he wasn't exactly a student, you see. That's why he wasn't listed anywhere."

"That makes sense," Sweeney said, thinking. "I was trying to figure out how he could have escaped being listed."

"I hope it helps," Bennett Dammers said. "May I ask if you've discovered anything?"

"Just that it seems as though Baladin must have made

Mary Denholm's gravestone." She wouldn't tell him until she knew exactly what had happened.

He smiled. "Well, congratulations. Isn't that what you were trying to find out?"

"Yes, I guess so. It's just that there are still some . . . unanswered questions."

"There usually are. Are you having a good time?"

"Yes. I keep thinking about your description of the parties in your book. The modern-day version must seem very tame to you."

"It does," he said, smiling. "Though I suspect the music's better. In the old days, Gilmartin always insisted on singing. Apparently, he was not gifted with a particularly melodious voice." They talked about the accounts of the parties in his book for a few minutes and then Britta came over and announced that it was time to eat.

Sweeney went and filled her plate, and took it over to the couch, where Sabina and Rosemary were sitting with a big group of people.

"Isn't Bennett wonderful?" Sabina asked as Sweeney came over.

"I think I have a little bit of a crush on him," Rosemary said in a whisper, and Sweeney said that she did, too.

They ate happily for few minutes, and listened to a story one of the guests was telling about a trip to Morocco on which she had been robbed at knifepoint. Sweeney turned to ask Sabina if she wanted anything more to eat and found her sitting straight up on the couch and staring at the big window on the wall across from them.

"Sabina?" Rosemary asked after a moment. "Are you okay?"

"Did you see someone outside?" Sweeney stood up and looked through the window. There was nothing but the party, reflected in the glass. When she went over and cupped her hand against the window, she saw only the empty black night.

Sabina said nothing. She just stared. And after a moment,

she put her plate down and started talking again, assuring them that she was fine.

The moment passed, but the tension wasn't broken until Patch came in dressed in boots and a parka. His face was ruddy from the cold. "Anyone want to go for a sleigh ride? I just brought it around."

Britta was standing at one end of the room, holding a plate of food. "Patch," she called out. "You're drunk. Be careful."

"I'm not so drunk," he called back cheerfully. "And I'm always careful."

Toby and Rosemary had put on their parkas and boots, too, and they stood beside Sweeney arm in arm.

"Come with us, Sweeney," Rosemary said, grinning. Willow and Ian and Gally and Trip had gotten dressed to go, too.

"Come on, Sweeney," Toby said. "Let's go. You'll love it. It's just like in Russian novels. You'll feel like Anna Karenina, racing across the steppes. And I promise there aren't any streetcars."

They were being kind to include her, and though she felt a thin rivulet of distilled fear snake its way down her spine, she nodded and let them lead her to the door.

# TWENTY-SIX

*The highlight of any Christmas gathering at the Gil-
martins was a sleigh ride up to Maple Hill. Herrick
Gilmartin loved to drive his little German-made sleigh
and he made a tradition of taking his guests up to watch
the stars from the summit, one side of which formed a
modest cliff above the river and offered pleasing views of
The Island.*

*He wasn't content merely to squire his passengers, but
would ask the cook to pack a basket of snacks and flasks
of hot chocolate fortified with brandy. If there happened
to be a musically talented guest at the house, passengers
might be serenaded atop Maple Hill as they viewed the
night sky.*

—*Muse of the Hills: The Byzantium Colony,*
*1860–1956,*
by Bennett Dammers

THE WENTWORTHS' SLEIGH was painted a glossy black, with
red velvet upholstered seats and crimson blankets folded on
the floor. It stood nearly ten feet tall, a gorgeous, strange
insect that did look as though it were out of a Russian novel.

"It can seat twelve," Patch said as he climbed in and took
the reins. "We got it from a bed and breakfast that used to
take guests on sleigh rides. Isn't it great?" Sweeney, Toby,
Rosemary, Willow, Ian, and the twins settled in, tucking the
blankets around their legs. Sweeney had put on a pair of

Patch's high winter boots and her parka over her dress, but she shivered in the cold air.

The two giant Clydesdales harnessed to the sleigh pranced and snorted impatiently. They were handsome animals, their chestnut coats and bell-laden harnesses gleaming under the driveway lights. Patch murmured something soothing to them and turned around, holding up a silver flask. "Anybody? There's only one way to stay warm on a sleigh ride."

"I'll have a drop," Ian said. "I think it'll be really good to be drunk as we careen wildly across the landscape."

"Oh come on, Ian. Where's your sense of adventure?" Willow teased him. "Patch has only lost a couple of passengers."

"My grandfather actually did lose one," Patch said. "Fell right out as they went around a turn. But I probably shouldn't be telling you that."

"What, some artist?" Ian said. "He was probably a depressive and decide to off himself by leaping from the sleigh. You know artists, always offing themselves." He passed the flask back around the sleigh and it struck Sweeney that he was very drunk. The twins and Toby each took a swig as the flask came around to them.

"Ready?" Patch called. And with a great heaving the sleigh started off, two battery-powered lanterns on the front showing the way through the night.

The horses pulled the sleigh down behind the house and across the back lawn, the runners whistling as they skated across the frozen snow. Sweeney took another gulp of the brandy and felt it shoot a warm path to her stomach.

As they reached the open field, they gathered up speed. It was exhilarating, the cold wind whipping at her face, the other bodies pressed against her. The night was clear and the sky was filled with stars. Sweeney raised her face up to the dark, cold air.

They sailed across the frozen fields as if borne by a great wind and she watched the cemetery and the Kimballs' house fly by in the moonlight as the sleigh glided along the edge of the woods and then, suddenly, came out into another open field. The broad, opalescent expanse of it lay out in front of them like a huge, white sheet.

"How's everybody doing?" Patch called out. It was almost impossible to hear him in the wind. Trip let out a whoop and stood up halfway, his arms in the air. Sweeney knew exactly how he felt. She never could have imagined it would be so much fun.

As they came up on the edge of the field, she could feel the horses start to speed up. Patch must have pulled on the reins then because the horses bucked and the sleigh leaned to the side. Sweeney could feel all the bodies shift toward her, as though they were on an amusement park ride.

She loved them all, she thought, drunk with the alcohol and the cold night air. She loved Toby, and his uncle, and Rosemary, who had been so kind to her, and the twins, their lives ahead of them. She loved them all and they loved her.

They sped on gracefully across the snow.

At the end of the field, the sleigh slowed and she could see a dark mound looming in the distance. "That's Maple Hill up ahead," Patch called back to them. "There's a great view of the river from the top." They began to climb and by the time they reached the top of the hill and came out onto a little plateau, the horses were walking ponderously, pulling the sleigh with great effort. Sweeney felt sorry for them.

Patch pulled them up next to the dark silhouette of a pine tree. "Now," he said, lifting a box from the sleigh. "Hot chocolate, anyone?"

He poured the steaming chocolate from a plastic thermos into Styrofoam cups and added a few drops from the flask to each. Then he reached into the box and brought out a portable tape player, pressing a button on the top. A waltz—Strauss—started up and they all got out.

Above them, the stars were brilliant in a black sky. It was so dark, it was almost impossible to see anything beyond the sleigh, where Patch had placed a small flashlight on one seat. The Styrofoam cup was warm in Sweeney's hands. She gulped the steamy liquid and felt the spirits rise against the back of her throat.

"That's the river down there," Willow said, pointing to a glimmering serpent of ice and water below them. "Be careful. It's a good drop down." They all approached the edge and looked over. There was something magical about the sight of the water, the dark night, the stars above. The music floated out across the hill, mingling with the gentle wind. Patch grabbed Willow and waltzed away with her across the snow. Toby and Rosemary followed, laughing as they disappeared into the dark.

Sweeney felt suddenly dizzy. She was tired and had had too much to drink. She breathed in the cold air and wandered a couple of hundred yards away from them, to stand under a tree where the hill fell away. She tipped her head back to look up at the sky. The Little Dipper shone brightly, and she picked out the other formations she knew, Orion's Belt and the Big Dipper. It was so beautiful. She closed her eyes and felt peace wash over her. She heard Toby's voice calling out, "Where'd you all go? It's so dark," then Patch's laugh.

Suddenly she heard a crunch of snow behind her and just as she opened her eyes, someone pushed her from behind. It was a surprisingly gentle push and she felt herself fall in slow motion, her upper body teetering over the edge of the hill, her arms flailing as she tried to keep her footing. For a moment, she thought she might be able to regain her balance, but then she felt the snow give way beneath her and she fell backward and started sliding. The hill was steeper than it appeared from the top, and she gathered speed as she slid. Grab something, she told herself. Just grab something. And at that moment her right shoulder hit something hard and she reached with her other hand and got hold of a small tree. It bent discouragingly, then held. She tried to catch her breath, and tried to block out the pain in her right shoulder. Then she was able to get a firm footing and could stand as long as she hung on to the tree.

"Hey!" she called out. "Help me! Please! Someone pushed me over." She felt her hold on the tree slip a little, her boots slide on the snow and she called out again.

Patch's voice came out of the darkness. "What? Sweeney?"

"It's Sweeney." That was Ian's voice, directly above her. "Sweeney, where are you?"

"I'm right here. I grabbed hold of a tree, but I think I hurt my arm. I can't hold on much longer."

"Shit!" That was Patch's voice. "Wait, let me get the flashlight."

But she heard a crashing above her and then Ian's voice saying, "Where are you? Say something so I can find you."

"Here," she said weakly. "I think I can get back up. It's just my shoulder."

"No, wait. You might be hurt." Suddenly, he was right in front of her in the dark and he put an arm around her, holding her up.

"Did you hit your head?" Patch shone a light down on them and she turned to find Ian's eyes searching her face.

"No, I don't think so. Just my shoulder."

"I've got my foot braced against a tree," Ian said. "Hang on and I think I can get us both up."

They made their way slowly, Sweeney holding his gloved hand and allowing herself to be towed along, her shoulder throbbing, her teeth chattering from cold and shock.

"Are you okay, Sweeney?" Patch helped them up the last few yards.

"I think so." She was shivering violently and Willow brought a blanket from the sled to wrap around her shoulders."

"What happened?" Toby asked.

"I . . . I think someone pushed me."

"What?" Toby sounded incredulous.

"We were all right here," Patch said. "Nobody would push you. That's ridiculous."

"It was dark," she said quietly. "You wouldn't have known."

"You must have lost your balance. It's so dark and we were standing too near the edge."

Sweeney's mind raced. Was it possible she had just

stepped over? She supposed it was. Yet, she thought she remembered someone standing there, the feel of a hand on her back. But now she wasn't sure. Had she imagined it?

"Let's head back really slowly," Patch called out once they were settled in the sleigh again. Toby put his arm around her and let her lean into him, her face against his chest.

They started for the house in silence, the cold air whipping at the sleigh. Sweeney huddled against Toby for warmth and comfort, wanting to cry.

When she saw the police car, its blue and red lights swirling in front of the house, her first thought was that someone had called ahead to say there had been an accident. But before she could work through the assumption and realize that there was no way the news could have reached the house so quickly, a second, much worse thought entered her head. Something had happened at the party. The house was alight and through the first floor window she could see a Christmas tree here, a couple dancing there.

"It's Cooper. Wonder what he wants?" Patch said as they pulled up alongside the driveway and the sleigh came to a halt.

"Maybe he's here to arrest you," Willow said, then laughed a little too loudly.

"Mr. Wentworth," Cooper called out.

"Is everything all right, Chief Cooper?" Patch jumped down and Sweeney could see in the low light from the house that he was scared, too.

"Oh yes, just fine," Cooper said. "It's just the bridge. The ice floes are up quite high and I think we may want to close it tonight. I thought you could make an announcement to your guests."

The party in the sleigh listened and Willow said, "This happens nearly every winter. When there's been a heavy rain, chunks of ice come rushing down the brook and get all jammed up underneath. You'd think they'd fix it instead of closing it every December. What a pain."

"Of course," Patch told Cooper. "You want everyone off now?"

"If they want to go at all tonight," Cooper said. "It's getting bad. The fire department thinks we'll have to close it up within the hour to avoid doing any damage. I'd appreciate it if you could make the announcement."

"I will." Patch helped the rest of them get down off the sleigh. When Sweeney walked past Cooper cradling her right arm, he looked at her suspiciously and nodded.

Patch asked Cooper if he wanted to come in for a drink, but the police chief just shook his head. "Got to get back to the bridge," he said and turned to go.

"Sweeney, are you okay?" Britta and Sabina came over as she entered the living room, their faces full of motherly worry and she reassured them that she was just fine. Sabina studied her for a moment, as though she were trying to put together the elements of Sweeney's face like a puzzle.

"I'm fine," Sweeney told her, taking her hand.

Rosemary came back with a glass of brandy and a little plate of hors d'oeuvres for her, toast with caviar and salmon and a couple of cookies. "That should help," she said kindly. "Caviar's a good balm for just about anything."

"Thank you," Sweeney said to her, downing the brandy. "I'm much better now."

Patch was standing in front of the Christmas tree, knocking a fork against a champagne glass as though he were calling for a wedding toast.

He explained about the bridge and said, "You may think I'm just trying to get rid of you and trying to get you to stop drinking my champagne, but Chief Cooper tells me that in fact you really must shove off. So put down your glasses, come on . . ." Everyone laughed.

His guests filed out slowly, saying their goodnights and thank you's and exiting into the cold air. Toby came over and put an arm around her, then whispered that he was taking Rosemary and Electra home. Sweeney raised her eyebrows at him and smiled.

"I like Rosemary," she whispered. "I wanted to tell you that."

"Are you sure you're okay?"

"I'm sure."

He smiled at her. "You know that you owe Ian a giant thank you?"

"I know, I know." She wasn't as sure as Toby was, but she let it go. She hugged him goodnight and, through the front windows, watched the long row of car headlights crawling toward the bridge.

In her dreams that night, Sweeney was standing on the platform of the tube station, watching the faceless commuters drift slowly from the train, seeking out Colm among them. She waited, watching the crowd, looking for his black hair, the red sweater he'd been wearing.

He walked past her, striding very quickly, his red sweater stained with blood, his trousers in tatters. His face, its sharp lines and laughing green eyes, his twisted, crooked smile, was untouched.

"Colm!" she called to him. But he only turned and smiled at her, then lowered one dark eyebrow in a rakish wink.

"Colm!" she called again. "Are you okay? There was a bomb on the tube." But still he kept walking. She followed him out of the station and suddenly they were in a summer field, tall grass and wildflowers undulating in the breeze. She recognized the landscape as Byzantium and she called out to Colm to ask him what he was doing there. But he kept walking very fast and she had to run to keep up with him. Then they were in the cemetery and when she came through the gate, she saw him sitting on Mary's stone, holding a book of Tennyson's poetry.

In an instant, Charley was there, too. Sweeney was watching her swimming in a pond or a lake, everything seemed perfectly normal except that she was wearing all her clothes. All alone, she laughed and splashed in the water. It was brilliantly sunny and hot and Sweeney wanted to go swimming. Then Colm ran by again, as though he was chasing someone. Once again, she followed, yelling after him, asking him what was going on.

But he disappeared into the woods. She kept running, and came out onto a bluff, overlooking the water. Charley wasn't there. She called her name, but there wasn't a sound in the silent forest. She looked around for Colm, but he was gone, too. She was all alone.

And she woke alone, her heart racing, her head pounding, her hands clutching at the sheets. Her feet were cold, and she got out of bed to put on another pair of socks.

Awake with adrenaline and the middle-of-the-night beginnings of a hangover, she wandered over to her window and looked out over the Wentworths' back gardens, down toward the cemetery. At first, she mistook the figure coming over the snow toward the house for a shadow, drawn in the moonlight by the profile of a fir tree, but as it drew closer, it took on the aspect of a man, bundled up in winter clothes and walking quickly, his arms swinging at his side. The clock by her bedside table read 4 A.M.

As he came closer, into the halo of light given off by the fixture next to the back door, Sweeney saw that the figure was Patch. She hadn't heard him go out, and what could he possibly be doing walking around in the woods at almost midnight? Maybe he'd taken the dogs out. Or gone to check on the bridge. That was it, he'd probably gone to check on the bridge.

She found another comforter in a blanket chest at the foot of her bed and wrapped it around her shoulders before getting back under the covers. It had been a long time since she had dreamed about Colm, and it was awhile before she was able to sleep.

# TWENTY-SEVEN

*December 22*

SWEENEY WOKE UP the next morning piteously hung over, her shoulder throbbing from her fall, and lay in bed for a moment, only partly conscious. From downstairs, she heard the sounds of the household, faint voices calling to each other, a radio blaring hoarsely somewhere. An overwhelming urge to roll over and go back to sleep started to take hold, but the clock on her bedside table read 10 and her ears told her that the household was awake. She put on jeans and a sweatshirt and closed her bedroom door behind her.

"This is awful," Britta said as Sweeney came down the stairs, one hand to her pounding head. "The house is a mess." She looked as though she were about to cry and Sweeney murmured something sympathetic as she looked around at the post-party carnage: half-full champagne glasses everywhere, marked with oily lipstick kisses on the rims; plates covered with food scraps, bones and skin and fruit rinds. It made her nauseous and she closed her eyes as the floor rose up to meet her, squeezing her temples to make the throbbing stop.

Toby and Rosemary were working on the living room, picking up glasses and plates.

"We just told the caterers to go home because of the bridge," Britta was saying. "We didn't even *think*."

The bridge. Sweeney had forgotten about the bridge. "Have they fixed it yet? I was thinking about going downtown for some Christmas presents."

"No. But it should be clear soon." Britta shivered a little.

"I hate it. It makes me feel claustrophobic. At least Carl Thompson's in jail."

Patch came in from the kitchen, holding a giant garbage bag. "Okay, let's do this. I want to get outside this afternoon."

"Can I help?" Sweeney asked bleerily.

"You look like you're going to be sick," Toby said. "How's your shoulder?"

"Sore. But not as sore as my head." Sweeney rubbed her temples.

Patch said, "Why don't you have some coffee, Sweeney. Brit and I can handle clean-up duty. Everyone else is down by the river, watching the cops try and get rid of the ice. You might want to head down and see what's going on."

"Actually," Sweeney said. "I think I'll go for a walk. The cold air will be good for my head."

Britta looked as though she wished Sweeney would grab a garbage bag and get working. But she said, "Go ahead. By the way, there's a paper bag on the table in the hallway. Charley Kimball came up and dropped it off for you this morning."

"Charley Kimball? Did she say what it was?"

"No. Oh, Patch. Don't throw those away. We can wash those. . . ."

Sweeney, feeling she had been dismissed, got dressed to go. On her way out, she tucked the little bag into the pocket of her parka.

The wickedly cold air *was* good for her head, and the headache passed after the first twenty minutes or so of hard walking. Despite the thin layer of new snow that had fallen during the night, she was able to follow the deep tracks left by the runners of the sleigh, and she walked along in them, on the path they had taken last night.

When she was a couple hundred yards from the house, Sweeney took the small bag out of her pocket and retrieved from it a blue, faux leather bankbook, a note paperclipped to the front. The note read, in extremely neat printing, "I thought about it and I thought I should give you this. Love, Charley." Sweeney folded the note into her pocket, then stopped and held the little book in her hands, turning it over.

She wasn't sure what she had been expecting, but it certainly wasn't this. The book had Ruth Kimball's name on the inside cover and listed a balance of $12,762. On a piece of masking tape stuck on the back someone had written, in red pen, "Charley's College Account."

The first page was faintly printed with a record of deposits that started in July and went on quite regularly from there. Each one was $1,500. When she flipped through the little book, she found, stuck in the back, a small scrap of paper with some dates jotted on it. They were different from the dates in the book, and didn't seem to have any significance that Sweeney could identify.

Why had Charley given it to her? It was sweet that her grandmother had established a college account for her, but what could it possibly have to do with Mary Denholm? She slipped the book back into her coat, disappointed, and when she felt the quick twinge in her shoulder, her mind was suddenly back on Maple Hill.

She went over the list of everyone who had been there. Patch, Willow, Toby, Trip, Rosemary, Gally. And Ian, of course. Ian had been there, too.

How had he gotten there so quickly? How had he known where to go? It only made sense if he had pushed her. The more she thought about it, the more convinced she became.

He had lied about when he arrived. And he had followed Sweeney to Boston. Kissing her had been a ploy to distract her from the sheer silliness of his stupid excuses.

But why? That was what she kept coming back to. The police were saying that Carl Thompson had killed Ruth Kimball and until she found out differently, Sweeney was going to accept that. So was it possible that Ruth Kimball's murder had absolutely nothing to do with Mary Denholm's? Was it possible that Ian had come to make sure that the truth about the older mystery didn't get out?

Anything was possible, Sweeney told herself sardonically.

But not everything was true. She decided she'd head over to
Gilmartin's studio. She hadn't seen it yet and it might be
inspiring to see the place where he'd carried on his liaisons,
the place where Mary's body had been found.

She took the path through the woods, taking the fork that
Ian had pointed out to her that first day in Byzantium. As
she came out on a little ridge, she could see the river below
her. The morning sun and warmer air had loosed the ice floes
a bit and the water ran swiftly by, dark and bottomless. She
stood for a moment, looking down at it and gasped when
she saw a dark form floating by, the face stretched into a
grimace, the flowing hair trailing in the water, the hands
folded demurely over the lap.

But it was just a log, a frozen chunk of ice at one end, a
plastic bag dragging like hair, icy hands twisted from a few
leftover branches at the other. The log bobbed a bit on the
water, innocuous now, and Sweeney admonished herself for
being so skittish.

The path sloped down to the river and after a few minutes
she saw, up ahead in the trees, the small brown form of
Herrick Gilmartin's studio. It was like a little log cabin, built
up on stilts. Underneath was piled firewood, and off to one
side was a telephone booth-sized structure Sweeney assumed
was an outhouse.

She stood and looked at the little building. It was in a
pretty spot, just above the river, with views across to the
other bank and a path that led down to what must have been
a small beach. In winter, under a thin and unattractive covering of snow and ice, the studio looked a bit forlorn, but
she could imagine it surrounded by leafy trees and gardens,
the green banks of the sparkling river beckoning a tired artist.
She climbed three wooden stairs to the porch and tried the
front door, but found it well secured with a shiny padlock.
The windows were obscured by curtains and when she stood
up on tiptoes to try to look through the narrow pane above
the door, she saw only molding, the top of a wall. Darn.

She climbed down off the porch and studied the building.
So this was where he had carried on his *affaires de couer*,

Sweeney thought, or his affairs of something else. It was also where Mary had modeled for Gilmartin on her last day of life.

The wind blew through the trees, stirring up the bone-bare limbs, which clacked against each other alarmingly. A branch that had been wedged in a little tree next to the studio flew and skittered down onto the ground. The wind came hurrying through the trees again and she felt suddenly afraid.

She turned to go. But the outhouse stood there like an unfinished sentence. She would just make sure there wasn't anything there of interest. She wasn't sure exactly what she was hoping to find, but it had been Gilmartin's and who knew, maybe there was some Victorian graffiti scrawled on the walls: "I killed Mary." "Mary and Herrick forever." Sweeney allowed herself a small smile.

She made her way across the little yard between the studio and the outhouse, and stood there, gathering her courage, then strode over and threw the door open.

She saw blood.

Red blood, frozen on the wooden floor of the outhouse. Eyes staring lifelessly at nothing, the body stilled in an improbable position.

She screamed and almost fled, then forced herself to look.

An unfortunate ermine—she only knew its name because she had studied art and she had seen countless of those snowy white pelts in European portraits of royalty—had retreated here after being attacked by some predator of the woods. Its throat had been opened. The blood had pooled beneath it and frozen. Its white coat was absolutely pristine, though, and its eyes looked somehow peaceful. Sweeney checked to make sure that there wasn't anything else to see in here, and shut the door.

She walked quickly back toward the house and felt better as she came out into the sun, her shirt sticky with perspiration inside her layers of winter clothes.

As she caught sight of Birch Lane, she decided to go visit with Sabina. She had been wanting to ask her about last night, about what she had seen in the window that had scared her so. She walked along the road and in five minutes, she was striding up Sabina's driveway.

The door was already open, just a crack, but through the thin aperture, she could see Sabina's cat. It had one paw around the edge of the door as though she were trying to open it, and she mewed plaintively at Sweeney.

"Sabina?" Sweeney called out, the door yielding to her gentle pressure. It was very cold in the hallway, probably because the door had been left open, and Sweeney shivered as she called out again. "Sabina? It's Sweeney. I just wanted to see if you're okay. You seemed pretty shaken up last night."

Silence. Sweeney stepped carefully over the cat, who was rubbing desperately against her legs. As she came into the morning room, she saw that it was very messy. Papers and magazines lay on the floor, and then as she stood there, she realized that it wasn't just messy, that someone had knocked these things from the coffee table and the bookcases. Paintings and picture frames lay broken and jumbled on the floor. Shards of glass from a broken vase glittered on the oriental carpet.

"Sabina?" she called again, more desperately this time, going quickly toward the library. "Are you okay?"

In the moment that she saw Sabina's body lying on the floor of the library, Sweeney felt as though Death had finally shown his face. He had been stalking her all this time, leaving small clues, titillating her with his mysterious ways. But now here he was, in the flesh. And it was Sweeney he sought. She was sure of that now.

She went to Sabina's body and kneeled down beside her to peer at her eyes, which stared heavenward, dead and empty. Her face was purple and around her neck was a red satin cord. Sweeney saw that it had come from the drapes in the morning room, the strands of glossy crimson rope wound together, the silk tassels hanging ridiculously by Sabina's waist.

She was wearing only a blue terrycloth bathrobe and it

had opened in front to reveal a peek of grotesquely mottled breast, silvery gray hair between her legs.

Sweeney looked up quickly at the wall where the relief by Jean Luc Baladin had been, and when she saw that it was bare, she got up and she began to run, away from Death, away from the evil that had been done here, away from her chaotic confusion about what it all meant.

She ran from the house and didn't stop until she reached the bridge.

# TWENTY-EIGHT

"So THE RELIEF was missing?" It was much later and Sweeney was sitting in Chief Cooper's office at the police station,
curled in a chair, hugging herself as if she could get warm
again. One of the state investigators—she didn't remember
his name—sat in a chair at the other end of the room, listening.

"You're sure of that?"

"Yes. I looked up and the whole wall was bare. It's definitely gone. I looked around the whole room, after I'd realized she was . . . that there was a body." She was seeing
once more the image of Sabina's eyes, staring up at her.

Cooper said nothing. His eyes were tired and his hands,
Sweeney noticed, tremored slightly. "Had anything else been
taken?"

She was so tired, she had to fight through a veil of exhaustion in order to focus her eyes on his face. "I don't
know. I'd only been there once. You'd have to ask Willow,
or someone who knows. I just don't . . . I can't remember."

He watched her. "Have you ever seen a body before?" he
asked quietly. "It can be very disturbing if you haven't."

The radio on his desk buzzed suddenly and Sweeney listened to a voice say something about securing Sabina's house
after the body had been taken away. "You'd think so, in my
line of work. But I haven't. It was different than I thought
it would be, you know? I think I'd always figured that a dead
body would look the way they do in horror films. Grotesque.

Violated. But it was just a person, it was just her. Except I knew she wasn't alive anymore."

"What made you go and see her?" She had been waiting for him to ask the question and she swallowed hard before telling him about the way Sabina had suddenly stared at the window at the party, and the look of fear that had passed across her face.

"So you think she must have seen something reflected in the window that scared her?"

"It's the only thing I can think. I was going to make sure she was okay and ask her what it was. But someone . . ."

"Someone got there first." He met her eyes and she nodded.

She thought for a moment and said, "It means that it wasn't Carl, doesn't it? Because he was in jail."

He looked up at her in surprise, then said. "You're right. I think it's pretty safe to say that Carl Thompson wasn't responsible for this." The state investigator cleared his throat and Sweeney got the idea that Cooper had said something wrong.

"I don't know anything about this. She was . . . she was strangled with a cord. From the curtains. I don't know how it works. Would you have to be strong, to do that? Or would the cord . . . ?"

He raised his eyebrows at her and she could see that he wasn't going to tell her anything. "Tell me a little bit more about what happened last night. There was an accident?" he said finally.

She looked up quickly, wondering who had told him. "Yes. But I'm not sure if . . . It was probably just an accident."

He raised his eyebrows. "I don't know. You were coming back from the sleigh ride when I saw you. Is that right?"

"Yes. You'd just shown up to announce about the bridge." She saw something flash across his face and in that instant, she understood why he seemed so grim. "I just realized. About the bridge. Don't you see? It had to be one of us. It had to be someone on The Island."

"Yes," he said slowly. "It had occurred to me. That's why we're trying to pin down what everyone did after the party. You went to bed, I take it?" She nodded. "What about the rest of the household?"

Sweeney swallowed, remembering Patch's figure returning home at 4 A.M. "The kids went to bed, too, at least I think they did. I think Britta and Patch went to bed about the same time I did."

He must have heard hesitation in her voice because she prompted her with a "And . . . ?"

"And I woke up from a bad dream at four and saw Patch coming home. He was walking."

Cooper sat up a little straighter in his chair. "At four, you say?"

"Yes. I figured he had gone to check on the bridge."

Cooper didn't confirm or deny that. "According to our interviews, your friend Mr. DiMarco took Electra Granger and Rosemary Burgess home. Mrs. Granger says he and Rosemary talked out in the car for a while and that she came back in around one. What time did he get home?"

"I don't actually know. I was asleep by then."

"What about Ian Ball?"

"I don't know. I assume he went to bed, too."

"But did you see him? Up on the third floor?"

Sweeney hesitated for a moment. "No," she said. "I didn't see him and his door was closed."

It was Britta who picked her up at the police station. She was waiting in the lobby when Sweeney came out of Cooper's office, reading a magazine, her right foot tapping out a nervous rhythm on the linoleum. Outside the windows, the twilight sky was the loveliest shade of blue Sweeney had ever seen. A few early stars shone brilliantly above.

"Thanks for coming to get me," Sweeney said as they got into the Land Rover.

Britta had been crying and she looked up and said, "That's okay. Toby wanted to, but I felt like I just had to get out of the house. I couldn't stand being strong anymore. For the children."

"I'm sure no one expects you to be strong all the time. Sabina was your friend."

"I know. There are times I think it's better for them to know that you don't stop being scared or weak just because you're an adult, that I should let them see what our problems are, where all the fissures lie. And there are times when I think the most important thing I can do for them is to let them be scared while we keep things going."

"You're right. I had parents who let me see how weak they were all the time. It was terrifying."

Britta started up the car and pulled out of the parking lot. "Where does your mother live? Why don't you see her at Christmas?"

"She lives in England. We haven't talked in two years." Sweeney thought for a moment, remembering. It was as though she could smell Ivy's perfume. Gardenia. Heavily sexual, sickly sweet. "She couldn't rise to the occasion when I needed something from her. I'm stubborn. She's . . . we disagree about something. We've never worked it out."

"What do you disagree about?"

Sweeney wasn't sure why she told Britta the truth now, but she looked over at her and said, "It's nothing particularly interesting. She's an alcoholic."

"I'm sorry." They were out of town now, Britta driving too slowly along the road. Normally, Sweeney became impatient when stuck in the passenger seat with a poky driver. But today, she didn't mind. She felt she wouldn't mind if they never went back to The Island.

"How's everyone doing?" she asked.

"Not very well. Rosemary and Electra and Willow have been at the house most of the day. I think Toby's going to stay with them tonight. Anders is coming back from Boston to be with Willow."

"That's good," Sweeney said. "I wouldn't want to be alone tonight."

It was dark in the car and so she didn't notice that Britta

was crying again until she pulled the car over and bent her head to the steering wheel, her body shaking with sobs.

"Britta? What's the matter?"

"I need you to drive. Okay? Just, can you . . . ?" She got out of the car and leaned against the hood for a second, staring out past the dark shoulder of the road. When Sweeney went to touch her shoulder, she could see that Britta was shaking. "Let's just get in the car."

Sweeney got behind the wheel and pulled back onto the road as soon as Britta had put on her seatbelt. They drove in silence for what seemed like hours until Britta stopped crying and said, "I thought I could handle this, but I guess I can't."

"It's understandable, Britta."

"No. You don't understand. You see, I was diagnosed with MS. Years ago, and I've been fine for the most part. It's just that when I'm tired or stressed I can feel . . . it's hard to describe. It's like I can hear a train coming from miles away, feel the vibrations. I got scared this afternoon, because I could feel it. That's why I had to get out of the house."

"I'm so sorry. Should you go to a doctor? I'd be glad to . . ."

"No!" Britta cut in. "The kids don't know and I don't want to tell Patch right now."

"But, Britta . . ."

"No!" Britta grabbed Sweeney's arm. "Please, Sweeney. You don't understand. We just have to get through this. As a family. There are things I can't tell you. Please don't say anything."

Sweeney promised with a nod.

By the time they got home, the house was quiet. Apparently everyone had gone to bed. Britta went upstairs and Sweeney sat down at the kitchen table, surprising herself by being ravenously hungry. When she had finished off three bowls of the chicken soup Britta had left simmering on the stove, she wandered into the laundry room to find a pair of sweatpants Toby had said he was going to wash for her.

She couldn't find the sweatpants, but as she turned to leave the laundry room, she saw the door to Patch's studio, painted red and decorated with a little artist's palette, at the end of the hallway and went to investigate. It was slightly ajar and she listened for a moment to make sure that no one was coming, and pushed it open.

It was the studio of a hobbyist rather than a full-time artist. For one thing it was too clean, and for another there was a lack of the clutter that filled every well-used studio she had ever been in. But the smell of turpentine and stale coffee brought her back with a painful jolt of memory to her father's studio. She had always liked sitting on his spare chair while he worked. The rule had been that she wasn't allowed to talk, but she hadn't minded, as long as she could watch him paint.

She looked at the canvases stacked upright against the far wall, boring landscapes and still lifes that would have been perfectly at home on the waiting room wall of her dentist's office.

But on another wall was a framed collage of black-and-white photos of the kids, Trip grinning and holding a tennis racket, Gwinny looking beautiful and ethereal in a sundress. Gally's photo was strange. He was sitting on the porch and looking out over the back lawn, where a blurry group of unidentifiable people were playing volleyball or badminton. His profile in focus, his chin resting on his hand in an unconscious mimic of "The Thinker," he looked very worried, Sweeney decided, and very alone.

At the back of the studio, there was a closet door and she went to open it, fumbling with the pull on the dangling light-bulb.

It was a walk-in storage area that Patch had retrofitted with upright storage racks that held ten or so canvases each. They were wrapped in clear plastic and Sweeney could see that they were mostly landscapes, similar to the ones leaning against the wall. But when she felt along the back wall, she detected that there was one that had been pushed down between the end of the rack and the back wall. She slid it carefully out of its wrapping and brought it out into the light.

It was a portrait of Willow, a nude done with a sublime combination of painstaking care and abandon. The blues and pinks of her breasts and arms swirled and climbed the canvas. She looked up at the artist with something that could only be love and in turn the artist had looked at her—and rendered her—with such passion that Sweeney was compelled to look away.

For the painting was very, very good and because of the way it had been hidden away, she knew that he would never show it to anyone. She knew that he would not hurt Britta or his family, that he was unlike his grandfather in this central way, and she understood a number of things very suddenly.

"It's good, isn't it?"

She turned around suddenly, the painting still held out in front of her, and found Gally watching her from the doorway.

"Gally, I . . . the door was open and I . . . I'm so sorry."

"You shouldn't be sorry," he said. "You're not the one who's doing something wrong."

He reached into his pocket and came toward her. Sweeney put the painting down and held her breath.

"I found these in the hallway," he said. "This morning."

She reached out to take her earrings, cold and sharp on her palm. As he turned to go, she stammered out "Your Dad said I could look at his work sometime. I . . ."

Gally stopped and turned to look at her. "You don't understand anything," he said. And he left her standing there holding the painting, the plastic wrapping around her feet on the floor.

# TWENTY–NINE

*December 23*

WHILE THE HOUSEHOLD huddled at breakfast, grief stricken and afraid—Britta and Patch nervous and grim, Gwinny and Trip bickering, and Sweeney feeling deserted by Toby who was still at Rosemary and Electra's—the day was exuberantly beautiful. The sky was the blue of cornflowers or faraway oceans, a summery unseasonable blue. And the sun shone brilliantly down, sparkling in the trees, which seemed to have been decorated by hand with garlands of ice and snow.

Trying to cheer them up, Patch and Ian made pancakes and sausage, but no one was very hungry and as soon as she could, Sweeney said that she needed to pick up some things at the drugstore and headed for town.

She had not been able to get the image of Sabina's bare library wall out of her head as she'd tried to sleep the night before. And her conversation with Cooper only intensified her curiosity. He had seemed very interested in the fact that the relief was gone and she knew that he was wondering if whoever had killed Sabina had taken the relief, if it was related to Ruth Kimball's death and the other burglaries in the colony after all.

She had not thought of the burglaries as being very important—other than as a motive for Carl to kill Ruth Kimball—because there had not actually been one at the Kimballs' house, but the fact that Sabina's house had been burgled had to have significance.

"We close at noon, you know," the librarian told her as

she came in the front door of the library. If she recognized Sweeney from town gossip, she didn't let on.

"That's fine," Sweeney said. "I've just got a couple of things to do."

"Okay. Can I help you with anything?"

"You showed me where the older papers were a few days ago. Do you have more recent editions? I was interested in looking at the last year."

"Go downstairs and take a left into the first room you see. They should be stacked in chronological order, but sometimes people mess them up. I'm afraid they aren't indexed."

Sweeney thanked her and went down to the dank basement.

The newspapers were stacked in a case that ran the length of the wall and had compartments into which the issues for each month were kept going back about fifteen years. She took out the papers for July through December of the current year, and sat down at an unstable metal table in the middle of the room.

There was nothing in the first paper, except for strange little stories about small-town life that she found delightful even if she didn't really have time to read them all. "Mega Squash Wins First Prize!" proclaimed one headline. "Lucky Pooch Escapes From House Fire," was another, with a dramatically rendered tale of an Airedale that had hidden himself under the kitchen sink as his family's home burned and then burst out as firemen were cleaning up the mess.

The next paper, dated July third, however, had an item on the second page about the ongoing investigation into a burglary a few days earlier at the home of George Farnsworth in Byzantium. "Carl Thompson of Byzantium was questioned by the police, according to confidential sources. Stolen from the house were an assortment of books, electronic equipment, and artwork. According to police, an original sculpture by Byzantium colonist Bryn Davies Morgan was also among the items taken."

She read aloud. "Thompson has prior convictions for burglary, possession of an illegal substance, and possession with intent to distribute. Reached at his home Tuesday, he denied any involvement with the burglary. There was another blurry picture, this one of Carl standing in front of what looked like a supermarket. He had a hand up in the air and was half turned away from the camera.

None of the other July newspapers yielded anything interesting, but August was a different story.

The weekend of the ninth, there had been another burglary. This time, it was at Upper Pastures, "the home of Jack Morgan, also of Byzantium." The Morgans, the article noted, were summer residents of Byzantium and had already gone back to their primary residence in New York.

That was Willow's uncle and aunt, who spent summers in the colony. The burglary had been discovered by Alan Hancek, a caretaker, when he entered the house to adjust the thermostat. The items taken ranged from stereo equipment to a vase to clothes to "a few pieces of original artwork and a small bust by Mr. Morgan's father, the Byzantium sculptor Bryn Davies Morgan."

Once again, police sources had apparently told the paper that Carl Thompson was under investigation for the crime.

She went on with the papers.

During the last week of November, the day after Thanksgiving, there had been a burglary at the home of Dennis Parsons. The items stolen were essentially the same as before, including some paintings and small sculptures by Morgan and, once again, police had questioned Carl, but hadn't made any arrests.

November didn't offer up any more incidents, though during the first week of December, shortly before she and Toby had arrived, she found an account of the burglary at the Rapaccis' house. Again, the stolen items had been small, decorative pieces, a few paintings.

And that was it. There didn't seem to be any connection with Mary, though it was hard to tell from the newspaper accounts what had been taken.

She thought for a moment. The items seemed completely random. Could the burglar be mentally ill? She hadn't

considered the possibility before that it was someone who
was driven to steal and then had to murder so he or she
wouldn't be found out.

She hurried up to the reference section and pulled down
*Taber's Cyclopedic Medical Dictionary* and went to the Ks.

> Kleptomania—Impulsive stealing, the motive not be-
> ing in the intrinsic value of the article to the individ-
> ual. In almost all cases, the individual has enough
> money to pay for the stolen goods. The stealing is
> done without prior planning and without the assistance
> of others. There is increased tension prior to the theft
> and a sense of gratification while committing the act.

Oh well. It had been a long shot. The burglaries were obviously well planned. The burglar would have to know what
was in the houses, then find out when the occupants would
be gone. She discounted the notion of her crazed kleptoma-
niac, robbing houses for some dark gratification, and went
back to her idea that the burglaries had something to do with
Mary's murder.

But what exactly it was, she couldn't begin to imagine.

They spent the rest of the day in front of the fire at Birch
Lane, Toby suggesting intermittent games of Scrabble that
went on and on because no one's mind was on the game.
Ian had asked her once if she was all right, but mostly left
her alone, and Gwinny sat behind Sweeney on the floor and
braided her hair. It would have been a pleasant day if they
didn't kept remembering that Sabina was dead.

Sweeney was so tired she thought she'd collapse into un-
consciousness as soon as she got into bed that night, but
instead she lay there, her heart pounding, the events of the
day flooding back along with the sounds of the noisy old
house, the mechanical whirrings and hummings and the
sounds of old wood settling at night. She fell asleep once,
but awoke again when the digital clock on her bedside table
read 3 A.M., and knowing there was no way she was going

to rest, she decided to go downstairs and try to read. She put on a sweater over her pajamas and found her notes and the copies she'd made of Myra Benton's diary pages.

The dogs started as she came down the stairs wrapped in the comforter from her bed, then quieted when they saw who it was. She switched on a table lamp in the living room and wandered around looking at the Wentworths' art and photographs. On a table behind the couch was a group of black-and-white baby pictures. She picked out the twins, sitting on a beach blanket, one smiling and one scowling. On the walls were paintings by Gilmartin and a beautiful portrait that Sweeney knew was of Patch's mother, Delia Gilmartin Wentworth. It had been painted just before she got married, Britta had told her.

There was a small bookshelf over by the window, filled with antique volumes of poetry and drama. They looked fragile, their spines frayed, the gold-leafed pages covered with dust, and Sweeney hadn't dared to touch them, but now she ran a finger along the old books and read the titles, *Ralph Waldo Emerson's Works, The Roman Century, Aristophanes, Tennyson's Collected Poetry.* She carefully lifted the Tennyson from the shelf and opened the thin, red fabric cover. On the title page was a woodcut of Sir Lancelot, and the words, *"Lancelot said 'That were against me; what I can I will;' And there that day remain'd, and toward even, sent for his shield."*

Tennyson! What was it about Tennyson?

Sweeney replaced the little book and looked again at the portrait of Delia Wentworth. She was a beautiful woman, a real blushing bride, Sweeney thought, smiling.

That phrase, *blushing bride*. It rang a bell somewhere. The diary. Sweeney sat down on the couch and flipped through the photocopies she'd made of Myra Benton's diary.

> *July 6, 1890—The girls and I went for a lovely picnic today at the pond and asked the Denholm girls to come along as they do not have much fun on account of their father's strictness. We brought cold meat and*

> *drank water from the little spring on the way and*
> *Ethel said it was the first picnic she had ever gone on*
> *and that she was enjoying herself immensely.*
>
> *It is just the time of year when the wildflowers are*
> *blooming and as we walked, we saw flowers of every*
> *variety. They were so beautiful, I could hardly believe*
> *they were of nature and we plucked them up and made*
> *little crowns for ourselves. I came upon Mary picking*
> *the petals from a daisy and saying, to herself, he loves*
> *me, he loves me not, and I asked her who her sweet-*
> *heart was and she said she would not tell me and then*
> *flushed so deeply I could not help but laugh and tell*
> *her that she looked exactly like a blushing bride.*

There it was, a blushing bride. Had Mary had a lover? Sweeney had assumed the first time she'd read the section that the
love was unrequited. But why did brides blush? Well, not to
put too fine a point on it, but it was about sex, wasn't it?
What if Mary's love wasn't so unrequited, after all? She
thought about what Dammers had said about the sexual ap-
petites of the colonists, about what Sabina had told her about
Gilmartin.

So perhaps Mary had been involved in a sexual relationship with Gilmartin. If she had gotten pregnant and threatened to reveal the relationship, maybe he'd decided that
killing her was the only option. Under that scenario, Morgan
and Jean Luc Baladin would have helped him cover it all up,
pretend that Mary had drowned.

She paced around the room, trying to think it through.
What about Morgan and Baladin? Maybe Mary had been
having an affair with one of them. She thought back to the
picture of Baladin and Mary, the way his hand gripped her
shoulder, his handsome face and flowing mustache. He was
much nearer her age. Maybe they had been having a relationship and she had gotten pregnant. But why would Baladin have killed her? He was presumably a single man . . . but
then she didn't know that. It was entirely possible he had a
wife back in Europe, wasn't it?

There was also the possibility that he wasn't married, but had no intention of marrying a poor girl from Vermont. How would Mary have reacted to the news that she was to be abandoned, pregnant, and alone?

Might she have killed herself? It was possible that she had drowned herself in the river, wasn't it? But if Mary had committed suicide, then why had someone resorted to murder—twice!—to prevent the truth getting out. Suicide had been considered somewhat shameful in those days, but, really . . . The only person who might have a reason for keeping it quiet was Jean Luc Baladin. But none of his descendants lived in the colony.

Or did they? She hadn't thought about that. What if . . . ?

Sweeney thought about the three deaths that were now all a part of this. Her father had loved engines and had entertained himself when the painting wasn't coming by buying small appliances or lawn mowers and disassembling them into a heap outside his house in Boston. She'd hated it when he did that. It had always made her feel unsettled, empty inside. But she recognized now what the appeal had been and wished she could put this thing together like an engine, the many disparate parts, perfectly oiled, working together as a practical unit.

She heard the dogs rushing toward the stairs and then footsteps sounded in the hall. She stood up suddenly to find Ian watching her from the doorway.

"I guess I'm not the only one who can't sleep," he said casually, coming over and sitting down in a chair across from her. Her heart sped up a bit.

"Guess not." She forced herself to stay calm and she wrapped the comforter around herself more tightly.

He leaned forward, and she saw a scratch on the side of his face. She hadn't noticed it. It must have been from scrambling down over the brook to help her the night before. "Are you okay?" he asked. "You must be very shaken."

"I'm all right."

There was an awkward silence and then he said, "I came down to read. I couldn't sleep, after . . . everything."

She nodded. "Me, too."

"What are you reading?" He stood up and came over to sit next to her on the couch, his hands folded in his lap. He was wearing a bathrobe, sweatpants, a pajama top and dark leather slippers—an old man's slippers. It was hard to think of him as anything other than a shy, intelligent Englishman who seemed to have a crush on her.

"Nothing." She tucked the hand holding the notebook under a fold of the comforter.

Ian watched her for a moment, then said quietly, "Why do you seem so scared of me? You make me feel like Mr. Hyde."

"I'm not scared of you."

"Then why do you act like it?" He was trying to keep his voice down, but he was angry and his anger pissed her off. What right did he have?

"You ask me questions about why I'm here and what I'm doing like you're some kind of a detective or something. I could ask the same of you, you know."

"Look, I know, I know."

Watching Ian, she was aware that the line of thought she'd been pursuing before he came downstairs had pushed itself again to the surface of her consciousness and was forcing her to come back to it. She didn't think Jean Luc Baladin had any relatives in the colony, but . . .

He turned on the couch so he was facing her. "Look here," he said. "I'm sorry about what I said at the party. When we were in the sleigh."

"What do you mean?" She had no idea what he was talking about.

"What I said about artists offing themselves. I didn't know who your father was until Patch told me today. I'm sorry."

"Oh God. I didn't even . . ." But now she did remember him saying it. Strange, it hadn't even registered. "That was a long time ago. I've pretty much dealt with all that stuff," she told him nervously.

"So you didn't answer me. How are you holding up?"

"Not very well. I keep seeing her face. Every time I close my eyes."

Pain crossed his face; he almost winced, and something about his eyes made her think of the picture of Jean Luc Baladin and Mary. Ian's brow had the same brooding set to it that Baladin's had. In fact, when she thought about it, Ian looked remarkably like Jean Luc Baladin. She hadn't seen it until that moment.

And suddenly, her mind was a confusion of thoughts. She could hardly put them into order.

"Ian, remember when you said that you were from Sussex? Did you mean that you lived there or that it's where your family's from?" She took a deep breath, trying to make sense of everything that was running through her head. "I mean, where is your family from?"

He flinched and then watched her for a few seconds, blinking once before saying carefully, "Sussex."

"And are they all English?" It was quiet in the living room and her question seemed very loud to her, a disruption of the silent room.

Ian looked down at his hands, then up at her, his eyes darting away nervously. "Why the sudden interest in Ball family history?"

She sprang up from the couch. Ball, Baladin. Of course!

She looked down at him, her heart racing, uncertain if she should be afraid or triumphant. "I think I know who you are."

Ian stared at her. "What do you mean?"

"I think I know who you are," she said again. "I think you're related to a French sculptor named Jean Luc Baladin."

He looked so surprised that at first she thought she'd gotten it wrong. But then he smiled a small, sad grin and looked into her eyes. "Yes," he said simply. "Jean Luc Baladin was my great-grandfather."

Sweeney stepped back. "But, was there something between him and Mary Denholm? Did you know that . . ." She wasn't sure now what to ask him. "Did you . . . Did you come here to kill Ruth Kimball?"

"Kill Ruth Kimball?" He looked genuinely shocked. "Why would I . . . Sweeney, Ruth Kimball was my cousin."

He smiled when he saw her face. "You see, Mary Denholm was my great-grandmother."

Sweeney paced up and down the room while Ian watched her in the low light, a small smile on his lips. She tried to put it all into order—the stone, and Ruth Kimball's death, and then Sabina's—but it refused to fall into place.

She sat down next to him on the couch. "Help me out here. Obviously she had Jean Luc Baladin's baby before she died. Or wait, did she die? Or did they . . . ?"

He said, "No, she didn't die. She lived to the ripe old age of seventy-eight in England. I think they decided to run away to Europe when she found out she was pregnant and they staged the death so it didn't cause a scandal. I'm still putting it together myself. But this will explain a lot. This is what brought me here." He took a manila envelope out of his bathrobe pocket and handed it over. Sweeney opened it and found a stack of handwritten diary pages inside. They had been torn out of a bound book and she recognized the handwriting as Myra Benton's.

"My father died last year and when I was going through his things I found this. It had been sent to his father—Jean Luc's son—years before by Myra Benton's son and I don't know if he knew what it was or what it meant.

"The way I always heard the story was that Jean Luc swept Mary off her feet during the summer he was invited to Byzantium by Morgan and brought her back to England. That's where they anglicized the name. For the rest of their lives, they lived between Paris and Sussex.

"There was always this sense of something unexplained when my father talked about his parents and his grandparents. I always felt like there was something there that wasn't whole, if you know what I mean. Before I found the diary pages, all I knew was that Mary was from New England. But no one ever talked about America, about her family. I'd always been curious. Then when I found these, I figured out part of it. Obviously there were still a lot of unanswered questions. I had been friends with Patch and Britta and after I did a little research into who Myra Benton was, it seemed like such a coincidence that they would be from Byzantium. I arranged an invitation and . . ." He shrugged. That's why I came early, so I could find out more about the family. I panicked when you said you were looking into it, too."

Sweeney took out the pages. "I've read everything leading up to this," she said. "You can't imagine how frustrated I was when I discovered these pages were missing. And all the time you had them. . . ." She began to read aloud.

> *August 31, 1890*
>
> *If I thought that the events of yesterday were strange, then I was mistaken, for today they grew even stranger. I awoke early, intent on going down to the studio to work for a few hours before breakfast, but when I got there, M. was already there and refused to let me in.*
>
> *I know not whether it was the events of the past days or the snub I had received at the hands of J.L.B., but I found myself seized with a violent storm of anger and I pushed through the door, telling him that he had hired me to do a job and had no right to stop me from doing it. I scolded him for treating me so poorly and said that if he persisted in his behavior, I would assume that he had something to hide and I would accuse him publicly of murdering Miss Denholm. I blush to think of it now. I was so angry, I did not stop to weigh my words, and I went on at him like a fury, scolding and shrill. I said that I thought it was very strange that J.L.B. had left so suddenly and that I had overheard that conversation between him and G. and J.L.B. and that I had my suspicions about Miss Denholm's death. And then I burst in to the studio and sitting there in the center was the oddest statue I have ever seen.*
>
> *It was a life-sized likeness of Miss Denholm, lying*

*in a shallow boat and looking quite dead. Hovering
over her was a horrible figure of Death, leering and
grinning and looking down at her as though he were
about to seduce her. It was such a strange thing that
I gasped and looked up at M., accusing him of terrible
things.*

*But he only laughed quietly and told me I had got
it all wrong and that he was going to tell me a story
but that I musn't ever tell the story to anyone.*

*Quite soon after J.L.B. arrived in Byzantium, he
said, he had asked Miss Mary Denholm to sit for him
and they had fallen in love. M. said that he knew I
wouldn't be so silly as to ask questions about that or
about why he hadn't gone to her parents to ask for
her hand or something like that. The truth was that
they had fallen in love and within a few months, Mary
found that she was going to have a child.*

*Now, this was a problem for everyone. People in
town would have been horrified, of course, as I was.
Mary's parents were against the artists and this would
have given them more ammunition against them. But
that wasn't the biggest problem. The biggest problem
was that Mary and J.L.B. announced that they
wouldn't just get married and pretend that the baby
had been born early. They would be honest, they said,
and tell anyone who asked the truth about themselves,
because they didn't think there was anything shameful
about their love. They were going to tell the truth and
run away to Europe, they said.*

*M. hadn't ever gotten along with her parents, but
he knew what the news of their daughter running away
with an artist would do to their reputation in town.
Then there was Ethel Denholm. As much as M. and
G.—who had been told of the difficulty as well—disapproved of what they liked to call "our goddamned
society's morals" they couldn't be a party to ruining
the marriage prospects and reputation of an innocent
girl. So M. and G. came up with a plan. They would*

pretend that Mary Denholm had met with an accident and had died. It would be easy for Gilmartin to report that he had found her body in the river. Dr. Sparr, who was a doctor, after all, and knew all about delicate situations, would do whatever was necessary to make it all right and they would weight the coffin and have a sham funeral. Mary's parents would have to be told, of course, but M. said that he had believed that they would go along with it—it was better than the truth—and they had.

It took me some moments to absorb this grand deception and I had many questions that I asked M. about.

Then I turned to the fantastic stone and asked him what on earth it was. He smiled and said that Mary and J.L.B. had gone along with the plan, but on one condition. They wanted to be able to make Mary's gravestone. And they wanted to make a gravestone the like of which had never been seen before. J.L.B. and Gilmartin had lately gotten very interested in what they liked to call "drawing the dead," but was really just painting or sculpting people to look as though they were dead. They had gotten the idea from some painters J.L.B. had known in England when he was a boy and they had been mucking about with it all summer, making people pretend they were dead so they could sketch them, and so they could get an idea of how dead limbs fell and how dead skin looked. Gilmartin even had Mary get into a cold tub and waited until her skin was blue and wrinkled before he let her go. She caught a terrible cold and J.L.B. said it was her sacrifice for art.

In any case, J.L.B. and Mary decided that this was the stone that was to mark her grave. He had been working feverishly at it for the weeks before they were to leave and toward the end, as he was finishing it, J.L.B. was in such a hurry that he forgot to sign it.

It was such an incredible, fantastical story that by

*the time I returned to the house, I could scarcely be-
lieve it had not been a dream and I sat down immediately to write these words, in order to convince
myself.*

*September 3, 1890*
*Today, Mary Denholm's very odd gravestone was put
in place down in the little island cemetery. We were
quite an odd party watching its installation and her
parents looked embarrassed by it, as though it were a
monstrosity. Afterward, I heard G. and Louis Denholm
saying something about a piece of land and when I
asked M. about it, he said that Louis Denholm had
been trying to get G. to buy a worthless strip of land
between the two properties for years and that now it
looked as though he would have to do it, to secure
Mr. Denholm's silence.*

*M. and G. have once again implored me to be si-
lent on the subject of J.L.B. and Miss Mary Denholm
and I have decided to tear these pages from my diary
in order to keep them from being read by unintended
eyes. I shall keep them in a secret hiding spot, should
I ever need proof of these events.*

"Ruth Kimball didn't know," Sweeney said, thinking out
loud. "At least I don't think she did. She believed that one
of the artists had killed Mary."

"Ethel might not have known," Ian said.

"You're right. The parents probably wouldn't have told
her. But I think she must have picked up on something,
thought there was something odd about her cousin's death,
and I think she must have talked to her granddaughter, Ruth
Kimball, about her suspicions. Why didn't you say something?"

"Well, once I'd figured this all out, I was a bit paralyzed.
I thought if I could meet Mrs. Kimball and kind of see what
the situation was, it would be easier to figure out what to do
next. Then it got complicated, you see. After researching the

family at the historical society, I realized that Ethel was a cousin, not a sister, and that Mary was the only direct descendant. I didn't know if they knew this or not and I didn't want them to think I was after their house or something. I don't know. It seems so silly now, but I just thought that I should break it to them more, I don't know, more gently. After Christmas."

"And then Ruth Kimball died."

"Exactly. And there seemed to be some suspicion about whether it was suicide. By then, I couldn't come out with this big announcement, you know 'Surprise! Mary wasn't really dead. Hello! I'm your long, lost relative.' "

"God, it's incredible. So what happened to Mary and Jean Luc? He was so talented. Why haven't we ever heard of him?"

"He was talented. But his career seems to have ended when they moved back to Europe. I always had the idea that she became his art. It was a great love, you know. Unusual in those days. But, of course, they'd married for love, and they'd sacrificed much for it. He came into some family money and they were able to live on that. Mary, I'm afraid, wasn't a very good poet, but they had this little medieval society and they put on plays and made little books and things. I have a few of them. What are we going to tell Patch and Britta?"

"I think we better keep it between us for now," Sweeney said. "It might just muddy the waters."

He nodded and they were both silent for a minute.

"So that's that then," he said. "You know my secret. Have you stopped thinking I'm a murderer?"

"Yes." She smiled. "But what I can't figure out is why you always seemed to be watching me. And why you went to Boston."

"I thought—I think—that you're interesting," he said simply. "I was telling you the truth before. I had to go to Boston anyway and I just . . . I just wanted to see where you lived." He was unashamed, and his open face made her shrink back as though she had seen something ugly or predatory there.

He saw her do it and he stood up and went over to the fireplace, where he fiddled with a little brass Buddha sitting on the mantel.

"But what about the murders?" she said, thinking out loud, trying to fill the awkward silence. "Ruth Kimball's death—and Sabina's—they must be related to something else. Unless someone found out that you were related to the Kimballs and . . . But that doesn't make sense."

He took her hand and she found herself terrified, wracked with vertigo and uncertainty. And when he led her upstairs and took her pajamas off, carefully as though he didn't want to wrinkle them, and then lay her down on his bed and kissed her, not quite so carefully this time, she found herself crying, from relief and release and for the sadness of the world, and the futility of knowing what she now knew.

He kissed her face, his lips tasting the saltiness of her tears, and stroked a circle around the nipple of her left breast. He looked into her eyes as she shivered underneath him. Then she wrapped her legs around his waist, kissing him and pushing down his pajama bottoms so he could move into her. They struggled together on the bed, making love until they remembered what could happen and he pulled away from her just as her body exploded in joy, light breaking through the shadow of death.

# THIRTY

*December 24*

THAT NEXT MORNING they went out the back door into the fresh air, holding hands, still sleepy and shy with each other. The sun hovered low over the river. The air was cold and dry. A granular layer of new snow had fallen during the night and it lay on top of the frozen crust that had been there, blowing this way and that when the wind came up.

"It's lovely this early in the morning," Ian said awkwardly. Her stomach fluttered with nervousness. She felt suddenly panicked. What did he want from her now? What would he expect? She had never felt this way with Colm. There had never been a moment of awkwardness or strangeness after that first pint of Guinness, which had turned into a drunken twenty-four-hour festival of sex, talking and singing after which they had drifted into love and couplehood. It had been impossible to feel awkward around Colm. For one thing, he was always talking, carrying you along on his crazy tide of conversation. They had never been silent together, never been still.

Now, walking along the wooded path to the cemetery, he said, "I dreamt of you last night."

"You did?" Sweeney felt a flash of irritation. If he said, "And then I woke up and there you were," she would scream.

But he said, "Yes. Quite a dirty little scenario, actually. I don't think I'll tell you."

Sweeney laughed. "I'm wondering what was left for your subconscious to imagine, after the actual events of last night."

"My subconscious has quite a good imagination."

When they reached the cemetery, they went to stand in front of Mary's monument—Sweeney realized she would have to stop thinking of it as a gravestone—which had started it all.

"Isn't it odd to think that it doesn't really mark a grave?"

"It is odd," Ian said. "She has a real one, you know. In Sussex. It's a much more typical stone, some flower garlands at the top and her name and dates. She's buried next to Jean Luc."

They turned to the stones of the rest of the Denholm family. "I wonder what it was like for her parents," Ian said. "Never seeing their child again, but knowing that she was alive somewhere, that she had a child they would never see. I suppose if they were proper Victorians, they would have blamed her for being of loose morals and kind of written her off. But it must have been hard."

Sweeney had been rereading the words engraved on Elizabeth Denholm's simple marble stone. "Her mother's stone. Look. I didn't really *read* it before."

"*O' Artful Death*," Ian read.

"It's everything I needed to know," Sweeney said softly.

"What do you mean?"

"Just that it's lamenting what they did, I think. *Artful Death*. Lying Death. Mary's death was a lie. Perhaps it reflected Louis's sadness, too. They thought that Death, i.e. Mary going away, would bring them peace, or resolution at least. But that was a lie, too."

Ian turned to Louis Denholm's stone. "Her father's was awfully dark wasn't it? The first time I saw it, I felt quite sorry for Mary."

He cleared some snow away from the stone and read out loud.

> *Think my friends when this you see*
> *How Death's dark deed hath slayed me*
> *He is a thief and taketh flight*
> *Beneath the cover of the night*

"It's . . ." Sweeney stared at it, confused.

"What?" He had heard the strangeness in her voice.

"Nothing, it's just that it's very odd."

They walked around, looking at some of the other stones. "Is it weird for you to think that you're related to them?" she asked him.

"I suppose it is. I hadn't thought of it like that."

"Will you tell Sherry Kimball? You'll have to."

"I've been thinking about that. I'll have to tell Patch and Britta as well."

"I think Patch may have suspected that there was something wrong anyway," Sweeney said. "I've had the feeling, ever since I got here, that he didn't want me to look into this thing. Do you suppose he suspected that his grandfather had had something to do with Mary's death, the way I did?"

"It's possible. He may also have been nervous about you looking into old family history because of this thing with the land and the condominiums and all."

She looked up at him.

"Sweeney?"

"Yes?"

"What's wrong? You've an odd expression on your face."

"I'd forgotten about the thing with the land. That's all."

"You look as though you'd seen a ghost."

She walked around in a little circle, something that helped her to think. "It's just that I had been assuming that Ruth Kimball and Sabina were murdered because they knew something about Mary's death. But we now know they weren't killed because of Mary. So I have to ask myself why they were killed. And it just occurred to me that I'd forgotten about the whole thing with the land."

"And . . . ?" He was looking at her with a concerned expression on his face.

"And, it's in the missing diary pages. Remember? Myra Benton asked Morgan about the land and he said that Gilmartin was going to buy it from Louis Denholm."

Sweeney paused. "What did Patch tell you about it?"

Ian hesitated for a moment. "What he told you, I think.

That he had always thought he owned the piece of land, but when they went and looked, no deed had ever been recorded and it looked like it was actually still owned by Ruth Kimball. So he decided to fight this condo thing from the angle of its intrinsic historical value. State regulations against development and all that. You were there, weren't you? Sweeney?"

But she had gone back to Louis Denholm's gravestone and now she was standing in front of it and reading the words over and over again to herself. "Come here," she said. "Take a look at this."

She pointed to the words on the stone. "The language is wrong. 'Hath?' 'Taketh?' That's eighteenth century, not nineteenth. It's like he was drawing attention to it. And 'Death's dark *deed.*' Now, I have never in my entire life heard of the physical experience of death described as Death's dark *deed.* It's wrong. It doesn't make sense."

Sweeney took off her right glove and traced four letters with her bare finger. The stone was smooth and cold.

"I'm saying that it's a puzzle. The word *deed* is in there for a reason. Maybe Mary was more her father's daughter than we thought. Maybe he's trying to tell us where that deed is."

Ian looked skeptical. "But why would he want people to know where the deed is? Or, what I mean is, why would he hide the deed in the first place?"

Sweeney said honestly, "I don't know. Patch said that his father told him that his grandfather bought the piece of land off Louis Denholm. But when they went to look, the deed was never recorded. Now, according to Patch, if they could find the deed, they could stop the development. So it's important."

"But Louis Denholm wouldn't have known that."

"I know, but I *feel* like it's important."

"Sweeney . . ."

"Look, just humor me, okay? I once wrote about a gravestone where the name of the man's wife was spelled out by the first letter of each line of the epitaph," Sweeney said.

" 'Bertha.' And the epitaph was framed as a question, asking if anyone knew the name of the 'fiend'—that was the word it used—who was responsible for his death by poisoning. And if you put it together, it says 'Bertha.' So what do the first letters spell, if you put them together?" She took a pencil from her jacket pocket and wrote them down on a scrap of paper as she read out loud. " 'T-H-H-B' I don't think that's it."

"All right," Ian said, resigned. "If it is a hidden message, I think you've got the right idea. When I was a boy, I was obsessed with codes. The thing about a code is you have to find the key, the clue to how you're going to decipher the whole thing. So, if it's a nonsense sentence hiding the real message . . . Let's see, the first letters don't make a word, but the key could be a particular letter or, how about this . . . ?"

He wrote something down on the paper and Sweeney, who couldn't see it, said, "What? What? Let me see it."

Ian pushed the paper over to her. "One of the simplest kinds of codes has to do with word placement. 'Deed' is the operative word here and it comes fourth in its sentence," he said. "So if we take all of the third words in *their* lines, what do we come up with?"

Sweeney turned the paper around and read the words written on it. "When Deed thief of." "What does that mean?"

Ian grinned. "I don't know. I just decipher them."

"What if we start it with 'Deed'? No, that doesn't work either."

She was suddenly dejected. It had seemed so promising. She had been expecting it to tell her that the deed could be found in safety deposit box number 56 at the Byzantium Bank, or in the third drawer of the bureau in the dining room of the Kimballs' house.

For the next fifteen minutes, Ian worked on the epitaph, trying different combinations of letters or words and coming up with nothing.

"Where would you hide something like a deed?"

"If I didn't want anyone to be able to find it?"

"Well . . . no. He did leave the message. If you wanted someone to have to work hard to find it. If you wanted to make a game of it."

"I'd hide it somewhere where it would be safe, maybe in something that would never be thrown away or damaged. Something in plain sight. Something that could be pointed to in the hidden message."

Sweeney stared at him. An idea was beginning to form in her mind. "Ian, you don't think that the burglaries . . . Remember how Patch described the burglaries. That the burglar took an assortment of things, statuettes, knickknacks, but also a variety of paintings."

"You mean that whoever is responsible for the burglaries was looking for the deed. But the only person who wants the deed is Patch."

"I know. But . . . actually, that isn't necessarily true. Everyone in the colony wanted to stop Ruth Kimball from selling her land to put up the condos. It could have been anyone. And come to think of it, the Kimballs had a reason, too. They might have wanted to find it before Patch did. Maybe Carl Thompson was looking for the deed. He was taking things from the houses. . . . what?"

He looked skeptical. "It just seems kind of far-fetched. And he's been in jail, so we know he didn't kill Sabina."

"You're right. Damn." They were walking back to the house when Sweeney said, "Look. I just feel like the burglaries are the missing link here. If Carl was responsible for them, then who killed Sabina? And if he wasn't responsible for them, then where did he get the stuff? See, there's got to be someone else involved. Someone from the colony who would know when people were going to be out, who would know what was in the houses."

She thought for a moment. Her thoughts were swimming around madly in her head.

She put a hand in her pocket.

"You okay?" He was watching her, concerned.

"Yeah. Listen, I'll be back at the house soon. There's

something I have to go do." She tried not to look at him.
She didn't want him to know.

"Well, let me . . ."

"No. I want to go on my own." The only way to dissuade
him was to be rude.

He flinched and said, "All right. Will you be back soon?"

"I don't know, Ian. Look, just go. I'll be back."

# THIRTY-ONE

ON HER WAY to the Kimballs' house, Sweeney took the little bankbook out of her pocket again and looked at the slip of paper that had been stuck between the back cover and the last page. She read the dates to herself. They were scrawled with different pens—one blue and one black—but all in the same hand. "7/1. 8/9. 11/28. 12/10," the writing read.

It hadn't struck her the first time she'd seen them because she hadn't been to the library yet, but the dates corresponded exactly with when the burglaries in the colony had occurred. Then she looked at the deposit dates. They hadn't seemed to follow any particular pattern, one in late July, two in August, another two in September, three in October, four in November. But now that she'd compared them with the dates of the burglaries, she could see that they started very soon after the first one and increased in frequency as time went on.

If it had been physically possible, Sweeney would have kicked herself. Why hadn't she gone to ask Charley about the book when she had given it to her? She wouldn't have gone to the trouble of leaving it for Sweeney if she didn't know or at least suspect why it was important. Sweeney was starting to have an idea of what it might be that Charley could have told her.

Sherry answered the door in her bathrobe. She looked as though she'd just gotten up and her face clouded when she saw who it was.

"What do you want?" she asked.

"Sherry, is Charley here? It's really important that I talk to her."

"If you talk to her, are you going to tell the police and get her arrested?" Sherry turned around and went into the house, leaving the door open. Sweeney followed her inside. She had been cleaning. The hallway smelled of lemons; wood surfaces gleamed from a recent dusting.

"I know it must have looked bad, but all I can tell you is that I had no idea that Carl was going to get arrested. In fact, I don't think Carl had anything to do with your mother's death and I think Charley might be able to help me prove it."

Sherry looked up at that. "She went for a walk. I got her a puppy, a couple of days ago. Carl had promised her one for Christmas. She took him out for a walk, to get him used to his leash."

Sweeney had to resist screaming at her, "Why did you let her go alone?" Instead she said, "I'm going to go out and look for her, okay?"

Sherry nodded. "She just went for a walk," she said, as though trying to convince herself.

She started across the back field, calling out Charley's name. It was almost noon, and the sun was high above her, offering a little welcome warmth as she ran. She made a wide circle and came out by the cemetery, yelling for Charley all the while. But no one answered back.

Sweeney was about to turn around when she saw the entrance to the path through the woods. It was steep as you went down to the river. Suppose Charley had been walking and slipped. She wrapped her scarf more tightly around her neck and started into the woods.

When she reached the point where the path veered off toward the river in one direction and Birch Lane in the other, she started calling out Charley's name again. Her voice echoed across the river and back again. "Lee-Lee-Lee-Lee," it mocked her. A chickadee scolded her from a low-hanging pine tree and she watched it flit across the path, land, and scold her again.

The path was slippery beneath the new layer of snow and she had to go carefully so she didn't fall. She was almost to the studio when she saw the puppy. It lay on its side about thirty feet below her on the riverbank, its body half-buried in the snow, its head twisted back grotesquely, and she knew it was dead without going down to see.

It was five or ten minutes before she found the small form, curled into a fetal position beneath a spruce tree, the Christmasy, wonderful smell filling the air. Sweeney saw the red of her coat before she saw that it was Charley and she stopped, afraid to discover what had been done to her. She remembered the way Sabina's eyes had stared up at her, the unnatural way her body had fallen.

But when Sweeney leaned over her and touched the bloody gash on her forehead, Charley's body jerked a little and her eyes opened once, fixed on Sweeney and shut again. She had wrapped Charley in her own jacket and picked her up before she remembered about spinal cord injuries and not moving people who had fallen. Charley's body was limp, but when Sweeney touched her skin, it was warm and she breathed as though she were sleeping, rhythmically and steadily. Sweeney felt the warm moistness of it against her neck.

And then she was running—it seemed improbable that she could run carrying the weight of the girl—running over the snow, holding Charley against her body.

"When she was born, I felt as though she had been given to me so that she could save me," Sherry Kimball was saying. They were in Charley's room at the regional hospital in Suffolk, watching her sleep, watching the beeping and whirring of the machines and the dripping of various liquids into her blood. "I was into all kinds of stuff then, and they said she probably wouldn't even come out normal, you know. But she did, she came out perfect. More than perfect. And she was mine, although she always made me feel that I didn't know what I was doing. She always made me feel like I shouldn't have been trusted with her or something."

"I think everyone must feel like that," Sweeney said. "I bet if you could have asked your mother how she felt when she had you, she would have said almost the same thing."

"Yeah. Maybe." Sherry stood up and went over to the bed. "I shouldn't have let her go alone," she said to Sweeney. "With everything that's happened. You wouldn't have let her go, would you?"

"I don't know. I have no idea what kinds of good or bad choices I would make. But she's going to be okay, so it doesn't really matter." She knew that she should have said something about learning from mistakes, but instead she said, "She's going to be okay. You get a second chance." Sherry looked at her, tears in her eyes. Sweeney said it again. "You get a second chance."

# THIRTY-TWO

*The storm of 1890 arrived a couple of days before Christmas, as the colonists who stayed were getting ready for the holiday and those who came north for the parties had just begun to arrive.*

*Morgan later said that he could feel in his bones that something was coming, but he didn't have any idea how bad it was going to be. By the time it had stopped on Christmas Day, it lay as deep as a child or small woman and we told the children not to go outside for fear they would be buried.*

—*Muse of the Hills: The Byzantium Colony,*
*1860–1956,*
by Bennett Dammers

THEY DIDN'T CELEBRATE Christmas Eve. Britta had already made oyster stew, and they were all eating halfheartedly when Sweeney came home from the hospital. Ian jumped up and asked her how she was and Toby tried to give her a hug, and get her to sit down, but she couldn't stand to sit there at the table and she told them she didn't feel well and wanted to go to bed.

The day after Christmas she would tell Cooper what she thought had happened. She would give them Christmas at least. She would do that for Toby.

Now she was tired. Now she collapsed into the armchair

in her bedroom and picked up the first book on the bedside table. She wanted to distract herself with words.

It was the collected Tennyson and she opened to the poem that had started all of this, and read it to herself.

> *On either side the river lie*
> *Long fields of barley and of rye,*
> *That clothe the wold and meet the sky;*
> *And thro' the field the road runs by*
> *To many tower'd Camelot;*

Sweeney found herself thinking of Mary, who had gotten her into this in the first place. Mary, who had fancied herself a kind of Lady of Shalott, pining away on her island until she was rescued by her own Lancelot, Jean Luc Baladin. But unlike the Lady of Shalott, he had taken her away.

> *There she weaves by night and day*
> *A magic web with colors gay.*
> *She has heard a whisper say,*
> *A curse is on her if she stay*
> *To look down to Camelot.*
> *She knows not what the curse may be,*
> *And so she weaveth steadily,*
> *And little other care hath she,*
> *The Lady of Shalott.*
> *And moving thro' a mirror clear*
> *That hangs before her all the year,*
> *Shadows of the world appear.*
> *There she sees the highway near*
> *Winding down to Camelot:*

She had always liked that line. *Shadows of the world appear.* It was true, looking at things through a mirror was a misrepresentation. She thought of her mother, who had always put on her makeup for the stage using a double mirror, so as to negate the switching-around effect of looking into a single mirror. It was a common theatrical practice, so you would see yourself exactly as the audience did.

Wait a second.

She dropped the book onto her lap. Her mind was racing.
Mirrors, shadows, it all danced around in her head, a dervish
of images. There was something . . . a window. Oh God.

She had been stupid. They had all been stupid. She felt a
cold fear settle over her shoulders. The figures in the little
book. She had thought she knew, but she hadn't. Not really.
This time she really knew.

She read the rest of the poem.

> But Lancelot mused a little space;
> He said, 'She has a lovely face;
> God in his mercy lend her grace,
> The Lady of Shalott.

She waited, unsure what to do, and paced around the room,
trying to put it all into order. After an hour or so she heard
Ian come up the stairs, pause outside her room, and then go
into his own room, carefully shutting the door.

Then she went and lay down on her bed, where she waited
for an excruciating thirty minutes, the numbers rolling over
slowly on the digital clock.

Finally, when the house was silent, she got up and put on a
heavy sweater and a pair of ski pants over her sweats. She
found a hat and gloves, grabbed a flashlight out of her bag, and
tiptoed quietly out into the hall. She'd decided that she
wouldn't use the flashlight until she was outside so that she
wouldn't wake anyone up, so she felt her way down the stairs,
shushed the dogs when they got up to greet her and stood there
in the hall for a moment, gathering her nerve.

Then she took the set of boots and cross-country skis
she'd used that first day out of the hall closet and slipped
out the back door, shutting it softly behind her. Thankfully,
the dogs stayed quiet, watching her for a moment through
the glass and then dropping their heads to the kitchen floor.

She'd made it.

She snapped the boots into the skis, switched on the flashlight and looked out into the whirling snow.

# THIRTY-THREE

LATER, SHE WASN'T sure how she'd reached the studio. The beam of the flashlight gave her only a foot or so of visibility in the whiteout. Every time she put a ski forward, she feared she was going in the wrong direction, searching for the path through the dark, snow-cloaked trees.

But then the light caught the silvery length of the half-frozen river, and she hugged the bank as much as possible, knowing the path led straight to Gilmartin's little studio.

It was bitterly cold and the driving snow made its way under the collar of her parka and down into the ski boots. She kept going, pushing her feet forward, even when they began to throb, when the muscles in her arms began screaming for relief.

Just when she thought she was going to collapse, she saw, up ahead, a brown block in all the white. She was there.

Sweeney stepped out of the skis and huddled on the porch for a moment relieved to be out of the driving wind and snow. When she'd recovered, she tried the windows, finding them locked, and pulled fruitlessly at the padlock on the door.

It took her a few minutes to find a rock under the snow, but once she had one in her hand, she wrapped her right arm in her scarf and punched the rock through the glass. Then she used it to break away the shards of glass along the window frame and placed her parka over the rough edges of glass, carefully climbing over the sill. Once she was inside, she put her parka back on and shone the flashlight along the ground and then up the walls. There was no one there.

The studio was a large room with a fireplace against one wall and a row of shelves against another. It was empty of any furniture except for an old easel, covered with splashes of multi-colored oil paint, and an army cot pushed against one wall.

But it wasn't empty. On the floor in front of the far wall, Sweeney could see an irregularly shaped heap. She went closer and lifted a brown tarp from the pile of stolen artwork.

She quickly found what she was looking for and she piled the paintings up to the side, wrapping them in the plastic garbage bags she'd put in her coat pocket. It wasn't an ideal way to transport art, but it would have to do. She was wrapping the parcel when she heard footsteps out on the porch and she shut off the flashlight, pressed herself against the wall next to the door, and waited.

After what seemed like an eternity, a figure came through the window. She turned the flashlight on, shining it at where she imagined the face would be.

"Hey." It was Gally. He squinted at her, holding a hand up to shield his eyes from the light.

She had not expected to see Gally.

"What are you doing here?" She continued shining the light at him. He was wearing a parka and ski pants and his legs and arms were caked with snow.

"Don't be scared," he said. "I followed you. I want to talk to you."

She didn't trust her voice, so she just kept the light on his face.

"How did you figure it out?" he asked her.

"I went to the library," she said. "I looked at when the burglaries were. It couldn't have been a coincidence that they only happened when you and Trip were home from school. And my earrings. I started to see that there was a pattern. One thing followed another." He seemed to understand what she was saying.

"I don't want you to go to the police. I'll pay them back for it."

Stay calm, she told herself, just stay calm.

"But what about the other stuff? The stuff that's been sold already. The stuff that was dumped and that Carl Thompson found and fenced."

"I'll figure something out. Look, he doesn't know what he's doing. He's always liked taking stuff. Ever since we were kids. It's like a sickness. He can't help it."

Sweeney stepped a foot closer to him. He was upset, almost crying, and she felt sorry for him.

"I know," she said.

"He doesn't know any better," Gally said, running a hand through his wet hair. "Look, if you're not a twin, you can't understand. He's gotten caught a few times and my parents have had to bail him out. If he gets caught again, he'll definitely get kicked out of school. He doesn't even know why he does it. He doesn't need the stuff. He can afford to pay them back. He has money from my grandparents."

Sweeney went along, not knowing exactly where it was going to go. "What about the blackmail, and the murders?"

Now Gally looked genuinely surprised. "What do you mean, blackmail? And he didn't have anything to do with the murders." Gally looked around the room, desperate, as though he expected someone else to be there.

"Are you sure?" Sweeney watched him think about it.

A motor sounded outside.

"What is it?" she whispered.

Gally turned and looked. "It's one of the snowmobiles." Sweeney shut off the flashlight and told him to be quiet and stand with her against the wall. They listened to the footsteps outside, and the sound of a key in the padlock, then the squeaking of the door hinges. And then a light came on.

It was Trip. He was holding one of the hunting rifles, the same one Britta had trained on Sweeney the day she'd arrived in Byzantium. It struck her that this had been the cause of Britta's fear, the knowledge of what this boy, her son, was capable of.

"Hey," he said. "What's going on here?" He watched them, his eyes wide, his hands shaking.

"She's not going to the police, Trip," Gally said. "Don't worry. She promised she wouldn't go. We'll bring back all the stuff and no one will know." His voice had an edge of desperation.

Sweeney turned to him. "Look, Trip. You're in big trouble. But if you tell the police about it, you'll get off easy. You're a juvenile. You probably won't even go to jail. Gally thinks you've been burglarizing the houses because of your sickness, but if you tell them the truth, if you turn her in, things won't be as serious." Trip kept staring at her, the barrel of the long rifle pointed at her forehead.

"What do you mean 'her'?" Gally asked, turning to his brother. "Trip, what does she mean?"

"Nothing," Trip said. "She doesn't know anything."

"Yes, I do," Sweeney said. "I know about Rosemary."

Trip turned and almost dropped the rifle.

"It's okay, Trip," Rosemary's gentle voice came from the porch. She had been standing out there in the snow, listening to them. "Just keep it on them. You're doing just fine. I can handle this now."

Then she came around the corner of the door and walked slowly over to Sweeney, her hands in her pockets. "Just relax," she said again to Trip, as though she were talking to a scared child. "It's okay."

Rosemary took off her hat and ran her hands through her hair. Then she got another flashlight out of her coat pocket and shone it around the studio. "You looked through our things," she said, looking up at Sweeney. Sweeney had expected to see someone else in her eyes, but she looked just the way she had the first time Sweeney had met her, pretty and lithe, her blond hair spiky, her cheeks pink from the cold.

"They're not your things," Sweeney said calmly, though she was very afraid. "They don't belong to you."

Rosemary stared at her for a moment. "So how did you know?" she asked quietly. "How did you find me out?" She unzipped her heavy parka, which was also caked with snow.

"Rosemary, shut up!" Trip yelled. "Don't tell her anything."

"Tell me," Rosemary said. "Doesn't seem like it could hurt now."

Sweeney's desire to know if she had gotten it right was so overpowering, it felt like a black hole she wanted to sink into. She moved slightly to the side and looked into Rosemary's very blue eyes, at the pretty little birthmark.

"There was a lot more to this than you and I kept getting confused by other pieces of this, by gravestones and deeds and word puzzles. But once I had boiled it down, I wondered about the burglaries," Sweeney said simply. "They seemed so random. Britta made a comment about magpies at some point and I thought to myself that it seemed we had a magpie for a thief. It was such a strange combination of items, mementos, keepsakes, then the electronic equipment sometimes. But every time, the paintings. It was stupid of me not to put it together sooner.

"It was strange, though, because no one made a big deal about which paintings were stolen. The names weren't in the paper and it seemed that they must not have been very valuable or famous paintings. There wasn't any obvious link. The only thing was that I knew a couple of them had been of you as a child, though I didn't put it together until tonight.

"I went to have tea with Sabina shortly before she was killed and while I was there, I saw a painting by Gilda Donetti of two teenage girls and a toddler. It was hanging in Sabina's house when I went to visit her the first time. The date on it was 1969. Sabina said it was a picture of Rosemary at the age of three or four."

Rosemary was staring at her, her eyes afraid, and Sweeney found it gave her courage. She went on.

"At the Christmas party, Frances Rapacci told me that he had owned a picture of you when you were a child, but that it was one of the ones stolen from his house when it was burgled. It didn't hit me until tonight that the pictures of Rosemary as a child might be the connection I was looking for in the burglaries.

"Marcus Granger's daughter had visited the colony once after her marriage, with her young daughter, Rosemary.

She—Rosemary, I mean—was a beautiful child and it seemed that at least a few of the artists around the colony painted her that summer. When I started thinking about it, I realized it was possible that Rosemary Burgess was in a number of pictures that had been given as presents to colonists by Gilda or Gilmartin or other artists. There were probably pictures of Rosemary all over the colony. That's why she had to get them. Or get Trip to get them. I think she had caught Trip taking things from people in the colony, little things, things like my earrings, and I think she knew it must be part of a larger pattern of kleptomania and she told him she would go to the police if he didn't take the pictures of her from the houses and take other things, too, to make it look like a string of burglaries."

"I don't understand," Gally said, looking from Trip to Rosemary and then back at Sweeney. "Why would she want pictures of herself?"

"That's what I was wondering. The burglaries coincided with Trip and Gally's school vacations. At first I thought that Trip had taken them because he was obsessed with her, something like that. But there was something else about the timing. *The burglaries only started after Rosemary arrived in Byzantium.* I didn't see that. But then something happened tonight that made me see why Rosemary didn't want anyone to see a picture of her as a very young child.

"I read *The Lady of Shalott* tonight and all the stuff about mirrors and seeing the world through mirrors got me thinking. And it made me see that I actually knew everything I need to about this. I remembered the painting that I had seen hanging in Sabina's library and I remembered that the toddler in that painting had a birthmark on her cheek, just like Rosemary. *Only it was on the wrong side.* It was on the left cheek. And yours"—she pointed to Rosemary's face—"is on the right. It isn't the kind of thing you notice, you know. If you remember someone as having had a birthmark, you don't really remember what side it's on.

"Rosemary had only recently come to live in Byzantium. In fact, no one had seen her since she was three years old,

and the only person who might actually remember what she
had looked like was her grandmother—who is nearly blind."

"Go on," Rosemary said.

"Her name isn't Rosemary Burgess," she said to Gally
and Trip, then turned back. "I don't know what your real
name is but I think you must have known Rosemary Burgess
in London and when Rosemary died shortly after her parents
did—in an accident or maybe not—whoever you are took
over Rosemary's life, having heard stories about the wealthy
grandmother. All you had to do was get back in touch with
the grandmother, get a fake birthmark, since people would
remember that, and show up in Vermont. I don't know if
you just did it for fun, for what you could get out of it, or
if you were going to take it all the way and Electra Granger
would have died before too long."

As she talked Sweeney was looking around the room, trying to find a route of escape. There was nothing but the front
door, and Trip was standing in front of it, holding the rifle.

"I think you felt that you could trick the grandmother and
that there wouldn't be anybody else who would remember
you as such a young child. This is the part I've been trying
to figure out. I think that you got the birthmark wrong because you had been used to looking at the real Rosemary the
same way we look at ourselves in a mirror. You thought of
it as being on the right cheek, because that's what you saw
in the mirror, so to speak. But it wasn't. It was really on
Rosemary Burgess's left cheek.

"You arrived in Byzantium and everything was fine until
you realized that you'd gotten it wrong. You could get rid
of photographs, but then you discovered that Rosemary had
visited the colony as a child and there were paintings. That
must have been a shock to you," she said, looking up at
Rosemary, or the woman she knew as Rosemary.

The woman said, "Yes. The first week I was here, my
grandmother—Electra—took me up to the attic and showed
me a box of photographs of Rosemary as a child. I panicked
when I realized I'd gotten it wrong." She stood up and started
pacing around the room. "It was so stupid. And it was just

like you said. I had this image of Rosemary, with the birth-mark here. . . . It was because it was so last-minute, you know. I didn't even think I was going to pretend to be her until I was in Boston. I thought that I would just come and meet the grandmother, tell her about Rosemary, you know. And then I was in Boston, and I thought to myself, 'Why not tell her I'm Rosemary.'

"We became friends in the first place because we looked so much alike. I was dating this guy who knew her from school or something and we were standing next to each other at a party and someone said, 'You two could be twins.' She was fun, you know, we always had a good time together, and I liked her, and we would go around and tell people we were twins.

"We moved in together about six months before her parents died. She didn't even talk to them anymore, hadn't for years. She was a complete druggie. I didn't realize it for a while, she was good at hiding it. But like her parents, I started to see signs, and like her parents I realized pretty quickly that there wasn't anything to do. She was one of the ones who die from it. She was determined to die from it, I think.

"But they died first. I took the call from the police and I sat up until she got home and I told her. She seemed okay. But a couple of nights later, I came home from work and I found her in the bathroom. The needle was still in her arm and everything."

"How did you find out about the colony?" Sweeney asked quietly.

"God, how could I not? She had always talked about the colony, about her grandparents and the beautiful houses and about how her parents had taken her away from it. She had all these books and everything. It was kind of an obsession, but I liked to hear her talk about it. It sounded so nice. Like the kind of place where everyone would treat each other well, where everything would be beautiful."

Trip had started to cry, but the woman seemed not to hear him. She went on.

"She had written a letter to her grandmother, to tell her about the accident. And a couple of weeks after she died, a return letter came from Byzantium. I opened it, because there wasn't anybody else to send her things to, and it was this wonderful letter, a sad letter, asking Rosemary to come and visit."

She looked at them. "I swear. I was just going to come to tell her in person. I didn't see how I could tell her about Rosemary in a letter, or on the phone even, after what she'd been through. And then I started thinking, what if I showed up and said I was Rosemary. I worried about my accent, but then I realized that she wouldn't know where Rosemary had spent her childhood. It was easy to tell the truth about myself, that I'd been born in England and that my father had gotten this crazy idea about having a farm in South Africa. That was easy. And we looked alike. I thought there might be some money in it. And I didn't remember about the birthmark until I was in Boston. I got a little tattoo. It was easy. But then I was so terrified when I saw those pictures. I didn't know what to do."

Sweeney said, "There wasn't anything you could do. You had already met all the neighbors with a birthmark on one side of your face, and you couldn't go and change it."

"That's right. I got rid of the photographs, pretended there'd been a flood in the attic. But then I realized that there were paintings. I hadn't counted on that. I almost left then. But I had started to love Byzantium. And Electra. That was the problem, you see." She looked very sad all of a sudden.

"It wasn't the kind of thing people would notice right away," Sweeney went on for her. "But one day, you'd be standing in someone's living room and they'd realize. You had to get rid of the paintings."

"It would have been fine if it hadn't been for Ruth Kimball," the woman said.

Trip was watching her in horror. "But you didn't kill her," he said. "That was Carl."

Sweeney looked at him and then went on. "Ruth Kimball has a nearly photographic memory. Just like I do. She must have looked at you one day and remembered what you'd looked like as child. Then she went to the Historical Society looking for proof in a book of photographs from the '60s. That confused me. But she must have found a picture of Rosemary as a toddler in the book and shown it to you. And instead of turning you in, she started blackmailing you. I thought she was blackmailing Trip because she knew he was the burglar, but in fact she was blackmailing you because she knew what was behind them. She had made the connection between your arrival and the burglaries and she threatened to go to the police. Instead you paid her. She used the money to set up a college fund for Charley. I think you must have gotten it from your grandmother. You had started handling the household finances and you figured she wouldn't notice."

Sweeney looked into the very blue eyes. "And you killed Sabina because she realized about the painting. At the party. She saw you reflected in the window and she remembered the painting and realized the birthmark was on the wrong side. She must have confronted you about it sometime at the party and so she had to die. But first you had to scare me. You pushed me off the edge of the ridge because you realized that I wasn't satisfied Carl had killed Ruth Kimball. And this morning, you came very close to killing Charley Kimball because she was snooping around down by the studio."

"I didn't know about all of it," Trip said. "I swear to God. I didn't know she was going to kill anyone. I thought it was just taking things."

"Okay," the woman said. "I think we should go outside now. Hand me the rifle, Trip."

He hesitated and she turned around to look at him.

"No," he said. He was crying. He dropped it to the ground, at Gally's feet. Sweeney watched, aware of every muscle in her body, every pulse of blood through her veins. The woman lunged for the rifle and Trip pushed her away. "Get away, Rosemary," he said. "I just want it to end."

"It will," she said. "This is it." She moved slowly toward

him, smiling, her hands out in front of her as though she were approaching a dog.

And in the instant she had turned her attention to Trip, Sweeney pushed past her and through the front door, yelling for Gally to follow her.

She had taken off her hat and gloves while she looked for the paintings and the freezing snow lashed her bare skin as she stumbled into the trees. If she could just find the path, if she could just get on the path, she might make it back. She stopped, but she had lost her bearings and she couldn't find an opening in the trees, couldn't find anything to set one patch of swirling whiteness apart from another. It was disorienting, like being under water, and when the wind died for a moment and she saw the silvery length of river below, she headed for it. If she followed the river, she would be okay.

When she reached the edge of the woods, she sat and slid down the little slope to the riverbank. Out on the river, she could see patches of ice interrupted by the swiftly moving water, dark and oily, and she could smell its peculiar scent. Even half-frozen, it exuded a green, live odor, like some awakening creature, waiting in the storm. The mist that the warmer snow made as it hit the cold water was like the breath of the beast, encircling and hovering.

Sweeney ran, but the snow by the side of the river was deep and it was hard going. She'd gone a few hundred yards when she turned to see if Trip and Gally were behind her. She stopped. The snow whipped at her skin.

All she heard was the howling wind.

And then she saw the rifle, raised, and the small figure standing very straight and still, only twenty yards behind her. Sweeney turned, but the riverbank had started to rise and she kept slipping as she tried to scramble up the bank. She was trapped. The woman was coming at her and the only thing she could think of was the water. She waded in, the iciness climbing her legs as she tried to run in the thin strip of unfrozen water at the river's edge. There was ice on the riverbed, too, and Sweeny kept slipping.

It was only a couple of seconds before her legs began to go numb. They got heavier and heavier, the way they did in her nightmares, and she slowed, trying to talk herself out of it, but knowing there was nothing she could do.

She stumbled in the water, felt it come up around her like a blanket, and when she turned, she saw the woman, standing on the bank and leveling the rifle at her. Sweeney's waist was tingling. She turned and looked at the dark water as it rose up to meet her. She turned back and waited for the shot.

But out of the storm, a figure came leaping off the riverbank. It was Trip and he landed behind the woman, knocking her off her feet. She fell into the water and he went in after her, struggling for the gun. She regained her balance stood up, then seemed to lose her footing.

Sweeney watched it happen, paralyzed. The woman slipped and screamed. And then the current drew her under the ice. Trip lunged for her as she was sucked under and she grabbed the edge of the ice and Sweeney saw the white of her hands, gripping the dark floe before she let go and disappeared.

Sweeney screamed and her legs gave way as Trip rushed out to catch her. The snow came down and they stumbled from the river.

# THIRTY-FOUR

"BUT HOW DID she do it?" Cooper asked them. "We went over and over the alibis. She was with her grandmother the whole time. I know the old lady's blind, but . . ."

It was much later the next morning, Christmas Day, Sweeney realized, and they were sitting by the fire in the Wentworths' living room, drinking hot chocolate. She was wrapped in a wool blanket, trying to get warm. Patch and Britta, after going to make sure that Trip was all right at the police station, had come back and demanded that someone explain to them what had happened.

Slowly, for she was very tired, Sweeney had told them about Rosemary. Toby had not believed her at first, but Cooper and Gally had convinced him and now he was sitting next to Sweeney, looking very sad and very scared. Then, with help from Ian, who was sitting on the floor next to the couch, rubbing Sweeney's frozen feet, she had told them about Mary and Jean Luc and about how she had gotten interested in the murders and the burglaries.

"It was the hat," Sweeney said. "We thought they'd been together the whole time, and in a way they had, but when I was talking to Electra Granger, she said they'd picked up Ruth Kimball's hat and they'd had to go back and drop it off on the porch. I realized that probably she didn't mean that she had run all the way back. She stood in the snow and waited and Rosemary ran back.

"Later I asked Sherry if she had found the hat the day her mother died and she said no, so I assumed that it had been lost. But there was another possibility that only occurred to me after I realized about the birthmark. What if Rosemary pretended to find it, told her grandmother she was going to return it, and instead ran into the cemetery and shot Ruth Kimball with the gun she'd taken from the Kimballs' barn earlier, then quickly arranged it to look like a suicide? Trip had told her the twins would be target shooting and she knew that their guns would mask her shot. She took Ruth Kimball's hat. Then she ran back and they continued on their walk."

"But I don't understand how you figured out about the burglaries. And the blackmail," Cooper was saying.

Sweeney took out the little bankbook and showed it to them. "It was a matter of looking at the numbers, at the patterns they made. Ruth Kimball had been keeping track of the burglaries and then she had received consistent amounts of money, increasing in frequency from the time the burglaries started. At first I didn't see it, but then once I'd focused on the burglaries, and realized that they only seemed to happen in the summer and school vacations, I started to think about Trip and Gally. Until I realized about Rosemary, I thought Ruth Kimball had been blackmailing one of the twins. My earrings had been stolen by someone in the house and when Gally returned them to me, I started thinking that he wouldn't have done that if he'd taken them, that it must be Trip."

She looked up at Patch and Britta and then at Ian. "That's why I couldn't say anything to anybody. I didn't want to. . . . It was Christmas and I needed to know if they'd been responsible for the murders before I did anything."

"But Carl was caught fencing the stuff from the robberies," Patch said. "He must have been involved."

"Trip dumped what Rosemary didn't need and he didn't want in the woods. Carl found it."

"Yes, that's what he told us," Cooper said softly.

"But what about the stolen items that weren't electronics or the paintings? Why did he take that stuff? The pictures that weren't of Rosemary."

"Rosemary told him to take them, so that no one would realize that the paintings of her were the true target of the burglaries. As for why Trip was willing to do it, I think Rosemary had found him taking something out of her bag, or her grandmother's. Something like that. And I think she knew that he had a problem. She used it against him."

She turned to Britta. "Early on, you told me that the burglaries struck you as strange. That the person who was doing it was like a magpie, picking things from here and there. 'They like glittery things,' you said. Did you know then that it was Trip?"

Britta looked up with tired eyes. "There had been a few incidents at the boys' school about a year ago. It didn't surprise me, necessarily. He had been taking things since he was a little boy. But this was the first time it had been outside the family, so to speak. The school wanted to go to the police, but Patch and I were able to keep it quiet. Trip promised that he would never do it again.

"Then when Sweeney's earrings were stolen, I just knew that it was him. They were exactly the kind of thing that he used to take when he was a little boy, glittering, sparkling things. I used to find my own jewelry under his bed, stuffed behind books, stuffed in his pockets. I was terrified that if you figured out it was him, you would go to the police and they would find out about the burglaries."

Gally, who was sitting on the couch with his father, said, "So was I. I used to follow him around when we were playing at other kids' houses and replace the things he'd taken."

"Did you suspect that Trip had anything to do with Ruth Kimball's death?" Cooper asked Britta.

"Maybe, no—I don't know. He's my son. I couldn't have, I don't know, I couldn't have lived in the same house with him if I'd really thought that. But there was a part of me that thought . . . I was so afraid." She broke down crying and Sweeney watched Patch lean over to put an awkward arm around her shoulders.

"But I don't understand how Rosemary thought she would

get away with it," Patch said after a moment. "Wouldn't Electra have figured it out at some point?"

Cooper said, "We think that she planned to have something happen to Electra. We discovered this morning when we were going through the house that she had begun transferring large quantities of money into her own account by forging Electra's signature. She knew that she might have had trouble claiming an inheritance because she didn't have any documents showing that she was Rosemary Burgess, though she might have been working on that, too. But she had taken over all of the finances for the house and Electra wouldn't have known. All she would have had to do was either wait for her to die or arrange for an accident and disappear with the money.

"I disagree," Sweeney said very quietly. "I think that may have been her intention originally, but I think that once she got here she fell in love with the colony and with her grandmother. I think she would have been very happy to stay here. And I think she had fallen in love with Toby."

"We heard from the authorities in London just now," Cooper added after a moment. "It's just as she told you. The real Rosemary Burgess died of a drug overdose in May. The police got in touch with her landlord and discovered she had been living with a South African woman named Fiona Vierbeck. Immigration and Naturalization confirmed that Vierbeck entered the country back in June on a temporary tourist visa."

"How's Electra doing?" Sweeney asked. She had been thinking about Electra.

"Willow's with her," Britta said. "And we'll be here for her. I worry about her, absorbing something like this. She says she had no idea, that she wanted so much to have her granddaughter back."

Sweeney thought suddenly of Patch's painting of Willow and wondered what would happen between Britta and Patch.

"What about Trip?" Toby asked very quietly.

Cooper said, "It will depend on whether the people whose houses have been burglarized want to press charges. I don't

know. As for you," he turned to Sweeney, "I don't understand why you didn't call the police. It was pretty stupid,
you know?"

"I know. I know. It was just that it had to do with Toby.
And if I'd been wrong, well . . . I felt like I had to know
before I said anything."

Toby took her hand and squeezed it.

It wasn't until much later that night that they told Patch about
Louis Denholm's gravestone.

Patch said, "But why would he hide it?"

Sweeney said, "It's in Myra Benton's journal. After Mary
and Jean Luc left for Europe, Gilmartin offered to buy a
seemingly worthless piece of land from Louis Denholm for
a large sum of money. Louis Denholm had been trying to
convince Gilmartin to buy it for a long time and I think that
after what had happened, Gilmartin felt that he had no
choice. So he paid the money.

"But, of course, Gilmartin didn't care about the land and
so he didn't check to make sure that the deed had been recorded. Louis Denholm thought he'd play a trick on him. I
think he was that kind of personality—there's something in
the journal about him loving puns—and I think he passed
that love for tricks and puzzles and puns on to Mary. Anyway, he hid the deed in a place that Gilmartin would find
entirely appropriate, if he ever went to look for it, and he
left a clue to the location on his gravestone."

Sweeney recited aloud.

> *"Think my friends when this you see*
> *How Death's dark deed hath slayed me*
> *He is a thief and taketh flight*
> *Beneath the cover of the night"*

"I always thought that stone was odd," Patch said.

"We thought it was a code," Sweeney told him. "Ian
and I. But it isn't. It's a pun. Louis Denholm loved puns.

"Beneath the cover of the night with an 'N.' Beneath the cover of the knight with a 'K.' "

They all looked over at Sir Brian, who stood silently at the bottom of the staircase.

"It wasn't very nice, hiding it in Gilmartin's own house. But I think Louis Denholm must have gotten a kick out of that. Can I . . ."

Patch nodded and she opened the faceplate, peering awkwardly into the helmet. "There's something tied on the inside," she said, reaching back and untying a string and coming up with a small cloth bag. She handed it to Patch.

"I wondered about whether I should tell you," she said. "I thought that Sherry and Charley should be able to sell it, if they needed to. But now I think that the colony is her legacy, too, Charley's. I still don't know if it was the right thing to do."

Patch took the small bag and went over to Sir Brian. He lifted the helmet and dropped the little bag back inside.

"Let's see what happens," he said. "I think it should be up to Charley."

Sweeney stopped by Bennett Dammers's house the next day, before she and Toby started for Boston.

She told him about Rosemary and about Mary and Jean Luc and she told him about the deed and Louis Denholm's joke.

He expressed his surprise at it all and then he said, "Do you know, I wonder what will happen between you and that nice Englishman."

Sweeney blushed.

"If I had known you under other circumstances," he said very quietly. "In a different time, in a different life where I'm not old enough to be your grandfather, I believe I should have fallen in love with you myself. It doesn't end, you know. The excitement of love. It never stops mattering. Don't make that mistake."

Her eyes welled with tears and before she knew what she was doing, she was blurting out to him, "I don't know what's wrong with me. I should want that. I know I should. But I'm so mixed up. I don't want to mix anyone else up, too. I feel as though I'm a disease, that I'll infect someone else with it and I should stay away, alone."

He smiled kindly and he took her hand and let her cry. "I expect you'll be all right," was all he said.

The car was packed and Toby was waiting discreetly, listening to the news on the radio. She and Ian stood in the cold driveway, leaning against each other.

"So you're going to go down and see Sherry and Charley today?" she asked him.

"Yes. I think I'll invite them to come to England for a visit sometime."

"She resembles you a little. Charley. I didn't notice it before." She reached up to straighten his glasses.

"Why don't you come to England," he said suddenly. "We can go for walks in Hyde Park and get married and have lots of babies who will have dual citizenship and lead strange binational existences."

He was kidding, or half-kidding, but he kissed her and looked hopefully down at her through his glasses, his eyes blue and very serious. She wondered what it would take for her to say yes, for her to get on an airplane and . . . and what?

She stood against him in the crisp, cold air, the deaths hanging between them as hard and cold as metal. Something she had once written in a paper about European funeral rituals came into her mind, "Death must have his due."

There had been so much death. She breathed in the cold, dead winter air and, with a small fluttering, she felt something loosen deep within her. Her breath caught in her chest.

"Not yet," she said, trying to smile. "But maybe I'll come visit. In the spring."

As Sweeney and Toby drove south a light snow started to fall, then grew heavier and heavier again, the giant flakes twisting in the cold air and falling to earth, making a thick shroud over the ground.

Just north of Boston, Sweeney pulled the car over and they got out to watch the sun set in the parking lot of a rest stop. When the sun, brilliantly pink and violet, had cleared the horizon and disappeared, she turned to Toby and hugged him hard, letting him cry, the pain between them a kind of anchor, pain she leaned into the way a sailor leans his boat into the wind.

# ACKNOWLEDGMENTS

MANY THANKS TO my agent, Lynn Whittaker. Her enthusiasm, expert agenting, and friendship throughout were indispensable. Everyone at St. Martin's Minotaur was wonderful. Thanks especially to Kelley Ragland and Ben Sevier, who were tirelessly kind, smart, and helpful in every way.

A number of people helped with the details of their own particular fields, though any mistakes or false notes are mine and mine alone. Thanks to Bob Dance, Robert Sand, and Phil Nel. Thanks also to a fabulous group of readers and friends who provided very helpful criticism, assistance and/or support: Vendela Vida, Olivia Gentile, Kathleen Burge, Sarah Piel, Andy Jen, Geoff Hansen, Deborah Perry, Jennifer Hauck, Vicki Kuskowski, and Rachel Gross.

And finally, many, many thanks to Susan and David Taylor, who have provided love, support, and cheerleading for this, and all of my endeavors; to John Judson Taylor, for all of his love; to Tom Taylor, a stunningly good writer, editor, and brother; and to my husband, Matt Dunne, who makes all things possible and fun. And many, many thanks to Faith Dunne, who should have been here.

# MANSIONS OF THE DEAD

## PROLOGUE
### 1863

*It was Belinda's favorite time of year, the three or four weeks of early spring when winter was transformed into something else, some halfway season that smelled of percolating earth and trickling streams. The grass was still brown and sickly looking from the long winter, but when she bent her head to inhale the wet scent of the ground below, she could see a fur of pale green growth below that promised a stronger green, could feel the hesitant sun that whispered its promise in the cool air.*

*She was on her way to her family grave plot on Asphodel Path, in one of the newest sections of Mount Auburn Cemetery. They were expanding the cemetery and she was aware of the movements of the workers as they carted soil to build more new roads. On the weekend there had been visitors thronging the little avenues—it was the custom now to come for a stroll among the headstones, seeking respite from the busy city, from news of sons and brothers and sweethearts killed by the Confederates—but today the grounds were silent. While she'd heard the workers laughing together as she'd arrived the first day, they seemed to be trying to respect her privacy now.*

*She had come nearly every day since he had died. And*

*she had found that she had begun to look forward to her trips to Mount Auburn, the only time of day when she was really alone. She liked wandering along the little lanes and reading the stones. There was one that she found herself walking by nearly every time she went, a simple white marble likeness of an angel with the words, "My wife and child."*

*The ground had not thawed sufficiently for burial and it would be months before Charles's monument would be ready, but she had been trying to tend to the plot with a dull little pair of sewing scissors, eventually giving up and using her fingers to pull up the dead weeds and grass by their barren roots.*

*Belinda smoothed the necklace that she wore at her throat, made of hair carefully braided into a chain. Charles had possessed such dark hair, a rich brown lit with auburn, and it hadn't grayed much at all, even during his long illness. It had grown out in those last months—he had had a strange superstition about cutting it—and by working the locks of hair around a mold to make twenty intricately netted balls and then stringing them together, she had been able to make a necklace that reached the third button of her dress. After preparing the locks of hair with soda water according to the instructions in Godey's Lady Book, she had sat alone in the parlor night after night with the strange little hairwork table that the gardener had made for her. When she was finished, she had taken the necklace to her father's jeweler, who had put on the clasp.*

*The pursuit had pleased her; it had been something to do during those strange evenings when if she didn't miss him exactly, she missed the bulk of him across the dinner table or in the parlor, where he had always sat and read the paper, drinking port while she read or worked at her embroidery.*

*She shook her head to clear away the image of his sickbed, the stained rags littering the floor, the housemaid scurrying around nervously, crossing herself as his time neared. It was funny how she had become attuned to his condition in those last few days, and she had known he was going to die before the doctor did. His color, and the way the room smelled, had told her that she would soon be a widow.*

*"I'm sorry, Ma'am, I have to bring a load of earth by and I wouldn't want to be disturbing you, Ma'am." She started and turned to find one of the laborers behind her, standing behind a cart. Irish. She stepped back.*

*"That's all right. Go ahead. It won't bother me," she said, looking into a pair of blue eyes, a boyish face. He wasn't very old. Not much older than she was. Twenty-three, she said to herself. I am only twenty-three and already I am a widow.*

*It was her own fault, what had happened. She had married a man as old as her father because she had wanted an easy life. She had been just a girl, prone to daydreaming. She had liked to sketch. That was how she had known he had an interest in her. They had met in Newport, at the Ocean House, where her father liked to go for the sea air. She had been sketching in the music room of the hotel one evening and he had wandered in. Her father knew him through business and they had spoken the evening before. When he came in, holding a newspaper and looking uncomfortable, she had had the idea to sketch him in his discomfort, and had asked his permission. He had smiled as though it surprised him, and agreed, and it wasn't until later that she had looked at the sketch and seen something in his face that made her stomach knot.*

*That night she had played cards with him and chatted flirtatiously. She felt somehow that she was acting out a script and when she examined her own actions she was ashamed. The next day she had agreed to stroll along the cliffs with him.*

*When they were back in Boston, her father had asked her to come into the library and he had told her about the proposal. "He is aware that the age difference is a problem," he told her, stammering a little. "It is up to you. I admit that I always thought of you marrying for love, someone who could match your high spirits. I wish that your mother were still alive to talk to you about the demands of marriage, about the difficulties in living with another person. But he is a good man and I don't have to tell you that we have been hard hit in the markets. It won't be many months before we have to sell this house. It's up to you to decide how you want to live."*

She had told him she would think about it, but she had known, even as she left the room, what her answer would be.

It was her own fault. God would punish her. She knew this now. God would punish her for her thoughts and . . . for her actions. She had not been a good Christian wife to him.

She sat down on the grass, feeling the dampness soaking through the wool of her dress. The cold shocked her skin. But the dress was dark and the stain would not show. She smiled a little at this. No, she had not been a good Christian wife to him at all. Still . . . if she was truthful with herself, she had never felt so free.

The first thing Becca Dearborne noticed was Brad's Angel fish.

It had flipped onto its side, its eyes staring into the bubbling water, its catlike whiskers trailing. The other fish—a few more Angels, a swarm of tiny, flashing Tetras, a grumpy catfish—swam around nervously, as though they knew something was wrong. She extracted a little green net from the jumble of supplies Brad kept next to the tank, bottles of chemicals and fish food, thermometers, a pair of rubber gloves, then scooped out the dead fish and took it through to the bathroom where she flushed it down the toilet and rinsed out the net.

"It must have died in the night," she said softly to Jaybee. "Otherwise, he'd never have left it there." She put a finger to the glass and felt something in her stomach, a pang, of sadness perhaps, for the fish.

"Yeah. He'd probably have taken it to the hospital." Jaybee, who had been Brad's friend since ninth grade and his roommate since their freshman year of college, liked to make fun of Brad's obsession with the aquarium. He spent a fortune, buying special plants and various concoctions that were supposed to kill bad bacteria or add good bacteria, or change the pH of the water. And he spent hours testing the water and taking notes on how various changes affected the health of the fish. Becca, who had known Brad even longer than Jaybee had, thought she understood. She could stare into the depths of the aquarium for minutes on end, mesmerized by their movement in the water, lazy one moment, quick the next.

"I'm taking a shower," she said. Jaybee reached for her arm and pulled her toward him, kissing her long and hard. Dizzy, she pulled away and escaped into the bathroom.

Under the hot spray of water she arched her neck, soaping her hair and body and feeling the tightly knotted muscles along her shoulders give way. It felt so good that she turned the tap toward "hot" until she could feel her nerves scream and stood under the scalding spray for a few seconds before twisting the handle to "Off". Drip, drop, came the final water from the tap.

Becca dried herself off, wrapped herself in a bath towel, and wiped a little window in the steam on the mirror. Her face seemed blurry to her, her eyes too big, the whites cloudy, the color of weak tea. She squeezed her eyes shut, then opened them again, but she looked the same and she turned away from the mirror, going out into the living room where Jaybee was standing in the middle of their area rug—a cast-off from his older brother's apartment—looking perplexed.

"What's the matter?" she whispered, coming up behind him and pressing her body against his. Jaybee—his long back, his grin, his soft, auburny hair, his right index finger, bent from a childhood accident with a car door—made her feel somehow at a loss. She felt displaced, almost sick when she was with him, a completely new experience. The three other sexual relationships she'd had in her 20 years—with her boarding school boyfriend and two casual college flings— had seemed a sort of kindly, benign prostitution. By sleeping with those boys, for they were boys, she had secured companionship, affection, dates for important events and presents on her birthday. It had seemed, in each case, a worthwhile exchange. But this was something else. She had woken up the night before to find him gone—he'd gone outside for some air, he told her when she located him—and she had felt the most profound panic she had ever experienced. She had felt that she would do anything to feel his back against her arms again as she did now.

"I don't know," Jaybee said, looking around the room. "The apartment looks different. Weird." Becca looked around too. As roommates, Jaybee and Brad were well-matched in their messiness. There were books piled on every surface, dirty dishes in the sink, bikes and helmets tumbled on the floor behind the black couch. But he was right: There was something different about the room. All of the kitchen cabinets were open, as were the doors of the entertainment center in the living room. There was a jumbled pile of tools and videotapes and odds and ends on the floor beneath the television stand. The room smelled of vomit.

Becca felt cold all of a sudden. "He was really drunk, and really out of it. Maybe he just . . ."

"Yeah." Jaybee tried to smile. "That's right. He was pretty trashed, wasn't he?"

"I'm going to get dressed." She walked past Brad's closed door and into Jaybee's room, where she hurriedly put on her clothes, toweling her hair for a second and then going back out into the living room. Jaybee was standing in front of Brad's door.

"You going to check on him?" She was making a conscious effort to stay calm, though she knew something was wrong. Later, she would wonder if it was Jaybee's pale, terrified face or something less tangible that had made her so afraid.

Jaybee didn't say anything. He just put a hand on Brad's doorknob and turned it, hesitating a few minutes before pushing the door open. "Brad?" Over his shoulder, she saw the gravestone photographs that Brad had all over his walls. The black-and-white images seemed to crowd the room.

And then she heard nothing but the waterfall rush in her

own head as she followed Jaybee in and saw Brad, lying there on the bed.

"Jesus!" Jaybee whispered. "Jesus!"

Detective Timothy Quinn stood in the doorway, preparing himself, as he had only done a couple of times in the year he'd been working homicide, for his first sight of an unnaturally deceased human body.

This one was male, young, lying face down on a large double bed pushed against one wall. The body was naked except for a pair of boxer shorts. The shorts, which Quinn fixated on for a moment in order to avoid looking at the rest of the body, were blue madras, well made. A working-class, Hanes-briefs-wearing boy from the part of Somerville where people didn't shop at Brooks Brothers, Quinn thought back to college and knew this was high-quality stuff. Though he was later ashamed to recognize it, they made him sit up and take notice.

The boy was thin but muscular, a tennis player or runner perhaps, his back still dark with last summer's tan. Because his arms were tied to the bedposts—with bright striped neckties, Quinn saw—the lean muscles across his back stood out in stark relief. His arms looked oddly stiff. Rigor setting in, Quinn thought, checking his watch. It was now 2 P.M. That meant he'd been dead for at around twelve hours. Early this morning. He'd taken his last breath sometime before the sun came up this morning.

Beneath the clear plastic bag that covered his head and was secured around his neck with another tie, a jaunty red and blue striped one, the boy's longish hair was a dark shadow. His face, pressed into the bedspread, could not be seen.

But Quinn could see the jewelry the kid was wearing. Around his neck, trailing down to the middle of his back like a snake, was a long, dark chain, made of twenty or so beads. Pinned to his boxer shorts, just over his left hip, were two brooches. One was white and had a drawing of a woman sitting in a graveyard, her head in her hands. The other was

smaller and darker and had a criss-crossed design on the
front. He remembered suddenly buying a shamrock brooch
for his mother the Christmas he went away to college. "What
a nice brooch," she'd exclaimed, pronouncing the double o.

"No, Ma, it's 'broach,'" he'd corrected her, pronouncing
it like the clerk in the store in Amherst. She'd shot back that
now he was a college boy he thought he knew everything.
He almost smiled, thinking of the way she liked to take her
American son down a peg in her Dublin brogue.

Someone had tried to put the last piece of jewelry, a gold
locket on a chain, around the boy's neck, but the chain had
caught on the plastic and was kind of half slung around the
back of his head.

"You got any idea what this stuff is, Quinn?" Marino
asked, a small smile on his lips. He was testing him. Quinn
had already heard the kids who had found the body telling
Marino what it was. They were sitting out in the living room
now, the girl crying, the boy looking terrified. Quinn had
made a note of how terrified the boy looked. The roommate,
he'd told them. He was the dead boy's roommate. The girl
was a friend of both of theirs, the dead boy and the roommate, though from the way the two of them were locked
together on the couch, Quinn decided that they were a little
more than friends. They'd come back because the shower in
the girl's apartment wasn't working.

But Marino didn't know that. He just wanted to make
Quinn look stupid. They had been working together for a
year, ever since Quinn had been moved over to homicide
after Marino's partner was stabbed by his wife during what
the Cambridge Police dispatcher would have referred to as a
"domestic" and what Quinn had heard was a knock-down
wife-beating session.

Quinn had been hoping for the transfer to homicide for
four years, and he'd been—he realized now—a little eager
probably. Marino was a compact, barrel-chested guy with a
salt-and-pepper crew cut, a cauliflower ear from high school
wrestling, and eyebrows that peaked in the centers. He loved
paperback westerns and he always had five or six piled up

on his desk, a couple tossed into the back of his car in case he got stuck somewhere without something to read. He didn't seem to read anything else and Quinn had always liked the idea that Marino got off on cowboys and rancher's daughters and desert sunsets.

Marino resented the death of his partner, resented that because of the way the guy had died, he was prevented from talking about him with the reverence that his colleagues used talking about their own dead partners, killed heroically in the line of duty. And he resented his own place in the department, which Quinn had soon realized was somewhat insecure. Marino and Quinn got pulled off cases by the lieutenant in charge of the homicide division when they got thorny and Quinn knew that they weren't the first choice for anything, that they'd been put on this one because it was Sunday morning.

He also knew that Marino disliked him. Quinn's second week on the job, he'd come back from a coffee break and overheard Marino referring to him as "college boy" and he'd been careful around him ever since. But Marino knew the job and he had good instinct. Quinn could learn from him.

He inspected the brooch for a moment, trying to look thoughtful, then said, "I took this class once about English history and I remember this whole thing about mourning jewelry. It wasn't quite like this, but I think that's what it is."

"Okay," Marino said. "Now tell me what else you see."

Quinn took his time, studying the boy's back and the ties before speaking. "Well, the obvious cause of death is suffocation, but we'll have to wait for the post mortem to be sure."

"Good," Marino said. "Anything else?"

Quinn sniffed the air. "Well, I'd do a tox screen. He reeks of booze. Tequila."

"Sure does. What else?"

Focusing on the details of the room and letting the noise in the apartment fade away, Quinn turned his gaze around the bedroom. He squatted down and looked at everything from waist level. "Well, there's the source of the Tequila," he said, pointing to the half-empty bottle pushed under the bed. He dipped his head and surveyed the floor. The kid had been fairly neat. There were a couple of dusty, but neatly labeled boxes—"BOOKS," "SWEATERS," and "MISC."— a pair of dress shoes with dust kitties in them, and a small notebook. "And there's a notebook under there," he said. "Check it out. It looks less dusty than the rest of the stuff. It may have been pushed under there more recently."

"What? Shit! You're right. Good one, Quinn." Marino was grinning and Quinn felt inordinately satisfied.

"What about suicide? You think he did this himself?"

Quinn went to the bed and stood next to it with his feet wide apart. He leaned over the body and put a hand just over each of the low bedposts, taking care not to touch the posts, the hands or the ties holding them there. "I don't think so," he said. "I'd be able to get this one tied." He waved his right hand. "But not the left one. It's too far away. He had help getting tied up. And someone put the jewelry on after the bag was already over his head. This might be sex-related. He got drunk, invited someone back here, asked them to tie him up."

"Yeah," Marino said. "I think you're right. We better check for signs of sexual contact—heterosexual and homosexual. In the meantime, it's a good bet the jewelry was just some weirdo thing he liked to do while he got off, but I want you to check up on it, just in case it points to a ritual murder. Try someone at the university or the museum. We'll ask the family about it but I want to get an expert's opinion first."

Marino waved him out into the hallway, dismissing him.

The phone calls didn't take long, though since it was Sunday, it took some doing to get the home number for the chair of the art history department. But the switchboard operator gave it up when Quinn explained that he was from Cambridge P.D. A few minutes later he was talking to the chairman's wife, who said that he was out but gave him the number of the department secretary. Once he had the secretary on the phone, he asked if there was anyone who specialized in mourning jewelry, if that's what it was called.

"Oh, that's Professor St. George you want. Professor St. George knows about death. Give me your name and number and I'll call her and tell her to get right back to you. I'll have to go into the office to get it, though. She might even be there. She's in the office a lot on the weekends." Quinn heard a note of disapproval in her voice.

He gave her his number at the station and was just hanging up the phone when one of the uniformed cops came back into the room. "They're talking to the kid who found him, the roommate. He told us the kid's name when he called but no one put it together until now. The kid's a Putnam."

"As in . . . ?"

"As in."

The cop was almost grinning.